"Read it for twists on twists, meditations on faith, and a deeply thoughtful treatment of an evangelical community."

—*Glamour*

"Bewitching. . . . [A] tender but cutting coming-of-age story."

—*Elle*

"McKinney is a strong and compelling storyteller and has crafted a captivating small-town world full of gossip and intrigue. *God Spare the Girls* beautifully explores the challenges of young womanhood in the context of a religion that has its own very strict ideas about what it means to be a good daughter, sister, and wife. Above all else, *God Spare the Girls* is a touching and powerful story of a bond between two sisters navigating a world and life they never chose. It is a beautifully rendered spin on classic coming-of-age tales, with the characters navigating intricate layers of relationships with themselves, with each other and with their faith."

—Associated Press

"Every family has its secrets. . . . *God Spare the Girls* is an exploration of individuality, family, religion, community, and how when one family secret is revealed, many more follow."

—Oprah Daily

"A fascinating look at the moment in a young woman's life when she starts to forge an identity separate from her family's."

—*Real Simple*

"Kelsey McKinney's debut is a timely exploration of the moral contradictions of contemporary Evangelical Christianity. But the accomplishment of this canny novel is in positing coming of age itself as a loss of faith—not only in the church, but in our parents, our family, and the world as we thought we understood it."

—Rumaan Alam, *New York Times* bestselling author
of *Leave the World Behind* and *Rich and Pretty*

"*God Spare the Girls* is an incandescent novel. The book is a clear-eyed, breathtaking exploration of sisterhood, faith, and love and loss. McKinney broke my heart a million times with her beautiful and unflinching exploration of two sisters caught in a repressive world of religion and even more repressive love. I couldn't put it down. I found myself lost in the world of Texas heat and the fires of faith. McKinney's world is both familiar and engrossing, compelling and poignant. *God Spare the Girls* is a dazzling debut."

—Lyz Lenz, author of *Belabored* and *God Land*

"This coming-of-age debut about sisterhood, faith, community, and Evangelical Christianity is sure to delight."

—The Millions

"Compelling. . . . Both a coming-of-age book and an examination of belief, identity, and family, *God Spare the Girls* is unflinching and entrancing, and a reminder of the dangers of blind faith, but also the power of love."

—Refinery29

"The writing is evocative, and McKinney masterfully captures the nuanced dynamics of sisterhood. I wish it had been ten times longer."

—The Atlantic Daily

"Kelsey McKinney's debut novel asks a difficult question: Why does God's love often feel more conditional when it comes to women? . . . With a story about family, womanhood, and the question of goodness, readers will not be able to put *God Spare the Girls* down."

—Shondaland

"A story of sisters, family, faith, power, performance, secrets, and betrayal, *God Spare the Girls* is a gorgeously written exploration of what it means to attempt to love and trust when the foundations upon which we've built those words have been torn down, the particular thrill and risk of trying to form a self on one's own terms, and the courage it takes to still want and need out in the world. It's a book that pulls you deep into the particularities, the desires and vulnerabilities, of a culture and family—two sisters I won't soon forget—such that you might, too, feel closer to your own."

—Lynn Steger Strong, author of Want and Hold Still

"Scandal, promise rings, hidden family secrets—what more could I want in a novel? But yet, there is so much more. This is a heart-filled exploration about faith, family, and loyalty, and what it means to strike your own path amid the church-run world of Hope, Texas. Told with such tenderness, humor, and, yes, hope, this is a novel for anyone who's felt broken down over faith and love and who has questioned what they thought they knew about life, which is to say, all of us. A coming-of-age tale that feels fresh and untold, *God Spare the Girls* is a fearless uncovering of the secrets that keep us small and the bravery it takes to choose differently, to choose better, and to stand up for what you believe in, no matter what. These characters will be on my mind for a long time."

—Chelsea Bieker, author of Godshot

"Kelsey McKinney has written a real whopper of a novel with *God Spare the Girls*, a book that explores the ultimate cost of love within a family and the secrets people keep. I felt deeply touched by these characters as I read; both hopeful for their relationships and also wishing for their success. It is a precious thing to find a novel that allows for both the sweetness and the sour—McKinney writes it all deftly, beautifully, and fearlessly."

—Kristen Arnett, *New York Times* bestselling
author of *Mostly Dead Things* and *With Teeth*

"Kelsey McKinney has wrought an elegant tale of sisters, yes—but its greatest success is in accommodating a story of evangelicalism that speaks to both its strengths and all-too-human heartbreaks. A compelling read."

—Esmé Weijun Wang, *New York Times* bestselling
author of *The Collected Schizophrenias*

"*God Spare the Girls* is a thoughtful and candid meditation on faith, family, and forgiveness; it's also a tender portrait of two sisters reluctantly on the cusp of adulthood. McKinney's writing is sonorous, unsparing, and deeply generous—this is a fabulous debut."

—Claire Lombardo, *New York Times* bestselling
author of *The Most Fun We Ever Had*

"I don't know what I was more moved by in *God Spare the Girls*: the depths and twists of family love, the complexities of faith, or the failures of both faith and love. A devastating and large-hearted novel."

—R. O. Kwon, author of *The Incendiaries*

"A deeply felt book about love—love for family and community, for people who sustain you and people who disappoint you. And love for God, too, which Kelsey McKinney writes about with humane and incisive frankness."

—Linda Holmes, *New York Times* bestselling
author of *Evvie Drake Starts Over*

"A compelling and beautifully written tale, a book that captures the hubris and hypocrisy that can come from institutionalized faith while also finding ways to acknowledge the value that such circumstances can bring. Delicately heart-wrenching, driven by sad realizations and quiet humor, it's an unforgettable read. . . . An exceptional piece of fiction."

—*The Maine Edge*

"A feminist rewrite of Lot. . . . *God Spare the Girls* is, in short, delightful."

—*Texas Observer*

"The novel's strength lies in its note-perfect depiction of conservative white Bible Belt church culture, and what happens when that culture's image of perfection clashes with reality. Kelsey McKinney's powerful first novel takes on Texas summer heat, church politics and complicated family dynamics."

—*Shelf Awareness*

"The highlight of McKinney's authentic narrative is her treatment of relationships, and Caroline and Abigail's growing connection as the rest of their world threatens to fall apart is at once engaging, witty, and heartbreaking. A loss of faith gives way to something much stronger."

—*Kirkus Reviews*

"This stirring debut about faith, secrets, and familial bonds will keep readers turning the pages."

—*Publishers Weekly*

GOD
SPARE
THE
GIRLS

GOD
SPARE
THE
GIRLS

A NOVEL

KELSEY McKINNEY

WM

WILLIAM MORROW

An Imprint of HarperCollins*Publishers*

P.S.™ is a trademark of HarperCollins Publishers.

GOD SPARE THE GIRLS. Copyright © 2021 by Kelsey McKinney. All rights reserved. Printed in the United States of America. No part of this book may be used or reproduced in any manner whatsoever without written permission except in the case of brief quotations embodied in critical articles and reviews. For information, address HarperCollins Publishers, 195 Broadway, New York, NY 10007.

HarperCollins books may be purchased for educational, business, or sales promotional use. For information, please email the Special Markets Department at SPsales@harpercollins.com.

A hardcover edition of this book was published in 2021 by William Morrow, an imprint of HarperCollins Publishers.

FIRST WILLIAM MORROW PAPERBACK EDITION PUBLISHED 2022.

Library of Congress Cataloging-in-Publication Data

Names: McKinney, Kelsey, author.
Title: God spare the girls : a novel / Kelsey McKinney.
Description: First edition. | New York, NY : William Morrow, [2021] |
Identifiers: LCCN 2021010498 (print) | LCCN 2021010499 (ebook) | ISBN 9780063020252 (hardcover) | ISBN 9780063020269 (paperback) | ISBN 9780063020276 (ebook)
Subjects: LCSH: Sisters—Fiction. | Pastors—Fiction. | Evangelicalism—Fiction.
Classification: LCC PS3613.C5628 G63 2021 (print) | LCC PS3613.C5628 (ebook) | DDC 813/.6—dc23
LC record available at https://lccn.loc.gov/2021010498
LC ebook record available at https://lccn.loc.gov/2021010499

ISBN 978-0-06-302026-9

22 23 24 25 26 LSC 10 9 8 7 6 5 4 3 2 1

For Trey, for everything

Look, I have two daughters who have never slept with a man. Let me bring them out to you, and you can do what you like with them. But don't do anything to these men, for they have come under the protection of my roof.

Genesis 19:8 (NIV)

For that whole brutal year, Caroline Nolan had begged God to make her life interesting. He sent a plague instead: grasshoppers emerged from the earth in late June, crawling across the dry grass, multiplying too quickly, staying long past their welcome. Now they carpeted the land she'd inherited with her sister, vibrated in the sun like a mirage. As Caroline drove the ranch's half-mile driveway, she rolled over hundreds of them. She threw the car in park, stepped out into the yellowed grass beside the gravel drive, and crushed their leggy, squirming bodies beneath her sensible heels.

It was Saturday, the morning of her sister Abigail's bridal shower. They had spent weeks readying the drab, cluttered ranch house for the event. Caroline climbed the creaking wooden porch steps paled by decades of harsh sun and ran a hand over the garland of pink paper flowers they'd wrapped around the railing. Abigail had wanted them draped just so, carefully inspecting every detail. Caroline bent to plug in the white twinkle lights that their mother, Ruthie, had insisted were tacky. That is, until she'd seen them suspended over the door. According to their mother, this was going to be the best shower Hope, Texas, had ever seen.

Caroline inserted her key into the chipped brass lock; as usual, it refused to turn for her. She jiggled the key until it gave way, and pushed so hard the door banged open, almost dropping the framed engagement photos she'd been warned a half dozen times not to break. She wiped the sweat from her forehead, careful not to smear her foundation, and stepped into the frigid air-conditioned entryway. She set the stack of photos on the table.

An hour earlier, Ruthie had pulled Caroline out of Abigail's room while they waited for her sister to finish primping and begged her to rush over here before their guests arrived. Her mother's bracelet was supposed to be a surprise shower gift for Abigail, Ruthie said, and no one had remembered to retrieve it from the ranch. Caroline had rolled her eyes at her mother's urgency, but she'd sped the whole way over.

Now she hurried past the gold-framed family photos that hung in the dim hallway, smacking her elbow on the wall as she turned. She didn't remember the hall being this narrow, barely wide enough for her to walk down it with her elbows untucked. Lately, it felt like the whole world around her was shrinking, when she wanted it to grow with her. Caroline sucked in her stomach, shifted her too-wide hips, and squeezed between the dozens of chairs they'd arranged in semicircular rows like an amphitheater in the living room.

She lingered at the door to her grandmother's bedroom. It had been two years since Nannie's death, and even though the high grass, wavering cedar trees, and cattle gates—basically everything below this huge swath of blue sky—now belonged to her and Abigail, entering Nannie's room still felt like trespassing. Nannie had willed the ranch to the two of them, skipped over her own daughters. She'd explained the decision in her will. She said that Caroline and Abigail were the ones who loved it. The only ones who would keep it safe. But Caroline wasn't sure she wanted the responsibility anymore.

She told herself that all she had to do was enter the room, unlock the bedside table drawer where Nannie had always hidden her jewelry, and pray the bracelet was there. "Think how happy Abby will be," Ruthie had said. Caroline gripped the knob, twisted, and swung open the door.

A room left alone defines its kingdom. Dust settles across surfaces like a morning dew that never burns off. Caroline took a deep breath and stepped down into the dated plush purple carpet. She'd expected to be overwhelmed by memories of long Saturdays spent reading with Nannie in her big bed. Instead, the room felt fresh and foreign. The curtains were drawn. A gardenia candle with an ashy wick sat in front of the simple circle mirror on Nannie's antique vanity.

Caroline and Abigail had agreed to allow their father to offer the ranch house as lodging for his church guests, but Caroline had assumed he meant the other two bedrooms. There was no need for anyone to stay in her grandmother's room, to leave the light on above the vanity and their summer sweater, too new to have possibly been Nannie's, draped across the rocking chair.

Caroline unlocked the bedside table drawer and sighed with relief when she saw the black velvet box. It was soft in her hand. She snapped it open and the gold bracelet with small inset rubies went flying, landing under the bed. "Shit," Caroline said, and then, feeling guilty about it, "shoot."

She dropped to her knees and thrust her hand underneath

the floral dust ruffle right as she heard her name echo through the house. Her fingers brushed against something square, plastic, wrong somehow. She pulled it out, looked down, and unclenched her fingers. There, in her hand, was a single gold-packaged condom.

"Ollie ollie oxen free!" Abigail called out. Caroline knew from a thousand games of hide-and-seek that her sister was still in the front hallway. She shoved the condom into her pocket, lifted the dust ruffle, spotted the bracelet, crammed it back into its box, stuffed that into her other pocket, and rushed from the room, heart racing, breath jagged, closing the door tight behind her. Her satin dress hung unevenly now, weighed down by the bracelet.

Abigail stood in the center of the living room, her blond hair curled uniformly. She was wearing white, of course: her Coke-bottle shape filled out the wide skirt of her sundress, the perfectly fitted top sprinkled with flower eyelets. Her shoulders were back and down, chin parallel to the floor, her confidence well-practiced. A white sash with pink script slashed its way across her breasts. Caroline tugged at the flat skirt of her own pale blue dress, suddenly aware of its awkward color and too-tight, overflowing top, and remembered how she'd once assumed her chest would look like her sister's someday. She slowly navigated her way toward Abigail, careful not to knock any of the bows off of the chairs.

"What were you doing in Nannie's room?" Abigail asked. Caroline heard the accusation hiding behind her smooth tone. She felt a bead of sweat drip down her back. Abigail's need to control everything was exactly why Caroline hadn't wanted anything to do with this shower.

"Oh, nothing," Caroline said, attempting to sound cute as if to imply she had some secret task.

Her sister's eyes turned hard above her gleaming smile. "Why are you here early, anyway?" she asked. "We could have used a hand loading everything at the house."

It was a challenge, to be sure, the beginning of a fight waged a thousand times. To Abigail, Caroline was ungrateful, reckless, babied. And Caroline was tired of Abigail always trying to mom her. They each pulled back their familiar arrows, ready to take verbal aim when Ruthie yelled from the kitchen. "Abby! Leave it be!" Adding: "Some things are supposed to be a surprise."

Abigail rolled her eyes and flashed a warning smile at her sister. They could hear their mother's agitation from the living room—plastic lids crinkled as they were lifted off vegetable trays, plates clinked as they left cabinets, ice clanged as it fell into pitchers.

"Are you actually going to try and seem happy today?" Abby asked, her voice so bright no hesitation was permissible.

"Of course I will," Caroline said. But when she turned away to head to the kitchen and make herself useful, Abigail grabbed the soft part of her arm and pulled her back.

"Ow, wha-at?" Caroline whined.

"She's acting weird," Abigail said, quieter now, looking toward the kitchen. She leaned closer. Caroline was a full head taller and could detect the faint scent of singed hair beneath her sister's subtle lavender perfume.

The two of them were always trying to be close. Every year on Caroline's birthday, Abigail would write her a note about how she wanted to work on their relationship, or how she wished they could speak to each other in a language no one else knew, or text each other first with good news. But it never lasted past Caroline borrowing a cute top without asking or forgetting to hang up her towel in the bathroom, which is to say a few days at most. Then Abigail would return to correcting Caroline's grammar, rolling her eyes whenever she spoke, and reminding her that she was six years older. Caroline still saved all of Abigail's cards in a box that she hid under her bed, a reminder that it was her own fault.

"Weird how?" Caroline asked, removing her sister's acrylic nails from the back of her arm and pinching the fat there herself.

"I dunno. Mrs. Debbie called before we left the house and Mom was, like, really silent on the phone and just said, 'Thank you so much for letting me know,' and then wouldn't tell me anything about it the whole drive over." Abigail crossed her arms. Her eyes narrowed.

"Abigail." Caroline sighed. "It's probably a surprise for later. Can you please just chill?" But Abigail's intuition had always been good. In small-group Bible studies, the other girls said prophecy was her spiritual gift—and sometimes it seemed like they were right.

"It's not like her," Abigail said.

She would know, Caroline thought. She and their mother were so much alike. They were the wives of noble character promised in Proverbs 31, constantly quoting their favorite verse: "Charm is deceptive and beauty is fleeting, but a woman who fears the Lord is to be praised." Caroline looked at her mother in the kitchen, noted her hunched shoulders and unfocused eyes. Abigail was right. This wasn't like her. Ruthie Nolan was a woman who always served with a smile.

"Yeah, I guess she does seem a little off," Caroline said, glancing at Abigail out of the corner of her eye. "Do you want me to ask her about the call?"

Before Abigail could answer, they heard the first crunch of tires over gravel and the clapping of a car door closing, and already another crunched behind it.

Abigail's curls swayed as she shook her head. "Later, okay?" she said, because they were here: the women of the Hope Church.

They poured through the front door like fire ants from a demolished hill: forty-five women, all on time. They came in holding the front door for one another, kissing cheeks, pointing at the lights and the flower garlands suspended from the hall ceiling. Abigail and Caroline faced them together. By the time the women hit the end of the long hall, both girls would appear happy and humble. For they were, above almost all else, Luke Nolan's daughters.

As Abigail hugged and flashed her big teeth, Caroline traded flutes of champagne for gift-wrapped boxes. The women pointed at the pictures Caroline had brought in, now artfully arranged on the kitchen island; they fingered the lace table runners, exclaimed over cupcakes with the couple's initials piped in buttercream. The temperature of the room rose five degrees. Caroline fanned her face with her hand. She wished they could have narrowed the guest list, though she knew that was never an option. It's impossible for a pastor's family to host a small event. There are too many people to potentially offend, too many church members who act more like aunts and uncles than neighbors. Everyone's hips were up against chairs, hands on one another, purses knocking into lamps and side tables. It all felt excessive and nauseating. Caroline answered the same questions over and over, smiled politely, each interaction like a bloodletting, draining a bit more of her energy.

Her entire life, this had been Caroline's role: Luke Nolan's younger, less important daughter. And today was no different. She listened as Abigail told a humorous anecdote to three women about how she'd had to call seven different flower shops to find the perfect yellow roses for the ceremony. Caroline knew these women because each of them had sent her sons against their will to ask her to the senior prom this past spring.

In a way, the Nolan women had been preparing for this day, this summer, for Abigail's engagement, their entire lives. As the daughters of a famous and beloved pastor, the girls had attended hundreds of bridal showers, each one held at the church in the women's ministry room with soggy sandwiches, dwindling juice pitchers, and oft-repeated if unconvincing meet-cute stories. Luke Nolan officiated, on average, thirty weddings a year, and his daughters were invited to most of them—their every Saturday from late May to early September booked with double-header showers so similar they blurred together in Caroline's memory, showers that were followed by equally forgettable weddings. Abigail had made it her personal mission to surpass them all. She wanted her long-anticipated season to be one that girls in Hope, Texas, talked about for years to come. To Caroline, it felt like a fantasy set aflame.

"So you're off to the big city for school next month, I hear?" a woman asked. Caroline donned a smile and spun around to find Mrs. Brody. Somewhere in the walls, the air conditioner kicked back on and women around the room cheered at the promise of cool air.

"I am," Caroline said with practiced confidence. A corner fan blew a strand of hair into her lip gloss. She struggled to remove it for long enough that Mrs. Brody averted her blue-shadowed eyes. Caroline continued smiling, tried to play it off, but she could feel her cheeks reddening.

"I hafta admit I'm a bit surprised you aren't going to Texas Christian like your sister," Mrs. Brody said in the same chiding tone Caroline had heard from just about everyone in town since she'd made her decision a few months back.

Of course you are, Caroline thought, *it's all anyone ever says to me*. She smiled. "They don't have as good of an advertising program. I think it will be a good fit for me." What she wanted to say was that anything would be a better fit than these dresses that hit at a demure but unflattering length right above the knee, and these women she'd loved all her life but who'd never really known her. Her mother always said she should be grateful to have a community that cared so much about her, even if their meddling annoyed her most of the time.

"I know it's far, but I really want to have a career," Caroline said, and steeled herself for the next part of this conversation, where she might be warned about the dangers of a big city like Austin and the creep of liberalism, or be subjected to some drawn-out account of how this woman's son's best friend's sister had found a church there despite all odds, and would Caroline like her email? Mrs. Brody fingered the large cross pendant that hung almost to her belly button and opened her mouth—likely to tell some version of the same overblown horror story—when Mrs. Debbie appeared behind her, silencing whatever Mrs. Brody had been about to say.

Caroline focused on keeping her body still and her smile genuine as she greeted Mrs. Debbie, whose large frame was draped in layers and layers of floral fabric despite the Texas heat. Mrs. Debbie said a quick hello to Caroline as she steered Mrs. Brody toward the chairs at the center of the room. Mrs. Brody smiled at Caroline on her way past. "Just don't let that big city make you forget where you come from," she said.

"It's time for gifts," Mrs. Debbie sang as she shepherded the women one by one, a hand placed between their shoulders, the other pointing away from the snacks and into the circle. It was said that Mrs. Debbie held the heart of the Hope Church tightly in her fist. She ran the small group that organized their volunteer events and coat drives, Bible studies and women's lunches. She alone decided whose secrets would be held close to the chest and whose scattered to sprout like wildflower seeds. The elders called her a force. The young mothers swore she was a baby whisperer. Even the teens admitted that she gave good advice. Basically, if the Hope Church had believed in saint-hood, Mrs. Debbie would have been the first one canonized.

Caroline hurried to her place at the front of the room but remained standing, fumbling with the plastic trash bag that hung on the back of her chair, looking around for her sister. She knew there was no point in sitting until Abigail had taken the seat next to hers. She watched the women sweep their dresses beneath them, cross their legs at their ankles. Abigail slowly made her way over to the front of the semicircle, placing a hand on the backs of chairs to squeeze past, joking about the tight quarters. With every few steps her eyes flitted toward the kitchen. Caroline followed her gaze and saw that their mother was leaning against the kitchen cabinets facing Mrs. Debbie, her lips tight. Then Abigail was there beside her, poking Caroline's shoulder, asking her to move. Caroline leaned against the chair in front of her and her sister slid past, plopped down into her seat with a smile. A navy box with a white bow appeared in Abigail's lap. Caroline sat and bent to pick up the notebook and pen they'd hidden underneath her chair. She jotted down the giver's name.

Abigail's friends, many of whom had driven from the nearby towns they'd moved to with their husbands after their own weddings, cooed at the wineglasses and gravy boats, passing the items clockwise so each guest could marvel and declare that these were the best and she should know because she had them too. A few women snapped photos of the bride-to-be, backlit by the window, flushing to the breastbone when she opened a lace baby-doll nightie and ducked her head to keep from making eye contact with her fiancé's mother, sitting in the second row.

Abigail opened a pasta maker and raised it for the crowd to see. Caroline snatched the wrapping paper from where it landed at her sister's feet and shoved it into the now bulging trash bag beside her. Then she rescued a pink bow from the mass of torn paper and placed it inside the gift bag under her seat. She wrote *pasta maker* and *Meredith Jones* in the notebook. As she waited for Abigail to finish tearing open the next present, she slid her phone from her pocket to check the time. Abigail noticed.

"You have somewhere better to be?" she asked through a smile.

For a fraction of a second, Caroline saw that her sister's eyes seemed overly joyous, her muscles too rigid. She wasn't happy, Caroline thought. Or at least, she wasn't as happy as she was pretending to be.

"Oh no," Caroline said. "Just checking the time."

Here was the pause in the action the women had been craving. "So . . ." a mother begged, dragging her words into a plea, "tell us the story . . ."

Everyone clapped, and Abigail positioned herself in her chair the way she did in her classroom: tilting up her chin, placing her hands upon her knees, lowering her voice. "Well . . ." she began, and every body in the room leaned in to hear her.

Any love story can be a fairy tale with enough encouragement—and Abigail gave them one worth swooning over. She left out the part about how she'd only agreed to a first date with Matthew because the weekend before she'd watched her own father officiate the wedding of her high school sweetheart to some girl he'd met at college. She chose not to mention that at the age of twenty-four she was already considered an old maid in this part of Texas, the last of her friends still wearing her abstinence ring.

On the four-month anniversary of their first date, Abigail hadn't expected a thing, she told the crowd.

"Of course, in retrospect, I should've known," she said, and raised an eyebrow to her audience. "He did bother to put on a tie. A dead giveaway." The room laughed.

She really had been surprised, though. That part was true. Matthew and Abigail had been dating for a month when he took a job in Midland on a recently tapped oil well and left Hope seemingly for good. She told the shower that she'd expected to forget about him, to return to her work at the elementary school begging her students to learn their multiplication tables.

"But he pursued me," Abigail said, and that too was true.

He came back for her fall break, and for every subsequent weekend that he could after that, sleeping in the Nolans' guest room and never (though Caroline always listened for it) sneaking out in the middle of the night to climb into bed with her sister.

Caroline had spent months trying to understand what Matthew could have done to convince Abby to marry him and then to move away from Hope, a place she'd sworn she'd never leave. Abby's decision to flee the town, the church, the land she'd always loved sat unsteadily in Caroline's stomach. Maybe, Caroline thought, her sister's commitment was one of desperation: to just be married, for better or for worse.

Abigail told the women that Matthew had taken her out for a fancy dinner last Christmas, where he'd ordered steaks and a bottle of wine, hers medium rare, his well-done.

"I know. I know," she quipped, "I probably shouldn't have said yes to a man who'd ruin a perfectly good steak." But she had said yes. There had been cake and a surprise bottle of champagne and the cork was popped and there, in the crystal glass the waitress set in front of her, was the ring. Abigail poured it into her hand, and when she looked up, he was kneeling before her, tears in his eyes, saying, "Please, darling, I'd be honored."

With every telling her sister's timing was better, her jokes landed cleaner. This story was so expertly crafted over dozens of recountings, it seemed like she'd started to believe it herself. It was a skill Abigail had inherited from their father. But Caroline knew better. She'd overheard Abigail tell their mother about how she'd zoned out that night, blanked on how to respond to a diamond ring, stared right past Matthew crying until the people began to clap and he placed his hand on her knee and asked again. Then she'd nodded, and so it was decided.

Here Abigail sat smiling, arriving at her grand finale. She looked into the eyes of those girls who were younger than she was, the daughters of their mother's friends for whom this brought not memory but fantasy, and said, "With a move that classic, what could I possibly say but yes?"

The women clapped, and a few wiped tears from their eyes. Love made a sucker out of them all. It seemed everyone in Hope, Texas—even those who didn't belong to their father's church—had been waiting years for Abigail Nolan to marry. They'd watched her as a small child, a ponytailed middle schooler, a teenager they wanted their sons to date. She was already the best bride. Caroline noticed her sister's knee jittering beneath her white skirt, something Abigail did when she was stressed, frustrated, or lying. There were only five short weeks until the wedding.

More gifts appeared in Abigail's lap. She tore at the paper, revealing candlesticks, towels with her new initials monogrammed, champagne flutes, everything she could possibly need to finally move out of the Nolan house. All the while she told jokes and kept the conversation going, her strip-whitened smile shining, her head high.

The women watched as Abigail opened table runners and decorative bowls, candles for special occasions and ice cream scoops. They looked straight into those big green eyes she'd inherited from her father to see if somewhere in there she felt any of the disappointment that they did. Because every one of them would have bet money that when Abigail Nolan walked down the aisle, it would be straight into the arms of her high school sweetheart, Connor Boyd. They had the decency not to bring it up, of course, though they still whispered about it behind hands and closed doors. Abigail Nolan was going to marry someone else. Well, they'd say, God's plan was better than any man's. Though many of them knew well enough that following God's plan didn't necessarily mean you'd end up happy.

"He's here," Ruthie said as she buzzed by, refilling glasses. Matthew.

Caroline stood, leaving her notebook on her chair, and walked quickly down the hall to the entryway. Through the stained-glass window, she immediately saw that he'd chosen the wrong flowers—gerbera daisies, pink and yellow like a grocery store frosted cookie, even their shadow wilted as he walked from his car. She grabbed the bouquet of yellow roses that Abigail had arranged in a blue ceramic vase on the table near the door and stepped outside. The sun burned her face. She raised a hand to shield her forehead—she had enough freckles already—and descended the porch stairs to greet him.

"Hey, Caro!" he said. She bristled at the nickname, a term of familiarity he hadn't earned.

"Hi," she said, and reached one arm out to accept his side-hug, both of them holding their bouquets away from their bodies. He was so eager, like a golden retriever in want of a treat. She took the daisies from his hand and replaced them with the roses. "These are better," she said. He just nodded in agreement.

Caroline slid her hand into her dress pocket and felt the sharp edge of the condom wrapper. She blushed, plunged her hand into her other pocket, and presented Matthew with the velvet box that contained her grandmother's bracelet.

"Do you remember what you're gonna do?" she asked as they climbed the stairs.

"Mm-hm," he said. "Walk in, give her these *much better* flowers, present this gift, wave to the ladies, and then skedaddle. Right?"

"Right," she said. "Except there's also a game. You're not supposed to know."

"Can I kiss her?" He seemed to be asking his shoes.

"On the cheek," she said, and opened the front door for him. "Oh, Matthew," Caroline said. He turned back. "Tell her it's something old when you hand it to her."

"The bracelet?" he asked. Caroline nodded; the shrieks had already begun. She breathed out through her nose as she shut the door behind her. If he did exactly as she said, took the lifetime of knowledge she'd just handed to him and passed it off as his own, everything would go smoothly. She hurried down the hall to keep an eye on things in case he stumbled.

She watched from the end of the hallway as Matthew wove between the chairs, kissed Abigail on the cheek, and handed over the velvet box.

"I thought you'd need something old," he offered, and the room cascaded with *aw*s, the women looking at one another, placing a single hand across their hearts. Over a dozen hairsprayed heads, Caroline watched him sit in the chair she'd vacated, wrap his arm around her sister's back, and accept her thanks as Abigail explained to the room that the bracelet was their grandmother's and that it had been given to Nannie by her own mother for her wedding day. All while Matthew beamed like he already knew the story.

The women allowed him to sit beside his fiancée, smiling with all of his teeth, for only a few minutes before they moved his and Abigail's chairs back-to-back and told them to remove their shoes. Now they each held one Nike Air Jordan and one tasteful Mary Jane nude heel as they were quizzed on their relationship. Which one of them was neater? Two nude heels rose. More beautiful? Up the heels went again. More excited? Matthew raised his own shoe and the women squealed with delight. In the end no one won because no one was keeping score. Matthew left right afterward, raising his hand to high-five Caroline on his way out the door.

The voices in the room escalated in his wake. Fingers pulled a strand of hair from a bun, brushed the edge of a scarf, gripped the stem of a wineglass. This was a time-honored Hope liturgy. Had the shower ended right then, the women would have left satisfied.

There were, however, still more games to play, Mrs. Debbie reminded the room. They were instructed to refill their glasses and grab a piece of thinly sliced cake. Their mouths curved around shining real silverware, lips painted the color of roses, strawberries, and rust. All done up for one another.

Caroline dropped into the chair where Abigail had been seated earlier and tried to catch her breath. Women scootched by, their hips knocking her chair, hands resting on her shoulder, stroking her hair, leaving a wide variety of scents in their wake—vanilla, pine, Dove soap, coffee breath. "We are so excited," their mouths said, "and so happy for her." Caroline's head felt light. She closed her eyes for a moment. "Excuse me," she said to the woman nearest to her, and wove her way out of the room.

In the hall bathroom, she splashed water on her face, totally forgetting about her makeup. She dried her cheeks on the hand towel, and sighed when she realized that she'd left a giant beige smudge across it. She turned the towel around. She leaned closer to the mirror and saw that she could just make out the bulge of a rising pimple. She tried out a fake smile like her sister's, but even that she did poorly. Everything seemed easier for Abigail.

She jumped at a rap on the door.

"Caro," Abigail said, "can I come in?" Before Caroline could respond, her sister opened the door. "What are you doing?"

"Just needed a minute," she said. Abigail knew that Caroline was never as comfortable as she was in crowds.

They both stood in front of the mirror, angled toward each other in the small space, Abigail's spine so straight that Caroline lengthened her own. "We have to get back out there," Abigail said to her sister's reflection.

"Yeah," Caroline said. At least she'd tried to say it nicely. Abigail hated picking up her sister's slack, and usually snapped at Caroline when she tried to duck out of their familial obligations. If Abigail could perform so easily, she thought everyone should be able to.

"Your bra strap is showing," Abigail said, and tucked it under Caroline's dress.

Caroline watched as her sister turned to study herself in the mirror. Abigail scanned her dress for stains, her skin for imperfections. She stopped suddenly, leaned forward over the counter, and swiped her smeared eyeliner into a straight line with her pinky finger. Maybe she didn't want to go back in either, Caroline thought.

But they were examples—extensions of their father—and expected to behave like it: to be gracious and humble and quiet and holy. For most of her life, Caroline had thought this a privilege. Now she wasn't so sure. After a few seconds,

Abigail stepped back, opened the door in one motion so she stood flush with the wall, and herded Caroline out with her left hand. "Smile," Abigail told her as she passed, and Caroline forced the corners of her mouth to turn up, though she still felt the balls of tension in her cheeks.

They entered the living room and saw that the chairs had been stacked against the wall to make room to play games. Abigail rushed away to entertain her guests. Caroline reached her hand into her dress pocket, traced the square outline, overheard a few of her mother's friends reminiscing about their own bridal showers. Later, she pricked the pad of her pointer finger with the foil's sharp corner as the women wrapped her in a toilet paper wedding dress. When her mother raised a champagne glass to toast her sister, she kept her right hand in her pocket and raised her glass of sparkling grape juice with her left. By the time the women had finished writing their recipes for a healthy marriage in a cookbook and transformed themselves into a choreographed cleaning brigade, Caroline had softened three of the wrapper's four corners from wear.

AFTER THE MOUNTAIN of leftover food was carted away in individual gallon Ziploc bags and the chairs returned to the garage, Nannie's house was just a house once again and would remain so until the balloon festival the following weekend. Caroline watched Abigail lock the front door behind them in one try.

But before they could descend the porch steps, the girls noted the firm set of their mother's mouth as she turned to face them, clearly uncomfortable. "Girls," Ruthie said, rubbing her forehead, "I know we were planning to swim in the pool this afternoon, but I need some alone time with your father, would you mind?" She said it as one sentence without pausing for breath. Abigail said, "Not at all," so Caroline said it too.

"I'll stop by the ·house and grab Matthew," Abigail said. "We need to make a Target run anyway, so we'll probably do that."

Caroline looked over at her sister, noticed that the curls on the left side of her face had loosened from Abigail running her hands through them. She pulled her phone from her purse to check for any notifications, but there were no bars, no Wi-Fi. She put the phone back in her pocket and felt the remaining sharp corner stab her thumb. "I'll just stay here," she said.

"Oh no, Caro." Abigail blushed, embarrassed. "I didn't mean you couldn't come with! Of course you should come too."

"I have a book to read," Caroline lied. "Don't worry about me."

She waved as her mother and sister drove down the driveway, and again when Abigail hopped out to close the cattle gate behind them. Once their car was out of sight, she went into the kitchen, opened the contacts on her phone, and dialed his number with the landline. She listened to it ring.

"Hello?" he said. She felt his voice on the back of her neck and told herself to relax, to be chill about this.

"Hi. I know you hate phones but I'm at the ranch and there's no service, and I thought you'd like to know that I'm here alone if you wanted to come over." She said it so quickly that by the end she had to take a sharp inhale to recalibrate.

There was some noise on the other end. He was in his car. Caroline could hear the click of his blinker. She tapped her forehead with the base of her palm. So. Stupid.

"Sure," he said. "I'm about twenty minutes away."

She shouldn't respond immediately, she knew, and tried to count to four; she didn't make it.

"Great," she said, "see you soon," and went back out onto the porch alone. It was hot enough to fry an egg on the sidewalk, hot as the hinges of hell. Caroline pushed away her doubts and waited for him to arrive.

2

Taylor McGregor and Caroline Nolan were not, and never had been, dating—and they never discussed what they were because they weren't anything at all. They'd known each other since childhood, attended the same Sunday school, though they didn't share any friends.

It's true that every teenager has their secrets, but for the children of prominent Hope Church families, a secret could be catastrophic. Caroline had seen deacons booted from leadership positions over sons who smoked pot, elders reprimanded for daughters who wouldn't take the abstinence oath. A few years before, a pastor had been required to step down after his college-aged son refused to repent and attend a Christian counseling group for ex-homosexuals. So rebellion was risky, not because she might be lectured, but because it could create a ripple effect that endangered her parents' leadership role within the church.

Had Caroline and Taylor wanted to date—to go to early dinners and keep their hands to themselves in a movie theater, or pray next to each other every Sunday—their parents would have been thrilled. But there was no scenario in which either set of parents would have approved of Taylor driving his Jeep onto the ranch property alone.

Caroline was sitting on the porch steps. She stood when she saw him climb out to lock the gate behind him. Smart, she thought. She pulled her dress from where it had stuck to the backs of her thighs, raised her right hand to shade her eyes, and watched him park his Jeep beside her car. His back muscles rippled under his thin T-shirt as he stepped out, closed the door, and beeped it locked over his shoulder. He was the same height as Caroline—she was tall for a girl—and had they fought, it probably would have been fair. But right now, he was walking toward her like he had somewhere to be.

"Hey," he said, holding her gaze as he came closer. She matched his look and smiled. Well-raised Christian boys always stared so deeply into your eyes that you knew all they could possibly be thinking about was your body. *This right here*, she thought, *is power*.

"Hey yourself," she said back.

It had been almost six months since they'd run into each other sneaking out of youth group during the final prayer, an accidental encounter that told them both more about each other than a thousand Sunday hellos. Abigail had gotten engaged the weekend before, and when Caroline had tried to explain why it bothered her to the girls in Bible study, they hadn't understood. She was lonely and there he was: this boy who'd seemed to grow five inches overnight, and learned to lean with one hand against his locker in a way that felt like a personal attack. They agreed to keep the sneaking out of church a secret from their parents, and then they'd wordlessly agreed to keep more.

At first, they were careful. They kissed with their mouths closed at prearranged locations where they knew no one could see them. Caroline would park her old Toyota and walk a few blocks into the darkened area where he'd parked his Jeep. She'd scan for eyes before opening the door. She knew that his back seat could be laid down, that you didn't have to have sex to end up with rug burn, and that his lips tasted like Carmex. It would have been illicit if it hadn't been so ordinary. They knew they were doing what every unsaved high schooler does, but for them it was dangerous. Still, Taylor McGregor—despite his rebellions—was a church boy. He was, after all, Hope Church royalty himself. He was Mrs. Debbie's youngest son.

"Are you sure?" he'd asked the first time she'd climbed into his back seat in early February. "Are you sure?" he'd asked as she'd pulled a bra strap off her shoulder. "Are you sure?" he'd whispered in her ear as he'd climbed on top of her fully clothed, and reached his hand down the front of her jeans, as he sucked not gently enough on the pale skin beneath her collarbone. Now it was late June and Abigail was getting married. The ground was littered with a thousand pulsing grasshoppers, and Caroline was determined to make her life more interesting.

CAROLINE LIKED TO believe that she'd been corrupted by her one true love: television. As embarrassing as it was to admit, a show about a comic book character with infinite abs had done her in. She had never read a romance novel, or harbored a real crush, or allowed herself to type a few choice words into the search bar late at night. But she had watched that show on her laptop while lying in bed and, afterward, seemed to be mesmerized by the dip in boys' shoulder muscles when they raised their arms to grab a book from a locker, by the stark defined U shape on top of their knees when they climbed the stairs, by the way their eyes closed when they ran a hand through their hair.

Of course, she'd felt guilty about it. For most of her junior year, she'd prayed that the Lord would take these feelings away. Surely a woman was not supposed to be this horny. But the Lord never responded and Caroline continued watching until she found Taylor, and then she forgot about the show entirely. It had been easier to be meek and self-controlled before she'd known the soft pain of a boy's bony hips inside her thighs.

After their first kiss, she'd started questioning whether she even wanted to be the kind of woman she saw all around her. When she helped Abigail address her save-the-dates in careful calligraphy, Caroline realized that she'd never tried to envision her own wedding, couldn't see herself in the white dress. The Bible promised a version of womanhood that was all sweetness and goodness. But Caroline wanted wet, sloppy kisses. She wanted to make quick retorts and harness the power of her body like the women she saw on TV. She didn't want a prime-time sitcom life. She wanted cable. She wanted a parental advisory warning. Or at least, she thought she did. There was only one version of womanhood she knew, and when she tried to imagine a future without children, or a husband, or a modest home with a well-groomed lawn and a golden retriever and three trips to church every week, she came up with nothing.

But she knew for sure that she wanted sex more than she'd ever thought she would, and that she didn't want to leave for college a virgin. She knew it was a big deal, your first time, but if she couldn't see herself with a husband, why wait? She could easily justify her slippery slope with Taylor if she wanted to. Jesus loved her despite her sins, she could have said. Hers was a faith of grace and forgiveness, she could have reasoned. But she didn't. She tried not to think about it at all.

Taylor followed her up the porch steps and through the front door. Caroline's desire led them down the hallway, guided them into the second bedroom, lifted her dress above her head, and stood there between them just long enough for him to ask.

"Are you sure?" He seemed unable to look up from the curve of her waist in the sunlit room, the bed behind him vast and far less shameful than a back seat. He tripped as he tried to take off his jeans, still looking at her. Caroline swallowed his helplessness whole. She slipped one bra strap down.

"I didn't," he stammered. "Bring, um, anything."

Caroline bent, sucking in her stomach, and retrieved the condom from her dress pocket on the floor. She handed it to him. It had been a sign. All year they had been building toward this inevitable act. What did it really matter, this sin?

Caroline stood in front of him in her underwear, the one bra strap limp around her biceps, waiting for him to make a move. He was nervous, so after an infinite ten seconds she made the moves for him. She unfastened her bra behind her back. He released all the breath in his lungs through rounded lips and sat down on the bed. She climbed on top of him and kissed him firmly on the mouth.

"Caro, hold on, wait," he said, holding her at arm's length. Her heart sank. She placed her hands behind her on his knees and forced her back straight, her body long. She tried to keep her face from falling.

"I just . . ." he fumbled, shook his head. "I know this has been kind of a chill thing"—he motioned between them—"and I know that's, like, every guy's dream."

Caroline wrapped a hand around his neck and pulled herself closer.

"I think I'm . . ." He looked away from her. "I think I might want it to be more than that."

She laughed, and instantly her body knew her mistake. Her hand flew to her mouth. He looked up and she saw the small boy with big eyes that he'd once been.

"Oh no, Taylor. I'm sorry. It's just, you are maybe the only boy in the world who would stop . . ."—she couldn't say *sex*—"*this* to confess you have a crush."

"Is it okay?" he asked.

She kissed him then, covering his lips with her own, unsure if she didn't want to respond because her answer was a lie or because it was the truth.

"Are you sure you want to do this?" he asked again.

"I'm sure," she said, and in that moment it was the only thing she knew to be true.

IT LASTED BARELY long enough for Caroline to realize she was no longer a virgin. When it was over, the only evidence that anything had happened was the knot in her hair at the base of her neck. All her life, Caroline had been promised that her first time would be painful, that her husband would have to lay down a towel on their marital bed and be very, very

careful with her. But they hadn't been gentle, or soft, or careful. It wasn't the lack of orgasm that disappointed her. It was
the lack of blood. She had been promised blood. He twirled
a strand of her hair between his fingers. "I'm sorry," he said.

She sat up. "For what?"

"For um . . . for going so fast," he said, not looking at her.

"It was great," she lied. "Don't worry about that." She
handed him the box of tissues from the bedside table like
she'd seen the girls on TV do.

She rose from the bed and waddled down the hall to the
bathroom. At the very least, she thought, she should feel guilty.
A good Christian would feel guilty. Caroline felt nothing at
all. She looked in the mirror, and saw that the girl looking
back at her was the same one from earlier that morning.

By the time she returned to the bedroom, Taylor had pulled
on his jeans and was straightening the comforter. He had been
raised right. He fluffed the pillows while she took the trash
bag out of the bedroom and deposited it in the empty kitchen
garbage can. Plenty of young couples used condoms even if
they were married, Caroline reassured herself. No one would
find it. But just in case, she took a couple of paper towels from
the roll, crumpled them between her hands, and tossed them
on top. The landline phone rang on the counter. Caroline hovered a hand above it for a moment before deciding to let it ring.

"You all right?" he asked as she returned to the room and
stepped into her dress.

"Yeah," she said. "Can you zip me?"

He pulled the zipper up her back, patted it twice when it
reached the top. When she turned to face him, his eyes were
wide, his lips parted.

"Can I ask you something?" she said.

"Of course," he said. "What's up?"

"Do you feel guilty?" The question came out sounding more vulnerable than she'd meant it. She wished she could take it back.

The light from the window was harsh and bright, his shadow long behind him on the wood floor. He looked away from her, and for a moment, she worried. If he felt guilty, shouldn't she? The sun overexposed his face. She searched it for any signal of how he'd respond; he gave her nothing. She focused on the bump on his nose, the only part of his face that wasn't sharp or angular. She knew it was from a childhood break. He ran a hand through his thick hair and shook his head. "I don't," he said. "But we don't have to do this again. I don't want to do anything that makes you feel guilty." He placed a kiss on her forehead.

She pulled away. "No," she said. "I don't feel guilty either." She looked at this long, lean boy before her, and missed the control she'd felt only moments before. "I think I'd like to do this again."

He laughed as he pulled his T-shirt over his head. "Guess our parents were right after all." He bent over and laced his shoes. "Without Christ, we really are living in sin." He looked up at her then, and she noticed how much lighter the top of his hair was from the sun, a soft brown.

"What?" she asked, and was proud of herself for keeping her voice so steady. No one had ever implied she was without Christ before. Because she wasn't. She'd been saved ever since childhood. But then again, she thought, so had he.

"Like now that we don't believe what they believe we've gone off the deep end or whatever," he said. And then, when she didn't laugh, he straightened up. "Caro. It's a joke."

"You're an atheist?" she asked, and turned to walk out of the room so he wouldn't see her reaction. He couldn't be an atheist. He was so good.

"Nah. More like agnostic," he said, following closely behind her. His voice echoed as they walked down the hallway toward the front door. "I know I don't really believe in the Bible or whatever. I think the whole thing is kind of naive, closed-minded."

They stepped out into the heat, the light golden and unchanged. Caroline felt a familiar question rise in her mind and shoved it down, deep down into her stomach, where it sat heavy and unwieldy like a cast-iron skillet. "Just a second," she said as she struggled to lock the door, grateful this time to have a moment to compose herself.

When she turned, she saw his face drop from a crooked smile into a look of concern. Somehow her expression had betrayed her fear.

"Oh man, you're still a Christian, aren't you? I'm sorry, Caro. I didn't realize." His lips were set in the same pout she'd seen a hundred times before from the more popular girls, the ones who pitied her without understanding her at all. But his eyes were soft, his hand reaching out to touch her arm instead of pushing her away.

She nodded. She and Taylor had said so little to each other over the past six months. Caroline rested a hand on the porch railing to steady herself. She had to be a Christian. It wasn't just her faith, it was who she was. Right? She was nothing without the blood of Jesus. She was in the world, not of the world. Wasn't she? She tried to reconstruct every conversation she'd ever had with him to see how he could have thought this about her. She found nothing, which meant it must be something she couldn't even see. If he thought this, what did everyone else think? No, she thought. No one would ever find out.

"I'm so sorry. I just—" Taylor took a couple of steps toward her. "I totally respect whatever you believe. I just thought . . ."

"No, it's okay," she said, waving both hands in front of her. "It makes sense you would think that."

She let him pull her into a hug and laid her head on his shoulder. She looked out across the long empty stretch of land to the west of the house. It was brown and hard from the summer sun, bordered by the darkening silhouettes of trees. Above them, the clear blue sky was stained with a spill of orange around the sun, and wisps of clouds drifted north. The high grass swayed in the warm breeze and matched the rhythm of his thumb as it moved up and down her back.

"You okay?" he asked after a few minutes, holding her away from him by the shoulders.

"Yeah, totally," she said.

He turned and climbed into his car, leaned out the window. "Caro," he said, waving her over. When she was close enough, he pulled her toward him by the forearm, grabbed her neck to kiss her with soft lips. "Think about what I said, okay?" His arm rested on the windowsill, bronze in the soft sunlight; beads of sweat along his hairline glimmered. Caroline wanted to reach out and stroke his cheekbone.

"About being a Christian?" she asked.

His eyes fell. "No," he said. "About having feelings. We don't have to talk about it now, but maybe soon?"

"Of course," she said, and hurried to her car before he could say anything further.

AS SHE DROVE home, Caroline tried to sing along with Johnny Cash on the radio to avoid thinking about what she'd done. Outside, the endless fields were barely visible, a small flat line of yellowed earth beneath a giant domed sky. She rolled the window down despite the heat and ignored her driving school rules, resting one hand at the twelve o'clock position. The sun caught the ring on her left hand. She rarely noticed it anymore. She'd slid it on sophomore year like every other teenager in the Hope Church Youth Ministry. Now it felt tight, pinched the skin of her ring finger. It also felt like a shining reminder of her sin. Her father had popularized this abstinence ring, encouraged more than a million teenagers to slide them on and say their vows, to join the movement. It was his legacy.

Caroline had been nine years old the day her father had become a household name. She was squeezed into a pink dress so itchy she remembered it irritating her collarbone as she sat in the front row of the large, circular arena at the Southern Baptist Convention's Annual Meeting in Dallas. There were almost ten thousand people in attendance, crowded into curved lines of chairs, two levels of stadium seating. Above her head, rows of stage lights hung suspended from the high ceiling, and three giant screens showed the pulpit. When Luke Nolan emerged from the door at the back of the stage to give the opening night's keynote address, the applause he received was tentative; a few conversations continued. Caroline had looked at Abigail, noticed her biting her lip, her knee bouncing under her dress.

Back then, Caroline never had any real alone time with her sister. Their six-year age difference meant that Abigail was too old to play with Barbies by the time Caroline was old enough to want to, and then seemingly overnight Abigail was a teenager. If she wasn't praying at church with her youth group, hair falling like a veil over her face, then she was at track practice. And if she was at home, so was her boyfriend, Connor, the two of them clinging on to each other as if afraid the other might float away.

The night before the conference in Dallas was supposed to be the girls' night. Abigail was fifteen and they'd been allowed to stay home alone for the first time. They had a stack of DVDs and ordered a pizza. But before the food arrived, before they could even hit play, the phone rang. Caroline answered with her chipper "Nolan residence, this is Caroline!" It was their father. He sounded disappointed that she was the one who'd picked up. He wanted to speak to Abigail. Caroline handed the phone to her sister and Abigail's face brightened. Their father kept her on for hours, discussing his sermon. Caroline watched her sister pace back and forth in the kitchen, cold pizza beside her, until she finally fell asleep on the couch. Abigail was like a rib taken from his side.

That was the greatest secret about Luke Nolan's name-making sermon: he'd needed his daughter's help to write it. "I just answered his questions," Abigail later told the reporters. She was a girl of strong faith with a killer stage presence, a sermon cadence baked into her bones. She knew there was no point in asking for credit. There would never be a leadership role for her within the church.

The next afternoon, Luke had sent Ruthie to fetch the girls. They were led into the freezing arena by their mother and seated in the front row, where they waited, hands folded in their laps and mouths closed until their father prayed to open the service. Caroline remembered watching his every movement—one man walking toward the edge of the stage, face stern, his right foot tapping below the pulpit. His voice started out low like a growl as he told a story of himself as a young man and a sermon he'd once hated.

It had been a simple sermon, he explained. The pastor had thrust out a single, flawless rose. "Imagine," the pastor had said, "that this rose is the sanctity of your virginity."

On the stage, Luke had paced as he explained how the rose was then passed around the congregation. He held his hands cupped before him as he described how he'd delivered the rose, its broken stem hanging between his pinkies, back to the pastor. "I felt so ashamed," he said. "And I'm ashamed that I didn't say anything then." As soon as the pastor had the rose in his hand, he'd asked the congregation: Who would want this rose? Who would choose this broken thing over something pure and whole?

Luke paused then for effect. He looked out at the audience. It wasn't included on the video of his sermon that would later go viral—viewed millions of times online by evangelicals all over the country—but Caroline's most vivid memory was of the moment before he erupted, when she looked over at her sister. Abigail was beaming up at him, green eyes sparkling in the aggressive stage lighting, her body pitched forward. The roughness of his whisper against the mic grated itself over the audience with each question he posed:

"Who could want something so broken? So ruined? So tarnished? Who could want that rose?" their father repeated, his voice rising. "It made me so furious. Because I knew. I know who wants that rose."

His glare flitted down to the front row, where his wife sat between his daughters, holding their hands. He waited. Five. Four. Three. Two. One. His gaze lifted to the back wall, and he bellowed out at his audience: "JESUS DOES.

"Jesus," he yelled, "wants the rose!" The hair on Caroline's arms stood up. "Our Savior. Our Messiah. Our God wants us. All of us. You and me." His voice dropped, and he finished softly, "Who wants that rose? Jesus. Does."

The room erupted into applause. Caroline clapped too; the roar of their approval filled her heart with pride. She looked around to see if they would give him a standing ovation. From the stage Luke Nolan raised both his hands. He wasn't done.

"I have two daughters," he said. Caroline waved when the camera panned to her. "I believe that they are saved, and that they love the Lord. But I don't want that sermon to be how they're taught about sexual purity."

"Amen!" someone in the audience shouted. Luke Nolan took a breath and continued. He was sweating by then, his light blue shirt darkening beneath his armpits. "I want to teach my daughters, and all the children of God, that they should remain sexually pure not because He won't love them if they don't, but because He already loves them so much."

He motioned to the front row. Abigail rose from her seat, smoothed the skirt of her light pink dress with her hand, tossed her hair behind her shoulders. Caroline too moved to stand. Her mother's strong hand held her in place. Caroline watched as Abigail climbed the stairs at the side of the stage and stepped into the spotlight.

"My daughter Abigail and I wrote this next part together," Luke said into his mic. "We've had many discussions about purity in our house."

On cue, Abigail rolled her eyes in a giant arc. The crowd laughed. Caroline had never been invited to join these conversations. She saw the pride and love in her father's face in that moment and hated her sister for it.

He smiled at his daughter conspiratorially. "We want to vow, both of us"—he smiled at the audience—"to seek more than happiness, more than sex, more than what this world has to offer us. We want to Hope for More."

It was the ideal tag line to start a revolution. People in the crowd whooped. A microphone was handed to Abigail, who flipped it over and switched it on before holding it close to her belly button. They faced each other—father and daughter—and she began to repeat the vows he spoke.

"I believe," she said, "that God has a plan for my life that is holy." The room was so silent a sneeze could be heard on the online video. "I commit today to remain sexually pure until I am married. I promise to turn from anything that could sway me from this commitment until I am bound to another, knowing that my Savior loves me, even if I fail."

Again the room erupted. The two of them ignored it. The clapping ceased when Luke handed Abigail the card in his hand so she could read him his lines to repeat. She held the card steady with both hands, four fingers wrapped deftly around the microphone.

"I commit . . ." she said.

"I commit," he repeated.

"To show you the Gospel by the way I live my life," her soft voice said, his booming one following right after. Caroline could see the wideness of her sister's eyes. "I promise to Hope for More from you than the world does," she said, and by the time his echo finished, the applause had already begun.

It was the kind of sermon a pastor spends his entire life dreaming about, divine inspiration that spreads like wildfire, a movement that millions of people can relate to and that they're happy—thrilled, even—to pay for. Almost immediately Luke Nolan became an evangelical celebrity. Young preachers began to style their hair with a heavy side part like his, matching his casual uniform of Wranglers and button-ups, no tie. The Nolan family moved into a bigger home in a nicer neighborhood, where they had their own pool.

Famous preachers looked at him and saw their younger selves. They invited him to preach in their churches—first around North Texas, later in Houston, New Orleans, Atlanta. Luke Nolan's First Hope Baptist Church was rebranded "the Hope," and it exploded in size. They built a second campus. People drove for hours to hear Luke preach. His first book, *Hope for More*, sold faster than any other released by a Christian publisher since the *Left Behind* series; its sales boomed as the movement infiltrated hundreds of youth groups nationwide. It even had a growing group of young celebrity endorsers. Abigail was the face of his movement; she was stopped on the street by people who recognized her.

Then, in the fall of her sophomore year, Caroline bought her own light pink dress and stood on the stage of the new auditorium and spoke her vows. She received more applause than any of the other teenagers in her group. She stood across from her father, smiling, basking in his approval, believing with all of her heart that she meant every word. She could not imagine a world in which she'd want to do otherwise.

AT THE NEXT stoplight, Caroline pulled the ring off her finger. She was still holding it when her phone began to vibrate in
the cup holder. Alerts appeared one after another, pushing their
predecessors down before she could even read them. She glanced
at the light, still red, and picked up her phone. There were half
a dozen missed calls from Abby. What was so urgent that she'd
tried so many times? Abigail never wanted her around when
Matthew was in town. Caroline was about to call her back when
her sister's name flashed on the screen: incoming call.

"Hello?" she said as the light turned green. She dropped
the ring into the cup holder and switched the phone to her left
hand so she could drive with her right.

"Where have you been?" Abigail said. She sounded like
their mother, Caroline thought. Her sister didn't have any
right to interrogate her about where she'd been.

Caroline sighed and signaled to turn. She let herself sound
annoyed and said, "Uh. At the ranch, like I said I would be."

"You need to come home," Abigail said. "Right. Now."

Caroline resisted the urge to whip the steering wheel to
the left, skid her tires into the other lane, and speed back to
the ranch, where her sister couldn't bother her. Instead she
rolled her eyes and said, "Okay, Mom."

She waited for Abigail to huff, to call her a brat or concoct
a lecture so good even their father would be impressed. Her
sister only said, "Please, Caro."

There was an unnerving desperation in Abigail's voice. "I'm
driving right now," Caroline said. "I'll be there in twenty."

"Okay. Hurry," Abigail said, and then, "I mean, don't like,
speed, but you know, come straight home."

"Okay," Caroline said. The pleading tone was scaring her
now. She pressed the gas pedal harder. "I'm coming."

"Love you," Abby said.

"Love you back," Caroline said, and placed her phone in the cup holder with the ring.

Caroline worried as she drove past fast food stand-alones and strip malls, school zone signs, two-story houses with sprinklers pivoting on already green lawns. She bit at the cuticles on her left hand. Could Abigail know already? Gossip traveled fast in Hope, but it's not like she'd had sex with Taylor in the parking lot of a Goody Goody Liquor. They'd been careful.

The Nolan house was situated at the end of a cul-de-sac, on a big triangular plot of land, its front door flanked by four columns: Corinthian, Caroline had learned in school. The house was brick, except for the large flat stones embedded on the second floor and its bright white trim. The roof was so steep that every Christmas they hired someone to hang their decorations. The sun hid behind a cloud and cast the whole structure in a deepening blue light, in contrast to the warm golden windows, every one of them ablaze through their sheer white curtains. She pulled into the long driveway and parked behind her sister's car, next to the side entrance. Only strangers used the front door.

She could see through the kitchen window into the house. Her mother and sister were sitting at the table, their shoulders hunched, eyes empty and swollen. A box of tissues sat between them. Caroline snatched her phone out of the cup holder and slammed the car door behind her. She forgot the ring, and by the time she noticed the nakedness of her left hand, she was already inside. Abigail stood to meet her before she even reached the door.

Someone must be dead, Caroline thought. And in a way, she was right.

3

Caroline had never seen her mother undone. By the time her daughters awoke each morning, Ruthie Nolan had her hair fixed, makeup set, dress ironed and zipped all the way up the back. Even when she was sick. While other mothers loitered around for after-school pickup in oversized sweaters and jeans, their hair in ponytails, Ruthie never looked anything less than immaculate. She was Tami Taylor before *Friday Night Lights* even aired, only better dressed. When she was interviewed for *Christianity Today*, she told them her full-time job was to be a wife and mother, and then, after pausing for emphasis in classic Nolan fashion, added, "While getting all dolled up doesn't make me a better mother, it certainly makes me a better wife." And she was the model pastor's wife: ever hospitable and happy to remain in her husband's shadow.

Now Caroline's mother sat at the kitchen table in her bathrobe. She'd removed her makeup and twisted her hair into a banana clip. She looked both twenty years younger and five years older. For the first time, Caroline noted the lines that extended like fans from the corners of her mother's eyes, the uneven redness on her chin and forehead. Caroline looked quickly at the ceiling to check the wave of tears she felt brewing, pulled out the chair next to her sister's, and sat down. In the window to her right, she could see her own reddened reflection and ruffled her sweaty bangs off her forehead.

Ruthie leaned forward and looked straight at Caroline, both hands flat on the table. "Your father had an affair," she said as if reading from a teleprompter.

She hadn't said *hello*. Or *This might be hard*. Just eye contact and the truth: Your father had an affair. *Had*. As if it had somehow been thrust upon him like a football he'd caught and then realized he shouldn't be holding. Their mother had always been direct. She was the one, after all, who pulled the girls aside following their father's lectures to deliver their real punishments.

"What?" Caroline said, even though she'd heard her.

"Mrs. Debbie called this morning and told her," Abigail said. Caroline recalled how Abigail had tried to warn her about their mother's weird behavior before the shower. "She told me when we got back from the store." Abigail reached out to cover Caroline's hand with her own. "We called and called, but you didn't pick up."

Caroline imagined her mother telling Abigail earlier, the two of them alone together, crying and comforting each other. She moved her hand from beneath her sister's and swiped at her tears. They fell in a steady stream now. She went to dry her hand on the skirt of her dress, but caught her mother's raised eyebrows across the table. The dress was satin. Abigail saw her hand raised, her brow furrowed, and pushed the box of tissues to her. Ruthie and Abigail no longer needed them; they'd done their mourning without her.

"Why didn't you wait for me to tell her?" Caroline asked her mother. Ruthie held a hand to her chest, mouth open, eyes wide. She hadn't even thought to wait, Caroline realized. Her mother hadn't thought about her at all.

"Baby," Ruthie said, "you weren't here."

They sat quietly, waiting for Caroline to compose herself. She blew her nose, wiped her eyes with tissue after tissue, each one coming away with less mascara.

"It's been over for a while," Abigail said, her eyes so big and sympathetic Caroline couldn't even look at her. She turned to Ruthie instead. *You tell me*, she wanted to say, but her mother was barely there, flickering in and out of focus through her tears. Abigail reached for her hand again, and Caroline noticed that she too had changed after the shower. Now she wore a Texas Christian track T-shirt with Nike athletic shorts.

"He ended it this time last year," Abigail said, as if that detail made the news any easier to take. "There's nothing to worry about, okay?"

Nothing to worry about, Caroline thought. This could destroy their entire life. She so desperately wanted to rewind the day and replay it in slow motion; that way she couldn't be caught off guard. She needed to know everything—who it was, when it happened, and why—but refused to ask her sister for information that they should have learned together. She turned to her mother. "How long did he have . . . the affair?" Ruthie turned away, as if just hearing the word was a slap to the face. Caroline pinched the inside of her leg. *Maybe this is all a nightmare*, she thought.

"A little over a year," Ruthie said, looking down at the

table now, her dark roots visible on the top of her head. Caroline's eye caught on the wooden cross that always hung on their refrigerator, the word *Blessed* painted across it.

"Where's Matthew?" She directed the question to her mother again, saw Abigail's brow wrinkle in confusion.

"He's upstairs. Don't worry about him," Abigail said.

Caroline cut her eyes at her sister and turned to her mother. "Who was it?" She wanted every ounce of information. If her life was going to be ruined, she at least deserved to know how it had happened.

Luke Nolan strode into the kitchen right then, stepping directly into one of the orangey beams of light from the window and cutting off whatever Ruthie's response might have been.

"There are my daughters!" he said, a refrain more common than their names. His face dropped when he saw his youngest in tears. "You told her already," he said, turning to his wife.

Ruthie nodded, which made Caroline wonder if he'd already taken Abigail aside, if the two of them had reconciled before she even knew about the affair, and now she'd be expected to do the same.

"Caro," he said, sliding into the chair beside Abigail's and stretching out his hand to rest on top of Caroline's. Even their movements were the same, Caroline thought. "I am so, so sorry. I would take it back if I could. I hope you can find it in your heart to forgive me."

Caroline pulled her hand away and tried to meet her sister's eyes. Abigail looked down at the table.

It was the shortest sermon Caroline had ever heard him give. The man had once lectured her sister for an hour after seeing her legs draped across Connor's lap, and somehow he managed to sum up his entire apology for having an affair in a matter of seconds.

Forgive him, Caroline thought, for what? He hadn't confessed to anything. She barely knew anything. She'd been in the house for less than five minutes when her mother and sister had dropped this bomb onto her life, and now it felt as if the three of them had conspired before she'd even arrived. She noticed that Abigail and Ruthie were both looking at her, though, and neither offered to fill the silence that followed his little speech. Maybe she should make him say the words, pretend she didn't know, ask so many questions he'd be forced to describe everything in lurid detail. Her father never would have accepted an apology like that from her. He would have called it thin, told her she wasn't taking responsibility for her actions. He would have made her try it again and again until she'd apologized in the manner he found most appropriate. Caroline imagined setting up these same hoops for him to jump through now, but the thought of staying at this table and being forced to listen to him was too nauseating. So she merely nodded.

"Your mother and I have spent the afternoon in prayer. We are going to meet with members of the elder board tonight," he said. The bags under his eyes were muted purple and green. "I assume you two would like some time alone to process this?" He looked between the girls. Caroline said yes, even though it hadn't really been a question, and she didn't actually want time alone.

"What are we supposed to do?" Abigail asked, staring directly at their father. The look was so intense Caroline thought she might cast a fireball from her eyes and burn him into a pile of ash right there. He ignored his daughter and turned to his wife.

Ruthie closed her eyes, rubbed her forehead with her hand.

"Just stay here and have a calm evening. Swim or get some rest," she said, and pushed away from the table, brushing a wisp of hair out of her face.

Luke stood too, his chair screeching across the linoleum, his height throwing a shadow across the girls. "We're planning to tell the congregation tomorrow," he said. He gripped the turrets on the back of his chair with both hands and slid it under the table.

Ruthie lifted her chair to push it in quietly and left the kitchen, her husband following close behind. Neither Caroline nor Abigail moved. They didn't say a word and instead pretended to look at the cedar table or the white kitchen cabinets or the lemons stacked in a precarious pyramid in a teal bowl on the counter as their parents grabbed their things, said their goodbyes, and left using the door Caroline had just entered through.

Caroline turned back to her sister, opened her mouth to ask what they were supposed to do now, but the words emerged as a sob. She covered her face with her hands. Abigail never cried or lost control of her emotions like this. She felt her sister move to the chair closest to hers, wrap her arms around her shoulders, and squeeze.

"Oh, Caro, we're going to be okay," Abigail said, stroking her back now.

She could feel Abigail's leg twitching against her knee. "Are we?" Caroline said, looking up to search her face for reassurance.

"I don't know." Abigail sighed, her remorse so heavy it seemed to secure them to their chairs.

Finally, after Caroline's legs had started to fall asleep, Abigail stood and went to the fridge. She opened the freezer drawer and returned carrying a gallon of Blue Bell under her arm like a basketball, two spoons threaded through her fingers. She sat in the chair where their father had been, tightened her ponytail in the reflection of the window, and turned to her sister with a smile.

"Eat our feelings?" She said it the same way she'd said it earlier that year when their parents had told Caroline for the thousandth time that their money was the church's money and they couldn't throw it away on some frivolous personal preference so she could attend a state school rather than Texas Christian. The night their parents finally agreed to let Caroline go, with the caveat that they wouldn't help her pay for food or housing, Abigail had raised a similar spoon heaped with light yellow ice cream, clinked it against her sister's, and said, "To your future." Caroline remembered how happy and hopeful she'd felt then as the vanilla flavor spread soft and thick across her tongue, a balm if not a celebration.

This time, Caroline spooned the ice cream into her mouth until she felt stuffed and gross. And when the phone started to ring, neither girl moved. "You've reached the Nolan household," their father's voice boomed through the answering machine. "God's always available to chat, but we aren't right now. Please leave a message after the beep!" Caroline cringed. Overhead, the pull on the ceiling fan clicked against the light. Caroline watched it swing back and forth as an automated voice from the church announced an emergency meeting at the main Hope campus the next day. The morning services would be canceled. Instead, there would be a meeting to discuss "family matters."

Abigail stood and went to the machine, pressed a button. The message played again. "Stop it!" she yelled, smashing various buttons with her finger.

"Whoa, chill," Caroline said, and Abigail stopped, hung her head, and waited for it to end. When it finished playing the second time, she left it there, a blinking red light announcing a new message.

Caroline watched the spot appear and disappear as Abigail left the kitchen. She counted out its rhythm—five steady blinks and a pause of two seconds, long enough to hope it might be gone, and then five more. She heard her sister thump up the stairs, then her muffled voice echoed down through the atrium. Abigail returned a few minutes later wearing jeans, her pink leather trapezoid purse swinging from her shoulder, with Matthew following so close on her heels, Caroline thought he might trip her. He stood a half step behind her in the kitchen doorway, his face in shadow behind her illuminated one. Caroline stood from the table and felt her knees pop from sitting so long.

"We're going out for a bit, if that's okay," Abigail said, her voice gentle, as if Caroline might snap at her. Caroline looked down. She was still wearing her heels and dress from the shower and assumed the *we* her sister had used did not include her.

"Can I come?" she asked.

Abigail seemed to think about it for a moment, adjusted the strap of her purse. Behind her, Matthew said nothing. "No, I don't think so," she said, shifting her weight uncomfortably. "We need a little time alone together. I'm sorry."

"It's okay," Caroline said, though she wasn't sure that she meant it. She watched them turn to leave, Matthew darting ahead of Abigail to open and hold the door for her. At the last second, her sister turned back and wrapped Caroline in a tight hug, so that her arms were pinned at her sides.

"We'll be back soon," she said, kissed her on the cheek, and disappeared out the door. Matthew closed it behind them with a little wave. Caroline felt the space their absence left behind fill with fear.

She refused to sit here alone and left the kitchen, flipping off the lights in the living room and entry hall, stomping up the plush carpeted stairs. She stalked across the open corridor and locked herself in her bedroom, where the fluorescent teal paint she'd chosen her freshman year now made everything feel too cheery and bright. She changed into an old T-shirt, flopped onto the bed, and grabbed her phone. She needed to talk to someone. Her instinct was to text Taylor. She hovered over his name. But she couldn't talk to him about this. A crush was something different.

She pulled her computer from under her pillow, opened it, scrolled to a show she'd seen a hundred times, and pressed play. She stared up at her ceiling; the fan chopped the air as the sound of the laugh track filled the room. She held her phone above her head, scrolled through her recent text messages. Hannah was away working at a Christian camp in East Texas, and even if she could be reached, she'd only encourage Caroline to pray for guidance. Her friend Anna Grace wasn't even allowed to watch PG-13 movies, so she definitely wasn't prepared to handle this, and Emily's parents were huge donors to the church. Caroline's finger hovered over Jennifer's name. For years, Jennifer had been at the top of her list, her closest friend. Jennifer would have driven her beat-up Camry over here and climbed into bed with her. But a few months back, when Caroline had told her about Taylor, she hadn't been understanding. *As your sister in Christ*, she'd said, *it hurts me to watch you make this mistake.* She hadn't told anyone, but since then their relationship had devolved into waves before Sunday services and the occasional text. Caroline clicked back to her contacts and continued to scroll.

Lauren. They hadn't messaged each other since April, the closing night of the school play. Lauren was who she needed, though. Lauren was in the world *and* of the world. She drank beer at parties. She wore a tight dress to prom. Her parents were divorced. Caroline had been the one to talk her off the ledge before the opening night of *Pride and Prejudice*, to reassure her that everything would be okay. Now Lauren could do the same for her.

I just found out my dad had an affair, Caroline typed, adding a frown emoji, and pressed send.

Lauren saw it immediately. That's fucked up, she responded.

Ikr? Caroline typed, and I don't know what to do, and added lmao to lighten it.

Caroline stared at the screen, waited for a call, a reassuring response, anything. She watched as the message changed from sent to read.

She rolled to her side and tried to focus on the sitcom, then glanced at her phone again. Still nothing. The characters' voices seemed too high-pitched, jovial. She turned the episode off, flopped back onto the mass of pillows, and lay there, staring up at the ceiling. It just didn't make sense, she thought. Her father couldn't even remember which days she had rehearsals or how many kids were in her class. He didn't seem capable of the kind of plotting and manipulation required to have an affair. The danger of sin, he'd always preached, was how easy it was, how you could just slip and fall into it. Maybe he'd really meant little sins, though, like impatience, lack of compassion, roughness. Because it didn't seem easy to carry on a yearlong affair. But it must have been, since he'd ruined everything so quickly.

4

Overnight, Caroline Nolan's previous life had ended. When she stepped out of the house the next day, the grasshoppers were crumbling husks as she walked across the driveway to her car. It couldn't be normal for them all to die at once like that, she thought, their remains dry and brown like a winter leaf.

She watched as each of her family members stepped outside and winced. "Gross," Ruthie said. Abigail was usually the first one out the door on Sundays, but Caroline hadn't seen her all morning. Now everyone was ready to pile into the car except for her sister. Even Matthew was waiting.

Her father looked at his watch. "We're going to be late," he said, and Luke Nolan was never late.

Caroline glanced down at her phone. It was twelve thirty. They had to be at the church in thirty minutes for a meeting with the executive pastor, followed by the emergency meeting. It was only a five-minute drive. Her parents climbed into their truck and blasted the air-conditioning. Luke drummed his fingers on the steering wheel, glanced up at the door every couple of seconds. Caroline let her eyes roll at him.

"We'll take a separate car," she finally said.

Her father backed out of the driveway, one arm thrown over her mother's seat, his body twisted around, as Ruthie sat staring forward at the concrete driveway.

"I'll go get her," Caroline said to Matthew, and left him there in the heat.

She took her time walking through the kitchen, the formal dining room with the cream chairs they never sat in, to the front atrium, where a cedar plank with the word *Family* painted across it in cursive hung above a dozen family photos. She bounded up the stairs two at a time, tapped her knuckles on Abigail's door. "It's me," she said.

Abigail wore a denim skirt, high-waisted with numerous buttons, and a white blouse. Her face shone pink, reflecting the soft color of the walls of her room. In front of her, an open palette of eye shadow and a straightener with the red light still on lay on her ornate white vanity with its large seashell mirror. They were the only things out of place.

"Dad just left," Caroline said. "We're late." Her sister didn't move.

"Why didn't you tell me?" Abigail said without turning away from the mirror.

Oh no, she knows, Caroline immediately thought. Her older sister knew she had slept with a boy and Caroline hadn't even been the one to tell her. How had she found out? Caroline wiped her sweaty palms inside the pockets of her dress.

"I could have hurried," Abigail said. "Just one second while I fix this eye and then we can go."

Caroline sat on the edge of the bed and took a deep breath. She hadn't realized how anxious she was about Abigail finding out. In the mirror her sister made imperceptible adjustments to what looked like two identical eyeliner wings.

"Are you worried about how today will go?" Caroline asked.

She'd noticed the way their mother had watched their father drink his coffee that morning, her eyes flitting to his right hand, which shook no matter how flat he pressed it against the table. Marriage, he had always preached, was a reflection of Christ's love for the church. So this wasn't merely a failure or an ugly scandal, it was a blow to his credibility. Caroline wondered how the congregation could ever take him seriously again. The more she thought about it, the more it seemed like this was a done deal: they'd fire him today at the meeting. Her sister seemed surprisingly calm, though.

"Hmm," Abigail said, closing her eyes and spraying something on her face. "I'm worried about the church for sure. Something like this can really make people question their faith."

"Yeah, but what about Dad?" Caroline asked.

Abigail sighed. "I think if they were going to oust him, they wouldn't be giving him this chance," she said. "My guess is that the meeting we're having today with Pastor Mark is to discuss strategy. How to steer through the skid." Abigail put the cap back on the spray and shooed Caroline out of the room, as if she were the one who was late.

"Daddy is too important and too beloved for them to let him go," Abigail said, speed walking through the first floor and turning over her shoulder to add, "Even for something like this." She stepped out into the heat and exclaimed, "Yikes, what happened out here? Gross." She ran on her tiptoes through the insect husks that covered the drive and threw herself into the passenger seat of Matthew's car. Caroline climbed into the back and leaned over the headrest to check her sister's legs—they weren't shaking.

Everyone was silent as they drove to the church, passing empty sidewalks, houses with eight-foot solid oak fences and metal garage doors that were closed to hide Audis, BMWs, Range Rovers, a few Porsches. Almost every green lawn sported a purple sign declaring it the home of a Hope High School football player or band member or thespian or (Caroline's personal favorite) mascot. They went by the park with its expensive sun canopy and neighborhood watch signs. The car jolted over speed bumps the community had installed to ensure the streets were safe for their children. Four stop signs and two left turns later, they reached the granite stone that announced the name of the subdivision and pulled onto the main road, continuing past two strip malls before arriving at the main campus.

The front entrance was the only reminder that the church's location had once been a grocery store. After their father's viral sermon, the congregation had outgrown its small chapel and the pastoral staff had begun a season of prayer that led them straight to the bankrupted Tom's Grocery, which happened to be the biggest available space in the area. They renovated the produce section and turned it into the children's ministry, the meat section became classrooms, and everything else—the shelves and the checkout counters—was transformed into an auditorium big enough to seat 1,400 souls. But no amount of renovation could save the exterior. It was still located in a strip mall with a decent Mexican restaurant, a dry cleaner, and a store that was called simply DONUT. Above the wide double doors they'd installed to replace the grocery's automatic ones, white Gotham type declared this building: THE HOPE.

Caroline could barely remember the church before her father was named head pastor there. She knew First Hope Baptist Church had been a seventy-person congregation when he was hired, and that by the time she was born had grown to nearly five hundred. She also knew the elders liked to say the church's popularity was due to the fact that people could feel God when Luke Nolan spoke.

She couldn't help but wonder, though, if the church's expansion was in some way tied to the influx of upper-to-middle-class moms and dads pouring into their small community. Most of these families had moved into subdivisions built where wildflowers had once grown and they had chosen the Hope. By the time Caroline hit high school, her father's church held six services each weekend: four live and two streamed, every single one of them at capacity.

But the Hope had never felt like a megachurch to Caroline. She had grown with it. As children, she and her sister had counted heads for attendance. They'd emptied offering buckets as teens. The girls hadn't just seen behind the curtain; they lived there. Caroline often stared at her father's name on the banner proclaiming his Genesis sermon series and wondered why he, of all men, had been chosen by God. Her whole life, people had told her that he was a great man—holy, righteous, talented. So what had happened to that man? She wondered if he had ever truly existed.

LUKE AND RUTHIE Nolan were waiting for them inside the first set of doors. Caroline wasn't sure why her parents hadn't gone straight to the executive offices until she stepped into the atrium and saw the gaggle of women gathered around the large coffee table, the holy book sitting before each of them, scattered with highlighted phrases, pamphlets sticking out between the pages.

"Good morning, Pastor Luke," one of the women called out, echoed by a few others. He waved in response and they all waved back. Caroline watched them smile at her father, with their big straight teeth and matte rose-tinted lips, tucking a curled hair behind an ear here, adjusting a cardigan there. *They really love him*, she thought.

A photo of the Nolan family as tall as a kindergartener hung slightly crooked on the wall behind the women, near the kiosk that had once been the bakery and now sold Luke's books. The picture had been taken in the golden light of late spring at the end of Abigail's fifth-grade year, the week before Luke was named head pastor. Caroline was four years old at the time, Abigail ten. They were nestled in a field of bluebonnets: all legs and heads and hair as white and bright as sunlight. Abigail was crouched between their parents, long hair in pigtails, hands on her knees, and Caroline, face still swollen with baby fat, was sitting on her father's lap.

It was a calling card that never aged: the first family of the Hope. Even as the girls grew older, the church always pulled this photo for the directory, newsletters, and press hits. "Oh!" newcomers would exclaim when Caroline introduced herself at events, "I thought you were younger." And just as quickly, they'd recover: "You're so beautiful, though." Of course, they'd seen Abigail at fifteen in the famed "Hope for

More" sermon. But not Caroline. She'd never had a public role in the church.

"Girls," their father called, beckoning them with his whole arm like he was throwing a basketball over his head. Caroline looked at her sister, who'd already turned to speak to Matthew.

"Why don't you get some coffee and I'll find you in the atrium when we're done," she instructed, and Matthew obeyed. He wasn't family yet and he didn't have to bear this cross.

The girls followed along behind their parents, up the stairs, past the receptionist and into the executive hallway, all the way to Pastor Mark's office in the back. Pastor Mark was the church's executive pastor, second in command, and Luke's oldest friend. He was seated at his desk, head in his hands, mouth moving in prayer. When he heard the door open, he attempted to adjust his face, though his eyes still looked weary and sad.

Pastor Mark glanced back and forth between the girls. "Oh, um, actually, I think it'd be better if you two hear the details from a woman. Mrs. Debbie is waiting for you in her office." Both her parents nodded their agreement.

"Mrs. Debbie?" Caroline squeaked. She didn't want to talk about her father's affair with any of the church elders, but she definitely preferred Pastor Mark over Mrs. Debbie.

"Wait, what?" Abigail said, and Caroline silently blessed her. "So we come up for a family meeting, after being told absolutely nothing, and now you're sending us out of the room?" She looked pointedly at Pastor Mark.

"Abigail," their father said, rubbing his forehead with his hand. "Please."

Caroline watched her sister. There had to be a way to convince them—and if so, Abigail would find it. Caroline and Abigail deserved to hear whatever Pastor Mark was going to say, didn't they? But her sister only said "Fine," and headed out into the hallway, leaving Caroline stunned and standing in the doorway.

"Shut the door behind you, won't you, Caro?" Pastor Mark said.

She tried to close the door softly behind her. Even the small thump it made seemed too loud. Early on, Luke Nolan had instituted a rule at the Hope that a pastor's door should always be open unless a member required a private audience— a couple considering divorce, a teen caught smoking pot, two young lovers dealing with an unplanned pregnancy. Caroline heard heels clicking behind her and looked back. A deacon's wife carrying freshly printed bulletins for the service raised an eyebrow at the closed door but said nothing. How long would it be, Caroline wondered, before that information made its way to the women sitting in the front atrium? Five minutes? Ten?

Her stomach rumbled. She regretted not eating breakfast. Her feet felt long and heavy as she made her way down the hall to Mrs. Debbie's office. Caroline had expected to see her today, of course, and she could handle seeing her in the atrium or at the service. But this? How on earth was she supposed to face the most revered woman in the church less than twenty-four hours after sleeping with her youngest son?

Mrs. Debbie's office looked exactly like her house, where both Caroline and Abigail had spent every Wednesday night their sophomore years for Bible study. She opened her arms to greet the girls. Abigail stepped into her embrace.

Caroline closed the door behind her. Everything about Mrs. Debbie was soft—her silk caftan and curly hair, her curved clear plastic glasses and warm brown eyes—so it was only right for Caroline to hug her now too, and her embrace was so much gentler than her son's. Caroline felt her face turn red as soon as the thought arrived and she quickly pulled away.

She sat beside her sister on the far side of a deep couch. Mrs. Debbie handed them each a cup of tea in a light pink mug with a cross on one side and *The Hope Women's Ministries* in gold script on the back.

Mrs. Debbie spoke with the long *A*'s of a family who'd lived in Texas for six generations. "They thought you two might have some questions. I want y'all to ask me anything you can think of," she began. "I'll start with the basics and then we can go from there, okay? We don't have much time before the announcement." The clock behind her said there was still an hour before the atrium would begin filling with people. Caroline tried to focus her attention on Mrs. Debbie, to not think about her son at all. She looked back at the clock: fifty-seven minutes still to go. Taylor had his mother's eyes, she noticed.

Abigail didn't wait for Mrs. Debbie to continue. "My understanding," she said, "is that the affair has been over for almost a year."

Mrs. Debbie sighed, picked up the bottle of creamer from the coffee table, and poured some into her own cup. Her son's hand had curled that same way around the back of Caroline's neck. Caroline shook her head, tried to find a point to focus on behind Mrs. Debbie's desk, landed upon twelve neatly stacked copies of *Hope for More*, and turned to look at Abigail instead.

"Again, let's start at the beginning," Mrs. Debbie said. Caroline saw her sister's jaw clench.

Luke Nolan's affair had begun two years ago, she told the girls, the summer before Caroline's junior year. "In your father's testimony to the elders last night, he said the affair ended sometime around last August." She frowned at this.

"That doesn't make it less of a problem for his leadership role, as I know y'all know."

Both girls nodded.

"The problem is not only the sin," Mrs. Debbie said, "but the secrecy—"

"Did he seek counseling?" Abigail asked, cutting her off. Caroline couldn't imagine why that mattered. Mrs. Debbie's eyes widened, a warning. She answered the question, though.

"Not that we know of, no. We know the affair ended and that the woman with whom he sinned did not quite understand that it was over. She claims to still be in love with him." Mrs. Debbie took a sip from her mug to avoid looking at them.

She loved him? Caroline had assumed the affair was only physical. Somehow this seemed worse. A sin of the flesh was one thing. Men, she had been taught, were fickle, weak things. They stumbled all the time over women who made themselves available. But to fall in love? That was something else entirely.

"And him?" Abigail asked.

Mrs. Debbie adjusted her shawl, recrossed her legs, straightened her skirt to cover her knees. She hadn't prepared for this question. "He says it was a, um, mistake of the flesh. It wasn't . . . at least, I was told it wasn't emotional on his part." Her voice had tilted into a question at the end. The three of them sat in silence for a moment. Caroline released air from her lungs that she hadn't realized she'd been holding; it came out as a sigh. Mrs. Debbie looked over, lines of worry forming on her forehead.

"Are you all right, Caro?"

"Yeah, I'm fine," she said. She didn't want Mrs. Debbie to look at her, to notice her. She didn't want to see those same eyes. She didn't want to be here at all. She took a sip from her cup.

"Are you sure?" Mrs. Debbie asked, and Caroline choked on her tea. She'd said it exactly the same way that Taylor had the day before; even their inflection was the same. Caroline coughed into her elbow and felt her face flush red. She turned away from their worried looks and coughed into the couch until she calmed down. Abigail patted her twice on the back.

"Sorry," she said, once she'd regained her composure. "Yes. Go on."

Mrs. Debbie tilted her head as if to say more.

Abigail preempted her with another question. "Who was it?" It was clear who was leading this meeting.

"We are trying to keep her name out of this," Mrs. Debbie said.

"Why?" Caroline asked, unable to hide her disgust. "Didn't she sin too?"

Mrs. Debbie's eyes flitted to Caroline's hand on her mug. Caroline thought she might have noticed the missing ring, the lighter skin from where it had remained ever since she'd taken the abstinence oath. She switched the mug to her right hand, tucked her left beneath her skirt. Mrs. Debbie's mouth turned down at the corners. "Of course she did, Caro, but she is not responsible to a body of people and for their spiritual guidance."

"Okay," Abigail said, "but don't we have a right to know who it is? We aren't going to tell anyone, obviously." Caroline nodded along with her sister.

"You're right. You're right. Perhaps you can even pray for her as well," Mrs. Debbie said, and then, "It was Mary Campbell."

Caroline heard herself gasp. Mary Campbell taught at the elementary school in their old neighborhood. She had been Caroline's fourth-grade teacher. She'd taught her subtraction and complex sentences. Caroline remembered that she'd always looked nice and respectable—with a tiny waist and her V-neck just high enough. She wore round glasses with gold rims and sometimes cried during worship.

"Oh, so that's how you knew," Abigail said.

"Wait, how?" Caroline was lost.

"Mary is in Mrs. Debbie's Friday-night Bible study," Abigail said to her sister. She turned her green eyes to the woman across from her. "Isn't she?"

"Yes," Mrs. Debbie answered—and then, even though she'd said they didn't need to know all the details, she proceeded to tell them everything.

Every week for a year, Mary Campbell had prayed that the Lord would bless her with a man who loved the Lord and who loved her. Finally, the Lord had answered. She'd told the women of her group that she was in love and the women had cried with joy at the news.

In retrospect, Mrs. Debbie noted, it probably should have raised a red flag that Mary's man never had a name.

The group met every Friday in Mrs. Debbie's living room to study the Word together. But the night before Abigail's shower, they had been forced to pause their lesson about good marriages and Song of Solomon because Mary Campbell was sobbing into an embroidered pillow she had gripped in her hands like a life preserver.

She wasn't in a godly relationship, she told the women between sobs. The love of her life was married. And for the first time in almost two years, she didn't say *him* or *he* or *the man I love*. She said *Luke*.

Mrs. Debbie had halted the conversation right then and there, closed the group in prayer, and ushered the other women out the door. Once they were alone, Mrs. Debbie took Mary's hands in hers. She knew there had to be more married men named Luke in the area, but she also wasn't a dumb woman.

"Tell me," she said, "that you are not in love with Luke Nolan." And when the tears continued to roll down Mary's cheeks, wetting the top of her blouse, her breath disappearing into sobs, it was all Mrs. Debbie could do to mutter, "Oh, baby. What a mess you've gotten yourself into." The path from there was straightforward. Mrs. Debbie told her husband, who agreed she had to tell the elders. She called the board that same night and Ruthie Nolan the next morning.

"I'm sorry," she said to Abigail, "but it couldn't wait."

Abigail was quiet, chewing on the inside of her lip. Caroline's entire body felt cold. Her right arm itched at the elbow, but she didn't want to move her left hand from under her skirt. Why hadn't she remembered to put her ring back on?

"But that means their stories don't line up," Abigail said. "Daddy said it was over last summer and she said it's ongoing. What does that mean?"

Mrs. Debbie sighed. "Don't dig up more snakes than you can kill," she said.

Abigail pressed her on it. "Don't you think this is relevant and important?" She was clearly angry, her back straight, voice rising. And Mrs. Debbie couldn't chastise her for it this time; her anger was righteous.

"I will say this," Mrs. Debbie said, holding up a hand to indicate that Abigail should wait. "I think your father is a good man. There is one reason that good men fall into sins like this, and it is not love." Mrs. Debbie took a breath. "I don't think she's lying. But I think she is probably deeply, deeply confused." Caroline felt confused herself.

"Yeah," Abigail said, "but how can we know for sure that

she's not telling the truth? Isn't this the time to question him?" The memory of Caroline's own sin resurfaced then, crowding out all this new information about her father. She looked between her sister and Mrs. Debbie, tried to understand where this was going.

"I'm not saying we shouldn't question him, and trust me, honey, people will," Mrs. Debbie said. "I'm just sayin' that there's no reason for him to keep lying. What gain would there be for him?"

"Sure," Abigail said, her voice tight.

Here were the two greatest feminine forces in the church, powerless against a single man's decision. Mrs. Debbie loved the Hope enough to betray its leader and Abby loved it enough to believe it could still be saved. Caroline couldn't think about the future of the church right now, though. She was too busy thinking about the fact that she hadn't noticed anything amiss in her own family. If she hadn't been able to sense this coming, what else had she missed? What other secrets could come bubbling to the surface at any moment?

Mrs. Debbie sighed. "Do you want to know what happens next?" she asked. "Or do you want to fight about every little detail?" She was using her mom voice now. Raised eyebrows and tight lips warned that further provocation would not end well. Mrs. Debbie's power was soft but swift.

Caroline looked at Abigail, who stared at Mrs. Debbie. After a moment, her sister nodded, so Caroline did too.

"Okay then," Mrs. Debbie said. She folded her hands in her lap and told them the plan: Luke Nolan would confess to the congregation that afternoon and ask for their forgiveness. He would attend counseling sessions for the rest of the week while the elder board did some investigating. On Thursday, they would vote to have him resign or to place him on probation. At the next meeting they could vote to reinstate him.

"What?" Caroline and Abigail said, almost at the same time.

"I know it seems fast," Mrs. Debbie said. "But this is a strategy that has worked many, many times at other churches."

It didn't seem fast, Caroline thought, it seemed absolutely insane. And they were using a strategy? As if they were planning how to win a high school football game and not deciding whether her father was capable of guiding the religious beliefs of thousands of people?

"Where?" Abigail asked, her tone sharp.

"First Baptist Houston," Mrs. Debbie said, too quickly. "We hope it can be effective here at the Hope as well." It was clearly a canned answer. Mrs. Debbie had been told the plan and she hadn't questioned it. Was she here to counsel them or to brief them on their lines? Caroline crossed her arms. She wanted to ask: Effective for who, the congregation or my family? It seemed to her that the plan was most effective in maintaining the church's reputation.

There was a light knock. Pastor Mark poked his head inside the room. "Don't mean to rush y'all," he said, "but people are starting to arrive." The clock above the shelf had ticked all the way down.

"Shall we pray?" Mrs. Debbie said, turning to the girls. Mrs. Debbie was a woman who could pray without ceasing, as the Bible commanded. She held both of her hands across the table and the girls knew better than to refuse. Caroline willed her own hand to relax as Mrs. Debbie took it and began. She felt Abigail squeeze her other hand. Caroline squeezed back. "Please give them strength," Mrs. Debbie said. "Give Abigail and Caroline Your fortitude, and Your goodness, and Your holiness." Both girls sat stiffly now, heads bowed. "Amen," she said, and then, "Take your time, girls. I'll see you out there."

THE MINUTE SHE closed the door, Caroline jumped to her feet. She needed to corral her thoughts. She needed to move. She paced back and forth. Her legs felt as if they had fire ants crawling all over them, ready to bite at any moment. She hoped Mrs. Debbie hadn't noticed the missing ring. It would be fine, she reassured herself. She would be fine. She whipped around then and there was Abigail, head in her hands, crumpled forward on the couch.

Caroline rushed to her sister's side, reached out a hand and rested it on her back. They waited a few minutes, solemn and silent, enough space for them to begin swallowing their sorrow by the spoonful.

"What are you thinking about?" Abigail finally said, her voice soft but jagged. Even when she was the one needing comfort, she was always trying to serve others. Caroline twisted her lips. It wasn't fair, she thought. Abigail was so good. Why couldn't she be more like that? Abigail never would have slept with the son of a Hope Church elder in secret. But she couldn't tell her sister what she was really thinking, so she said, "I don't know what to think. What are you thinking about?"

"I know that the devil seeks to destroy people who God uses for His glory," Abigail said, her voice catching in her throat. She looked at Caroline, tears in her eyes. "I just never thought he could be so selfish, so—I don't know—stupid? Of all the ways to fail . . . I can't believe he'd do this to us, to the church."

"I don't think he was thinking that much about us or the church," Caroline heard herself say.

"Isn't that worse, though?" Abigail said, her tears falling quickly now.

Caroline hugged her sister, scrunched up her own face, and tried to cry. She wanted to feel upset too. She only felt anxious. "You're okay," she said. "You're okay." She didn't add *Everything will be fine*, or *It'll all work out*, because she didn't know if either of those things was true.

Abigail grabbed a tissue to blow her nose, afterward folding it into exact quarters. She looked up at Caroline. "I just don't know what to hope for now," she said.

Caroline wiped a tear from her sister's face with her thumb. The irony of the moment struck her and she just couldn't resist the joke: "Hope for More?" she said with a shrug.

"Caroline," Abigail said, trapping the laugh behind her lips.

Caroline looked at the clock on the wall. They had five minutes before they needed to be downstairs. "Abby," she said, "we have to get down there."

Abigail pulled her phone from her purse, flipped the camera around, and swept the smudged mascara from under her eyes. She reapplied concealer and lipstick. Then she stood, smoothed down Caroline's stray hairs, adjusted the hem of her own skirt, and replaced her sadness with a smile. The girls pulled down their masks together, more slowly this time, the fit less comfortable, and returned to their public personas as Luke Nolan's daughters and nothing else.

5

The voicemails had created a dust devil of rumors. Every congregant of the Hope Church had received the same automated call. Some had felt a strange sense of calm, deleted it easily, and went about their night; most had panicked. Phones vibrated on tables, families gathered around pizzas to pray, a glass of wine shattered, game nights dissolved into anxiety. They worried the church was out of money. They worried a missionary had died. They worried that Luke Nolan was sick. They were so worried that they left Caroline and Abigail alone. No one texted either of the girls, no one called. Even in the lobby that afternoon, they were handled with oven mitts, hugged gently, their dresses complimented. *How are your summers going? Let me tuck in your tag, sweetie.*

"You know, we are just so blessed to be able to celebrate God's love for us in such a personal and intimate way," Caroline heard her sister respond when asked if she was excited about her upcoming wedding. The atrium buzzed with voices, the volume rising, everyone shouting their small talk at one another. The entire congregation was wearing their Sunday best—fathers in button-downs, open at the collar with jeans; young men in graphic tees; the women in knee-length skirts. Each family huddled together, every conversation was holy. Caroline stood a few feet from her sister. She wanted to participate in the chatter, but she couldn't figure out what to say. When Ruthie swept into their circle, placed a hand on Caroline's shoulder, and whispered in her ear: "Do you mind grabbing the seats, honey?" Caroline felt unexpectedly grateful.

Every Sunday Ruthie asked Caroline to grab their seats, and every Sunday Caroline balked at being asked to serve the family in such a small, unimportant way. Today, she did it without complaint. "Yes, ma'am," she said.

There were no reserved seats at the Hope, and yet the Nolan women had sat in the second row, stage left, for the third of four services every Sunday for as long as Caroline could remember, even through the church's move and two auditorium redesigns.

The mood was more somber at the front of the room. Caroline heard snippets of conversation trickle in from the lobby. But mostly it was quiet. The rows appeared longer than they'd ever looked before, the stage higher, the cross behind the podium taller. She felt her face getting warm. Mothers entered carrying babies. Two young girls trotted down an aisle to commandeer a whole row for their family, standing guard at separate ends, throwing each other a thumbs-up. A few old ladies were led in by the elbow and guided gingerly to their seats. The members of the worship band wandered around near the stage, side-hugging friends and high-fiving children. All spoke in lowered tones, the roar of the lobby rushing in each time the double doors opened. Like every other Sunday, the lights began to dim ten minutes before the meeting was set to start and, for that moment, everyone looked lovely, reverent.

As the congregation took their seats, Caroline shifted uncomfortably. She scooted farther down the row to make room for her mother and Matthew. Abby took the aisle seat, leaning forward to make eye contact with her, and waved her over. Caroline stood on her tiptoes, hands on the backs of the chairs in the front row, and tried to squeeze past her mother and Matthew. "Scoot down," Abigail told them, and they listened. Caroline sat next to her sister, where Matthew had been sitting, and smiled.

There is a reliable liturgy even in a church as trendy as the Hope. Here there is no sacrament, altar call, rosemary incense, or confessional booths. There is only the liturgy of habit, knowing what comes next so that you are never pulled out of the constructed experience of worship.

If this were a normal Sunday, Abigail would be onstage as the lights came up to help the worship pastor lead the congregation in song. She had a beautiful voice, a commanding stage presence, and that rare ability to seem entirely genuine when she raised her hand above her head in exultation. The band would play three songs to start: two slow, one fast. Abigail would lower her hand, the chords would fade out, and one of the senior pastors would start to pray, and then Luke Nolan would ascend the stairs at the side of the stage.

"Follow me," he'd say as he greeted the congregation, and then he'd begin to read aloud from the Bible he held aloft in his hand. He'd read until he reached the verse he planned to focus on that particular day, and then suddenly Every. Single. Word. Was. Emphasized. When he was finished, he'd pause, the silence reverberating through the packed room.

"Ya got that?" he'd ask after a few moments. It was such a consistent trick that the church's volunteer shirts had I GOT IT plastered across the back in white block letters as tall as they were wide, the words bending and rising with their bodies.

A great pastor's style is so distinct that it shows up in everything he does—from his prayers to his descriptions of high school track meets. After twenty-five years of preaching, Luke Nolan's sermons were as predictable as a lullaby. This consistency made him easy to mimic, and Abby could do an exact impression of him, fake sermon and all. But when Luke Nolan was on, when his sermons worked, they were a force so strong it sometimes felt like the Lord had whispered them directly into his ear.

The afternoon of the family meeting, though, there was none of that. Pastor Mark stood center stage and welcomed the congregation. Luke stood over to the side, buttoning and unbuttoning his shirtsleeve. Caroline noticed a faint stain on his collar and that his pants were too long, frayed slightly at the hems—and when he bowed his head to pray, it looked like his hair was starting to thin on top. Caroline loved her father, but she'd also loved him as her pastor. It had been easy to love a steadfast and honest leader. Now she wondered if she'd ever be able to see him in that soft light again.

After Pastor Mark finished praying, Luke beckoned his family to join him onstage. The Nolan women rose and shuffled out of the row in single file, leaving Matthew alone next to their empty seats. For Caroline, the walk to the stage felt infinite, the steps insurmountable. She looked out at the audience and saw only a sea of bleached blond hair. She pressed her nails into her palms. This was like a nightmare that would never end. The spotlight made her sweat. She realized she'd forgotten to apply deodorant and pressed her arms tight against her sides.

"Pastor Luke," Pastor Mark said, once they had taken their places onstage, and after an appropriate pause, "has had an affair."

A gasp snaked through the audience. Caroline heard sniffling, noses blowing, the murmur of a dozen whispered questions. Most of the church's leadership crises had been dealt with privately at elders' meetings. A deacon whose daughter had an abortion retired quietly. An elder whose wife came to see Luke with a bruised hip and black eye switched to another church. Two summers ago, when the youth pastor had been accused of having an affair with a high school girl in Caroline's Bible study, the girl was reprimanded and the pastor transferred to a church in Arkansas. Caroline only knew about these issues because her father had talked about them at home. The congregation had no practice absorbing this kind of scandal.

Abigail slipped one finger and then her whole hand into Caroline's, breaking her tight fist. Caroline squeezed. Thank God her sister was here.

"Because he is a head pastor, and so clearly living in sin, the elder board met last night and came up with a plan," Pastor Mark continued. "Of course, if you have questions or need to talk through your grief, all of our doors will be open." He smiled to reassure his audience. "We have to trust Him to guide us through this period of trial and tribulation." At first, when Pastor Mark said *Him*, Caroline had thought he meant her father and struggled not to roll her eyes, then she realized he was talking about the Son of God.

It felt as if her whole family were on trial, standing there onstage. Caroline tried not to meet anyone's eyes. She thought maybe she would cry if she did. She scanned the room for a familiar face, spotted Mrs. Debbie sitting next to Taylor, and quickly averted her gaze. That's when she noticed the mounted television in the back of the room, the scroll of type across its screen. Pastor Mark was reading from a script. "God can do all things," he said, as Caroline read along. "And even this can be used to build up our congregation of His followers into a stronger community of believers." She wanted to ask him if he really believed the words he was saying, but the thousands of eyes held her in place. Her doubts would have to wait until after the meeting.

Confess your sins, the Bible teaches, before the Lord your God—and now it was her father's turn. Luke's fidgeting stopped when he stepped forward to address the room, though he struggled to find his distinct rhythm. Caroline read the words of his speech on the screen and imagined the delivery as he must have intended it. Over the past year, he had butchered several sermons. Caroline had blamed herself. She'd thought it was somehow connected to his disappointment in her decision to leave home for college. Now she realized that it had always been about the affair. She squeezed her sister's hand again and felt Abigail squeeze back.

Luke turned to face his family. He had come to the end of his speech. Caroline's right foot tapped anxiously on the stage while the rest of her body remained still, presentable.

"My wife," he began, and closed his eyes. "I have forsaken the covenant we made together before God. That is a mighty sin to forgive, but I hope that with the help of our Savior, you will try."

Caroline couldn't believe it. She had been shocked when

he'd asked for her forgiveness the night before—and now here he was about to do it again and in front of everyone? She hadn't agreed to this. She glanced at her sister. But Abigail's mask was on; it revealed nothing.

Ruthie strode across the stage and hugged her husband; the sound of his lapel mic hitting her chest echoed throughout the room. Luke's eyes widened in what seemed like real surprise, or gratitude. "Of course I will," the room heard her say. His mic picked up her response, muffled as it was by his shirt. There they were: this couple that was supposed to symbolize decency and goodness, now stitched loosely back together. His arm around their mother, he turned to his girls.

"My daughters," he said. Caroline felt Abigail squeeze her hand. "I have failed you, and failed to lead our family." He took a deep breath. "I know this will not be easy, but I hope that you will forgive me the way our Savior forgave you."

Caroline glanced at her sister again for some indication as to how they should respond. She hadn't been prepped for this. She looked to their mother, but Ruthie was looking at Luke. The lights were so warm on her face, she felt the sweat gather on her brow and beneath her arms. His eyes were wide, waiting for them to answer. Obviously, she and Abigail were supposed to walk toward him now, a show of solidarity for the good of the church. Caroline tried to release her sister's hand and step forward. But Abigail held her back. Her sister's eyes were fixed on their parents. She did not move.

"We promise to try to forgive you as the Lord forgave us," Abigail said. The stage mics barely picked up her voice, but the *try* rang in Caroline's ears. It wasn't a promise. Abigail was withholding her forgiveness and Caroline was happy to join her. She hadn't even realized that was an option.

She saw the flare of disappointment on their father's face. But before he could say anything further, Pastor Mark stepped forward to close the meeting. Abigail squeezed her hand.

"Let's pray," Pastor Mark said.

And Caroline wanted to pray. She truly did. She bowed her head and closed her eyes, grasped outward for God, listened to her sister's voice reciting her own prayer under her breath. Caroline searched for the Holy Spirit. *Please*, she prayed, *guide me*. But she no longer felt certain that anyone was listening.

Caroline had viewed the whole of her life through the lens of God. In her college acceptance letters, she had seen His perseverance. In her mistakes, His discipline. In her future, His promises. She'd always felt wonder easily, a sense of awe when gazing upon the beauty of the Lord's creation, like that feeling you get when you drive around a hairpin turn and the vastness of the earth spreads out before you.

But now it felt silly to bow her head, as if she were alone and adrift in the stillness of the room. She imagined Taylor's eyes on her and tugged on her hemline. She struggled to focus on Pastor Mark's words. She glanced at her father and saw that his own head was unbowed. He was staring out at the audience. Pastor Mark said "Amen," and everyone in the room remained in their seats as the Nolans descended the stairs. The girls returned to the second row. Luke went to stand at the side of the stage.

The worship pastor came out then, carrying an acoustic guitar, and played one song: "How Great Thou Art," a rendition so slow and somber Caroline could hear women sobbing between each verse. When he finished, the lights went up and the congregation milled about the room, hugging and reassuring one another. No one said a word to the Nolan women, though. It seemed they were not invited to participate in the communal grief. Caroline met eyes with Taylor across the atrium and he started toward her. She held up a hand, shook her head. *Are you okay?* he mouthed. *Yeah,* Caroline mouthed back, and turned quickly to face her sister. She didn't want him to see that her eyes had filled with tears.

Abigail looked over and noted her sister's expression. "Oh," she said. Caroline's shoulders stiffened, expecting a reprimand.

"Do you want to leave?" Abigail whispered. Caroline nodded. She desperately wanted to leave. Abigail grabbed their mother, leaned close to say something in her ear, and then proceeded to drag Caroline and Matthew from the room, through the front doors, and out into the afternoon heat, where the sun was shining so brightly it formed waves on the concrete.

6

No one in the Nolan family slept soundly that night. Caroline heard her father pacing the living room, her mother going to the kitchen for ice, Abby whispering good-bye in the hallway, the hum of a car starting to carry Matthew back to Midland. Caroline spent all night watching the comeback sermon from the Houston pastor Mrs. Debbie had mentioned. His church had shared it online. During her fifth view she noticed how happy everyone seemed, how they stood and clapped for him. She fell asleep with it on, tossing and turning throughout the night, unsure if she could ever support her father in the same way. When she awoke the next morning to the sound of the front door, she wasn't sure if she had slept at all.

Caroline went downstairs a little after ten and was surprised to find the kitchen flooded with light, the shadows of two Starbucks coffee cups stretched long and lean across the table. Her mother and sister were sitting next to each other. "Good morning," they said in unison as she turned the corner.

"I think I'm gonna make a pot of coffee," Caroline said. "Who wants some?"

They both raised their hands. "Your daddy is gonna need some too," Ruthie said.

Caroline held the glass pot under the water. Her hand quivered from its weight. "Wait, Dad's not up yet?" Their father was always "up with the Son," as he liked to say, another one of his dad jokes about spending the early-morning hours with the Son of God.

Abigail shook her head.

What's going on? Caroline mouthed at her sister from across the kitchen. Abigail shrugged and Caroline finished spooning the grounds into the filter. As she waited for the coffee to brew, she bent over the counter and rested her chin on her crossed arms. She only had two hands, so when the coffee was ready, she poured her and Abigail's mugs first. She set them down on the table right as their father entered the room. His hair was rumpled, his eyes dark, smile fake.

"There are my daughters!" he exclaimed, like it was any other morning and no one was mad at him. Neither girl greeted him. He sat down at the table before he realized there was nothing waiting there for him.

"No. No. Sit. I'll get it," he said when Ruthie hopped up to make him a coffee, as she had every morning for as long as Caroline could remember. "Do you need another cup?"

"Sure," she said, sitting back in her chair, as if the idea had never occurred to her and she hadn't just asked Caroline to make her a cup moments before. Caroline sat down too. Her mother was trying so hard, Caroline thought.

Caroline took a sip and watched her father pull two mugs

from the cabinet, clanking them together. He tore open a couple of Splenda packets for his own. Caroline then waited for him to reach for the fridge. He didn't. He stared at his wife's cup as if it might tell him the answer. Abigail's eyes seemed to be pleading with the back of his head.

He set the mug of black coffee in front of his wife and sat down. Ruthie and Abigail rose in an almost synchronized motion, spinning away from one another—Ruthie to add creamer and sugar to her cup and Abigail so he wouldn't see the tears in her eyes.

Caroline knew how her mother took her coffee. She liked vanilla creamer, so much of it that the coffee paled before it was even stirred. This was the least of the things Caroline knew about her mother. Ruthie Nolan was nothing if not a collection of habits. She was the purple pens she used to take notes in her Bible. She was the black (always black) purses she carried and filled with pink things: pink wallet, pink lipstick, pink journal. She was the grocery lists penned on the pad by the fridge, the smell of gardenias, the decorative hand towels she folded in half and then in thirds. Ruthie Nolan never changed. She'd had the same hairstyle, a (dyed) honey-blond bob cut to her collarbone and flipped away from her face, since college. She was always freezing, always dieting, always wearing flawless winged eyeliner. And the only sweets she ever ate—she had to maintain her figure, after all—were the two cubes of sugar she placed at the bottom of her mug every morning.

Caroline's eyes connected with her father's across the table. He shrugged as if to say, *Who could know what they want, the women?* Except Caroline was one of them. She stood and left the kitchen without a destination in mind.

She ran into Abigail in the hallway. "Where are you going?" her sister asked.

"I just—" Caroline fumbled, pausing when she saw their mother pass through the living room. "I can't be in there with him right now," she said, and waited for her sister's rebuke. Abigail kissed her on the cheek and headed back to the kitchen.

CAROLINE LAY ON her bed, turning over the last two days for the thousandth time. She slid open her phone. Still no messages. Lauren had read her text and never responded. Caroline opened Instagram, scrolled through photos of pool parties and pontoon boats, girls she knew in bikinis posed to make their waists look tiny, their big smiling selfies. They all looked so happy. She rested her phone facedown on her stomach. How was she going to survive until August?

From her bed, she could hear the conversation in the kitchen grind forward. Through some failure of engineering, Caroline had always been able to hear anything that was said in that room.

She listened to her father's voice drone on and on, and recalled one of the many nights when his words had been so powerful to her that she'd climbed out of bed to lie on the floor so she didn't miss a single one of them. She had been in middle school then. Abigail had started her sophomore year at Texas Christian—and her sister's life, to Caroline, had seemed just about perfect. She had a full-ride scholarship, an active social life, dozens of people texting her at all times, and even their father, Caroline was certain, loved her more. And she had Connor.

Back then, Connor Boyd and Abigail Nolan had seemed predestined. They were both tan and strong and optimistic. They'd been together for four years and were still figuring out how to handle the whole long-distance thing at their separate colleges, but then Connor came home at Thanksgiving and broke it off. Caroline had lain on her bedroom floor and listened to every detail—Abigail's key in the back door, her unsteady gasps for breath in between the sobs, and their father coaxing it all out of her.

It wasn't God's plan, he'd said. Connor had told her sister that he didn't believe it was God's plan for them to be together. And it was that claim, not his first daughter crying, or the fact that an egotistical nineteen-year-old had broken her heart, that had set Luke Nolan off. It was the best sermon either of his daughters had ever heard him give.

God's plan, any congregant of his should know, was not to be used as an excuse. God's plan was that His children be protected, and loved, and as capable as possible of spreading the Gospel. "God's plan is not a specific date you break up with your girlfriend," he said, "and God's plan certainly is not the feeling that makes you do it." He spoke of broad truths for about twenty minutes before he honed in on his daughter, made the sermon personal and specific just for her. Luke Nolan shifted his focus to God's grace, and how His love was so much greater than any earthly love.

"The Lord's plan isn't made to hurt you," he told Abigail. "It is the greatest gift you could have been given, and if that boy doesn't understand that, then he doesn't understand God." It was the Gospel tailor-made for Abigail, too specific to have been prewritten, too inspired to have been worried over.

Now Caroline's mind swam as she lay in her bed listening

to her father discuss his lunch plans downstairs. She couldn't figure out why the Lord had so divinely inspired someone who would fail Him so greatly. She still believed in God, though, right? Sure, her faith had weakened over the past year. It was difficult to both climb into the back of a Jeep half-naked with a boy and be transparent at Bible study the next night—and so she had split her life, forgetting God when she was with Taylor and forgetting Taylor with God. But she worried that she liked being with Taylor more, and this was why she was struggling with her faith. She turned onto her stomach and thought about praying.

Her phone buzzed. She snatched it up quickly. **Checking on you,** it read, **let me know if there's anything I can do.** It was from Taylor. How had she not noticed that this thing with him was becoming more serious? Her thumb hovered over the keyboard. It was a thoughtful text. Nice, even. But she didn't want to have a full conversation with him. Maybe she could just send a *thanks* and leave it at that.

She started to respond, but she heard her sister's feet on the stairs and shoved her phone under her pillow. Abigail came into the room without knocking, poking in her head, following it immediately with the rest of her body.

"Are you okay?" she asked.

Caroline's face flushed. "Yeah," she said.

While Abigail shut the door behind her, Caroline rearranged the pillows over her phone and leaned back to cover them. She glanced at her sister to see if she'd noticed, but Abigail sat down on the bed as if in a trance. Caroline noted that her jaw was tight beneath her ear from pushing her tongue against the roof of her mouth. She did that when she was trying not to cry.

"Are *you* okay?" Caroline asked.

Abigail took a deep breath. "Yes, Caro, I'm fine. The Lord is capable of all things, ya know, but I'm really worried about how He's gonna work on that." She motioned toward the kitchen below. "I also just . . ." She sighed. "I need to get out of this house."

Caroline heard the resentment in Abigail's voice, something she had never heard there before. Her sister was always the first to defend their parents whenever Caroline complained. If only the two of them could be alone, she thought, or run away.

That was it. The ranch. The girls had daydreamed about living at the ranch ever since they were old enough to be asked to pick up their dirty clothes or do the dishes. That's what Caroline wanted now—the two of them against the world. They could get away from their father and she could finally talk to her sister about the wedding and Matthew. Caroline's phone vibrated again. She snatched it out from under her pillow and turned it off, ignoring her sister's raised eyebrows. Maybe with enough time, she could even tell her about Taylor.

"It just feels so weird that we have to stay in this house and act like nothing has happened," Caroline said, dropping the hint. She wanted Abigail to think it was her idea. "Like, don't we deserve a change of scenery?"

"Hmm," Abigail said, like maybe she had an idea.

"What?" Caroline said, sitting up to face her. Abigail's eyes were unfocused. *Come on*, Caroline thought.

Suddenly, there was the spark Caroline had been waiting for and her sister said the magic words: "We could go out to Nannie's ranch. For real this time."

Caroline restrained her agreement to a nod.

"Do you want to?" Abigail pressed.

"More than anything," Caroline said, and tried to imagine a world where she could feel this close to her sister forever. She wanted them to be friends. She wanted to show her the texts from Taylor and get her advice. But then she'd have to explain the whole situation, and then what if Abigail didn't want to go to the ranch anymore? She would tell her after they were out there, Caroline decided. She needed the space to examine her beliefs and decide which ones she wanted to keep. She needed the space to breathe.

"Let's go, then," Abigail said.

Her sister had always been a woman of action, movement. And she must, Caroline thought, really want to leave.

"Pack, roomie," Abigail said, and stood and walked away. She turned in the doorway, seemed to sense Caroline's apprehension. "Look, it'll be fine. Just pack a bag. We'll stay the week and see how we feel."

But Caroline wasn't so sure it would be fine. She followed her sister out of her room and into the bathroom they shared, watched as she began putting her makeup into a bag. Caroline met Abigail's eyes in the mirror. She had always been the kid sister, the one who had to be taught how to draw eyeliner on the inside of her lid, or reassured that she couldn't lose her virginity to a tampon. This move was an opportunity for the two of them to be equals.

"We gonna do this or what?" Abigail said.

"Definitely," Caroline said, and returned to her room with a smile.

Caroline didn't know how to pack. She'd never traveled anywhere except on mission trips, and those came complete with a packing list. She shoved shorts and baseball hats, T-shirts, and a swimsuit into a duffel bag. She went to the bathroom and swept everything left on the counter in with her clothes. In the end, she packed as much as she could, and when she emerged from her room with her suitcase and duffel bag, she found Abigail waiting on the other side of the corridor with two large shiny white suitcases, looking down at her phone.

They thumped their way down the stairs. The noise of the heavy suitcases hitting the steps echoed through the foyer and into the kitchen. By the time they reached the ground floor, both of their parents were standing, eyes wide, in front of them.

"What are you doing?" Luke said, the look on his face tense and firm.

"We're going to the ranch," Abigail said. "We need some space to think, and it would be good for the two of you to have some time alone to reconnect."

Luke stared at Abigail. Ruthie stood beside him, saying nothing. Caroline could feel her father's anger radiating like a space heater, until there was no room for anyone else's.

SHE SHOULD HAVE known Abigail would convince them, Caroline thought as she maneuvered her suitcase out the back door and into her car. Once, when Abigail was in high school, she had fought with their father for over a week about the swimsuit she wanted to wear to a friend's birthday party. Abigail won, and she'd worn her two-piece, later admitting that the sides were too tight and the fit uncomfortable. But she had won.

In the driveway the girls argued over which car to take,

each of them wanting to take her own. They compromised by taking both. Caroline's shoulder burned through the window as she drove west in the late-afternoon sun. She watched their neighborhood, the high school, and the new developments still under construction fly past. She followed her sister's lead, copied her turn signal, pulled into the grocery store lot, and parked next to Abigail's car. Caroline still wore the same dingy T-shirt she'd slept in and hoped they wouldn't see anyone she knew.

It was too optimistic and the catastrophically wrong thing to hope for—they made it only four steps through the automatic sliding doors before a woman they vaguely recognized as a member of the Hope congregation set upon them.

"Well, if it isn't the Nolan girls," she said. "Aren't you two all sweetness and light!" Her voice dropped into a concerned whisper. "I am so sorry about your daddy. Are you two doing okay?"

"About as well as we can," Abigail said, her fingers tightening around the buggy.

"Well, good. That's good to hear," the woman said, her eyes lingering on Caroline's unwashed shirt and unbrushed hair. Caroline tried to smooth her hair with her hand. "Well, I will be prayin' for y'all."

Abigail released the air from her lungs as they wove their way through the produce section.

"Who was that woman?" Caroline asked.

"I have no earthly idea," her sister said.

Caroline prayed she would be their only encounter, but the girls were stopped again and again by similar voices, dripping with nosy concern and pity. Everyone was just so very sorry for them. Caroline knew they were considered the most likable characters in this hellish drama—no one sees themselves in the man who cheats, or the woman he cheats on, but everyone can see themselves in the betrayed daughters. The girls hadn't strayed and they hadn't let their father stray. They were "young and beautiful," the women said, frequently followed by: "Good luck, we'll be praying for y'all."

Caroline was certain they would be whispered about forever. *Did you hear that their father used to be a major leader of the evangelical movement and threw it all away to sleep with some elementary school teacher?* The stability she'd been too privileged to notice her entire life had crumbled so easily—and without the status of being Luke Nolan's daughter, who exactly was she?

Caroline glanced at her sister as she tossed three jars of smooth peanut butter into the cart.

You read my mind, Abigail's eyes seemed to say, followed by her whispering, "We really should stock up." So they loaded the cart with nonperishables: frozen pizzas, taquitos, cereal, canned beans, colorful Popsicles that came in individual plastic sleeping bags. They stacked bread on top of bananas, jam jars and boxes of macaroni and cheese on frozen vegetables and bags of chips. They were prepping for an apocalypse that only they were experiencing. They said nothing to each other the entire time.

Caroline finally spoke as they loaded the groceries into her car: "Woof."

Standing by her front door, Abigail responded, "You can say that again." They climbed in, started their engines, and set off in their caravan down the road to the ranch.

CAROLINE HOPPED OUT to swing open the cattle gate. She leaned against it and felt the warm metal press against her back, supporting her. The lake that bordered the northern-most edge of the property shimmered. She turned to watch her sister pull on through and drive up to the house. Caroline drove her own car through and left the door open while she locked the gate behind them. She turned and looked up at the house. The sun hovered just behind it to the west. In silhouette, it appeared small and full of promise. The roof's slope was gentle. This was now the oldest ranch house in this part of the county. The others in the area had been newly renovated to feature open floor plans, shiplap on their walls, 1,200-square-foot great rooms, and big-screen televisions.

Nannie's house was different, Caroline thought as she made trip after trip with the groceries and suitcases. It was one level and the long hallway that dumped out into the living room divided the house in half. On one side, the dining room led into the kitchen, which led into the laundry room, and on the other side, two bedrooms were smushed together with a bathroom in between them, and the master housed in the back. The house had wooden ceilings, wooden base-boards, and colorfully painted walls in all the bedrooms. It had a giant island in the kitchen and metal farm sinks in the bathrooms. It had a front porch and a back porch. And it had the beginnings of every memory she'd ever had.

Right now, the air inside the house was warm and stag-nant. The girls passed through the front hall, which was lined with photos of their grandmother at various ages—her skin bright, smile wide, an angel by any measure. Despite owning the house and having spent every Saturday of their childhoods there, they weren't actually sure how to work the thermostat. It took Abigail a few minutes to locate it in the dining room before they felt the cool air begin to trickle in from the vents.

Abigail grabbed her digital piano from where she'd placed it on the table.

"Are you going to start writing songs again?" Caroline asked. All through high school and college, Abigail had written and performed worship songs. And like everything she did, she was really good at it. Caroline realized that her sister hadn't written anything new since she started dating Matthew.

Abigail shrugged. She did not look up at Caroline, but her fingers pressed the silent keys as if trying on the idea.

Caroline dropped her bags in the front room and went to unload the groceries. For the most part, the girls were silent as they readied the house. They left their clothes inside their suitcases on the floor, as if giving themselves an out in case the transition wasn't as smooth as they'd hoped. When everything was finally unloaded, the cars moved, groceries put away, they looked at each other, both sweaty and out of breath, and realized they were hungry.

"Pizza?" Caroline said.

"Oh, great idea," Abigail said, and dug through the freezer. Caroline sat down at the table. Abigail took a frozen pizza out of its box, tossed it on a baking sheet, and slid it into the oven without preheating it. She searched around in the drawers for the timer, set it, and then drummed her fingers on the counter.

"How long will it take?"

"I dunno," Abigail said. "I set the timer for twenty minutes." The sun was dipping below the horizon outside the window and the cabinets glowed orange. Abigail's hair was bright and her eyes somehow looked greener here. Twenty minutes stretched out before them like a runway, with no end in sight and nothing to distract them but each other.

Abigail spoke first. "We made the right decision, don't you think?" And Caroline nodded. Abigail proceeded to fill the silence by recapping their meeting with Mrs. Debbie, rehashing all the things she'd said about forgiveness and about how "two souls forced apart by sin need time to be mended together again" (which Caroline had no memory of her even saying). Her sister seemed to be arguing with herself. "We aren't a part of their marriage," she said. "We're grown!"

But Caroline did not feel grown, and she was grateful when the timer finally went off. They ate without talking, long strands of cheese sticking to their chins, sauce staining their mouths. They ate seconds and thirds, and then sat at the table staring at each other. Maybe the silence was a good sign, Caroline tried to tell herself. It was still early, only nine thirty. She yawned and Abigail said, "I agree."

"Should we go to bed?" Caroline asked. She was so tired that her eyes felt fuzzy, as if they were already closing. Abigail followed her to grab their suitcases and then to the front bedroom where they'd always slept together as children. They changed into their pajamas, each facing a separate wall.

"Well," Abigail said, "I guess I'll just sleep in here."

That wasn't fair. Caroline wanted to sleep in here too. She wanted to curl up in the same bed with her sister and feel as she had when they'd slept here as children: safe and warm and happy. Plus, she didn't want to sleep in Nannie's room or the guest room where she'd had sex with Taylor.

"What?" Abigail asked.

"Could I maybe—" She felt so small. She rubbed the back of her neck. "Can I sleep in here too?" Her voice trembled slightly.

"Yes, yes. Of course you can," Abigail said.

They piled into the full bed and lay facing away from each other. After a long period of more silence Abigail's breathing slowed, became lighter.

"It's good to be here," Caroline said, and heard her sister sigh. But she wasn't sure if Abigail had heard her or not.

7

Caroline woke the next morning groggy and sweaty and trapped beneath the sandbag of her sister's left arm. Every noise she made was the only noise in the room—the sheets thrashed, the floorboards creaked, the doorknob whined. She looked back at Abigail, who had rolled over and tucked her hands beneath her cheek as if in prayer, hair splayed across the pillow. A single strand of light from the window illuminated her natural highlights. Caroline pushed her own dull hair behind her ear, closed the door as carefully as she could, and crept to the kitchen to make some coffee.

Most days, Caroline awoke to the thumping bass of a pop song blaring out of her phone and was greeted downstairs by a television turned to four arguing moms on a yellow couch, her mother and sister chatting over them, the sounds of the Christian family station filtering in from the radio in the kitchen. Here at the ranch, she held the glass coffeepot under the faucet and listened to the water running and the birds chirping. She remembered that her mother had always said the best thing about the ranch was how all that land and sky quieted the mind.

Her thoughts this morning were anything but quiet, though. They were so loud she lost count as she spooned the grounds from the red plastic canister. She had slept through the night for the first time since Friday, but she still felt bleary-eyed, exhausted. She couldn't escape the images of the auditorium and Mrs. Debbie's office, Taylor walking up the front steps at the ranch, hearing her father's voice say "I'll allow it" when Abigail had told their parents they were leaving. It was so embarrassing, Caroline thought, how much she still sought his approval. She would have stayed if not for Abigail.

She leaned against the counter, turning it all over in her mind. Her father had had an affair. Her father had had an affair. Her father's job was in jeopardy. Her father had had an affair and his job was in jeopardy and he might be put on probation and might be reinstated. After all, that seemed to be what everyone wanted: Luke Nolan forgiven and back on the stage. But she couldn't figure out who decided when her father was redeemed, because it certainly wasn't her.

The coffeepot hiccuped, spitting steam from one side. Caroline tapped her foot on the ground. Her head felt cloudy. Coffee would help. She folded her arms on the counter and watched it drip, drip, drip into the pot. The minute there was enough for one cup, she snatched it out, a few beads sizzling on the hot plate, and filled her mug to the brim. She did not add cream. She was determined to become the kind of woman who enjoyed the bitterness of black coffee.

Caroline sat at the kitchen table. The big window showed the stretch of land between her and the sky, the light at this hour soft and tenuous. Every bit of the ranch house was littered with signs of Nannie's life—her spot at the wooden table, scattered with water stains from her glass, the lip worn from the oil of her hands, haunted by a thousand solitary dinners. Caroline traced one of the water rings with her finger. She heard the door to the bedroom open, and the bathroom door close, water running in the sink. She got up and made Abigail a cup of coffee so it would be waiting for her when she arrived.

"Good mor-ning," Abigail sang, coming around the corner, hair already brushed and buoyant. But Caroline thought she heard a slight catch at the end of her lilt.

"Good morning," Caroline said. "How did you sleep?"

"Good," Abigail said. "You?"

"Good."

Abigail smiled down at her coffee and rubbed her left eye. She piled her blond hair into a bun on the top of her head. The sun rose over the house and the field to the west seemed to glow amber. Caroline looked at the glass canisters of flour and sugar on the counter, at the photo of her and Abigail near the back door, at the crack in the wood paneling in the living room. She hadn't even finished her first cup of coffee. They had three long, empty days beneath a high summer sun before the elder board decided whether their father would be considered for reinstatement. How on earth would they fill the time? There was no internet and she'd forgotten to tell anyone she was here. A panic started in the crease of her elbows and crawled its way toward her head. Beside her, Abigail frowned out the window.

"This isn't going to work," Abigail finally said, and Caroline felt her hope land with a thud in her stomach. She was bored too, but she didn't want to give up so easily! This morning was better than yesterday. Abigail slurped her coffee and set it in a ring on the table. "I think we need a routine," she said, and Caroline's shoulders loosened. She didn't believe in astrology.

She thought it was silly and heretical. The only thing that had ever made her question that stance was how every single Capricorn trait seemed to apply directly to her sister. Of course Abigail had a plan to structure their days.

"Here is what we should do," she said, as if she'd spent years ruminating on the topic. "I think we eat breakfast, take a walk, read our Bibles for a bit, have lunch, be a little lazy in the afternoon, take another walk around sunset, cook dinner, and spend the evening on the porch."

How dare she map out their existence without even talking to her, Caroline thought. Her inclination was to push back, to whine, but she didn't have a better suggestion and she was desperate for a distraction from her thoughts. So she went along with her sister. After they finished their cereal, Caroline slipped on her grandmother's boots, noting the softness of the worn soles, the gentle slope near the back of the heel from Nannie's uncorrected pigeon toe, the heaviness of the steel. She felt somehow smaller in these boots, reduced to something breakable.

Caroline followed her sister out of the air-conditioned house, into the dry, thick Texas heat. It was so bright she squinted, so hot she was sweating in minutes. The ground was covered in wildflowers, sunflowers stretched their spiky necks taller than their drooping heads, grass grew as high as a grown man's belt. They took a lap around the property, picking bluebonnets and Indian paintbrushes and milkweeds, running their hands across the bellies of trees, saying hello to the cows, watching them graze from the other side of the fence. Caroline felt the high dead grass brush her legs, the snap of twigs underfoot. They had 350 acres to explore together.

At first, there was only a tolerable silence between them,

but then Abigail began to share stories about the ranch, stories Caroline already knew, though she still found comfort in hearing them told out loud.

Once, long before they were born and the empty prairie turned into a suburb, the ranch had reached all the way down to the river. Six miles of nothing except land and sky and cattle gates sprinkled between barbed wire fences. Their grandfather, Marion Cullen, inherited the land when his father died, and then he married Nannie, who was eight years younger, and moved her here with a promise: that she would never be hungry or bored. Nannie was eighteen at the time, the same age as Caroline now, with a lifetime ahead of her. Four weeks after the day they met, Nannie and PawPaw were married right here on the land, at the highest point on the property, just as their daughter Ruthie would be years later, and Abigail five weeks from now. After PawPaw had died, though, a man came to the door and offered Nannie a chunk of money for most of the eastern property, enough that she'd never have to work or worry again about supporting her four young daughters.

"I can't believe she sold all of this," Abigail said, her hand running along the twelve-foot pine fence that marked the western border. "Even though she wasn't from a ranching family, I bet she felt the mistake in her bones. You know, like chopping off too much hair?"

"Uh-huh," Caroline said. Of course it would have been hard to sell the land, but Abigail always acted like she alone knew what was best for everyone. Plus, it felt like the hair comment had been directed at her. Caroline had chopped hers to her chin last fall and later cried to her sister about it. They'd only been here one night and Abigail was already making little digs at her, and explaining her own family's history.

"I mean, she did need the money," Caroline said, adopting her sister's condescending tone. "What was she supposed to do, hang on to all this land and let her daughters starve?"

"Caro, come *on*." Abigail rolled her eyes. "You can regret something even if you know it's the right decision."

Abigail didn't know anything. To her, life was a long, straight highway that disappeared only as the earth curved away from her, the road ahead of her always smooth, her future stable.

Caroline couldn't help but think about the loans she'd have to take out for college this fall as she turned to her sister to add, "It's just land, Abby. You may not need the money, but some of us do." She thought about the $1,000 she'd managed to save over four years of part-time work, watched the color rise in her sister's face. "Maybe," Caroline said, "*we* should sell some of it."

Abigail stopped right then, half her face covered by a tree's shadow. "We are not," she said through her teeth, "selling this land."

"But it's both of ours!" Caroline yelled. "Just because you're older doesn't mean you get to decide everything!" She heard her voice and knew that she sounded whiny and petty, but also that she was absolutely right.

"Well, you can sell it when I'm dead, then," Abigail said, and Caroline saw the fire in her eyes.

"Maybe I will," she said, crossing her arms.

"You are so immature," Abigail said, and turned on her heel to march away.

"I am NOT!" Caroline screamed at her sister's swishing ponytail. Abigail never took her seriously. Caroline didn't really want to sell the ranch, but she also didn't want to apologize for having an opinion. It seemed like every time she tried to even talk to her sister, she ended up in tears.

She watched Abigail walk away and noticed something. She squinted against the sun. With her hair pulled up like that, Caroline thought she detected a darker outline through her sister's sweaty white T-shirt. She blinked hard, trotted to catch up with her. How would Abigail have gotten a bruise at the top of her back? Her eyes focused and she realized it wasn't a bruise at all.

"ABIGAIL NANCY NOLAN!" Caroline shouted, and Abby turned back to face her.

"What?" Abigail said, hands on her hips. It was clear she wanted an apology, but Caroline had moved on from that.

"What is that on your neck!"

Abigail's hand flew to cover it. "Oh," she said.

Caroline lowered her voice. "Did you get a tattoo? Can I see it?"

The Nolan household was one of pure, undefiled bodies. Abigail had to fight for months to get her ears pierced in high school. "Your body," the Bible says, "is a temple." And Luke Nolan took that literally. You would not stab holes in a temple and you would not graffiti its walls.

Abigail turned around reluctantly, smoothed up her baby hairs, and looked down. Caroline hooked a finger under the collar of her shirt and pulled. There, on her sister's smooth white skin, was a tattoo: a cross designed out of the tiniest of roses, each of their petals shaded carefully, their leaves joined together. Caroline loved it immediately. She felt the envy rise in her like a blush and stay there.

"Why is it peeling?" Caroline asked, touching the flaking skin.

"It's new," Abigail said.

"How new?" she asked.

"New new. I got it Saturday night, after I left you at the house. I'd been thinking about it for a while and I just needed to do it." She turned to face Caroline. "Stop looking so shocked. You aren't the only one who's allowed to rebel."

"But I am shocked!" Caroline said. "I can't believe you got a tattoo."

Caroline spun her sister around to look at it again.

Abigail's shoulders fell a little. "Does it look bad?" she said.

"Oh Abby, no no no no no," Caroline said. "I love it. It's really pretty." Caroline loved it so much her own neck itched. She wanted one too. She wished they had gotten them together.

"Okay," Abigail said, "thanks," and the girls walked back to the house side by side, their hands brushing as they crossed the fields.

THAT NIGHT THEY sat on the front porch eating Popsicles, the sticky syrup dripping onto their hands and the pale wood, where it left small red and purple stains. The sides of Caroline's hips hurt from the long walk in heavy boots. She finished her Popsicle and left the stick on the arm of the porch swing. The sky in front of them was dark at the horizon, pink overhead. Abigail stood and dropped her heels off the edge of the top step, stretching her calves, holding the railing with one hand, her Popsicle with the other.

"Abby," Caroline said, and her sister looked at her from across the porch. "I'm sorry about earlier. I just . . ." Caroline paused. "I feel like sometimes you hear what you think I'm saying and not what I'm actually saying."

Abigail turned her stick horizontal to keep it from dripping down her hand. She stopped stretching and came to sit on the swing beside Caroline, facing forward. "I'm sorry too," she said. Her Popsicle broke then and she shoved a chunk of it in her mouth. "We're just so different." Abigail's words were muffled by ice before she paused to swallow.

"I feel like a bad sister," Abigail continued. Caroline could see the tears shimmering in her eyes despite her shadowed face. "I never know how to support you."

"That's not true," Caroline said. "You were really supportive when I didn't want to go to Texas Christian." She scooted closer, her foot on the swing, a hand on her sister's shoulder. She lightened her voice and smiled at her. "You were so supportive. I almost couldn't believe it."

Abigail didn't laugh, though. She turned to fully face her. "I never thought I'd want to leave Hope before last year," she said. "But I understand why you do." Maybe it was the dwindling light, or the sheen of sweat on her face, but when Abigail looked at her right then, her eyes appeared to be made of stained glass, her gaze so knowing and intimate that Caroline had to look away, afraid what Abigail might think if she knew her secret.

BY THURSDAY, THE heat had broken them. Their concerns had evolved from puckering skin on the backs of their legs and ingrown hairs on their bikini lines, past the petty fights and into a present where they lay on the couch all afternoon in their underwear, something they'd never done at home, never done ever. It was the third day in a row of triple-digit temperatures, and they had both agreed to move as little as possible. Every hour that passed brought them closer to the meeting. They did not chat. They did not do anything, the stress building inside their bodies until they both felt too nauseous to eat dinner. Luke Nolan's daughters did not believe in purgatory, but they found themselves trapped in one all the same.

Caroline felt restless with no new information. Their cell phones had no service and their parents hadn't called the house with an update. The Bible was pretty clear about the importance of forgiveness and the promise of redemption, but she also understood why the elder board might not accept their father's apology. Who could have faith in a church leader after finding out he'd lied to you for years?

"Do you think it's a good sign or a bad sign that we haven't heard anything yet?" Caroline asked as Abigail pulled yet another frozen pizza out of the oven.

"I don't think it's either, really," she said.

"But what if they don't accept his apology?" Caroline wasn't sure what she wanted the outcome to be. Really, it seemed too early to make this decision, and far too early for him to be reinstated. She shuddered. If forced to choose, she would probably vote against her father.

Abigail sighed. "Caro. It's going to be fine. If Hope doesn't give him a second chance, which I highly doubt, seeing as they're in the business of forgiveness and all, he'll transfer to another church and preach there."

"Oh," Caroline said. She hadn't thought of that. Their father was too talented. He brought in too much money to be unemployed. She was confused as to how she should feel about everything. Was this what was best for the Kingdom of God?

Her brain felt like a salad spinner, and for a moment, a dangerous thought flashed: If the church could brush off this kind of behavior, did that mean they could brush off anything? And if they didn't care about sin, then maybe they didn't care about goodness either? Caroline tried to repress these thoughts, but they had already planted themselves at the base of her neck. She rolled her head to try to release the tension there.

"They'll decide tonight," Abigail said.

That was all there was to say about the fact that their parents would face a group of wealthy men who donated a lot of money to the church, and these men would decide whether their father was worthy of a second chance. There was no call while they picked at the dinner neither of them wanted to eat, no call as they sat on the porch with the front door open until late in the night, waiting for the phone to ring. When there was still no call at midnight, they went to their too-warm room and climbed into the bed.

Abigail turned to face the wall. Caroline lifted her sister's hair up onto her pillow so that she could see the tattoo. "I want a rose too," she said.

"Go to sleep," Abigail said.

THEY WERE GENTLE with each other the following morning, glancing every few seconds at the phone until finally, as they were in the hallway pulling on their boots for their walk, it rang. Caroline ran to the kitchen to grab it off the counter. Abby was close on her heels. But when Caroline got there, she couldn't pick it up. It rang twice, three times. Abigail pushed her out of the way and answered it.

"Hold on, speaker," Abigail said, and pushed the button on the machine.

"Girls? Can you hear me?" Ruthie's voice asked the kitchen. Caroline laid her hands flat on the counter. They were trembling slightly. She'd lain awake for hours in bed wondering if any outcome in this situation could possibly be good. She was torn. She wanted her family to survive. But did he deserve it? Had he really repented?

"Yes. We can hear you," Abby said. "Tell us what happened."

But their mother didn't continue. Instead, his deep, melodic voice came on the line, echoing around the room. The hair on Caroline's arms rose. She wanted Ruthie back. She could still trust their mother. She looked at her sister, who laid a hand on top of hers and squeezed.

"Well, to start, it's good news," Luke said. Caroline inhaled sharply. "The elder board voted unanimously last night to begin the process of my reinstatement." Now that she knew the results, she was no longer confused. She slipped her hand out from under her sister's and slid down the cabinets to sit on the floor. She didn't think he should be reinstated. She put her head in her hands.

"That's great, Daddy," Abigail said. But Caroline heard the catch in her voice, saw the way she gripped the counter as if she needed it to hold her up. Caroline shook her head side to side.

"Yes. Your mother and I prayed fervently for this outcome and we are grateful that God saw fit to answer those prayers," he said. "My period of evaluation will begin today and last three weeks. If all goes well, the elder board will vote me back in as head pastor then."

His voice was too even, his pauses too performative. His speech was canned. They weren't the first people he had called with this message.

There was a pause before Abigail could find something to say. God, Caroline thought, how was she going to talk to Abigail about this? She listened closely to her sister's tone, tried to decipher whether she agreed with the board's decision, but Abigail was as unreadable as ever.

"So who will preach until then?" Abigail asked. Why did she care? Caroline wondered.

"Pastor Mark," he said.

Both girls nodded. Abigail realized their parents couldn't hear them and added, "Well, that's good news. We're happy for you." But Caroline wasn't happy.

"Thank you, girls," he said. "I'll see you both tomorrow at the festival and we can chat more then. I love you both."

No, Caroline thought. She'd forgotten all about the festival. She couldn't do it. She didn't want to see anyone except Abby until she figured out how to feel about all of this. She certainly didn't want to see their father and every single other person she knew.

"Love you!" Ruthie added from the background.

"Love y'all," Abby said, and hung up.

She reached down and offered her hand to Caroline, who took it and allowed herself to be pulled up from the floor and led out onto the porch. Abigail lifted the bangs from her sister's forehead and wiped the sweat there with the back of her hand. "Why didn't you say anything on the phone?"

she asked. It wasn't an accusation. The words seemed to float through the air like a blown dandelion.

"I didn't know what to say," Caroline said. "I don't know how to feel." And that was true. She wrapped her own arms around her as if they could provide comfort.

"I think we're supposed to feel happy," Abby said. Caroline looked for an emotion, any emotion, in her sister's face. If Abigail fell in line, she wasn't sure she had the strength to fight on her own. She wasn't even sure if she should want to fight. She wanted guidance, but the thought of praying made her chest feel tight. She was alone in this. The sun filtered through the leaves above and printed shadows across her sister's face, blotchy and dark.

"Do you feel happy?" Caroline asked.

"No," Abigail said. "Not really."

8

The worst part was that the girls had to be the welcome party for their own invasion. They heard the car horn at eight the next morning and pulled on their denim shorts, brushed their hair, and dragged their feet down the long gravel driveway. A few cars waited as they unlocked the gate and swung it open. Abby propped it there with a rock, and then they both sulked back up to the house.

They sat on the porch and let their legs flop down over the side and watched as people they'd known their entire lives crushed the grass beneath their wide tires, dragged tables across the dirt, interrupted the flat horizon line with their colorful booths and wooden stage and dozens of games and prize tables. Their voices punched the air, intruding on the morning silence. Caroline and Abigail had been on the ranch for only five days, but they had tasted solitude and now knew that it was sweet.

As more and more cars pulled in, parked, and began to unload, the girls retreated inside. Caroline sat on the toilet and watched her sister swipe concealer under her eyes, pin up half her hair so the other half fell long and loose nearly to her bra line, and tuck a collared long-sleeve shirt into high-waisted shorts. For as long as she could remember, Caroline had loved the Hope, Texas, Annual Balloon Festival. This had always been one of her favorite days of the year—nostalgic, magical, and sweet. But today, she felt none of her usual excited butterflies. Her stomach was heavy. She pulled on dresses and took them off. She sweated through a pair of linen shorts and a V-neck shirt. Eventually, she gave up trying to be an individual and found a collared long-sleeve shirt of her own and tucked it into a pair of high-waisted shorts. She looked in the mirror, straightened her shoulders, and lifted her chin. She could do this.

Abigail raised her eyebrows when she came out of their room. Caroline waited to be chastised, but her sister only sighed, handed her a can of Coke, and led her back outside. The sodas were fizzy and bright for only a moment before they turned syrupy and warm as lake water in the heat. Caroline's head hurt. "I don't feel good," she said.

"Physically or spiritually?" Abigail asked.

"Both?"

Abigail sighed and swatted a mosquito on her leg, leaving a smear of blood across her thigh. "We have to do this, Caroline," she said. "Whatever it is, you're going to have to power through." She sounded like their mother.

"Okay," Caroline said, feeling small and silly. "It's just that usually I don't have to power through the balloons because I'm happy and—" She cut herself off before she could say that their father had ruined the one thing their family had that felt like it had always belonged to her. She didn't have to say it, though. She saw the vacancy in her sister's eyes as she looked across the prairie and knew that she thought so too.

WHEN THE SUN seemed like it couldn't get any higher in the sky, the cars began to arrive in a rush, kids tumbling out of minivans. Their father's red truck pulled in closer to sunset and parked near the cattle gate. Caroline and Abigail watched their mother wait in the front seat for him to open her door. She emerged in a dress, light blue and ironed. Luke wore a short-sleeve button-up that he was already sweating through. Caroline almost didn't recognize them. Luke took shorter strides and Ruthie's movements seemed slower than usual, their waves and smiles too big, their hugs stiff as they embraced members of the congregation. Caroline was staring at her mother, trying to understand what had changed about her, when Ruthie shielded her eyes with her hand, looked toward the house, and spotted them sitting there on the porch. She waved to her daughters, a beckoning command, not a hello.

Caroline stood, tugged down on the hem of her shorts.

"Where are you going?" Abigail asked. Caroline, confused, pointed toward their mother. Abigail sighed. Her sister was always sighing, always expecting Caroline to know what she wanted without her having to say it, but she stood and they walked toward their parents together. The carnival booths, all evenly spaced and formed in straight lines, turned on their lights then, and children shrieked with joy as the games opened up—shooting tin ducks with pellet guns, bouncing balls into goldfish bowls. The air smelled like burning oil and corn. The girls made their way through the crowd and up the slight hill to where their parents stood among a few church friends.

Here was the Ruthie Nolan they recognized: forty-eight years old, dyed blond hair sprayed high above her cowlick, curled at shoulder length, turning her face toward the remaining sunlight to inspect her daughters as they approached. Their father beamed a too-big smile at them.

"Hi, girls," he said, and then added, "there are my daughters," when he realized his misstep.

Caroline and Abigail squeezed into the circle, chatting up anyone who looked their way. Caroline turned those two words over and over in her head: *hi, girls*. They had sounded like marbles in her father's mouth.

Every second the sky dulled a bit more, turning vast and empty, a sapphire above, hints of ruby along the westernmost edge. The clouds were thin and wispy, moving east just in time for the first glowing orb to appear. It drifted in over the trees that lined the southern border of the property, a rising sun first noticed by the children, their small fingers pointing high into the sky, and then by the crowd of adults. Slowly it grew until the red shape became a red-and-orange balloon filled with the exhaust of a fire no bigger than a man's torso, supporting two figures who waved to the onlookers below. Caroline heard the children scream with delight and longed to be one of them again, to shriek in awe at the hovering globes and roll in the grass with her friends, her only worry being how to convince her mother to let her have more cotton candy.

Luke placed his hand on the small of Ruthie's back to pull her attention from another conversation and raised his other to point. Caroline noticed how her mother jerked away from his touch before settling back into it.

There, above the lake, was a second balloon, bright and royal blue decorated with yellow swirls, the pilot waving with his whole arm. Behind that one came a bobbing rainbow, and a slyly dipped lightbulb, and one that was green with magenta flowers. The sky to the west was a gradation of pink fading to a light denim blue in the north, where the balloons now appeared closer and closer together. They moved so slowly it felt like time itself stood still, their hugeness masked by their height until, suddenly, they were descending.

Across the lake they came, and for a moment Caroline was tranquil. The orange sides of the first balloon were stark against the sky. It landed with a thump on the ground by the lake's shore, spitting out a disheveled young man, sweaty from not only the heat of the air but the giant fire that blazed right above his head. He tied his balloon to the stakes and left it bobbing up and down. Every few minutes another basket crashed to the ground to more raucous applause. Each and every one seemed a small miracle.

Abigail jerked her head toward the booths. Caroline tried to restrain her growing smile.

"Bye! Funnel cakes," Abby said to their parents, waving as she and Caroline left arm in arm.

Once they were out of range, Caroline lowered her voice a little. "Did you see her flinch?" she asked.

But before her sister could answer, Abigail swung Caroline around and pulled her behind one of the stands. They stood in a too-narrow pathway between the aisles that wasn't meant for pedestrian movement, facing each other, both breathing heavily. Caroline saw the back of his head as he passed their hiding spot, headed toward the hill where their parents were standing: Connor Boyd.

Caroline still liked Connor and didn't really understand why he'd broken up with her sister. She felt her own sense of betrayal that he'd left their lives so suddenly.

"What's he doing back here?" Abigail whispered.

"I don't know," Caroline said. After he'd gotten married last summer to some girl he'd met at college, he'd left Hope with his new wife and a car full of unopened presents quicker than a prairie fire with a tailwind. The girls waited, shoulders scrunched against the booths, each fanning her face with her hand as if it might help with the heat.

"Why are we hiding?" Caroline finally asked, but Abigail had already turned away from her, heading back toward the aisle, zoning in on the funnel cake stand manned by some thirteen-year-old boy neither of them knew.

Abigail sighed. "I just didn't want to see him," she said. "Do you want powder?"

"Yes," Caroline said, "but what's it matter anymore?" Caroline wanted to say hello. She wanted to be able to talk to Connor again.

"It just does. I don't know." Abigail shook her head. "One funnel cake with powder, please," she said, flashing the boy a smile. After a moment, Abigail took the outstretched funnel cake from the teenager and held it out toward Caroline as they walked away. "Matthew's perfect," Abigail said. "He's perfect."

But Caroline hadn't said anything about Matthew. She knew all too well the script her sister used whenever anyone asked about her fiancé. Their love, she would say, was a relationship with a defined goal: marriage. Abigail was not making the same mistake again. Matthew was a born-again believer who, unlike Connor, had built their relationship on the church's rule book. No kissing until they were engaged. No closed doors. No being alone with any member of the opposite sex. The rules, he said, were there to protect them.

Every time Caroline heard Abigail list these relationship rules for other girls, it was like she could feel Taylor's hands as she let him pull her into the back seat of his car, the softness of the flesh between his shoulder blades. The secret sat like a bowling ball on her diaphragm. Caroline pulled off a piece of the cake, the powder falling onto her shirt, and chewed it to avoid talking.

She didn't quite buy her sister's narrative. A love like Abigail and Matthew's was like a bay window at the front of a house, square and single-paned, allowing anyone from the street to see inside. Here, it said, are all of the things that we have. Watch us hold them in our hands and share them together. But a love like that was also fragile. All it would take was one rock. Caroline saw the distress on her sister's face as she watched Connor greet their parents and wondered how well she would have to aim.

Caroline's paper plate was saturated with oil now and starting to bend. She motioned for her sister to stop for a second. They stood in the center of an aisle picking at their funnel cake—people passing by, heading toward the stage that was being readied for the band, the crew plugging in the instruments, testing the microphone. A gentle tapping sound could be heard over the Christian rock that played softly from the speakers.

They were surrounded by their schoolteachers, first crushes, and childhood friends, a group they were used to belonging to not as members but as leaders, women afforded a position of power based on the secrets that their father had accepted and that the girls shouldn't, but absolutely might, know. But as they moved through the crowd tonight, they felt like live ammunition. "We are thrilled with the elders' decision," Caroline responded when asked. "I'm thrilled about the wedding," Abigail reassured a friend. "Feeling optimistic," they postured. "Thank you for your prayers. We need them."

More than anything, the girls heard the beginnings of rumors, and even though no one said her name, it was clear everyone knew it by that point. *That Woman*, they called her. *That Woman who led Pastor Luke astray.* That Woman was a widow and her son just nine years old. That Woman had been a Christian for three short years. That Woman wore V-necks a little too deep, shorts a little too short, and everything a little too tight for a woman of her age. That Woman made a bad brownie.

That Woman didn't attend the balloon festival, but she might as well have. Caroline tried to make eye contact with her sister, but Abby was too busy smiling and waving, playing her part to perfection.

"Five minutes till the welcome greeting, everyone," a voice said through the speakers. The balloons finished drifting in over the lake and the sun had now set. If she looked closely, Caroline could see a few stars beginning to wake up.

"Game time, I guess," Caroline said to Abby, and started toward the stage, only her sister didn't follow. Caroline took a few steps before she noticed, turned, and walked back.

"I want to talk to you," Abigail said, taking the rest of the funnel cake from Caroline and dropping it into the trash can. There was a little hitch in the way she said *talk*, as she brushed the powdered sugar from her shirt. Caroline had noticed her sister's movements becoming more fluid as the days went on; the tension had released in her jaw. She cupped wildflowers in her hands just to admire them on their walks. And for the first time in Caroline's life, she knew exactly what her sister wanted without her having to say it.

"We don't have to go home if you don't want to," Caroline said. "I'll stay here with you. I want to."

Abigail bounded over and hugged her around the waist. Caroline felt her sister's tiny bird bones contract as she wrapped her arms around her.

"Ugh. Sweaty," Abigail said, backing up now, her eyes gleaming.

"I feel different out here," Caroline said. "I don't know."

"I know," she said. "Me too. Plus, we're like, bonding."

Caroline smiled in response, but inside she felt the fizzle of Pop Rocks. She would stay out here on the ranch forever if that's what it took to keep Abigail close. Her sister was radiating with joy now, and it was all her doing. Caroline had read her mind the way Abigail had always wanted her to, and for once been able to grant her wish.

"Shall we?" Abigail said. She reached out a hand, and Caroline took it. Her sister's eyes lingered on her ring finger, bare except for the still paler line where her matching cross ring should have been.

She saw the question cross Abigail's face. "My hands were swelling," Caroline offered. Abigail nodded but looked skeptical. Caroline knew she would have to tell her eventually. She would wait until the time was right.

THEIR PARENTS WERE at the front of the crowd near the stage. The girls exchanged a knowing look and dove into the swarm. The ground was littered with families sprawled out on giant quilts faded long ago at various soccer games and practices. A couple of teenage boys were throwing a football. Abigail sidestepped to avoid their passing lane. *Excuse me, excuse me*, the girls said, placing a hand on a shoulder here and there. It was still close to a hundred degrees. The air pressed in; it almost felt as if they were swimming through it as they inched closer to their parents.

Caroline spotted Taylor in the midst of the crowd, sitting with his mom and dad. The lines of his chest muscles were visible through the thin fabric of his white T-shirt; the dip between his collarbone and shoulder muscles appeared big enough to hold a quarter. He had missed a spot shaving on the right side of his neck. The hairs there were longer, growing rebelliously. She could still feel his hands on her body from a week ago, still taste his cinnamon gum. He looked up then, his eyes meeting hers, and smiled with his straight white teeth. Caroline looked away and focused on following her sister.

It took longer than they expected to make their way to the front. Some areas were too crowded and they were forced to turn back, accepting hugs and compliments at every turn. Caroline didn't realize how close they were to their parents until she heard her father laugh, looked up, and there he was less than ten feet away, holding court, towering over everyone around him.

Luke Nolan always played host at this event, even though it was a secular gathering. When the elder board questioned why the church's money was being used to pay for tents for balloonists and stands for food, he'd remind them that people from all over came to the balloon festival. Some belonged to churches nearby; others might have left the church or never attended one, or might not know what they believed in at all. This was a ministry opportunity.

Caroline and Abigail took their seats on the quilt their mother had laid out in front of the stage. They opened the small picnic basket she'd packed and began shoving grapes by the fistful into their mouths, smashing them between their teeth as they watched their father chatting away happily, his huge gleaming smile. Caroline wished he looked less satisfied with himself.

Abigail was spinning her engagement ring around her finger so that it made a gentle clicking sound against her unchipped nails. There and gone. There and gone. Caroline felt almost hypnotized by the steady, even click. Their father climbed the steps to the stage. She reached out a hand to stop her sister's movement. People around them clapped and cheered. Ruthie sat beside them on the blanket.

Every year, their father concluded the evening with a re-telling of the festival's origin story. Caroline had always loved this part. She loved the story. But this year, all she heard were the many ways in which he butchered it.

In Luke Nolan's version, Nannie disappeared. He didn't mention that she had been pregnant for the very first time when a young man had crashed onto her land in a big blue balloon. He didn't mention that she had then fed that man a meal—one whole chicken, mashed potatoes, butter on every-thing, and a homemade pecan pie, the same meal Ruthie had made for Luke the night she told him she was pregnant with Abigail.

Instead, he stood on the stage with his legs spread wide, his back straight, the thumb of the hand he wasn't using to hold the microphone hooked through his belt loop, and spoke about how the balloons were a reminder that God can surprise us. No mention of the fact that Nannie and PawPaw had refused to accept any money from their visiting balloonist, or that they'd opened their home to a stranger and fed him with the same hospitality that was depicted in Jesus's parables.

And his cadence was off again. Caroline looked to her sister. Abigail's eyes were focused on their father. He was pacing the stage, struggling to get through an anecdote he'd told every year for more than a decade about how his first balloon festival was a sign from God that he needed to stay in Hope. Caroline realized then that he'd taken Nannie's story, one about heart and gumption and pain, and sterilized it. He'd made it safe and boring. Had he always done this, made every one of their family stories all about him? And if so, why hadn't she noticed it earlier?

Caroline knew that the first balloonist had returned every year after that accidental visit and brought his friends along with him, and that everything had been fine for the first five of those years. But during the sixth year, while PawPaw was clearing the land, moving the cows so the balloons would be free to land, he'd noticed smoke in the distance. He'd hurried to move the cattle onto a nearby hill, but one of the calves ran the other way, into a small clearing on the western half of the property. PawPaw was still there coaxing it out when the fire, traveling too swiftly following a summer of drought, engulfed the entire field. His horse bucked, he fell off, and the calf bolted.

Their father cut that part too. Caroline was still haunted by the way that balloonist, by then so old and sunburned his skin looked thick, had once described the burned land as the color of oil and the sorrow he'd felt when he'd first seen their grandmother, surrounded by three girls all under five and pregnant with Ruthie, the fire still alive in her eyes.

But Nannie didn't seem to exist at all in this version. Luke's story didn't feature fires or burials or grief, or the people who'd been hurt along the way. It only featured him, standing in front of the balloons, hearing from God. He'd made his public apology, and now there would be more articles and videos, and he'd be right back on top. This event was only one more stop on his redemption tour.

"That could have gone better," Abigail said as he descended from the stage. A gradual hum returned to the crowd scattered on blankets around the property.

Caroline turned to her. "Can we get out of here?" she said.

"I thought you'd never ask," Abigail said.

Caroline held her tongue as they wove between families folding up their quilts, picking up their dinner garbage, stretching their backs, and past boys playing pop-a-shot, shooting their toy guns to win a stuffed trinket. Caroline was quiet as they brushed by everyone who told them they "looked cute" or "sure were getting some sun" or "hoped they were doin' okay." She didn't say a word until they'd almost reached the house.

"He tells that story all wrong," she said.

"Caroline . . ." Abigail said.

"What?"

"He's always done that." Abigail laughed. "He just did a bad job of it this year."

"Oh," Caroline said. "Right." It upset her that she'd never noticed before.

They retired to the porch and waited for the whole thing to be over. From there they watched the balloons deflate, the stands fold up, a team of volunteers circling for trash. They waved goodbye to Mrs. Debbie and the other members of the elder board, to their teachers and middle-school crushes.

THEIR FATHER WAS always the last one to leave. His daughters had a lifetime of practice waiting, of finding a place to sit as his promised ten minutes stretched into an hour. Even now he stood in the middle of a crowd of people hanging on his every word.

It was nearly midnight, the last light coming from the small sconce on the side of the front door encircled by bugs, when he finally joined the girls on the porch, one hand on the railing, one foot on the second step.

"Well, that'll do it." He brushed his hands against each other. "Another successful year! Let's load up."

Caroline panicked. She hadn't thought she would have to talk to him. She squeezed her jaw tight and felt the tension at her ears. She looked at Abby for help right as her sister spoke.

"No," Abigail said, her voice firm and defiant, her left leg twitching.

"No?" he parroted back. "Listen, you two were gracious to give us the house for a week to be alone, but we are ready to have you back. We miss you, right, Ruthie?" His wife nodded along behind him. "We're all good now."

Caroline wanted to laugh. She wasn't "all good." He didn't have the least idea of how she was. Every inch of air between him and her seemed to shake in her vision. She wanted to be angry at him. She wanted to kill the part of her that still so desperately wanted the attention he'd always paid to her sister.

"I think we're going to stay here for a bit," Abigail said. "Caroline and I think it would be good for us to have some space this summer from everything. It's not really about you two at all." Her voice was defiant and yet submissive, the same tone Ruthie always used with him.

Luke Nolan was not a man who tolerated disobedience. You could ask him nicely for something, or suggest he prayerfully consider your opinion, but if you were angry at him, he would be angry right back at you. He wouldn't yell, though. His voice would tighten and he'd start to pace. He would preach at you with the full conviction that his position was right, and he'd have the verses to back it up. Plus, he was the man of the house, so he tended to win. Caroline saw him grip the banister of the porch, his knuckles turning white.

"Absolutely not," he said, climbing the steps so he was standing in front of the girls. Ruthie was still behind him, her lips pressed tight together so that they paled beneath her bright lipstick. "Families stay together. We need your support right now. We need to look like a unified front."

"Daddy, we're not asking permission. We're just telling you that you can find us here if you need us." Abigail looked past him to their mother. Ruthie didn't respond.

"Caro, come on. Let's go," he said. Caroline looked at him then. His eyes were finally fixed on her, and she might have been tempted if she hadn't been so distracted by his use of the word *look*. "We need to *look* like a unified front," he'd said. This wasn't about her at all. It was about getting reinstated. Her emotions didn't matter to him. Her desires didn't matter. He would drag them all through the mud to regain his position.

She forced her head to shake.

"What does that mean?" he said.

"It means I'm staying here with Abby," Caroline said.

His hand gripped the railing tighter. Caroline settled into the porch swing, prepared herself for the sixty-minute sermon he was about to deliver, the many reasons the Lord backed up whatever it was that he wanted his daughters to do. But it never came.

"There's no point having this fight now," Ruthie said. "It's late." Her voice was soft but firm, coming from the darkness behind him and right up onto the porch.

She so rarely spoke during their fights that all three of them startled a little. Luke was so thrown that he just turned around and headed back down the stairs to where the old red pickup truck was parked by the fence along the edge of the property. Ruthie stayed, leaned against the porch railing, pressed her forehead against the webbing of her right hand.

"You girls should stay if you want to," she said. She looked defeated. She would surely be forced to hear the sermon he had failed to deliver here on their drive home. "I know this can't be easy on you, and you've given up a lot for him already."

Caroline began to tear up. Her mother was referring to the sacrifices they had made for him this week, but they had given up a lot for him their entire lives.

"Please be careful out here," she said. "This land hasn't been kind to the women of our family. It holds a lot of bitterness."

Caroline shot Abby a look out of the corner of her eye. The land didn't feel bitter to her. She wasn't sure what her mother was trying to tell them.

"I love you both," Ruthie said. "You can always come home."

"We love you too," the girls said, their voices echoes of each other.

And Ruthie left, her sandals slapping down the stairs, the door to the truck slamming shut behind her, the click of the clutch, the crunch of the gravel, and the long whinnying screech of the cattle gate being closed behind the truck, followed by the bang of its lock. There was the shushing of their tires when they pulled onto the street, and then the quiet of the midnight air. The wind hummed over the grass and around the corners of the house. A warm, unsatisfying breeze whispered through the thick summer air something that sounded like a promise, but could have just as easily been a curse.

9

Caroline woke before her alarm and crept out onto the porch into the harsh morning sun. The light brightened the wide-open field and fires blossomed in colorful puddles as the balloons were inflated into buoyant orbs. A soft, heavy blanket of silence tucked itself around her, and when Abigail joined her a half hour later, rubbing her eyes, hair stuck to her face, the balloons were already fighting against their restraints. Caroline took the mug Abigail offered with a smile and patted the space beside her on the steps. They watched the balloons rise like a colorful rain in reverse, waving up at them as they floated away, their coffee cups balanced precariously on their knees, until their arms grew tired and their stomachs turned demanding.

The morning air seemed lighter without the balloons. The linoleum floor in the kitchen was smooth and cool beneath their bare feet. Their toast burned evenly. The tabletop smelled like lemon cleaner. Caroline fingered the delicate lace of the table runner. The day was alive with possibility and so was she.

They pulled on their boots and left for their walk. Caroline listened to the trees groaning in the wind that blew hot as a hair dryer. For the moment, everything seemed worthy of her attention—the glare of the sun on the lake, the bleached side boards of the house, the tall cattails spinning like hot dogs in the breeze. There were no clouds in the sky, and she felt all that emptiness was somehow trapped inside her rib cage. She was so enchanted by the things around her that she didn't notice Abigail's odd demeanor until lunch. Her sister was slouched over her sandwich, eyes unfocused, gazing out the window, hair swaying from the movement of her legs beneath the table.

Abigail stood to wash her plate in the sink and dialed Matthew. Caroline pretended to read the book in her hand until her sister shooed her from the kitchen. From the living room sofa, Caroline heard her tell him that they were staying on the ranch a while longer, then she hung up, walked to the bathroom, and turned on the shower. Later, there was the whirring of the hair dryer. Caroline left her place on the couch and tiptoed down the hall. She put her hands on the doorframe and listened through the door as her sister's crystal soprano lilted through various hymns as she finished getting ready.

Abigail opened the door then and screamed, a single piercing belt that ricocheted around the house and then back, right as she burst out laughing, bending over to catch her breath. "You scared me!" she said. But Caroline didn't laugh. Her sister's hair was masterfully curled from the ears down, eyeliner modestly winged, her tiny waist accentuated by a belt.

"You're leaving?" Caroline said, and though she tried to hide it, the anger in her voice spun between them like a wind chime.

"Hey," Abigail said softly. "Not for long," and then, "It's Sunday."

"So?" Caroline said.

"So . . . I'm getting ready for church," Abigail said.

"What? Why?" Caroline said.

"Uh—" Abigail said, raising her left eyebrow, "because I'm a Christian?"

Caroline scoffed. "I'm a Christian too, Abby, come on," she said without hesitation. "There is nothing in the Bible that says we have to go to church the literal week after our father embarrassed us forever." There was no way she could smile and sing and raise her hand and not acknowledge that everyone was looking at her. Last week had been bad enough.

"I know I don't *have* to go," Abigail said, and flipped her hair over her shoulder. "I want to go."

"How?" Caroline remembered her father's eyes in the porch light staring straight at Abby, tilted down from the weight of his disappointment. "Dad got to you, didn't he?" Caroline said quietly.

Abigail's face tightened. "What?"

Caroline crossed her arms. "Seeing Dad made you feel guilty and now you want to go and make him happy like you always do."

Abigail took a deep breath. "I'm going to church because this is a very hard time for me. Okay?" Her voice was firm and even. "I need to make sure I'm right with God and I suggest that you do the same."

"I'm not going to church, Abby," Caroline said. "I have no intention of helping Dad 'look good.'" She used air quotes.

Abigail glanced at her phone. "Okay, do whatever you

want, but I need to go." She turned her back on her sister and marched down the hall.

"Please don't be mad, Abby," Caroline said, trailing after her.

Abigail slipped on her flats, gathered her denim jacket from the front room. Caroline watched her throw open the front door. "Love you," her sister called over her shoulder, but her sweetness felt tinged with bitterness, like a ruby-red grapefruit.

"Love you back," Caroline called.

NO MATTER HOW many times Caroline told herself that she'd made the right decision, she still felt that tug inside that she'd always been taught to call conviction. She hadn't been praying. Every morning Abigail read her Bible dutifully, and Caroline found a way not to. She hadn't even really thought about God in over a week. Now she couldn't stop thinking about her conversation with Taylor about faith and went digging through her duffel bag to find her Bible, and took it with her out to the front porch.

Please, God, she tried to pray, *if You can hear me. I'm so confused. Please help me want You in my life.*

She sat on the swing. The book's gilded pages reflected the sun as she flipped to the passage in Genesis she knew the service would be focused on that evening. She read about Abraham and his wife, Sarah. She'd read this one a dozen times and basically knew it by heart. She read three verses, stopped, and started again.

It felt like the first half of the story had been shoved into her Bible when she wasn't looking. She followed along with her finger, hovering over each word. Abraham and Sarah are traveling through Egypt and Sarah is too beautiful, the Bible says. Abraham tells her to lie and say that she is his sister, that if she announces herself as his wife in enemy territory, he will be killed. Sarah lies and Abraham is rewarded: he is given sheep and camels and women to serve him. That part, Caroline remembered. But how had she never noticed that Sarah was then given to the Pharaoh for sex and might have been stuck there forever if the Pharaoh hadn't contracted a carnal disease from her?

Caroline flipped forward, tearing one of the book's thin pages in her haste. Here was the more famous story of Sarah. Caroline had memorized it when she was young, reading it over and over in her very first illustrated Bible. It said that Sarah had never been pregnant, and therefore must have been barren, her womb inhospitable. But when she was ninety years old, she overheard a conversation in which the Lord promised her husband that she'd bear him a son by the following year. When you are a woman, there is always a man between you and God. That much Caroline knew.

But her finger paused at the word *laughed*. "Sarah laughed." Caroline had never questioned its meaning before. Most pastors considered Sarah's laugh a sign that she did not have faith in the Lord. But perhaps it meant that Sarah had never really been barren at all. Maybe she just remembered how her husband had handed her off to the Pharaoh without hesitation and now wanted nothing to do with him. Maybe her laugh came from the bitterness of realizing that the Lord had now returned to ask her for more. Caroline had been taught that

Sarah wanted the baby, that it was the answer to her prayers. But had she ever really believed that? Did she believe it now? Did Abigail? Caroline took a deep breath and asked the Lord for passion. Of course, she had questioned the Bible's teachings before—and she'd always taken these questions, hands trembling, into her father's office and left reassured.

Caroline snapped the Bible closed and carried it back to their bedroom. She looked around the room for a distraction and there, on the dresser, she found one. She traded the Bible for her cell phone, opened her contacts, walked to the kitchen, and typed Taylor's number into the landline, drumming her fingers on the counter as she waited for him to answer.

"Hello?" he said. He sounded out of breath, as if he'd just run up a flight of stairs.

"Hi, it's me," she said, before he cut her off.

"Caroline. Hey. I've been trying to be patient and wait for you to call, but I've been really worried. I mean, is everything okay? I know it was a big step and then everything happened with your dad and I sent you, like, a dozen text messages and I'm not sure if you got them and—"

Caroline put her head in her hand, interjecting when he took a breath. "Taylor," she said, and then realized she didn't have much else to say after that. "I just . . ." She'd thought she'd call him and he'd come over like last time and make her forget about everything. But here he was, his voice saying "Yes?" and she knew things weren't so simple anymore. She sighed. She wanted to feel the way she had last week, like she still had power. Except now she was caught in something else. She heard the sap in his voice. Maybe, she thought, she could do this. Maybe it would be worth it.

"I'm sorry I haven't texted you back," she said. "I moved out to the ranch for some space. There's no service, but I should have told you."

"I know," he said, "my mom told me."

There was too long of a pause. Caroline pushed through it. "Anyway, I was just calling to see if you wanted to come out here for a bit."

"Oh," Taylor said.

She added, "No biggie, if not."

"I mean, I do, Caro. I really do. I would love to." There was that earnestness again. She could already hear the *but* in his voice, though. "But I'm on my way to church right now, and my mom is mad at me."

The adrenaline arrived faster than a sneeze through a screen door. "Did you tell her about us?" she blurted.

"Jesus Christ, Caro, no," he said. "She's mad because she caught me not bowing my head last week in service."

"Oh," Caroline said. "I'm sorry." How had this turned into a serious conversation?

"Don't be," he said. "And really. I promise I haven't told anyone. I don't think it's anyone else's business. Anyway, I'm pulling in, but I could come over later."

Caroline swallowed. She didn't want him to come over later. She had been wrong to call him at all. She didn't want anything serious. She just wanted him to come over and kiss her.

"No," Caroline said. "Abby will be back. But I'll let you know."

"When?"

"Soon," she said, and hung up before he could add anything further. The phone call had left her feeling even less in control than before.

SHE PULLED ON her boots and walked the fields. She moved fast enough to lose her breath, to silence her thoughts. In the late-afternoon light, the trees cast long shadows back toward the house, but they provided no relief from the heat of the blazing sun. She wove between them—a splinter lodged in her finger from brushing against one. She pulled it out with her teeth. She walked past the two marble crosses where her grandparents were buried. Here there was some shade. The ground was soft and cool. Caroline sat between the two crosses to catch her breath. She used the hem of her shirt to wipe away the layers of yellow pollen that covered their stones. The wind whispered across the tall grass, but it brought her no peace. She stood and continued on.

The property felt bigger without her sister. Caroline stopped at the lakeshore to splash water on her face and on the insides of her legs. When she lifted the edge of her denim shorts, she found two raised red lines on her thighs. She dabbed cool water there and rolled her shorts higher. It worked for a while, the walking, except now her bladder was full. She quickened her pace and her shorts rubbed at her irritated skin. She turned back toward the house. Her bladder grew heavier; the denim grated her skin more and more with each step. By the time she ran up the porch stairs, Caroline felt as if she might explode. She slammed the front door shut behind her, locked it, raced down the hall to the bathroom, jerked the shorts down her thighs, plopped onto the toilet. She put her elbows on her knees and waited for her bladder to empty.

Caroline looked to the right and realized there was no toilet paper. Of course, she thought, and smacked the empty roll so that the cardboard spun. Contorting her body as best she could, she swung open the cabinet door beneath the sink.

Nothing. She bounced a little to dry off, pulled up her underwear, and grabbed a pair of exercise shorts from the bathroom floor. She checked the hall closet, where they stored the flannel sheets, and the pantry filled with canned goods. Nothing. She checked the garage with its unlabeled boxes of junk. Nothing. Finally, she stood in front of Nannie's room, turned the knob, and let the door swing open. She hustled through the room and into the master bath. Beneath the sink, she found bottles of cleaning supplies. She opened the towel closet and there, finally, was toilet paper. She reached up her arm, grabbed one, two, three rolls. Stacked them so high they snuggled underneath her chin. She reached into the cabinet for more. Her fingers brushed something hard. *Weird*, she thought, and stood on her tiptoes, brushed it again. Whatever it was scooted back. She released her breath through her nose, set the toilet paper tower on the counter, and grabbed a chair from Nannie's room to stand on.

There, on the top shelf of the towel closet, was a box of condoms with its top indiscreetly opened. Caroline pulled it from the shelf and stepped off the chair. She turned it over in her hands, plucked one from the box, and dropped it back in as if it had burned her. She closed the top. Sure, she'd found the condom under the bed, but she'd assumed that a visitor had left it, some married couple. Now she felt her stomach gurgle. Why hide something if you have no reason to be ashamed of it? She carried the box of condoms into the bedroom, examined the space more closely now.

There were Nannie's perfumes, lined up in front of the large mirror that reflected a sweaty girl with bangs stuck to her forehead and a crazed look in her eyes. Caroline started to look away and then she noticed it, a pink globe with rhinestones, a perfume her grandmother would never have worn. She picked it up, pulled off the top. It smelled like something Abigail would have used in middle school. She wrinkled her nose. Who would have left this here? She spun around, searching for more evidence. She ran her finger along the top of the vanity. No dust. Shouldn't there be dust? There was the bed with its hospital corners, the light curtains open around the window. A lilac cardigan hung off the rocking chair. Caroline picked it up; it was new, cheap. She set the condoms on the bedside table. It wasn't a ghost her subconscious had felt the last time she was in here. It was the presence of another woman. She took three deep breaths and flopped back onto the bed, thwacking her head on something hard. What the hell? She pulled back the comforter and found a book tucked under the sheet, a novel, its pages dog-eared, sentences underlined, an active reader. Caroline flipped through it and landed on the title page, where, in all capital letters, her name was written: MARY CAMPBELL.

Caroline threw the book. It landed on the floor on the other side of the bed. If the sound hadn't echoed back to her, she never would have known that she'd screamed. Her breath was shallow. She sat back down on the edge of the bed. She looked at the condoms on the bedside table. Her mind pieced the truth together before she could stop it.

Luke Nolan was the one who had been here.

And he had been here with That Woman. Not at her house. He'd been here in the house that belonged to his daughters, the house where he had spent his wedding night with his wife, the house where his wife had grown up, on the land that held their family's entire history.

Caroline wondered then if the story Mary Campbell had

told in Bible study about them having a full-fledged emotional relationship might not have been a lie. What did this mean? That he had orchestrated the whole thing? Had he noticed her, a single mother among a community of wives who admired his teachings, and spun her like a top until, in her dizziness, she confused her faith and love for the Lord with a deep desire for him?

Caroline retrieved the book from the floor. She should have put it together earlier. How had she not seen these clues at the shower? She should have known that some visiting missionary wouldn't have needed condoms. Condoms were for people having sex outside of marriage. Condoms were for people like her father and—oh God, they were for people like her. She'd found one under the bed. It must have come from this box, which had been purchased by her father to use in his illicit affair with another woman, and she and Taylor had opened it and used it.

She ran to Nannie's bathroom and dry-heaved. She put her arm on the edge of the toilet bowl, rested her forehead there with her eyes closed. "Holy shit," she muttered. She closed the lid of the toilet and sat down, pressing her fists into her mouth. There was more to the story. Caroline threw open the shower curtain, and there on the shelf was a green bottle of shampoo. She grabbed it and flipped open the top. A whiff of synthetic roses filled her nose; she gagged and snapped it shut. Long brown wavy hairs were stuck to the wall of the shower.

An uncomfortable truth nagged at her. This was it. This was what she had inherited from her father. Abigail had gotten his charismatic personality and his leadership qualities and Caroline had his height and his sin. She covered her eyes with her hand.

She was still there, shower curtain pulled aside, the curl-taming shampoo in her hand, bracing herself against the shower wall, trying to steady her breathing, when she heard banging on the front door.

Shit, she thought, and self-corrected this time. *Shoot.*

Caroline carried the shampoo from the shower and flipped off the bathroom light on her way to the bedroom. She snatched up the cardigan and the perfume and threw the haul under the bed. She placed the book on top of the box of condoms and slid both underneath the dust ruffle. She remembered the toilet paper and bolted back to the bathroom, snatched it off the counter, and rushed from the room, slamming the door behind her.

10

Caroline ran through the living room and stopped before she reached the front door. She could see through the stained-glass window that Abigail wasn't alone. Each of their knocks seemed to bounce off the glass picture frames and into Caroline's ears, where they refused to settle. She stood there, goose bumps on her arms, listening to her mother and sister jostle for the key, their laughter ricocheting, both calling out her name. Caroline braced a hand on the wall to steady herself right as the key rattled in the lock.

"I don't think it matters how big the place cards are as long as—" Her mother stopped as soon as she stepped inside the entryway and saw Caroline. She adjusted the orange-and-white-striped fast food bag that sat on her hip like a toddler and pushed her sunglasses up onto her head. "Where were you? We were knocking."

Caroline looked down and saw that there was mud streaked across her leg from her walk and that her clothes were ratty. She gripped a roll of toilet paper in each hand.

"Oh, sorry, I didn't hear you," she lied. "I was getting more toilet paper."

Her mother brushed past her and Caroline was overwhelmed by the scent of gardenias. "Do we need to buy more toilet paper?" Abigail asked, and then noticed her sister's face.

"What's wrong?" she asked.

"Nothing," Caroline said, "just gonna put these away." She fled to deposit the rolls in the hall bathroom. *Calm down*, she told herself in the mirror. *You have to calm down*. Her eyes were unsteady; her arms were shaking. She took two deep breaths, maintained eye contact with the mirror until she felt sure she wouldn't faint. She heard her mother and sister chatting in the kitchen. Her mother was saying "Is she okay?" Caroline reached out an arm and flushed the toilet. She turned the faucet on and off, and left to join them.

She pulled out the chair across from her mother and sister at the table. They stopped talking about potential bridal bouquets and smiled up at her, their lips tight. Ruthie slid a striped box packed with chicken tenders and long, thin fries toward her, followed by a small Coke in a foam cup. Abigail and Ruthie snapped open the plastic lids of their salad containers and began to eat. Caroline wasn't sure her stomach could handle food yet. She stacked half a dozen small packages of sauce into an unstable tower in front of her.

She saw her mother inspect the peeling skin on her forehead, the pimple developing beneath her nose, while Ruthie chewed on a forkful of lettuce. "You two seem to have made yourselves at home," she said, raising her eyebrows at her youngest as her eyes took in the half dozen dirty cups on the table, the mugs caked with coffee residue, the paper towels scrunched into tumbleweeds.

"We miss having you two around the house," she went on, stabbing at her salad. Neither girl responded. Ruthie looked between them and continued. "I thought I would drop by. There's so much to do and the wedding is so close." And just like that, Ruthie and Abigail fell back into their conversation about everything that needed to be done for the wedding and who needed to be called and how many days were left. Caroline's mind darted from Nannie's room to her sister and back again. She wasn't a good actor, so she started shoveling fries into her mouth until her mother folded her hands on the table in front of her half-eaten chicken salad.

"I thought you two might want an update on your dad and me," Ruthie said, looking each girl in the eye. Caroline took a bite of a chicken strip and chewed. Abigail reached across the table and snatched one of her fries. Neither looked at their mother.

Ruthie sighed and continued. She told them their father was seeing a counselor at the church and that he was home praying for hours each night. Caroline tried to make eye contact with her sister, but Abigail was too busy nodding along. Caroline dunked another chicken tender in her barbecue sauce.

"Honestly, I'm really grateful you girls gave us the space to have these kinds of conversations," Ruthie said. "Your father is on the right track." Caroline grabbed for her Coke in what she hoped was a natural movement. "I understand that you didn't want to be at church tonight," she said to Caroline, though her voice said that she absolutely did not understand. "I hope you'll come next week, for your daddy and me."

Caroline tried to adjust her face to appear normal but felt

like she was doing a weird half smile. She took another sip of her soda. She shouldn't be having this conversation while she could still see the door to Nannie's room, while she was still thinking about her father carrying on his affair in this house. She set the cup down and almost knocked it over. Abigail grabbed it before it fell. Caroline looked at her with wide eyes.

"Caro . . ." Abigail said, and reached out a hand to hold it against her sister's forehead. "Is everything okay? You look a little pale."

Caroline looked between her sister and her mother. *Flee,* her brain said. *Run far, far away.* She could change her name and disappear and then someone else would have to tell them that his affair had happened right here. It would devastate them both. She couldn't be the messenger. She took in their soft, open, concerned faces and realized that she had no one of her own to tell, no one to ask for advice. Caroline began to cry. Her sister stared at her.

"It's gonna be okay, baby," Ruthie said. "What is it? What's wrong? You can tell us."

Caroline sniffled. She saw them exchange a worried glance. She couldn't tell them. She had to let them find out on their own, except now she couldn't stop crying. She wiped the tears away. She had to say something. She blew her nose to give herself a moment to think. A small wrinkle formed between Ruthie's brows and she remembered her mother's warning.

"What did you mean when you said the ranch was bad for women?" Caroline said through her tears.

"Oh, honey, I just meant that there's been a lot of hard times for our family out here." Unable to reach Caroline, whose hands were now in her lap, Ruthie grabbed for Abigail.

It was just too easy, Caroline thought, to get them to

stop paying attention to her. Caroline had always believed her mother's intuition to be better than a police detective's. Ruthie would look at her sideways and know she'd eaten a cookie for a snack, or gotten her first period. But in the last year, her mother must have misplaced it, because she didn't know about the B Caroline had gotten in physics, or the ding in her passenger-side car door, or about Taylor. And she definitely didn't know that her husband had been conducting his affair in her own mother's bed. Or did she? Maybe she did know, Caroline thought, and that's why she'd let them stay out here.

"Yeah, but like, what happened that was so bad?" Caroline said, searching her mother's face. She wanted a confession. If Ruthie knew the affair had happened out here, maybe she'd tell them. Caroline leaned back in her seat and watched her mother's pupils grow until her eyes turned black with guilt. *She knows*, Caroline thought.

Ruthie withdrew her hand from Abigail's and tears began to fall in straight lines down her cheeks.

"Mom, don't cry!" Abigail said, moving closer to comfort her. "Caroline's being really rude." She shot a look at her sister. Caroline shrank beneath her glare.

"No, it's okay," Ruthie said. "It seems like you already have some suspicions, so you might as well hear it from me." She dabbed at her eyes with a paper napkin, reached her arms out wide to touch both of them. Caroline realized she should not have eaten her fries so quickly. She felt them settle in her stomach as she searched Abigail's face for the appropriate response, a way to pretend that she didn't already know. She raised her eyebrows and scrunched them together. Her poor, beautiful, trusting sister, Caroline thought.

"Nannie didn't die of a heart attack," Ruthie said, her voice quieter now. Caroline sat back in her chair, straight, and gripped the sides of her seat. This was not the confession she had expected. Her mother continued, "In those last few years, she was very unhappy."

Caroline glanced at Abigail, who was staring hard at Ruthie. Abigail removed her hand from their mother's and placed it flat on the table. "What are you saying?" she said, her tone crisp, the ends of her long hair lying on the table.

"Your grandmother . . ." Ruthie's words were muffled behind her hands now.

"Are you trying to say she *killed herself*?" Abigail flung the words at her. Caroline inhaled sharply. *No.*

Ruthie's chin moved about half an inch up and down. Caroline felt as if she were floating above the table. She watched Abigail turn on their mother. "Why didn't—I mean, why did you lie to us? Why tell everyone she died of a heart attack if she didn't really?"

Abigail was on the edge of her chair now, her voice powerful and firm. She was David with his slingshot. She stood and paced the room, flinging question after question at their mother, so quickly that Caroline had barely processed one before she was hurling the next. After about a dozen had gone unanswered, Abigail stopped directly behind Caroline's chair, rested her hands on her shoulders. Caroline could feel Abigail's anger pouring right through her, directed at their mother.

"Who else knows about this?" Abigail's voice was low, barely above a whisper. Caroline did not look up at her. She kept her eyes focused on their mother.

Ruthie lowered her hands, eyes pleading, tears still dripping on the table. She looked over and addressed her eldest daughter. "Your daddy thought this would help preserve her memory."

All their lives they had been taught that people who believed in Jesus Christ would be reunited with their loved ones in heaven. No wonder, Caroline thought, Ruthie had been so inconsolable when Nannie passed away. She would never be reunited with her mother in heaven.

"Of course he did," Caroline said, her tone dipped in so much hatred that their mother stopped crying and looked straight at her.

"I am worried," Ruthie said, directing her attention toward both of her daughters now, "that y'all being out here alone is not good for your spirits, much less for your skin." She shook her head. "I saw what happened to my mother and I don't want that to happen to you. I worry that spendin' all this time alone will allow the bitterness to take hold of your hearts and turn you against your father."

So what? Caroline thought. Didn't they have a right to be bitter toward him?

"No, Mommy," Abigail said, and clenched her hands, squeezing Caroline's shoulders. Caroline reached down and flicked her sister's knee as hard as she could. "Don't you worry about that. We love you two," Abigail said, and then returned to her chair, her manner soft once again.

"There is a lot to do before the elders' final vote and we could use your help," Ruthie said. Caroline felt her face getting hot. Her mother was pivoting. Caroline saw the gleam of power returning to her eyes. She was already planning his reinstatement. "I know I said that I understood," she continued, "but I think maybe it would be best if you both came home now." Her voice was firm; this was a command.

Caroline wouldn't. She couldn't. Their mother didn't know what was best for them. She didn't have the slightest idea. She'd come out here under the guise of dropping off wedding crafts and dropped this bomb that she'd hoped would rattle them enough to bring them home. "No," Caroline heard herself say.

Ruthie blinked at her hard. Caroline saw the corners of her mouth twist up. She had expected her daughters to say *yes, ma'am* and pile into the car. She had no idea who she was dealing with now. If her mother wanted to be manipulative, Caroline thought, she would beat her at her own game. Caroline took a long sip of soda, set it down on the table, and cleared her throat. She opened her mouth and—a flash of pain shot up from her shin to her knee. Abigail had kicked her under the table. Caroline glared at her sister.

"She's just upset. It's a lot to take in," Abigail said. "You should go so we can think."

Ruthie looked at Caroline. "I didn't mean to upset you girls. I just think—"

"It's okay. It's a lot to process. We just need some space," Abigail said, and reached for her mother's shoulder. "I'll talk to her."

Talk to her? Caroline thought. Abigail wasn't even looking at her.

"Yes, yes, okay," Ruthie said, wiping away a final tear and patting where she thought her eyeliner might be. She looked between the girls. "I love you both," she said.

"We love you too, Mom," Abigail said. Ruthie hugged her, and Caroline was next. She stood to hug her mother and was surprised by her small size, how her bones felt made of reeds, like Caroline could snap her if she squeezed hard enough.

Ruthie headed down the hallway and out onto the porch. She stopped on the top stair to say, "Don't forget to finish the place cards! And Caroline, don't wear whatever this is"—she motioned to her outfit—"to church next week."

"We won't!" Abigail said, standing in the doorway, waving until their mother's car had started down the drive. She slammed the door shut and her shoulders dropped. When she turned to face her sister, Caroline saw that her hands were in fists, her eyes angry. Thank God, Caroline thought.

Abigail stomped back to the kitchen, picked up a paper napkin from the table, and began to tear it into pieces as she paced. The affair and the announcement and the elder vote she had handled with relative ease. This was different. Abigail loved the ranch. She'd loved Nannie. Abigail was the keeper of family stories, the one their parents told everything, but she had been left out of this. She had been lied to.

"Do we have to go?" Caroline asked.

Abigail stopped pacing and looked right at her. "We are not going to church next week."

AN HOUR LATER, the girls were out on the porch. Abigail was still pouting, sighing every so often, hitting the arm of the porch swing with her fist as it rocked. Over the banister, the sky was deep magenta, feathered with orange. There were bags under her sister's eyes that Caroline had never seen there before. Her hair was twisted into a bun on top of her head and her shoulders slouched. Caroline felt like it was her fault Abigail was so miserable.

"I'm sorry," Caroline said.

"For what?" She wiped her brow with her hand, curled one leg onto the swing with her.

Caroline moved to lean against the railing so she could face her sister. "I didn't mean to get so upset about you going to church. I didn't want you to leave . . . and I don't know. I feel bad." She squeezed her forehead between her fingers like it might free her frustration.

Abigail raised a hand. "Stop," she said. "I'm not going to church next week. If you want to you can, but—" She wasn't looking at Caroline. She was staring past her over the prairie, where the grass was still for once. "You were right actually, not to go."

Caroline raised her brows. Abigail was admitting to being wrong about something? Her sister's face was tight, golden sunlight highlighting the bridge of her nose. She rubbed her forehead and sighed again.

"What happened?" Caroline said.

"It was awful," Abigail said. "Absolutely awful."

"The sermon?"

"All of it. It was like a funeral. People kept coming up to me and apologizing for him, and I just . . ." She hugged her legs to her chest and rested her forehead on her knees. "It is really painful for me to be there." Her voice was muffled. Caroline leaned forward to hear her. "I think you might have had the right idea. I'll pray about it this week, but I'm not sure I can go through that again."

"I'm sorry," Caroline said, and moved to sit beside her on the swing. She was grateful Abigail didn't look up then because she couldn't help but smile.

"I couldn't get close enough to God. I felt really, really separated from Him," Abigail said.

"I feel that way too," Caroline said, and the tension she hadn't noticed in her shoulders loosened. Maybe she wasn't so alone. "It feels like something's missing."

Abigail looked over at her and frowned. "It was the first time I've ever felt like God was far away from me. It was terrible."

"Yeah," Caroline said, pulling her legs up to her chest too. "It feels lonely."

Abigail cocked her head. "What do you mean?"

Now Caroline was the one to sigh. She looked out at the waves on the lake, watched as they carried golden strands of sunlight toward the shore. "Just, like, I used to be able to talk to God and feel supported and safe, and that's gone and I feel empty." She looked back at her sister, saw the color fade from her eyes. Oh no, Caroline thought. Maybe she had misunderstood. She'd thought that after her experience at church Abigail might share her uncertainty.

"I don't understand," Abigail said, her lips a straight line.

"I guess I used to feel like I could talk to God and He was listening to me. Ya know?" Caroline said, running a finger back and forth across the railing. "And now I don't."

"Do you think going to church could help?" Abigail asked, laying the side of her head on her knees so she was fully facing her now.

"No," Caroline said. "I don't." She took a deep breath.

How could she explain that the thought of going to church made her feel like her limbs were full of sand? She wanted to explain the desperation she felt all the time these days, but only said, "I think it would make it worse."

The swing rocked forward and back, the iron chains creaking under their weight. Caroline wiped the sweat from her brow and stared straight ahead. She didn't want to see the look on her sister's face. She sat in discomfort until Abigail extended her legs, leaned forward on her arms as if to stand, and then just pushed the swing a little more.

"I want to take a little break from it too," she said. "Let's just be here together for a while."

Caroline wanted to hug her then, to kiss her on the cheek and say thank you. Instead, she reached out her hand. Abigail leaned back, grabbed her sister's hand, and squeezed. They sat looking out at their land, swatting the occasional mosquito, until the heat got the best of them. At some point, Caroline noticed that Abigail was smiling.

11

The girls did not talk about their mother's revelation that evening or the following morning. They placed two fingers on a shoulder, one hand on the other's back, only what was necessary to maneuver around the other without speaking. They walked down to the dock at sunset, sat on its edge, hovering their bare feet above the water that shone like a mirror, so flat it reflected the empty sky above.

"It feels like nothing will ever be the same," Abigail said, finally breaking the silence. Caroline glanced back up at the house, dark on the east side, overexposed on the west. It had been easier to enjoy the light and shadows of this land before she knew all the secrets it hid.

She looked away from the house and tried to imagine how her grandmother could have ended her own life. She knew that suicide was a sin, but Caroline wasn't sure how to process what that really meant. Sure, Nannie hadn't been a blissfully happy person, but she had still led a good Christian life. Caroline felt like she was drowning in questions and might never reach the surface.

She noticed then that her sister was crying big, dripping tears that ran down her face and landed on her bare legs. The small blond hairs around the edge of her forehead were lit up like a halo in the orangey light of the setting sun. Caroline pulled the sleeve of her T-shirt across her body and wiped her running nose. "I don't know what to say," she said.

"Say anything," Abigail said. "Anything that's not about any of this."

Caroline tried to think of something. But what else was there besides the affair, the suicide, all that was horrible and barely survivable? She wanted to take Abigail into their grandmother's bedroom and tell her the truth, that the affair had happened here, that this place they loved truly was cursed. But she also didn't want to leave. She couldn't bear the idea of staying in the same house as their father—and wasn't this better, she reasoned, to keep the secret, to let her sister be happy here? And what did it matter anyway, where he had chosen to ruin their lives?

Caroline stared out at the lake, watched the sun dip below the surface of the water, and swiftly dove in after it, swimming west, legs kicking out behind her, arms flinging forward, every stroke reaching until she was too tired to chase it anymore. When she stopped, she realized Abigail was there beside her, both of them gasping for air, treading water, smiling. "You followed me," Caroline said in between breaths, and dragged her hand across the water, spraying it at her sister. Abigail splashed her right back. Caroline laughed and blinked the moisture from her eyes.

They floated on their backs for a while and then swam side by side to the dock, heaving themselves up onto it, and lay there panting before they traipsed across the field, up the porch steps, and into the blasting air-conditioning of the house. Now they stood in the kitchen, shivering, towels from the hall closet encircling their wet bodies, dripping lake water onto the linoleum floor.

"What if," Abigail said, "we just forgot it all?"

"How?" Caroline said.

Abigail pulled her wet shirt away from her body. "Like we just, I dunno, be here." For once, her sister seemed to feel self-conscious.

"Yes," Caroline said, and left it at that. Because here there was no threat of running into anyone they knew, and the temperature was only hot, the time only morning or day or night, and the agenda only to walk. And those walks might be miserable—Caroline's bangs plastered to her forehead, shorts chafing against her skin, the tall grass of the western pasture itching her ankles, mosquitoes making molehills on her arms, the sun painting her pink—but each and every time she pulled on her boots, her sister was right there beside her.

FOR THE NEXT few days, Caroline and Abigail drank their coffees in the morning, walked the fields at midday, dragged their hands through wildflowers, sang as they did the dishes. They adapted so quickly that they forgot their lives had ever been different than this. They built habits like newlyweds. Every day they made decisions together—what to cook for dinner, not to talk about church, to leave the cleaning until Tuesday, and that Tuesday was in fact the worst day of the week. They acted as if they'd maintain these traditions for the rest of their lives, as if everything they'd built wouldn't be demolished in three weeks' time.

The heat hung in the air like it was clipped to a clothesline. The grass yellowed from the sun and crunched beneath their feet. Every once in a while, one of them would see a shimmer in the grass and reach down to reveal an arrowhead or an interesting rock. They'd carry these souvenirs back to the house, where they'd drop them in a clay bowl that Nannie had once used to serve them banana pudding. They ate apples with their dirty hands, pulled off their boots and left them lying in the middle of the floor. This was their Eden, and while they were aware of their sins—their unclean bodies, their selfish indulgence—they were no longer ashamed of them. The days dissolved, drawing them closer and closer to the wedding.

And then one afternoon, Abigail ran her hand through the high grass as they walked and turned to Caroline. "It's Sunday."

Caroline saw in her sister's eyes that she didn't want to go to church and so they chose to stay.

LATER THAT EVENING, a metal clang disturbed their peace for the first time in days. Both girls startled. They looked up from their spots on the porch and watched as Mrs. Debbie struggled with the cattle gate, the door to her Lexus left open behind her. Neither of them moved to help. She shouldn't have a key, Caroline thought. How was it that they owned this property and yet people were always entering it without their permission? She looked over at her sister. Her hand was shoved inside a bag of frozen blueberries. Both girls rushed to wipe their stained hands on the dish towel they'd wrapped around the bag. Abigail hadn't bothered to put on a bra and crossed her arms over her nipples. They were somewhat visible through the thin fabric of her T-shirt, though neither sister had noticed until now.

Caroline reached over and ripped the hairband from her sister's ponytail.

"Ow!" Abigail said, but her eyes said *thank you*.

Caroline wrapped the band around her own hair. Her ponytail was short and stubby, like a makeup brush. They were already in enough trouble without Mrs. Debbie finding out that Abigail had gotten a tattoo. The girls exchanged a glance as she stepped out of her car again, slammed the door, and approached, still wearing her greeter name tag from the evening's service.

"Oh good," she said without an ounce of happiness. "Glad to see you two aren't dead."

Caroline pulled her shirt away from her body and shifted, tried to rearrange her legs more modestly. Her shorts were too short.

"Good to see you, Mrs. Debbie," Abigail said.

Caroline said nothing. She couldn't look at Mrs. Debbie without seeing Taylor. She blushed.

"It's too hot for you girls to be sitting out here. I'm already gettin' eaten alive." She slapped a mosquito dead on her forearm, maneuvered her way past Caroline's outstretched legs on the stairs, opened the door to the house, and motioned for them to follow. Caroline couldn't believe it. This was their house. Mrs. Debbie had a way of convincing people that her ideas were their own, but that trick wasn't going to work on her anymore. Caroline hopped to her feet, ready to get in between Mrs. Debbie and the door.

Abigail stepped ahead of her, though. "Of course, Mrs. Debbie. Come on in."

Caroline followed along behind her sister, arms crossed.

"Now you both know I'm here out of love for you and love for your parents, right?" Mrs. Debbie asked as she entered the kitchen, poured herself a glass of water, and sat herself down at the table, right in Abigail's seat. The girls joined her. Caroline sat on her feet in her chair.

"Your mama and daddy were really surprised not to see you at church tonight. I was surprised too. I understand last week, but I don't want y'all falling out of practice." She said *y'all* but looked right at Caroline.

"We're having a hard time processing is all," Abigail said. "We just need some space."

Mrs. Debbie took a sip of her water and set down her glass. "And I understand that inclination, I do, but the place to do this processing is in the community." She drew out the word like she thought they couldn't understand it. "The Lord says that we are one body in Christ, that we need each other. That means you too."

Caroline thought of another verse that said where two or more gather in the Lord's name He is present. So didn't that mean that any moment she and Abigail spent together was holy? Weren't their dinners communion? Their walks prayerful meditations? Their conversations confessions? This guilt trip of cherry-picked verses might have worked on her before all this, but she was still Luke Nolan's daughter. She knew the Bible too. She also knew how easily it could be used to justify any action.

"Which of our parents sent you?" Caroline said. She had tried to make her voice sound sweet, but it came out resentful.

Mrs. Debbie raised a brow at her. "Am I not allowed to worry about you two all on my own? I feel like I might have plenty of reason to."

Caroline's face flushed. Taylor couldn't have said any-thing. He'd assured her that he hadn't told anyone. But could Mrs. Debbie know anyway? There was nothing in her posture that indicated anger. Caroline looked to her sister. Abigail's hands were folded delicately in her lap. She was waiting for Mrs. Debbie to say more.

When neither girl spoke, Mrs. Debbie continued. She was a woman who was used to filling pauses. "Your daddy wants the two of you there. He loves you both so much, and he misses you."

Caroline's skin felt hot. Their father only wanted them at church to prove that his family was fine, a whole united front. Pursue your wife, the Bible says. Lead your family. Love others the way the Lord loves you, enough to kill his own son for you. The path to heaven, it says, is lined with gold, gleaming like nothing on earth, and yet this path is not for everyone. The gate is narrow. Not all prophets are true. Their entire lives, the girls had been warned that their actions were a reflection of him. So their absence was a problem. A pastor's first church is within his own home. If his wife is not devout, how can he expect his congregation to be? If his children are not obedient, how will the church he leads present itself before the Most High God? The stakes are never low; the spotlight is always bright. The girls knew that they were making a big statement by not attending the service, but it had also been a natural one to make. Caroline could see the door to Nannie's room from where she was sitting at the table.

Mrs. Debbie shifted uncomfortably and Caroline looked her dead in the eyes. Mrs. Debbie met her gaze for a moment and looked away. Caroline realized she was the one with the power here. She sat up straighter.

"Tell our father," she said, "that if he wants to command us to attend church, we will. But he has to come here and do it himself."

Mrs. Debbie appeared stunned. Her face remained the same color, covered as it was in foundation, but her chest reddened. Caroline realized then that she'd been talking to her sister alone for too long. She'd forgotten to remove the hardness from her voice.

"Oh, I am sure he is not trying to *command* you to do anything," Mrs. Debbie said, turning to Abigail for support. Abigail was already staring at Caroline in stiff silence. Caroline looked down at the table.

"Plus, you know," Mrs. Debbie said, her voice lighter now, "you miss a lot more than a sermon when you don't show up. People talk."

Caroline met her eyes and blushed again. There was an uncharacteristic cheekiness to her tone, and Mrs. Debbie was no random gossip. If she was alluding to some sort of secret, that meant it was directly related to their lives. But she couldn't know about Taylor, Caroline reassured herself. No, she couldn't know. She bit her bottom lip.

But if she did know, then she might out her to Abigail and make her look like a liar. Caroline glanced at her sister. She was leaning forward, eyes wide. Mrs. Debbie looked between the two girls, a smile creeping onto her face. She gathered her many layers of floral fabric and rose from the table, chair scraping across the linoleum tile. She placed her glass in the sink and, without looking back over her shoulder, left the kitchen and headed down the hall. Abigail followed fast on her heels. Caroline darted out of her chair.

The front door was open by the time Caroline had caught up to them.

"Did we miss anything good?" Abigail asked.

Mrs. Debbie stepped out onto the porch. "Nothing *good*, I would say." She didn't know, then, Caroline thought. Right? *Please*, Caroline prayed, even if she wasn't quite sure who she was praying to anymore.

But Mrs. Debbie's voice was conspiratorial, not chiding. "For the second week in a row," she said, turning to the girls, "Connor Boyd was sitting in church next to his mama and without that wife of his."

"Sick?" her sister asked, and Caroline released the breath she'd been holding.

"Not what I heard," Mrs. Debbie said, and mimed zipping her mouth closed and throwing away the key. The motion set off a similar memory of Taylor rolling down his car window, throwing away his pretend key, after Caroline had asked him not to tell anyone. She tried to shake the image from her mind.

"I will see you girls next Sunday, okay?" Mrs. Debbie said. The girls only nodded. "I love you both so much." She hugged them one at a time and Caroline's body forgot how to relax. "Be good," she said, looking directly at Caroline, and then she was in her car, starting down the drive. The girls watched until the cattle gate closed behind her.

Caroline turned and headed back inside. Abigail caught her by the hairs at the base of her neck.

"Ow!" Caroline yelled, rubbing the back of her head with her hand.

"What is up with you?" her sister said. "You're acting so weird."

Caroline shook her shoulders, twisted her back to try to

get it to pop, and tried not to meet her sister's eyes. "No, I'm not," she said, the words falling flat out of her mouth and landing somewhere between them.

Abigail put a hand to her hip. She clearly knew Caroline was lying, but Caroline couldn't deal with that right now. She was too busy comparing her own failures to their father's, thinking about how he'd come here with That Woman. There were only six rooms in this house and between the two of them, a third of those rooms were now tarnished. Abigail's eyes were boring into hers so intensely that Caroline worried she might read her mind. *Think about something else*, she told herself, *anything else.*

Abigail opened her mouth, closed it again. "Okay," she said, rolling her eyes and raising her hands, pretending to let it go. Caroline knew she hadn't really, though. To have a sister is to watch the same movie on repeat until the end of time. You've seen every scene, every musical interlude, every action and reaction is predictable. You know which phrases are catalysts and which are checkmate. Abigail had merely decided to bide her time.

Caroline needed to change the subject. "Was Mrs. Debbie trying to say that Connor has moved back to town?"

"I don't know," Abigail said.

"But even if he has, what does that have to do with you?"

Abigail shook her head.

"Is it because you still have feelings for him?"

Her sister seemed taken aback by the direct question. "Caroline, he's my ex-boyfriend. I don't want to talk about him anymore."

"Okay," Caroline said, recognizing her sister's unfocused gaze, and knew that she too was lying.

12

For the next several days, Caroline watched Abigail watching her. Her sister didn't ask questions. She didn't beg, and yet every time Caroline opened her mouth to speak, she appeared to be waiting. And every time, Caroline's confession remained lodged in her throat like a Ping-Pong ball. By Thursday, she still hadn't told Abigail anything. *Maybe tonight*, she thought, as they stretched out long and lean on the dock in the afternoon sun. She was so consumed with her thoughts that she didn't notice her sister staring out across the lake at the darkening horizon.

At first, it was only a troubling line along the outer edges, growing thicker as it drew nearer. Abigail stood to face it. "Storm's coming," she said, and winked at her sister.

"Okay, Dad," Caroline said.

And Abigail just laughed.

One of their father's favorite stories was about the storm that only he'd predicted. Caroline had heard him tell it exactly the same way at least a hundred times. For as long as she could remember, it had always been built out of the same pauses, the same rhythm and tone. It was practically lore; it was his origin story.

And like every good origin story, Luke Nolan's began with the Lord choosing him. He had woken to the sound of water, even though the weather was supposed to be clear that day. He always began by describing how the sky had stretched all the way to the horizon, not a single cloud in sight, a gorgeous cerulean, and so Ruthie and Nannie hadn't heeded his warning. They had shaken their heads, pushed a pot roast into the oven. All saviors need to be questioned, Caroline knew this.

So that same evening, after everyone had already arrived to celebrate his new marriage, the sky had caved under the weight of his prophecy. Normally, when he was onstage and reached this part, he'd grip the sides of the podium and tell the audience how the clouds had darkened from white to gray to violet quicker than greased lightning.

"Faith is about that," he'd say. "Because the Lord never once promised that your skies would always be blue." God's promise, as he liked to preach, wasn't that there'd be no storm, but that He would always provide you with refuge.

Caroline wondered now if her father had been chasing that same feeling ever since, searching for some undeniable evidence that he was predestined. Maybe his affair would become yet another storm after so many retellings, evidence that even he was sinful. He'd point to his transgression as proof of God's forgiveness. She imagined how he'd frame it: "God knows I've had my own periods of struggle."

The sky above the girls darkened. The air turned sweeter; the humidity fell away for the first time in days. Caroline watched the navy clouds gather. She turned to her sister, who was still standing beside her, watched her turn and march away, her heavy steps reverberating across the wooden dock. Abigail turned back and stopped, smirked when she saw that Caroline was watching. She gripped an imaginary podium with her left hand, cocked her hip, reached her right hand out toward the storm clouds on the horizon like she was serving them on a platter.

"Storms are a promise," she said, "a reminder of my failures, my affair, my inability to own up to who I am." At first, Caroline was confused. She had never heard Abigail mock him before. But her pacing was as good as his ever was.

She unclenched her hand, thrust it toward Caroline. "Come thou," Abigail whispered. "Come thou," she said, a little louder. *"Come thou!"* she said, her scream falling into a laugh.

Caroline broke too, lying prostrate on the end of the dock, her face scrunched up, laughing until her sides hurt and the clouds had nearly reached them. It was an absurd story. It always had been an absurd story.

The sky opened up right then—as if someone had reached up and sliced open its belly with a bowie knife, giant raindrops pocketed the dry ground.

"Come thou inside for real," Abigail yelled and ran forward, pulling her sister up from the boards and dragging her, laughing, across the field and inside. The storm ate the sun and the silence. All around the house, the wind whipped itself into a frenzy. Branches fell from the trees and the lake slapped the dock in its fury.

The girls stood near the back door, shoulders touching, staring out through the big bay window, watching as the clouds turned from light gray to a dark brooding black, and then as they began to fade like a bruise, purple to ugly green to an almost putrid gray. The rain fell in sheets. At her side,

Abigail's face shone in flickers from the lightning, like a flash without a photograph.

Caroline counted the seconds between the closest strike and then *bang*. Five, four, three. Now two seconds. The tornado sirens started to blare.

"You have got to be kidding me." Abigail laughed, shaking her head. The window in front of them whistled in the wind. Caroline reached out a hand, but before she could lay her palm flat on the cool glass, her sister was calling to her. Abigail was already across the living room, throwing open the door to the guest room. Caroline had closed it the day they moved in.

"What are you doing?" Caroline asked, following her to the doorway, not crossing the threshold. Abigail pulled the pillows off the bed, tossed them on the floor. She tore off the comforter and piled it on top of the pillows.

She removed the sheets until the lumpy white mattress lay bare. "We need a mattress," Abigail said, raising an eyebrow at her. "Is there something wrong with this one?"

Yes, Caroline wanted to say. *Yes, I lost my virginity on it, and I'd prefer not to hide under it with my sister. I feel guilty enough.* But all she said was "Fine," and she grabbed for the foot of the mattress as Abby grabbed the top. They hauled it right off the wrought iron frame as sirens cried in the distance.

"Pivot!" Abigail yelled, and Caroline swung her body to the right. The flat side of the mattress pressed into her face as they headed toward the hall bathroom. Should she tell her now?

She was so distracted that when they turned the corner, she knocked every single thing off the bathroom counter and onto the floor. They left it all lying there and climbed into the tub, stretching their bodies out long, a mess of limbs and joints and skin. Caroline's shoulders were bent at a funny angle under the spigot. They heaved the mattress on top to cover them, their necks uncomfortable beneath its weight.

The lights went out and they were entombed in the dark whir of the storm. A single drip from the faucet fell onto Caroline's T-shirt. She tried holding the mattress away from her face. Her arms were too tired.

"Are you scared?" her sister asked.

"A little. You?"

"A little," Abigail admitted, and reached for her hand. Caroline grabbed it. Neither of the girls had ever had a tornado siren result in anything other than a wasted half hour, but still their muscles were tense. If she told her now, Caroline thought, she wouldn't be able to run away. They were trapped. But no, it still didn't feel right. If Caroline told her now, she wouldn't be able to see Abigail's face to know if she'd hold it against her forever.

THE MATTRESS WAS stuck in the doorframe, one corner pressed against Caroline's stomach, the other side wedged where the jamb met the floor. "You have to lift it," Abigail said, and Caroline tried. Her arms were shaking. She dropped her side and it sort of fell into the bedroom. "Oh, that works," Abigail said, and they lifted together. Caroline's left elbow scraped on the door as they carried it to the frame. They flapped the sheets in the air and shoved them under the corners of the mattress. Caroline threw all four pillows onto the bed in a stack. Abigail fluffed and rearranged them.

"I'm gonna make a couple calls," her sister said. Caroline

followed her from the room, closing the door fast behind her. Her body felt heavy, her movements restrained, as if the mattress were still on top of her. In the kitchen, her sister picked up the phone, tucked her hair behind her ear. Caroline went to the hall bathroom. She heard the sweetness of Abigail's voice as she spoke to their parents, and then to Matthew. "Oh, I thought I'd get your voicemail," she said, and Caroline could tell that she was using her fake smile, reassuring him that there had been a tornado but that they were fine, and that she missed him. "Is it really only that many?" she asked before hanging up the phone.

Caroline joined her afterward in the main room. "That many what?" she asked. Abigail was sprawled on the couch, a pillow wobbling on her stomach. Caroline lay on the couch facing the opposite direction, her longer legs bent, feet tucked under her sister's armpits.

"Oh, days till the wedding," Abigail said, pulling her arm from between the cushion and Caroline's leg and wrapping it around her knee. "There's only fifteen days left."

Caroline gasped. Two weeks was nothing. Her heart dropped. How had this happened? She felt like they should still have a whole summer ahead of them, the rest of their lives.

"I know," Abigail said. "It's wild."

"Do you feel . . ." Caroline fumbled for the right words. "Excited, now that it's getting so close?"

"Not really," Abigail said. When Caroline didn't respond, she went on. "I don't care about the wedding as much as I say I do." Her right leg began to shake then, betraying her lie. Caroline grabbed it with two hands to stop it. Abigail laughed.

"Hmm, why don't I believe you?" Caroline asked.

"I don't feel a lot of certainty anymore," Abigail said. "About anything, really."

Caroline knew she had only a limited number of days left to ask her sister these questions, so she asked the one she really wanted to know the answer to. "Do you feel certain about Matthew?"

Abigail's fist rested against her mouth, her index finger raised higher than the rest. She lowered her hand, sat up on her elbows, puffed the pillow behind her head. "No," she said, looking over Caroline's head and down the hall. "I mean, that's not fair. I'm pretty sure. I don't know how, like, sure a person can be about this kind of thing." She twisted a strand of hair around her finger. "It's like, I think about the love I had for Connor, which was so, so intense, and it tears me apart that I gave him so much of myself that I now can't give to this man who is going to be my husband."

Caroline squeezed Abigail's leg, reassuringly, she hoped. But she was confused by her sister's logic—if Abby knew she loved Connor more, why didn't she try to be with him instead? Matthew was nice and all, but she had always fantasized about her wedding. She should be more excited for it two weeks out. Caroline worried that Abigail was just too far along in the process and felt like she couldn't change her mind, and that was the only reason she was going through with it. Caroline wanted desperately to be wrong, but her sister had always cared too much about public appearances. And how could she not? She was a Nolan.

"Why him, though?" Caroline asked. "Of all the men in the world, why Matthew?"

"He loves me," Abigail said, as if it were a question she'd considered many times and had rehearsed the answer to.

Caroline's eyes filled with tears. She took a deep breath. "But do you love him?" *Please say yes*, she thought. *Please just love him back. You deserve to be happy and at least one thing should be good and pure this godforsaken summer.*

A moment passed and then another. Caroline stroked her sister's knee.

Abigail wasn't looking at her. "I'm not sure that matters anymore," she said, the tears running around her chin and down her neck. Caroline mocked offering her the sleeve of her T-shirt from the other end of the couch in an attempt to get her to laugh. They sat for a moment in silence as Abigail composed herself.

"I'm sorry," Caroline finally said. It was the only thing she could think of. What were you supposed to say when your sister told you that she'd given up on the one man she'd ever loved and was settling for a man who loved her?

"Me too," Abigail said.

Outside the house the air didn't move and a thin blue line could be seen creeping toward them along the horizon.

13

After the storm, the days fell away like petals. The girls painted white numbers on wooden blocks to act as table numbers for the reception. They hot-glued twine around tea candle holders to add to the centerpieces. Caroline still couldn't look at her sister without thinking of everything she hadn't told her and everything she wished she could say.

One afternoon, as they were working on the seating arrangement, Caroline's period arrived. She went to the bathroom and returned in dismay. They were out of tampons. Abigail looked up from the digital piano she was tinkering with at the table.

"Can't you just use toilet paper?" she asked, and played a series of ominous chords to match the atrocious suggestion. The smile on her lips twisted into a devious smirk. Caroline glared at her. They rarely left the ranch anymore. They both worried the sense of calm they were feeling would evaporate the moment they hit town.

"All right, all right," Abigail relented. "If we have to leave, we might as well go to the grocery store."

"Yeah," Caroline added, "we're out of Popsicles."

"Ooh, yeah. Good point. Let's go now." But Abigail didn't seem happy about it. Caroline noticed the slouch of her shoulders as she carried the piano back to the dining room.

They changed out of their sweaty shirts and slipped on their tennis shoes. Caroline grabbed her cell phone and wallet from the dresser in their room. They piled into Abigail's car and headed down the long westbound road. Abigail drove past two grocery stores, three, and then eight. Caroline didn't have to ask her reasoning for this—every mile they drove was another mile away from all the people they knew. Caroline rolled down her window and let her right arm hang out, the warm air pushing against it. Abigail normally reprimanded her for rolling down the windows when the A/C was on, but she said nothing. Caroline was grateful. Abigail could have made her go to the store alone and she hadn't.

"What?" her sister said when she caught Caroline looking at her from the passenger seat.

"Nothing," Caroline said. She wanted to tell her that she deserved better than this, than all of this. Maybe Caroline deserved some misery based on her questionable choices of late, but not Abigail. Abigail deserved the best in the world.

Caroline's phone buzzed. She pulled it out of her back pocket and slid it open to find a truly disappointing number of text messages, half of them from Taylor, asking if she wanted to meet and if she was okay. Caroline could feel the dread growing in her stomach already. She rubbed her forehead with her hand. Was this how Abigail felt about Matthew? Having someone else so interested in you, and you just feeling fine about it? Maybe, she thought, it wasn't too late to save her sister from committing to this marriage. But she couldn't figure out how to go about it. She shoved the phone back inside her pocket and left Taylor's messages unopened.

Abigail pulled into the parking lot for a Tom's Grocery three towns and forty-five minutes away. It was just like the one the elders had bought and renovated into the Hope Church. The girls sat in the car out front until they'd convinced themselves that they could handle the specific suffering of an awkward encounter with anyone they knew.

In some ways, the store provided the comfort of the familiar in the shine of its glowing fluorescent bulbs, buzzing like wasps, the nook for the carts the exact size and shape of the welcome desk at the Hope. The entrance on the left of the building dumped them into a colorful sea of produce— oranges precariously snuggled together in tight pyramids, wobbly stacks of potatoes in a variety of colors, dozens of peppers nestled between the lettuce and herbs.

Caroline looked around and all she saw were women: women standing on tiptoes to shout their deli orders across the glass countertops, lightly smacking their children's hands as they reached for a treat on a shelf, reading nutrition labels, sorting through cheese options, squeezing avocados to see if they were ripe enough. Standing in the middle of the produce section, Abby inspected the strawberries inside their plastic shells for any signs of decay.

"Can you help me, please?" she asked, her hand on her hip.

Caroline hurried to her side, the cold air seeping through her T-shirt, raising goose bumps along her arms. There was a hint of martyrdom in her sister's request that made Caroline bristle, a note that said she didn't ever help with anything. It seemed they were falling back into their old routine. Caroline thought she should call her on it, but then she took in the droop of her posture, the tension in her forehead. Maybe Abigail's tone said more about her than it did about Caroline. Maybe she really just needed her help.

Caroline was reminded of the New Testament story she'd always loved about the two sisters who host Jesus and his disciples for dinner. As the men are relaxing around the table, the one sister, Martha, is working—cooking dinner, pouring wine, cleaning—as the younger one, Mary, sits on the floor at Jesus's feet listening. "Don't you see?" the responsible older sister asks Jesus when she comes to serve the table, "that my sister has left me to do all the work myself?" But Jesus scolds the older sister and tells her to be more like Mary, to remember that you can serve so much that you end up missing the life in front of you.

And here are all these women pushing their buggies through overcrowded shelves of food, navigating packed aisles as toddlers scream. All of them doing so much, so busy taking care of everyone else. Caroline wasn't sure what they were waiting for—someone to tell them they didn't have to?

Maybe, she thought, that's what her sister needed: someone to help her do what she really wanted, to give her permission to be selfish for once. Caroline could do that. She would do it. She pulled out her phone and opened a new text message.

Can we talk? I'm at the ranch, no reception. Caroline typed, read it back, and sent the message to Connor Boyd.

He would come to the ranch, and once he was standing there in front of her, she would be able to tell if he loved her sister. They should be together if he did. It was insane for them not to be. Connor's family had let him marry the wrong person, but that didn't mean Caroline would let Abigail do the same. No, she could still fix this. It would take too long to convince her sister that she was making the wrong choice, and they didn't have that kind of time. Caroline looked up and saw Abigail leaving the produce section. She trotted to catch up to her, snatched three avocados from the stack, dropped them into the buggy, and just caught the miserable look that crossed her sister's face. Yes, she was right to interfere.

Abigail stopped at the butcher counter, stood with her shins against the metal cooler that was filled with sausages, steaks, and burgers, asking about the chicken on sale. Caroline wandered over to check out the six large brown lobsters in their tank, the claws on their front legs bound together with colorful bands. She'd always loved to watch them, ever since she was a kid, and was just about to wave her sister over when she saw her: That Woman, coming around the corner, a basket draped over one arm, a baseball cap nearly covering her face, her nine-year-old trailing behind her like a puppy. She looked tired, dressed in baggy jeans and an oversized T-shirt, her hair in a ponytail, and she certainly didn't look like the kind of woman a man cheats on his wife with.

Caroline's brain short-circuited for a moment. Her hips turned away; her legs shuffled through a pair of swinging metal doors next to the lobster tank. The doors swung back and forth. Caroline stood against the wall, trying to calm her racing heart, rubbing her bare arms with her hands. This was not an area for customers and it was significantly colder than the rest of the store, the shelves around her stacked with pallets of food. Caroline stretched up and tried to peer through the small circular window in the door, not exerting any pressure for fear it would swing open. Her view was dirty with cloudy smudges, so it took her a second to spot the long, thick ponytail pulled through the back of That Woman's baseball cap as she turned down the dairy aisle.

Caroline counted to fifty inside the storage room, prayed the coast was clear, and popped her head out the door. Abigail was standing in front of the lobsters, looking around for her, hands wrapped tightly around the buggy.

"There you are!" she exclaimed. "What are you doing?"

"I was, uh, hot," Caroline said, and her sister laughed. Caroline really wanted her sister to have more of that: joy.

Their buggy clicked across the tiles as they loaded it with dried pasta and cereal, Oreos and frozen pizzas. Caroline kept her hand on one side of it at all times to stop herself from running out of the store. She held her breath at the end of every aisle, made sure to step around each corner first, gripping the cart in case she needed to stop it before Abigail could go any farther. The overhead lights highlighted the pores on everyone's noses, the wrinkles burgeoning at the corners of their eyes. Caroline was looking around so much while sorting their groceries into bags that when she reloaded them into the buggy, she realized some were so heavy she needed two hands, and others held only one item.

"Can you slow down, please?" Abby asked as they walked to the parking lot. Caroline looked down. She was guiding the buggy with her left hand. She released it and made sure to stand on the side of the car closest to the store as they unloaded. Abigail hummed under her breath as she arranged the bags in the trunk.

"I'll return the buggy," she said, tossing Caroline the keys, "you drive." Before Caroline could stop her, Abigail took off across the parking lot, riding it like a chariot every few steps. Her sister's mood had seriously improved. Caroline climbed into the driver's seat and turned the key, watching Abigail through the window. The air conditioner blew hot breath into her face. Abby had pushed their cart into the line and then paused there for a moment, looking out across the parking lot, left hand shielding her eyes from the sun. Her body stiffened and she turned, walking quickly, arms swinging faster than usual, across the burning concrete to the car. She climbed in and pulled the door shut behind her. She sat staring straight ahead.

"What?" Caroline asked.

Abigail shook her head, bit her lip. Had she seen Mary too? Caroline didn't want to ask her outright. Maybe she'd just seen someone they knew from church. Abigail popped the knuckles on her right hand. Her eyes were vacant, staring past the car in front of them, her knee bobbing up and down. Something was wrong. Caroline reversed the car back into the lane. She wanted to leave through the side exit, near where Abigail had returned their cart.

Only then, slumped in her seat, did her sister speak. "I can't imagine why he would be all the way out here."

Caroline let her eyes drift out above the steering wheel, past the carts to where another car was parked near the back of the lot. A dark figure sat in the front seat of a familiar red Ford pickup truck. A woman was loading groceries into the back. Caroline checked the license plate. The Nolan family had it memorized. They had used it as a password for years. The girls had ridden in that truck thousands of times. They knew the back door stuck and that the ceiling was deteriorating so small particles fell in your eyes if you looked up at it for too long. Their father was at the store with Mary Campbell.

14

The car drove them home to the ranch, down back roads they'd forgotten they knew, across rusted bridges and past giant copper sculptures of men on horseback. The girls saw none of it. They didn't cry or speak and neither allowed her feelings the space they needed. The radio was silent. The sun was setting. Through the open window, the air blew hot and dry and the vinyl seats grew slick with their sweat.

They arrived at the ranch house feeling smaller than they ever had before. Abigail hopped out, swung open the cattle gate, the golden light of the setting sun behind her. Caroline knew it was time to tell her sister everything. The two of them were in this together now.

Caroline parked the car, climbed out, opened the passenger-side door, and grabbed her sister's hand, which was surprisingly chilled and shaking slightly. She guided her up the porch steps. The front door lock turned easily for her this time. She rubbed Abigail's hands between her palms as she pushed open the door and led her down the hall to Nannie's room. She paused inside the doorway, releasing her sister's hand, and entered the space alone. Caroline stood a few feet inside, watching her sister, still in the doorway, her head bowed and eyes closed, her mouth mumbling something to God. Caroline realized then that she hadn't even thought to consult Him, and remembered their groceries were still in the trunk. Their Popsicles would melt.

"I have to show you something," Caroline said. Abigail entered the room as Caroline knelt beside the bed, reached her arm deep under the dust ruffle, and withdrew the box of condoms, placing it on top of the bed. Abigail's eyes widened. Caroline reached under the bed for the book this time. She stood, holding it with both hands, and passed it to Abby. Her sister took it but looked confused, smoothing a hand over its cover, looking to Caroline for an explanation. "Open it," Caroline said. She took a deep breath as Abigail flipped the first and second pages, stopped for a moment, eyes moving over the signature, and then snapped it closed.

Abigail looked at Caroline, then she looked at the condoms on the bed. "He brought her here." It was a statement, not a question.

Abigail bit the inside of her cheek. The book was shaking in her hands now. Caroline took it from her, placed it and the box of condoms on the bedside table.

"Why didn't you tell me?" Abigail said, her eyes wide, a single tear waiting in one corner.

"I didn't think it mattered," Caroline said, and as she spoke the words, she knew they weren't true. "I thought if you knew, you might want to leave me."

"I don't want to leave you," Abigail said, her eyes still unfocused. "But you should have told me." She lowered herself to the bed, forcing her joints to bend like a Barbie. Caroline sat on the floor at her sister's feet, hands shaking in her lap, unsure how to comfort her, whether she should even try. The sun emerged from behind a cloud and light streamed in through the blinds, casting them both in golden stripes. Abigail reached out her hand. Caroline grabbed hold of it with both of hers.

"Are you mad at me?" Caroline asked.

"Kind of, to be honest," Abigail said. "Even if I am being a hypocrite." Abigail looked away from her, into the bathroom.

Maybe she thought Caroline hadn't seen the truck. No more secrets, Caroline told herself. "I saw her too, you know."

"Where?" Abigail said, the green of her eyes darkening to almost black.

"In the store. That's why I was hiding."

But her sister wasn't listening to her anymore. She snatched the box off the table and ripped open the top, pulled out a piece of fluttering white paper. It was a receipt the length of her arm. She unrolled it. "Oh my God," she said, slapping a hand over her mouth.

Caroline couldn't help but laugh at her sister's heresy. She'd never heard her use the Lord's name in vain before.

Abby didn't look up. She just turned the receipt around so that it lay face-up on the bed and pointed. There in faded block print was the address of the Walgreens near the church. Someone had paid for the box of condoms with a Visa card. She tapped the last four digits. "It's Dad's card," she said. "I have the number memorized from buying all the stuff for the wedding."

Caroline inhaled to steady herself. She wasn't sure why this was such a surprise.

Abigail waited for her to understand. She tapped the receipt again. "Look at the date, Caro." And there, in smudged type, it read JUNE 15. Two weeks before the shower. Their father had watched his family prepare for his daughter's wedding and continued to carry on with his affair.

"So he's still sleeping with her?" Caroline's heart was pounding against her sternum. Of course he was. How dare he? She waited for Abby to respond, to react on her own time. She pinched the pressure point between her thumb and forefinger and tried to calm down.

Abigail paused for a moment, seeming to consider. "At the very least, he lied about when it ended." Her voice was bitter. Her lips opened as if to say more.

Abby will know what to do, Caroline thought. *Please, let Abby know.*

"Caro, I have been so naive," she said, tucking the receipt back inside the box, moving it to the side table. Abigail bowed her head, closed her eyes.

"No, you haven't." Caroline hopped up on the bed and sat beside her, wrapped an arm around her shoulders, their legs touching. "How could you have known?" This wasn't what she needed, Caroline thought. Where was her confident, all-knowing big sister?

Abigail opened her eyes, looked straight at Caroline. "There's something I haven't told you," she said, and the tears began to fall in careful paths down her cheeks, rolling over her chin and down her neck. She used the back of her hand to wipe them away, her breath jagged now, catching on itself. Caroline felt her hope vanish.

"Abby," Caroline said, and shook her sister's knee with her hand. "Abby, it's okay." There was nothing left to ruin anymore. They knew everything now.

"It's not okay, Caro," she said. "None of this is okay. What I did is not okay."

Caroline's back straightened. She moved away from her slightly, removed her hands from her leg. "What do you mean? What did you do?"

Abigail collapsed back on the bed with a sob and rolled onto her side, facing away from Caroline. She bent her elbows and balled up her hands like a boxer protecting her face. She tucked her knees; her shoes were on the bed. Caroline patted her foot twice, and went to grab her some tissues, returned with another roll of toilet paper from the closet shelf. She slipped off her own shoes and climbed onto the bed, sat cross-legged beside her sister's head, ready with the toilet paper for whenever she regained control.

"You can tell me," Caroline said, stroking her sister's hair. Her voice sounded pleading even to her own ears. "Please tell me."

All she'd ever wanted was to be let into her sister's confidence, so if it had to happen this way, she would take it. It really didn't matter what she had done. And selfishly, Caroline hoped Abigail had a horrible secret too, because then she might forgive Caroline when she eventually told her about Taylor.

Abigail cried and cried until she was surrounded by a pile of crumpled, snotty toilet paper balls. Her eyes were red and swollen. She sat up, removed her shoes, and sat cross-legged facing Caroline.

She took a deep breath. "I . . . knew about the affair," she said carefully, each syllable like torture.

Caroline didn't know how to respond. She had meant to

be supportive, understanding, forgiving no matter what, but tears began to well in her eyes. "Knew when?" Her voice had an edge to it that she hadn't intended.

"This time last year, the weekend after Connor's wedding. Gosh, I was so stupid. I'm so sorry, Caro." She shook her head. "I was having a really hard time with his marriage, and Daddy was doing that series about families in the Bible. I was helping him with the sermon structures and everything had been going fine until I got stuck in chapter nineteen of Genesis. I just couldn't figure it out, and so I came out here to get some space, and that's when I found her wallet on the counter. Mary's."

Caroline was shocked. She hadn't known that Abigail was still helping their father write his sermons. She'd thought their conversations were more like theological discussions. She remembered when he had started that series of sermons last summer. It was supposed to focus on every family in the Bible, but he'd delivered only four before switching up their order.

"I was so wrapped up in the sermon, trying to figure out what to say. I went to the church to ask him about the etymology of a phrase, and I brought the wallet with me. I didn't think anything of it. I thought someone could give it back to her. But when I put it on his desk, he looked so—so guilty. He apologized before I had even put it together." She grabbed Caroline's hands, squeezed once before releasing them again.

Caroline tried to imagine Luke Nolan looking guilty. In all of his repenting of late, she'd seen sadness and regret, but never guilt. He'd shown Abigail this side and no one else. Typical. She shook her head.

"He told me that it was over, Caroline. I promise. He told

me that he had confessed to the elder board, and Pastor Mark, and that he was in counseling. He told me he had repented." Her voice evolved from softness into something sharper, more pointed, and much, much angrier. "I believed him," she said. This whole time Abigail had been blaming herself when she should have—when they all should have—been blaming him.

"Of course you did!" Caroline said. "Why wouldn't you have? You had absolutely no reason not to believe him!"

"No, Caro," she said. "I should have told someone. I should have talked to someone else about it. I should have told Mom . . ." Her voice trailed off then. She turned her head to look out the window.

Caroline patted her knee.

She blew her nose again. "The worst part," Abby said with a short, terrible burst of a laugh, "is that I never did figure out that sermon about Lot."

"You mean Luke Nolan didn't figure it out," Caroline said. She was furious. Of course their father had used Abigail's help all these years and never given her any credit.

"Oh yes, excuse me," Abigail said, using her fake Southern accent now. "Luke Nolan decided that the Lord led him to teach a different story that week."

Caroline felt her eyes widen, dazed by her bitterness, the two of them joining together against him, her sister choosing her for once—and Abigail knew as much about the Bible as any pastor on staff at the Hope. Caroline couldn't imagine her getting tripped up on a story that they'd known since childhood.

"So what was it about that passage?" Caroline asked.

Abigail returned from wherever she had drifted off to. "What do you think the story of Lot is about?" Her tone was measured, easily slipping into teaching mode now, the same one she'd perfected on a hundred third-graders.

"Isn't it a condemnation of homosexuality?" Caroline said, feeling unsure all of a sudden. That was how their father had always interpreted it for them.

Abigail's lips tightened. She shook her head.

Caroline fought to keep her eyes from rolling. "Okay, so what is it about, then?"

"It's about—" Abigail began, but she couldn't find the words. "Hold on," she said, and climbed off the bed. She left the room, hair swishing behind her. Caroline leaned over to try to see where she'd gone, to decide if she was supposed to get up and follow her. Abigail returned then, her Bible in hand.

"Okay, so," she said, and began to pace at the end of the bed. "The Lord sends two angels to warn Lot that God is upset with the Sodomites' behavior, right?" She looked at her sister.

Caroline nodded for her to continue.

"The men of Lot's town think the angels are sexy and demand to sleep with them, but Lot refuses." Abigail flipped rapidly through the pages. She looked up at Caroline again. "The Bible praises him for that refusal, and okay, sure, but then there's this." She turned the Bible around and laid it flat on the bed in front of her sister, coming around the side, sitting on the edge to point out a verse she'd underlined in blue pen. "Read it," she said.

"'I have two daughters who have never slept with a man. Let me bring them out to you, and you can do what you like with them. But don't do anything to these men,'" Caroline read aloud. It couldn't say that, she thought. She read it again, silently this time. "That's terrible," she said, and her sister hopped back up.

"Yes, exactly," Abigail said, and continued to pace. "Then the Lord orders them to flee and they do, and Lot's wife looks back as the cities burn, which, like, of course she did, it was her home, and she's turned into a pillar of salt." Abigail pivoted on her heel, gripped the footboard with both hands, and looked straight at her sister. "God didn't tell Lot's wife not to look back. He told Lot."

Caroline took in the fury in her sister's eyes. "He didn't tell her?" she asked, not quite sure where Abigail was going with this.

"Maybe, but it's not written here," Abigail said. "But what does God ask of Lot?"

"To flee," Caroline said without thinking.

"Yes, good," Abigail said. "And what does He ask of the women?"

Caroline looked at the Bible in front of her, scanning her finger down the page. "'Do what you like with them,'" she read again, and looked back to her sister.

"It's not a condemnation of homosexuality," Abigail said.

"So what is it, then? What does this mean?" Caroline heard her own voice echoing throughout the room.

"It's—honestly, I don't know what it is." Abigail came back around the side of the bed and sat down, looking at Caroline, her energy depleted, her head heavy. There was clearly no end to her sermon.

Caroline read a few more verses. She thought it meant that the women around Lot had given up everything so that he could have a relationship with God, and received nothing in return. Of course her sister hadn't been able to write that sermon, Caroline thought.

"Why are you shaking your head?" Abigail said, watching her look over the page.

Caroline felt like she'd swallowed a bitter seed that had just now taken root. She knew it would live there forever. "Do you ever think that all of the men in the Bible are kind of terrible?" And then, catching herself. "I mean . . . except Jesus."

Her sister shrugged. "Well, even Jesus caused a lot of problems," she said, and laughed. "I mean, imagine being Mary. He must have been the biggest problem child."

Caroline laughed along with her and felt her shoulders loosen. She watched as Abigail's smile faded, the light from the window highlighting her blond eyelashes.

"Does that mean you're not mad at me for not telling you sooner?" Abigail said.

"It makes me sad that you didn't tell me, but I understand," Caroline said. "How about this: I won't be mad at you for not telling me you knew about the affair, and you don't be mad at me for not telling you it happened here."

"That seems like a very good deal for me," Abby said.

"You should probably take it, then." Caroline smiled and offered her hand. They shook on it and Abigail pulled her up off the bed.

"I don't want to be in this room anymore," Abigail said, grabbing the box of condoms and the book off the bedside table and carrying them both to the hall closet, where she hid them behind a stack of clean towels. Caroline stumbled along after her.

"Black bean tacos?" Abigail said, turning to look back at

Caroline, her smile weaker now. With every step they took away from Nannie's room, the air seemed less suffocating, the light more golden hued. Abigail pulled a pot from the cabinet, the beans from the pantry, an onion from the basket on the counter. Every movement she made without looking at Caroline was another moment alone. But they couldn't just return to normal. At least Caroline couldn't. They had to do something about their father.

CAROLINE BROUGHT IN the groceries while Abigail cooked the tacos. She sat at the table drinking a glass of water after she finished putting everything away, and waited for the somber tone to resettle before bringing up their father again. "What are we going to do about this situation? Should we, like, tell someone?"

Abigail looked at her from across the island, where she was spooning beans from the pot into soft tortillas. "I don't know, Caro." But her sister always knew what to do. Who else could they ask?

"I just think we should decide kind of soon because they're voting to reinstate him in the next few days, right?"

"Yeah, we should," Abigail said, carrying over the two plates, setting one down in front of Caroline. "I'm just . . ." Her voice trailed off. She took a sip of water.

They'd agreed to be on the same team, and here she was wavering again. Everyone in this whole town was always defending him. "Why are you so hesitant?" Caroline said, each word as sharp as a spear.

"Whoa, chill," Abigail said, and took a bite of her taco,

holding a hand over her mouth as she chewed, and then swallowed. "I also think we should tell, okay? I'm just trying to figure out how we can do that and be sure they take us seriously."

"What do you mean? We know he lied about when the affair ended! You found the evidence!"

"Yes," Abigail said. "But it's not *damning* evidence. It's only evidence that he lied. It's not evidence that he's still having an affair." She took another bite. Caroline couldn't even think about food right now; her tacos remained untouched.

"Yeah, but doesn't the Bible say that all sin is equal? Doesn't that mean he's still living in sin and that they shouldn't vote to reinstate him yet?" She knew she was yelling. She couldn't help it.

"Listen," Abby said, setting her half-eaten taco down on her plate. "I agree with you. But I don't know that the elder board will care. So we need to be strategic about this. We can't get emotional."

Caroline wanted to throw her fork across the table and hit her sister right in her flawless, reasonable face. "Oh, you mean because we're silly little girls who don't know anything so we have to make sure the elders like the way they hear this truth from us that they are literally going to hate?"

Abigail picked up her taco and resumed eating. She finished her second, chewing slowly, wiped her hands on a paper towel, and said, "Yes."

Caroline tried to take a couple of bites, but she was too worked up. She picked up the rogue fallen beans with her fingers and ate those. She refused to meet her sister's eyes even when she heard her sigh across the table.

"I'll think more on it tonight and we'll decide tomorrow,

okay?" Abigail reached across the table to grab Caroline's arm in reassurance.

Caroline looked up and saw that her eyes were still sad. *She's trying*, Caroline told herself. "Okay," she said. She just didn't know how to stop fighting with her sister.

Abigail removed her hand, sat back in her chair, and looked around the room as if they hadn't been living there for weeks. "You know what?" she said. "We deserve to have a little fun. I'm going to make us some drinks."

She disappeared into the dining room and returned with two blue-rimmed margarita glasses in her right hand, their necks threaded between her fingers, a bottle of tequila and a bottle of triple sec cradled like a newborn in her left arm.

The Nolan family rarely drank—a glass of wine for Ruthie while she watched *The Bachelor* on Monday nights, a beer for Luke during college basketball games. Drunkenness was a sin and the easiest way to avoid it was not to drink at all. Caroline's mouth fell open as she watched her sister deftly pour shot after shot into a shaker and strain the liquid into two glasses. She did not spill a drop.

"But I'm not twenty-one," Caroline said.

"Who cares," Abigail said, rolling her eyes, setting a glass in front of her sister. "That rule is so arbitrary. Legalism is stupid."

Caroline lifted the drink to her lips, winced at the scorch of the tequila as it traveled down into her empty stomach. She'd seen teenagers drink on television and promised herself she wouldn't cough when she finally took her first sip. But here she was, face turning red, a hand over her mouth, coughing, sputtering, smiling. Abby laughed at her reaction. Caroline had always wanted this bond, secrets between sisters. She shoveled one of the tacos into her mouth, bean juice dripping down her arm. Abigail tilted the shaker, poured more of the light green liquid into their glasses.

Caroline was beginning to feel flushed, warmed from the inside out. She looked at her sister, watched her tilt her glass to her lips, twist her hair into a knot on top of her head. She was acting like this was something they'd done a million times. "I love you," Caroline said.

Abigail looked surprised, but her voice was soft. "I love you back."

Caroline's emotions felt so light in that moment, as if she might shatter. The margarita had made her confident. She wondered if now was the right time to share her secret. She took another drink. She wanted to feel light enough to float away.

Abigail stood to pour more triple sec and tequila into the shaker. She squeezed more limes. Caroline took another sip, and then another. She could do this. Her tongue felt heavy. She forced it to move.

"Why do you still wear it?" she asked.

Abigail raised her eyebrows. "Wear what?" she said, squeezing another lime.

"Your Hope for More ring."

Abigail shook the drink over her shoulder, the bottom of her arm wobbling with the tequila, back and forth. "Because I'm not married yet, silly."

Caroline looked down at her glass, but it was nowhere to be found. She located it in Abigail's hand, now full and floating toward her.

"Why do you ask?" Abigail said, setting both glasses on the table, sliding one over to Caroline, the drink sloshing over the blue rim to form a puddle on the table.

"I guess I just don't understand how you waited so long. How you made that work."

Abigail pursed her lips. "Well, I never really had to, I guess." She shrugged. Caroline had hoped Abigail would confess her failure and then she could too. But her thoughts were turning wispy. She licked the rim of her glass; the hard salt flakes dissolved on her tongue. She tried to remember what she'd been saying before Abigail had interrupted her.

"Don't let that stop you," her sister said, looking at her from behind the edge of her glass, taking a sip, her tone too casual.

Caroline reached for her glass with both hands. "Stop me from what?" She took another drink.

Her sister flung her arm across the back of the seat next to her and leaned back. "Stop you from whatever it is you're trying to confess to me right now." Her limbs were loose, her lips smiling, but her eyes were looking pointedly at Caroline's bare ring finger.

Caroline set down her glass, spilling some over the side. Her head felt too light now. She placed her palms flat against the table in front of her to stop it from moving.

"I had sex." Caroline knew she should have been more delicate about telling Abigail, but she also seemed to have lost that ability. Her confidence had turned into drunkenness. She tried to read Abigail's expression, but she just sat there. Her eyes didn't narrow, her limbs didn't tense. A little smile had crept onto her face. The slight uptick indicated amusement and not judgment, and that was all the permission Caroline needed to tell her everything.

She told her she'd felt so lonely after the engagement and that she'd found someone to be less lonely with, and that they'd kissed and been careful. She told her that on the afternoon after the shower, when she'd stayed out here at the ranch, she'd lost her virginity in the guest bedroom. Abigail's eyes flitted to the closed door across the living room.

Caroline wanted her to say something, anything, after revealing that detail. Maybe this would be the end, she thought. Maybe this was too much sin. Maybe Abigail would resent her the same way she resented their father. Caroline started to cry. "I just—" She was sobbing now. "It's the same sin. We did the same thing. You got his talents and I only got this, the worst of him. I didn't tell you because I didn't want you to . . . I thought you might think I was like him."

"Oh, Caro. Of course you're not like him." Abigail moved to sit in the chair next to her sister, sliding her drink across the table along with her. "How do you feel about it? Are you okay?" Abigail asked, stroking her hair.

"Yes," Caroline said, wiping her eyes. "I feel fine."

"That's good." Abigail smiled. "So stop crying about it."

"I'm trying," Caroline whined, but she couldn't stop. She had disintegrated. It was like the molecules in her body had floated off to be somewhere else. She no longer felt in control of them.

"How was the sex, though? Was it good?"

"Um . . ." Caroline blushed. She didn't know how to gauge whether the sex had been good or not. "It was fine, I guess. There wasn't, like, blood or anything, which I thought was weird."

"Yeah, but did you enjoy it?" Abigail's eyes were wide, gentle; her hand patted Caroline's leg.

Caroline realized she hadn't thought about that at all. At no point since she made the decision had she stopped to consider whether she'd had a good time. "I think I liked making out better," she said, and that was true.

Abigail threw back her head and laughed: a single, joyful bray.

Caroline knew then that everything was going to be okay between them. "It was weird, though," she said. "I really thought I would feel guilty. But I don't. Even when we went to church for Dad's announcement, I still didn't feel guilty."

"I never felt guilty either," Abigail said, and then seeing Caroline's reaction, her mouth hanging open, "Don't look at me like that."

"Wait, but you just said—" Caroline couldn't finish that sentence. "Matthew?"

Abigail let out a cynical laugh. "No, not with Matthew." She paused. "Matthew's too good."

"So it was Connor?"

Abigail sipped her drink. "Bingo."

"But the purity pledge!" Caroline was almost screaming now. She had watched Abigail her entire life, sneaking into her room at night to lie beside her in bed, listening for her steps on the stairs. Caroline had always hidden things from her sister, but she had never once considered that Abby might have so many secrets of her own.

"You had sex with him?" Caroline asked.

Abigail shook her head. "Oh, Caro, no. We didn't go all the way or anything. But further than we probably should have. I knew it was wrong, but I never felt guilty about it," she said. "That's part of why Matthew has these rules." She waved away the phrase. "We both know how easy it is to stumble."

Caroline tried to reconstruct the timeline of her sister's current relationship. She realized she was talking out loud.

"Wait, okay, so Connor got married last summer," she said, and Abigail nodded. "Right after that you found the wallet here. And that's what you were so upset about? Because you knew about the affair? Not the wedding?"

"Yes," Abigail said.

"And then you started dating Matthew because . . ." Here she ran out of thoughts. She looked to her sister for clarification.

"Because I realized that I needed to have a life as an adult. I can't just be Luke Nolan's daughter forever." Now it was starting to make sense: Abigail suddenly supporting her decision to leave for college, getting engaged to Matthew.

Caroline had assumed that her sister had gotten swept up in the engagement and Matthew's desire to get married because of her feelings for Connor. She was wrong. Their father was the one who had set her spinning.

Oh no, Caroline thought. She shouldn't have texted Connor. She felt sure that Abigail wouldn't want to see him. Where was her phone? She tried to locate it in her mind. She didn't remember what she'd done with it after the grocery store. It wasn't in her pocket. It must still be in the car. She would go to the car now, drive until she reached somewhere with service. Perfect, she thought. But when she tried to put her feet under her, her legs wobbled.

"Wait," Abigail said. "You never said who it was."

"What do you mean?" Caroline said.

"You didn't say who it was, the boy you *slept* with."

A sober Caroline would have dodged that question, begged for privacy. But she was too focused on her mistake and replied without thinking. "It was Taylor McGregor," she said, and covered her ears as her sister screamed.

"Caroline Nolan!" Abigail yelled. "Oh my gosh, no wonder you've been acting so crazy."

Caroline hid her face behind her hands and tried not to smile. She heard her sister laughing, opened her eyes and saw that Abigail had raised her glass from the table. She was holding it out to her.

"To figuring out what comes next," Abigail said.

Caroline smiled and raised her own glass, toasted with her sister. Just then, with their glasses suspended over the table, a blast rang out—and both glasses fell, shattered on the floor.

"What was that?" Abigail said. They stepped over the glass and went to the back door. The rain had stopped and another boom rang out. Across the lake, a giant red firework hung in the sky, its ends fizzling down like a willow tree. The girls walked back inside, giggling, and moved to the front porch to watch the display—Abigail sitting in the porch swing, Caroline leaning her elbows on the railing.

"Do you think this is a celebration of our confessions?" Caroline joked, and her eyes flitted to her car. It was maybe forty steps from the front door. She was so close. But it would seem suspicious to go to her car for no reason right now. She needed to think of an excuse to get her phone.

Fireworks exploded in rapid succession—greens and blues, pinks and golds. The sisters watched them with their eyes wide, their spirits dark. After a while, the sky quieted and stillness returned.

"Maybe you're right," Abigail said. Caroline turned around to face her. Her sister was twirling her abstinence ring around her finger. She'd moved it to her right hand after she and Matthew got engaged. "We should get rid of these."

"Really?" Caroline said.

"Do you still have yours?" Abigail said.

Caroline thought about it for a moment. It felt like she'd taken it off a million years ago, a lifetime ago really, before she even knew about the affair. She'd had it on the drive to their house. Oh, this was perfect. "I think it's in my car," she said. "I'll go get it."

She found her ring in the cup holder, exactly where she thought it would be, closed the door behind her, turned on the overhead light, and laid back the seat. She was pretending to look. Her phone was right there, in the door. She slid it open. Six more texts from Taylor. She had . . . service? One bar. She opened the text she'd sent to Connor. **Nevermind**, she typed. **Don't come here. Everything's fine. Hope you're well.** She hit send and watched it deliver. Thank God, she thought, and slipped the phone back into her pocket and the ring into her hand.

She climbed the porch stairs. Abigail was waiting for her by the railing, already holding her ring in her outstretched palm. Caroline joined her there. Abby drew her hand back and threw it as far as she could in the direction of the lake. The girls watched it twinkle through the night sky and fall like a star into the tall yellow grass. Caroline threw hers too, and didn't bother to watch where it landed.

"Do you feel anything?" Abigail asked her later, after they had climbed into the bed.

Caroline shook her head. She felt nothing at all.

15

Luke Nolan's daughters spent the next day deciding whether they should ruin his life. They were certain he had lied to the elder board, not only about when his affair had ended but also about having ended it at all. A pastor who repented could be reinstated. But a pastor who continued to live in sin? Someone like that was in no way qualified to lead a congregation, right? This kind of revelation was the whole reason the waiting period existed between the board's initial vote to begin the process of his repentance and their upcoming vote to officially reinstate him as head pastor.

Caroline and Abigail were perhaps calmer than they should have been while discussing the matter, bound together as they were in their rebellion. But they weren't sure how to go about it. The question seemed to float through the air like a gnat, and they knew of only one way to get rid of a gnat: clap it dead in your hands.

They didn't discuss the possibility of covering for him; neither would have wanted to at this point. But what did it mean for them to tell on their father? Then again, what did it mean for them not to?

Caroline was ready to act. She knew they needed to tell someone, and the only thing stopping her from doing so was Abigail. Her sister was being overly cautious. She wanted to make sure that whatever decision they made was the best one for the glory of the Kingdom of God. But Caroline didn't care about that anymore.

As the day wore on, the air around them grew tighter and tighter. Abigail excused herself in the late afternoon to go for a walk on her own. She returned an hour later, sweaty and sticky, sunburned on the left side of her forehead.

She came and sat next to Caroline on the couch. "We have to tell," she said, the rage simmering in her eyes.

"Finally," Caro said, and tried to cover her annoyance. She knew Abigail needed to talk things through. "What's made you so sure this is the right decision?"

"Last night," Abigail said, "I dreamed of deer, and I couldn't figure out what it meant. But just now, on my walk, I realized that it's probably prophetic, a reminder."

Caroline fought the urge to roll her eyes, and crossed her arms. Sometimes Abigail was so exactly like their father. She couldn't talk about an important decision that they were supposed to have made hours ago without relying on some sort of metaphor. Caroline should have known all along that she was helping him write his sermons. It seemed so obvious now.

Abigail looked annoyed at her response. "Don't you remember that time when we were kids? We were coming home from the pumpkin patch and Mom was driving. The car in front of us hit that giant buck and smashed up their fender, and the buck was lying there on the ground bleating. Mom pulled over and immediately jumped out of the car and ran to help. She brought the two teen boys over to wait with us in our car."

Caroline was nodding along, even though she mostly remembered the blur of tears and her mother screaming, holding a tiny pumpkin in her lap, squished between strangers in their back seat.

"And while Mom was comforting the two boys, waving down a sheriff, sending someone to call their parents—do you remember what Dad was doing that whole time?"

"Praying," Caro said. "He was praying for us and for them."

"Yes," Abigail said. "And prayer is important, but it wasn't what those boys needed at that exact moment. They needed help. Some problems are best solved with prayer and the Lord's intervention. Others require action. Jesus calmed the storm even though he knew his disciples were safe, because he knew it would help them."

Caroline nodded again.

"I feel like this is something we can do," her sister was saying, "an action that is holy. We need to tell even if it is hard for him, because that's what's good for the church, do you understand?"

Caroline knew her sister was trying to persuade her to see things her way, but she was surprised at how well it was working. "I think you're right," she said. "But who should we call? What day is it even?" She realized then that it was Wednesday, only ten days until the wedding.

Abigail frowned. "The final elder meeting is scheduled for tomorrow. That's when they'll vote on whether he should be reinstated, so you have to call now. Pastor Mark will need enough time to talk to Mary and to Mom and the elders will need space to weigh their choice. If we wait until morning, they might speed him through the process without looking into any of this."

She was talking fast, her plan unspooling so quickly, Caroline had to cut her off to interject. "What do you mean 'you have to call'?"

She sighed. "I can't call, Caro," she said, as though it were a fact.

Caroline wanted to defer to her, to say nothing at all. People believed in Abigail.

"Why can't we call together?" Caroline crossed her arms.

"Because," she said. "I didn't find the box or the book. We need to tell them the facts only. Nothing that could discredit our story."

Caroline wasn't sure she could do it. She swallowed her anxiety and followed Abigail into the kitchen. Her sister had already picked up the phone and dialed before Caroline could say anything further. She put the receiver to her ear. "Wrong number," she said, and started the whole process over again.

"Hi, yes, this is Caroline Nolan speaking," Abigail said into the phone. "No. Could you put me through to Pastor Mark? It'll be quick, but tell him it's kind of urgent."

She thrust the phone at Caroline then, who almost dropped it before cradling it between her ear and shoulder, holding the mouthpiece with both hands as if it might steady her.

"Hi," Caroline said when Pastor Mark answered. Her voice was shaking. Pastor Mark had been her father's best friend for as long she could remember. He'd come to every one of her plays, always asked her about school. She saw him as he'd been at his desk the Sunday of the announcement, appearing defeated, his head in his hands.

She braced herself against the cabinets and took a deep,

steadying breath. Abigail patted her encouragingly on the back and Caroline let it all out. "There's something I need to tell you before the elder meeting tomorrow night," she said in one breath.

"Okay, Caro," he said. "Thanks for calling. It's good to hear from you. I've missed you at church." He paused, as if waiting for an apology. She didn't respond, reassured herself again that she could do this. She just had to focus. "Tell me what's up," he said.

"I don't. I just . . ." Caroline fumbled for the right words. Of course he was more worried about her church attendance than her father's affair. She considered hanging up, and looked over at her sister, who threw her an encouraging thumbs-up.

"You sound nervous," he said. "Don't be nervous. Whatever it is, you can tell me. You can trust me."

Caroline took another deep breath. She *was* nervous. Here was her father climbing the stairs, about to step into the spotlight, and she was tying a noose to hang him with backstage. She was about to open her mouth and ruin his life. She was Judas Iscariot.

Abby scribbled something onto a notepad and slid it across the counter. "I don't believe," Caroline said, reading it aloud, "that my father has actually repented."

There was a sharp intake of breath on the other end of the line. She could hear the copier machine running in the background. "Hold on one second, okay? I'll be right back," he said, and then came the sound of his office door closing. "Okay, that's a big accusation. Tell me why you think so." His voice sounded open. He would hear her. He had to.

Caroline outlined it all: the book with That Woman's

name in it, the box of condoms, the receipt with his credit card number, the grocery store where she'd seen the two of them together. Pastor Mark was quiet on the other end. Caroline heard the scratch of his beard, his pen scribbling notes. Abigail rubbed her back.

"I just don't believe," Caroline said, "that he's repented. And I don't believe he's ready to return."

"Caroline, thank you for calling and telling me," Pastor Mark said, his voice soft. "It's okay to cry, but don't feel bad about this. You did the right thing. This was the right thing to do." Except Caroline wasn't crying.

"Okay," she said. "It feels terrible." But what she really felt was relief.

"I know," Pastor Mark said. "I feel terrible too. But you have been so brave, and so led by the Lord in following what you know to be right. Your father would be—" he started to say, as though Luke Nolan were dead. "I mean, I am so proud of you."

Abigail rested her head against Caroline's so they could both listen through the earpiece and squeezed her shoulder.

"I am going to spend the day trying to confirm everything you told me. Tell Abby that I'll probably call to talk to her later as well. And Caro," he said, "don't worry. I won't tell him who called. If it turns out you're right, only I'll know that it was you."

Caroline hung up the phone and returned to the table. She saw out the back window an endless, indecipherable cloud of gray. Her stomach lurched as if she were on a boat. Her head felt dizzy. "Did I do the wrong thing?" she said, turning to her sister.

"No, Caro. You did the right thing, I promise. You were brave."

THE NEXT MORNING, Caroline sat on the floor in the kitchen while Abigail talked to Pastor Mark on the phone. She confirmed the story for him, with a few caveats. Only Caroline had seen Mary at the grocery store. Caroline was the one who found the condoms, but Abigail had found the receipt. She had also seen the book and the box.

"I do," Abigail said, near the end of the call. "I believe her."

"What did he say?" Caroline asked when she hung up. She'd heard the conversation, but every detail seemed important. The tile was cold beneath her legs.

"He said he's going to talk to everyone today and present the findings at the beginning of tonight's meeting." *Tonight*, Caroline thought. *Findings*. It felt like some sort of police drama, and not the church she'd belonged to her whole life.

Caroline's stomach felt queasy in anticipation. It was 10:30 A.M. The long, open day before them felt oppressive, unendurable. Abigail must have some kind of plan. Abigail would distract her. "What do we do now?"

"We wait," Abigail said.

"No," Caroline said, shifting her stiff legs, stretching out over them. If she didn't do something, she might take it back. It was too dangerous. "I want to do something. I can't just sit here all day. I feel wild."

Abigail laughed. "Well, lucky for you we have to finish the table assignments for the reception."

"Oh God," Caroline said, but she gathered the pens and the clipboard and the list of names and the circles they'd cut out of cardstock, and brought it all to the table.

They wrote the names of all the wedding guests on small, sticky fluorescent tabs—pink for family, blue for close friends, green for everyone else. Caroline couldn't think about her father's red truck in the parking lot when she had to focus on details like which of Matthew's uncles always drank too much and therefore had to be seated as far away from the bar as possible. She couldn't think about the elder meeting while they were busy deciding between two crammed tables for the singles or three spacious ones. And she was more than happy to answer questions like: Do you think Pastor Cameron's daughter will dance? Instead of thinking about the one that was really on her mind: Do you think we ruined our father's career and possibly our own lives?

In nine days, it would all be over, Caroline reassured herself. Abigail would be married, and nothing would ever be the same. So, Caroline helped her sister decide the cutoff for the kids' table (fourteen), and silently agreed not to talk about their father. Outside, it was raining again, and the foam board filled up with penciled round tables and perfectly arranged colorful tabs. It felt wasteful, so much excess, this display of love in a family that had failed at it so publicly. It made no sense to do this now, to believe in it still. But across the table, her sister was looking down on their arrangement and smiling so big even her ears had lifted.

"Are you happy?" Caroline asked her then.

Abigail started at the question, but after thinking about it for a moment, she answered in a more measured, thoughtful tone than Caroline had expected. "Yeah, I mean, but in a different way than I thought I would be."

"How so?" Caroline said.

"I don't know. I mean, I thought for a long time that all I needed to be happy was to find my soul mate, ya know? And while I'm not sure if Matthew is my soul mate, I'm also not sure I believe in that anymore. I think I'll be happier with him." She moved one cousin's tab to the new third singles table. "The things that I want—" She stopped, and tried again. "I cannot have the life that I want if I don't get married. I need this to work."

"But why not?" Caroline asked. "Why can't you?"

"Caro," she said without looking up from the table, switching two pink tabs. "I want to have kids and build a home and be something more than just Luke Nolan's daughter for once." She sighed. "As a married woman, I'll be able to lead Bible studies and maybe even write songs that are sung in other churches. Without Matthew, I can't do any of that. The only thing I'm worried about even a little bit is leaving Hope."

Matthew wasn't perfect, Caroline realized, and he didn't have to be for her sister. He knew what she wanted and he wanted to give that to her. They both knew how women at church whispered when a single woman hit thirty. How sad, they'd say, she'd been such a pretty girl once. Abigail didn't want that future. Perhaps with Matthew, she felt like she wouldn't disappear, and that was enough for her.

Caroline finished copying the names for table seventeen onto a notecard for the setup crew. "It's hard for me, I guess," she said, "to have a whole lot of faith in the institution when our parents' marriage is such a failure."

Abigail looked up from her own notecard.

"But Caro, we don't know if our parents' marriage is a failure." She set down the ballpoint pen she was using.

Caroline scoffed. "How can you say that? He's been cheating on her." And if infidelity wasn't a failure, what on earth was?

"Yeah, I know," Abigail said, rolling her eyes as if she were talking to a child. "But isn't it kind of incredible that they are working through it together? Isn't there something beautiful in that effort?"

Caroline waited for her sister to say she was joking, or to laugh off the comment. It took her a moment to place where she'd heard this sort of talk before about marriage. Instagram, maybe? The way the older girls she followed talked about their relationships. Marriage, they said, was hard. Marriage was borderline miserable. You hate your husband and you fight all the time and you cry on your date nights. You are broken and sinful and so is he, and your marriage is one everlasting realization of your flaws. But you still have to fight for it. Fight for this relationship that will never be easy. Fight so that he can hand you over to the Pharaoh, or to a group of roving men (if you took the Bible literally), and all while everything you've worked for goes up in flames.

LATER THAT NIGHT the girls sat on the front porch listening for the sound of the telephone. Caroline could feel the cool air from inside the house seeping through the open door. Anytime they thought they heard it ring, they cut off their sentence midway. But it never did. Not after the sun had set or when the bugs came out or as the sky turned to navy and then black.

"Why haven't they called?" Caroline said, and the question hung there on the porch between them, unanswered for a while.

"I don't know," Abigail said, fanning her face. They could see the moon's reflection on the lake. There was a large swath of black land between them and it. Caroline focused on the light rippling across the water.

Abigail looked over her shoulder, followed Caroline's gaze down to the lake. "Okay, we are not going to just sit here and make ourselves miserable." And with that, she stood and marched inside. Caroline did not follow. She listened to the sound of her sister's feet walking to the kitchen and back again. Abigail returned with two juice glasses, each containing an inch of liquid so gold it refracted the light back up onto her face.

"I think it's time for us to be a little reckless," she said, and winked.

"Reckless?" Caroline asked. Who was this woman with the yellow hair falling uncombed over her shoulders, smiling down at her now? Caroline pulled herself up from her slouch and took the glass from her sister.

"Skinny-dipping," Abigail said.

Caroline laughed. "Absolutely not." She was thinking about the size of her boobs, how big they were compared to Abigail's neat, perfect ones, and the dimpled undersides of her thighs and her tummy.

"Oh, come oooon," Abigail said. "We grew up with a pool, you must have gone skinny-dipping before."

Caroline blushed. She hadn't. She'd never even considered it. She had always thought she was the rebellious one, choosing to leave for college, losing her virginity, and now here was Abigail dragging her to her feet, handing her the other glass to hold. Her sister pulled her shirt over her head and revealed a purple lace bralette and—because of course, Caroline thought—two well-defined ab muscles.

"You're gonna do it," Abigail said. "Who is going to see you?"

You, Caroline wanted to say. *You will see me.* Abigail slipped off her shorts, draped them over the railing.

She took her glass, clinked it against Caroline's, and threw back her head, downing the tequila in one go. She unhooked her bra and tossed it aside, put her hands on her hips and played her trump card. "Come on," she said. "Don't be such a baby."

Caroline knew exactly what Abigail was doing and yet she was powerless to resist her. She tilted her own head back and felt the tequila burn all the way down. She sputtered and coughed. "Aren't we supposed to have, like, limes or something?" she said, her face scrunched up. Then she set the glass on the railing and lifted her shirt.

Abigail clapped. "Limes are for babies. Come on." She jumped down the stairs two at a time and ran toward the lake.

Caroline could still choose not to follow her. She could stay here on the porch the way she always had, riddled with self-consciousness, swatting away the moths and mosquitoes. Or she could change. She wanted to be the kind of girl who swam naked in a lake. Didn't she?

She ran, shirt in hand, after her sister's blond hair in the moonlight and then stood at the end of the dock, watched as Abigail wrestled off her tennis shoes and cannonballed into the water. The distance between them was growing every second. Abigail would understand if she didn't want to partake. She always had before. But Caroline didn't want what they'd had before. She wanted something more than that.

She stepped out of her shoes, looked for her sister. Abigail was still underwater. Caroline flung off her socks and then, in one motion pulled off her shorts and underwear. She unhooked her bra, and tossed it behind her as she ran to the end of the dock. She jumped, tucking her knees, holding her nose with one hand, and prayed that she'd be in the water before her sister could see her. The water was comfortable, the same temperature as the air. She swam back up, heard her sister shouting before she even broke the surface.

"I knew you'd do it!" Abigail screamed as soon as Caroline's head emerged, splashing her with water.

Her sister's joy was infectious. Caroline smiled right back at her and screamed into the night air: "I DID IT!" She dunked her head, smoothed her bangs off her face, and tried to keep her body beneath the surface. When she grew tired, she hoisted herself up the stairs and onto the dock and turned her back to Abigail. She crossed her arms across her chest and stepped into her underwear and shorts, pulled her T-shirt over her head, and carried her bra and socks in her hand, shoes squeaking, as they trudged back up to the house. Abigail was still wearing only her underwear. They laughed as they dried off in the hallway and readied themselves for bed. Caroline fell asleep almost as soon as her head hit the pillow, her limbs entwined with her sister's. She did not think of her father at all.

16

It was Friday afternoon, twenty-eight hours after Pastor Mark called Abigail, five hours after the girls had jerked awake, three hours past when they'd stopped speaking and started panicking instead, and two hours after the thermometer on the porch had hit 103 degrees, when they heard the cattle gate creak open.

Caroline barely had time to look up before Ruthie Nolan came barreling into the house. Abigail pulled her hair out of its ponytail so it fell long down her back, fluffed it around her forehead. Caroline rearranged the dip of her V-neck. But their mother didn't look at either of them as she rushed through the living room and threw open the door to Nannie's bedroom.

The girls stood from their seats at the kitchen table, their chairs screeching across the floor. They watched their mother's blond hair disappear into the room, glanced at each other. "What is she doing here?" Caroline asked. They heard her opening drawers, banging cabinet doors in the bathroom.

"I don't know," Abigail said, straining her neck to try to catch a glimpse of her.

"We moved it, right?" Caroline whispered.

"Yes," Abigail said. "Shush."

They waited in silence. Abigail's right leg was shaking.

Ruthie closed Nannie's door tight behind her and returned to the main room. Her hair had been blown out, her nails blushed, her linen shirt artfully untucked. But Caroline noticed that the polish was chipped on every nail of her left hand, the lavender of her eye shadow painted on a little too brightly, and she'd missed a section when curling her hair. Caroline's heart dropped. She focused on her breath, out and in. Her mother's form was stiff, her expression impossible to read.

"Sit," Ruthie commanded, and both girls did, positioning themselves across from each other at the oval table as they had been all summer. Ruthie sat at the other end of Abby's digital piano, in front of a puzzle they had been puttering with for the past week. Caroline glanced at Abigail and saw her own fear reflected in her sister's eyes.

Ruthie sat in her chair, her back as dramatically straight as Caroline's was slouched. "Your father has been accused of something terrible," she said, her words plain and matter-of-fact. The girls waited as she took off her cardigan, draped it over the back of the chair, looked each of them in the eye. "As you know, the vote for your father's reinstatement was held last night," she continued, "and let me tell you, it was a mess."

"How so?" Abigail said, looking only at their mother.

"We-ell," Ruthie said, stretching the word into two syllables. "We walked into the elder meeting all smiles, and guess who was there? Can you believe That Woman would even consider standing in front of me?" That Woman, her voice intonated, who had tried to ruin her life.

Ruthie folded her hands on the table in front of her, crossed and recrossed her legs. "So we all sit down—me, your father, her, the elder board—and Pastor Mark gives this strange speech. He spent fifteen minutes rambling about his friendship with your father." She waved her hand to indicate this was utter nonsense, her eyes wide in disbelief. "And the whole time I am lookin' at That Woman, tryin' to figure out why in the God's great heavens she is here for what is supposed to be a joyous occasion." Ruthie looked back and forth between them. Her eyes settled on Abigail until it became clear she wouldn't continue unless prompted.

"So, why was she?" Abigail asked.

"Apparently," Ruthie said, hands flat on the table, leaning forward conspiratorially, "someone wanted to sabotage your father and called in to say that the affair was still going on. And That Woman told everyone that the liar who called was telling the truth!"

Caroline bit her tongue. Sabotage, she wanted to say, was attempting to take someone down without a reason—and she and Abigail had a very good reason. She looked out the window right above her sister's head, counted the large cottonball clouds in the sky to calm herself down. Her mother's voice droned on, dripping with disgust as she described Mary Campbell's confession. She had claimed that they'd never stopped seeing each other, never stopped greeting each other with kisses that bled at the edges, never stopped planning for their future lives, never stopped discussing their hopes and fears and dreams.

"What a load of hogwash," Ruthie said, shaking her head. "I think That Woman probably made the phone call herself to ruin your father's career, just like she meant to the first time."

Caroline looked to her sister, who was staring at the table.

It was clear from her tone that their mother wasn't upset at the accusation that her husband's affair was still ongoing. Because she simply didn't believe it. She told them about Mary Campbell's hysteria, how she'd reached for Luke, begged him to back up her story, and then turned angry when he'd refused, hitting him in front of everyone. Caroline realized that the truth didn't really matter anymore. Their mother had already decided what she wanted to believe.

"So what's going to happen?" Abigail prodded.

Ruthie ran a hand through her hair and looked at each of her daughters before opening her lined lips. "Nothing," she said with a smile.

"Nothing?" Abigail and Caroline said in unison.

"Yes, nothing," she said. "The elder board met and they didn't find anything to back up her story. All she had was her word and a pile of love notes and a lot of delusion." Ruthie sat back in her seat now, satisfied.

What could she possibly present, Caroline thought, that wouldn't be dismissed as some deranged woman's fantasy? Should they show their mother the evidence they'd found? Ruthie reached out to grab each of their hands. "I'm sorry this had to be drug back out. Your father is still your father."

Caroline and Abigail sat dumbstruck in front of her for a moment. Caroline's fingers felt numb. They twitched in frustration. She did not want their father to stay the same; she wanted him to change.

"So that's it then?" Caroline said.

Ruthie tucked a strand of hair behind her ear. Her two-carat diamond engagement ring shimmered in the sunlight.

Abigail looked past their mother, toward Nannie's room. *Please speak*, Caroline thought. *Say something, anything.* But her sister remained silent. Caroline took a deep breath.

"I'm sorry, but this is absurd," she said. Abigail's kick came swiftly beneath the table, a firm hit with the ball of her foot to the middle of Caroline's shin. Caroline took a sharp inhale and glared at her sister. Fine, she thought. She swung her own foot and missed, connected with the leg of the table instead. Caroline winced. Their mother looked back and forth between them, her features hard, her eyes questioning.

"What?" Ruthie asked.

"Nothing," Abigail said, refusing to meet her sister's eyes.

Caroline knew Abigail didn't agree with their mother's assessment, but if she thought it was best to let her ignore reality, that was different than staying silent about their father's reinstatement. No, Caroline thought, not this time. She would not let her mother sit here and be fooled by him.

"We are almost done with this trying period in our lives," Ruthie said, looking between her daughters again. She placed one hand on each of theirs. "Everything will return to normal soon."

Caroline jerked her hand away. "No, you don't understand." She felt her anger taking over and was helpless to stop it. "You don't know what he's doing! You don't know that he's lying to you." She had never raised her voice at her mother like this before. *Maybe this is what it will take to wake her up*, she told herself.

Ruthie raised her eyebrows a full inch at her daughter and cocked her head. "I have forgotten more about Luke Nolan than you"—she glanced at Abby to include her too—"either of you, will ever know. I understand that you think you're all grown up playin' house out here and that none of this matters, but both of you need to understand something . . ."

Her daughters knew what was coming next. This was the only sermon Ruthie Nolan ever gave. They'd heard it any time they'd tried to skip out on church or been caught in a lie. They'd heard it when they didn't finish their chores or played their music too loud.

"The most important thing in the whole entire world is the Kingdom of God. We, despite all of our sin, have been saved by His grace," Ruthie said, a hand on her heart. "If we aren't proclaiming that Truth, our lives are worth nothing. Nothing. Do y'all hear me?"

"Yes, ma'am," they said.

She continued: "What your father does is more important than any other priority that the three of us might have. He is in the business of saving lives, and I am in the business of supporting him no matter what. That is the job God gave me, and He—not me, and certainly not the two of you—knows best." She snapped her fingers at the girls. "Do you understand me?"

Caroline blinked. It was as if she had never really heard this speech before. She looked at her mother's self-satisfied face. Did she realize that she wasn't defending her own mission, but her husband's ability to do whatever he wanted as long as he claimed it was holy? Abigail's jaw was clenched behind her teeth.

They should have responded again with *Yes, ma'am,* and when neither girl did, Ruthie's anger was written all over her face. But before she could say anything, Abigail finally broke her silence.

"So you're saying that his affair barely matters, then?" her sister said, hands firm on the table as if to ground herself.

"That his mission is so important that his sins can be forgiven and forgotten like they're nothing?"

Outside the window a cloud, as if sensing her anger, covered the sun and the room grew dark. Abigail stood from her chair, walked to flip on the switch to the overhead light. Ruthie's eyes followed her, waiting for her to return to her seat at the table. Abigail stared her down.

"I am saying," Ruthie said, "that being lured by the flesh a couple of times doesn't make his purpose any less holy." The clock on the wall ticked and the faucet dripped. The wind slapped against the window. Caroline watched as her mother's face dropped from cream to milk to paper white, her soft smile set in stone, eyes unfocused and unrevealing. The pointer finger of her right hand tapped against her thumb, a nervous tic. As mild as it was, Caroline wished she'd been the one to make their mother uncomfortable. She forced herself to focus on Abigail, who seemed to be unfurling, taking up more space with every moment that passed.

"A couple of times?" Abigail said, each word precise, tinged with fury. "What do you mean 'a couple of times'? Has he done this before?"

Done what before? Caroline thought. She'd lost the thread of the conversation and looked to their mother for an explanation. Her face had turned a deep, deep red, her fury evident even through her coverup. Caroline sat up straight in her chair. Was their mother going to yell at them? She looked like she might drag them outside by the ears and force them to go straight home. But as she watched, Ruthie's eyes widened, her jaw loosened, and her smile returned. Caroline had never realized that she was doing it too, donning this mask in service of him.

Caroline shifted, crossed her legs the other way. She willed her sister to look over at her, but Abigail was still staring at their mother, seemingly without blinking.

"Done what before, honey?" Ruthie asked, using her overly sweet, fake phone voice.

Abigail did not falter. "Cheated on you. Had an affair. Whatever you want to call it."

The leafy wallpaper seemed to quiver right before Caroline's eyes. Her sister was fuzzy around the edges. The sun reemerged then and filled the kitchen with thick bands of light that shimmered with dust.

"Caroline, close your mouth," Ruthie said, turning to her youngest.

"Has he cheated on you before, yes or no?" Abigail was the only one standing. "Do not lie to us anymore." The echo of her accusation reverberated off the kitchen cabinets and right through Caroline's bones. She closed her mouth. She did not blink.

"Yes," their mother said. "He has."

Suddenly, Caroline's mouth felt like it was filled with sand. She wanted to get a glass of water and chug it while standing at the sink, refill it, and drink some more. But she was afraid to stand, afraid to miss a moment of this encounter in case no one ever spoke of it again.

"Why didn't you tell us?" Abigail asked. "Don't you think that's fairly relevant information?"

"Why would I have?" Ruthie said. "It is none of your business. Our marriage is between us and God. And besides, I have forgiven him." Caroline leaned forward in her chair and tried to look deeply into her mother's eyes. Had she really forgiven him? That was another one of his sermons: The Bible says that true forgiveness keeps no record of wrongdoing. True love is not only forgiving but forgetting. But their mother hadn't forgotten. Caroline didn't want to forget. She wanted to remember everything: his smile on the stage at his announcement, his fumble saying hello to them at the balloon festival, the way her mother's hair was curled tighter on the right than the left side as she sat here and pretended everything was okay, forever.

"Is that why you hid what happened to Nannie from us, because you didn't think it *concerned* us?" Abigail said.

Ruthie slammed her hand on the table, and a couple of the puzzle pieces bounced to the floor. "Abigail Nancy Nolan, you watch your tone. Don't be ugly. I am your mother and you will not speak to me that way." She glared at Abby.

Abigail sat back down in her chair, flipped her hair over her shoulder, and softened her face, closing her eyes for a moment. Her hands remained clenched. "Yes, ma'am," she said.

Ruthie's face softened. "No," she said finally. "That's not why I didn't tell you about my mother. I didn't tell you because I didn't want it to get out." Here they were again. Always back at the same tired, useless reasoning. It wasn't about the Kingdom of God or saving lives, it was about perception.

Caroline couldn't stop herself. Her eyes rolled.

"Did you just roll your eyes at me?" Ruthie asked. Caroline did not respond. "This is exactly what I was worried about. You two have clearly been out here too long."

Neither girl responded.

"It would be best if you both came home with me now, before your father's reinstatement on Sunday."

Caroline bit the inside of her lip until she tasted iron.

"Wait, what?" Abigail said. "He's getting reinstated on Sunday? Sunday as in two days from now?"

"Yes, honey, I told you already," she said, even though she had not. "The elder board voted him back in and he'll be re-instated on Sunday at eleven A.M. You're both gonna be there and you're gonna put on makeup to cover these sunburns and you're gonna wear some real clothes."

The girls looked at each other. This was supposed to be the beginning of his demise. They had been preparing for the worst, thinking he'd lose his position or maybe be hired by another church. But neither had imagined that his story would be believed and redeemed without repentance. Caroline had to remind herself to breathe.

"Neither of you seem very happy about this," Ruthie said, pointing her finger at each of her daughters. "Work on that."

"Okay, but we're not coming home," Abigail said. "What time do you want us to meet you at the church?"

Ruthie raised her eyebrows, but she didn't comment on her eldest daughter's tone. "If you're not there at nine forty-five for the eleven o'clock announcement, I will come out here to get you myself."

"Yes, ma'am," Abigail said. "See you at nine forty-five on Sunday."

Under usual circumstances, their mother would have hung around, made herself a coffee, engaged in small talk, but she seemed to understand that she'd dropped a bomb. Caroline took another deep breath when Ruthie rose to leave, held it in until her lungs began to hurt.

"Bye, girls," Ruthie said, stepping out the front door, waving a hand at her face, groaning at the wall of heat that pressed against her. "I'll see y'all on Sunday, all right? And don't wear black." She continued, "And Abby, baby, don't for-get to send me the names of Matthew's parents' friends so I can make sure we know them before the rehearsal." She slid her aviator sunglasses off her head, onto her face, and removed the car keys from her purse.

The wedding was a safe topic in this seeming minefield of family drama. Caroline knew their mother had pivoted to something innocuous on purpose to lighten the mood. She realized that Ruthie hadn't had any reason to drive all the way out to the ranch. There wasn't a festival to attend, or a bucket of crafts to drop off. She could have called to tell them about the reinstatement. So why had she come out here in person?

"Wait, Mom," Caroline said, running to the front door. Ruthie was at the bottom of the porch steps. She must have been looking for the evidence they had told Pastor Mark about. If she'd admit it, maybe Caroline could show her the book and the condoms and she'd change her mind, recant her support of her husband. They had to try. Maybe there was still a chance. "Why'd you come all the way out here to tell us about this?"

"Oh," Ruthie said, turning back with a laugh, one so laden with anger and bitterness it ate any of the hope Caroline had left. "That Woman, she said that they'd been"—she searched for the right word—"um, conducting their affair here, at my mother's house, up until the announcement a few weeks ago, when your father made it crystal clear that the whole thing had been over for almost a year. The nerve, right?"

"So a part of you believed her, then?" Caroline said. Abigail reached for her hand and squeezed. Her sister must have followed her to the door.

"No, Caroline." Ruthie's forehead wrinkled. "I believe your father. I only came here to grab some earrings from Nannie's jewelry box for the reinstatement."

It was a blatant lie, and both of her daughters knew it. She had come to look for evidence. But if she'd found any, she probably would have destroyed it. She was so convinced that God needed Luke, she would do anything to protect him. Abigail was digging the long nails of her right hand into the soft flesh on the back of her sister's arm. They both stood inside the doorway looking out.

"Mom thinks we agree with her. She thinks we want him reinstated," Abigail whispered. "We have to tell her." Their mother had turned away. She was walking to her car.

"Abby, no," Caroline said, and felt the dread paralyze her. She couldn't think of a way to stop her sister.

"See you Sunday," Ruthie called back to them. "So glad you girls understand."

Abigail's face was so close to hers that Caroline could hear her sharp intake of breath. Her sister released her arm. Caroline tried to grab her as she stepped forward. Abigail brushed right by her, now standing at the top of the steps.

"We made the call," Abigail yelled, and their mother, in her pink cardigan, with her coiffed hair, stopped to remove her sunglasses and turned back to face the girls.

"What?" she said. She was still smiling, her face open and bright in the sun.

"We made the call to Pastor Mark," Abigail said. Caroline saw their mother lose control of her face then; it transformed into an angry scowl she'd never seen before.

"Abby, stop," Caroline said. But her sister did not stop.

"I think it's important you know where we stand on this. That we don't believe him anymore."

Abigail whipped around, hair flying out behind her, grabbed Caroline, and dragged her into the house before

Ruthie could say anything further. She pushed the door closed behind them. Their mother's outline still standing and facing the house was visible through the stained glass of the front door. The girls waited for her to come back inside, to demand an explanation or to scold them at least, but Ruthie just stood there until, a few minutes later, she turned, climbed into her car, slammed the door, started the engine, and drove away, spraying gravel behind her. Only then did Caroline begin to breathe normally again.

17

They had bathed themselves in God's righteousness and holiness and it wasn't enough. They'd been wrong to believe the truth would matter to the elders. Luke Nolan's path was laid out before him. The Lord would listen and find him innocent and his daughters would be but two girls screaming into the void.

Abigail retrieved the book and the box of condoms from the hall closet. "We could bring these to Pastor Mark," she said. Her voice sounded flat, hopeless. Caroline cradled the evidence in her hands. She tried to imagine taking it to someone who actually cared. She set the items on the table, where they stayed for a few hours before Abigail returned them to the closet without asking about it again.

The next morning, following hours of silence, Caroline finally accepted the inevitable. "It doesn't matter," she said. The elder board had already voted. Their decision was made. The girls had played their highest card and lost. "It doesn't matter if we're right."

Abigail didn't respond. The bags under her eyes had deepened overnight. She drank her coffee and seemed to stare straight through her sister.

Caroline didn't notice that Abigail wasn't ready for their walk until she'd already laced up her boots and was waiting at the door. She clomped down the hall, but her sister wasn't at the kitchen table, or in the living room. She found her in their room in bed. "Are you coming?" she asked from the door. But Abigail didn't move. Caroline took that as a no and closed the door quietly behind her.

She walked down the dim hallway, through the front door, out onto the porch, where the sun beat down upon her face. It was only 10 A.M. and the air was already oppressive. Caroline felt a headache brewing behind her eyes and at the base of her neck; the revelations of the past week slammed inside her forehead. Their father had cheated before and their mother had covered for him. Abigail had known about Mary Campbell and told no one. He would now be reinstated, loved, and forgiven. None of it was fair. *Holy*, Ruthie had promised.

To Caroline, the day was bright and full of spite. Weeds with purple heads and scarves of green leaves grew on lanky, smooth stalks, their roots slithering underground, choking out the other life until they alone remained—malicious and dominating, albeit pretty if you really looked at them. The grass shifted in small ways, tiny creatures trying to survive. The air was quiet all around her.

She could never unknow everything she'd learned this summer. She would have to sit through his sermons silently. She wouldn't be able to ask questions. Every time he came home late, she would wonder whether he was still meeting her and never know the truth. She felt weary and sat for a while on the fence, looking out at their land. She was glad to be leaving soon, glad that she and Abigail both were.

She lay down in the tall grass and felt the bitterness their mother had promised begin to seep like a dew into the seat of her shorts, the back of her shirt. It mingled there with her sweat, absorbed into her skin, filled her with a chill she knew she'd never shake. The trees above her were a silhouette of leaves against the clear bright sky.

It's only right to be bitter, she thought, even if she was becoming the sort of woman the Bible had warned her about: one whose heart was a trap, whose hands were chains. Any man who pleased God would run from her. *Let him*, she thought. She never wanted to think of God again. All summer she'd let her faith fade, turn brittle, like a beach chair left too long in the sun. That afternoon, she let the bitterness course through her. It wasn't a curse, she decided. The bitterness was a blessing that would free her from this life.

It was early afternoon by the time she pushed herself to standing, steadying herself against a tree. She was thirsty and took a shortcut through the center of the property on her way back to the house, where she went straight to the kitchen and poured a glass of water, and then another, drank them both standing by the sink before going to the living room. Abigail was reading on the couch. Caroline sat down next to her and laid her head on her shoulder.

"You're awake," Caroline said.

"Yes, but I'm so tired," Abby said. "I'm glad you're back. I don't really want to be alone right now."

Caroline wrapped an arm around her sister's waist. They

were closer than they had ever been, bound together by sins revealed and secrets kept, their shock radiating through every pore of their skin.

"You're sweaty," Abigail said, and pressed a finger to the skin on Caroline's chest. "And no more sun for you. How are you feeling today?"

"Terrible," Caroline said. "Awful."

"Me too," Abigail said. "I really thought he wouldn't get reinstated. I keep thinking about him bringing her here, about how he was having sex with her in a space that didn't even belong to him, and I just feel so nauseous and tired."

"I know," Caroline said. "I can't stop thinking about the way he preaches. Every time I think about him I think about him with her, Speaking. Like. This. As. He. Ruined. Our. Lives." But her sister didn't laugh at her poor attempt at a joke.

"I think he might just be a bad person?" Abigail said. "But I don't know what to do with that. I've been praying all morning and reading my Bible and I'm not any closer to figuring out what to believe."

"I haven't prayed at all," Caroline confessed. She traced a finger in a circle on the back of Abigail's hand. "I don't think I'm going to."

"Oh," Abigail said. "That's sad."

"Not really," Caroline said. "I feel okay about it." She felt her sister lean her chin against Caroline's head. "What if we skipped again tomorrow?" Caroline said. "We could stay here."

Abigail was quiet for a moment. "We have to go this time. It's over. We don't decide if he gets reinstated, but we do decide how we behave."

"But we don't agree with it. Why would we go to support him?"

"Because he's our father," Abigail said. It was a terrible argument, but it was also true. They would go because they were his daughters, because that was what was required of them, and because the statement they would make by not attending would be held against them and not him. Never him.

What else could they say? They couldn't say they hated him, or that they hoped he would confess so they could believe he wasn't so terrible after all. They were bound together so tightly it felt eternal. Caroline lay with her head on Abigail's shoulder until they drifted off to sleep. It would be their last afternoon together like that, though they didn't know it then. That summer was all slow moments and nothing days, dream sequences that blended into sunsets and back again, and like all things once foreign, it had become so familiar that they'd forgotten to savor it.

He came so quietly to ruin everything.

THEY WERE NAPPING and didn't hear the cattle gate they had forgotten to lock swing open, or the car door slam. They didn't hear the sneakers on the gravel or the steps on the porch. They heard the knock and raised their heads, weary and disoriented.

"Is someone here?" Abigail asked, and stood to greet their guest. Neither of them was scared at the idea of an unknown visitor. The ranch was too remote to worry about break-ins, and they'd been raised in a culture that believed kidnappings only happened when strange men in white vans offered you candy and assaults only occurred if your skirt was too short.

Abigail swung open the door. Caroline was right behind her, a head taller, and there on their front porch was Connor Boyd.

"Hi," he said to one or both of them. Caroline wasn't sure who. He looked tan and was wearing jeans despite the heat, with a tight black T-shirt. He had grown out his facial hair in a well-managed way and smelled clean, like soap.

"Hi?" Abigail said. Her hair, Caroline noticed, was all knotted in the back. "What're you doing here?"

"Caro invited me," he said, and his eyes landed on Caroline. He opened his mouth as if to ask a question and then closed it.

Caroline felt her bones turn soft, like she could have melted right there in the doorway. She had texted him not to come. He couldn't be here. Sure, she had thought it was a good idea to invite him four days ago, but she had realized her mistake and taken it back. Days had passed since then. She saw her sister's shoulders tighten in front of her. Abigail instinctively took a step back and bumped into Caroline. She did not turn around to apologize.

"Oh," Abigail said, quickly amending it to "How rude of me. Come in. I'll just go change real quick. We weren't expecting company." She motioned him inside and down the hall to the living room. He ducked through the doorway. "Can you come with me?" she said, turning to her sister with a stiff smile, grabbing Caroline's arm, dragging her to their room, and closing the door behind them.

She gripped Caroline's wrists rope-burn tight and swung her so she stumbled back a little and ended up sitting on the bed.

"What is he doing here?" Abigail asked through her

teeth. She was undressing now, frantically searching through her suitcase on the floor, smelling each item to see if it was clean.

"I just—I'm sorry," Caroline said, and suddenly, she understood self-flagellation. If she could have, she would have beaten herself right then with a whip until her sister understood how sorry she was.

Abigail picked up a black dress with a tie waist, inspected it, and then shoved her head through it. She did not look up from tying the bow. "Why is he here?"

Caroline put her head in her hands, looked down at her own knees, which were shaking uncontrollably. They'd never done this before. She saw Abigail's bare feet in front of her own, felt her gaze burning the top of her head. Abigail reached her hand between her sister's arms, placed two fingers beneath her chin, and lifted her head until Caroline was looking at her. Abigail bent at the waist, their noses now less than two inches apart.

"What is going on?" she demanded.

"I texted him when we were at the grocery store, before we saw her. I didn't realize—" Abigail grabbed Caroline's cheeks with her hand, smushing her lips together.

"Okay, but why did you text him? Why would you invite him to come here?"

"I *uninvited* him, though," Caroline said, her words muffled now. Abigail released her face and backed away, crossed her arms over her breasts. She tapped her foot while she waited.

"I texted him because I thought maybe you wanted to see him but weren't letting yourself, and then I realized I was wrong and I told him not to come. I'm so sorry. I'll go tell him to leave. I'll do it now."

"You will not," Abigail said through her teeth. "He's already here."

"I'm sorry," Caroline said again.

Abigail didn't look at her again as she brushed her hair, reapplied deodorant, and adjusted her bra straps. She left the bedroom and headed to the living room. Caroline followed close behind.

"Water?" Abby asked him as a form of greeting.

Connor was seated on the couch. He stood to follow her to the kitchen. She raised a hand to stop him and he sat back down obediently. "Sure. That would be nice," he said.

Caroline followed her sister like a shadow, listened to the ice hit the glass, the faucet trickle, and then trailed her back to the living room and sat on the smaller couch facing him. He ran a hand nervously through his hair.

"So, you're back in town?" Abby said, sitting beside Caroline, crossing her legs at the ankles, her knees pressed together.

"Yeah, uh, I moved back in with my parents, actually," he said, and looked at the floor. "I'm sure you've heard."

"Heard what?" Abigail said. Connor looked between the two of them, his right hand massaging the back of his neck. Caroline felt her sister lean forward.

"Oh." His face brightened. "I figured because the gossip moves so quickly at Hope that you'd have already heard. But I guess y'all haven't really been around much." God, Caroline thought, was anyone ever allowed to skip church without the whole town noticing? "Bailey and I . . . we're, um, I don't think it was the right decision for us to get married."

"Oh. I'm sorry to hear that," Abigail said, and she did sound genuinely sorry. She pulled a strand of hair at the base of her neck with both hands, stretching it all the way to her rib cage. Caroline checked her sister's knees and saw that they were still. Abigail and Connor had spent so much time together in their formative years that they'd developed similar mannerisms, and then they'd forgotten to grow apart. Their vocal cadences were in sync, their hand gestures mirrored. They were good together, Caroline thought.

The conversation jerked forward. Caroline began to understand that she was the problem. She was the reason neither one of them had anything more than one-word answers, the reason Abigail kept glancing at the clock even though it had only been fifteen minutes. Neither of them acknowledged her presence in the room until Abigail asked what he had come to talk about, and he glanced at Caroline before responding, "Caroline, could I have a few minutes to talk to your sister alone?" He turned to Abby. "Is that okay?"

Her sister nodded.

"I'll just run to Sonic. Anyone need anything?" Caroline said.

"You will not." Abby was looking at her now. "Just go outside or something."

Caroline realized she couldn't leave her sister there alone with his car in the drive. Women weren't supposed to be left alone with men in general, but they were certainly not to be left alone with men they had once thought they were going to marry. She strained to hear their conversation as she pulled on her shoes by the door, but they didn't say a word until she was safely out of earshot.

There was nothing to do outside and it was 102 degrees. Caroline sat on the bottom step of the porch, kicking at the dirt. She thought about going for a walk, stood, and sat back down. She had betrayed her one and only sister.

She paced the porch, her boots clicking against the wood. Why hadn't she told Abby that she'd texted Connor? Why hadn't she apologized in advance and told her everything so she wouldn't have been surprised? Why couldn't she do anything right?

CAROLINE LAY ON the porch until the cattle gate creaked once again and a familiar Jeep came driving up the lane. Taylor didn't wave as he approached, and his brow was set in a frown. He turned to grab something from the back seat and emerged with a cake carrier, holding it in both hands as he walked toward the house. "Why haven't you responded to my texts?" he said when he stood before her. Caroline thought she could smell the cinnamon gum he'd always chewed during their make-out sessions.

"What?" Caroline said, blinking slowly.

He transferred the cake to one hand, pressed his lips together, and rubbed the back of his neck before responding. "You sent me this weird cryptic text at like midnight on Tuesday saying not to come out here and 'Nevermind' and then I texted you back like fifteen times and you didn't respond." He took two steps toward her. "What the fuck is going on?"

She had sent the text to Taylor by mistake. Caroline put her head in her hands and began to cry. She hadn't even uninvited Connor. She'd had those two margaritas and now he was here. They were both here. And her sister hated her. Everything was wrong. Taylor's body was blocking the sun and she cried harder. Her tears were hot too.

"Whoa, don't cry. I'm not that mad," he said, sitting next

to her on the steps, pulling her toward him with one arm. He set the cake on the porch and wrapped her up in a hug. She turned her face into his neck and cried giant tears. When she'd calmed down a little, he released her, and she saw the worry etched onto his face.

"Why do you have a cake?" Caroline asked through the sniffles.

"Oh, right. My mom sent me to bring this out here to y'all. She told me to tell you it was to celebrate your dad's reinstatement, since you guys wouldn't be going to the celebratory dinner tonight." He paused. Caroline raised her eyebrow at him. He continued. "Okay, fine. Mrs. Boyd called the house about an hour ago and told my mom that Connor was coming out here to see Abby, so she asked me to bring y'all this cake and to find out what this visit is all about." He waved a hand toward Connor's car.

"Ah," Caroline said. "So you were sent as a scout."

"Guess so," Taylor said, and patted her on the leg. "I'm going to put this in the fridge." He stood and climbed the last two steps. They heard hushed voices that faded as soon as they opened the door. Their footsteps echoed down the hall. Taylor steered them into the living room, carrying the container with both hands out in front of him. Caroline peered over his shoulder right as Abigail and Connor scooted apart.

"Well, Mr. McGregor, to what do we owe this pleasure?" Abigail said.

Taylor laughed. "Just dropping off a cake my mom made for y'all."

"Is it poisoned?" Abigail said, but only the lower half of her face seemed to be joking about this. Connor too was all tight and serious.

"Wow," Taylor said.

Abigail's mouth opened slightly, as if to apologize.

He held the cake up to the light, squinted at it. "You know what? It absolutely might be." He winked at Abigail. Her shoulders dropped then and she laughed, a real laugh this time. Taylor was charming, Caroline realized. Connor did not look up at them and he did not smile.

"We'll get out of your hair," Caroline said. Abigail's right hand rested between her and Connor on the sofa. His hands were in his lap, gripped tightly.

"Of course, no rush, though," Abigail said, but Caroline knew they were about as welcome as a skunk at a barbecue. Taylor led the way into the kitchen, looked over at Caroline as he set the cake down on the island. Caroline shook her head, opened the refrigerator door, moved a big bowl of cold pasta salad, and put the carrier on the middle shelf.

"We should go," she said. Taylor swept his left hand toward the living room and dropped into a mock bow, then followed along behind her. On the couch, Abigail and Connor had scooted farther apart. They stayed silent until Caroline and Taylor closed the front door firmly behind them.

"Well, that is certainly something," Taylor said. "Hope's Greatest Couple together at last."

Caroline hit him in the arm. He rubbed the spot. Her voice came out rocky and uncertain. "That's not what that is. Please don't tell anyone that." All it would take was him mentioning offhandedly that he'd seen Connor, and someone would ask where and he would say here and Caroline would wake up in the middle of the night to Abigail strangling her.

Taylor raised his hands in surrender. "Whoa," he said.

"Okay, okay! I won't tell, but what will you give me for it?" He winked, pushing at her shoulder with one finger.

She could feel the way his body pulled toward hers like a magnet. He took a step forward and she stopped him with a hand on his chest. She'd spent all year laughing at his jokes and returning his winks, bargaining with her lips and chest and hips. She looked at the shimmer of hope in his eyes and wanted to smother it. "Nothing," Caroline said. Her voice was flat.

He didn't step back, and the smile was still on his face. Caroline could smell the clean scent of his fabric softener. "Wow, tough crowd here today," he said, looking her over, their eyes at the same level. She couldn't help it. She felt her mouth turn up at the corners. "How 'bout just a conversation? I think I deserve that, at least." His tone was light, but she thought she detected a hint of sadness. She glanced at the house, and when she looked back, his smile was gone, his hands in his front pockets. She wasn't being fair to him, she thought.

"Okay," Caroline said. "But not here." They walked toward the lake, far enough apart that there was no way their hands could brush against each other. By now the grasshopper carcasses had almost completely disintegrated, and yet every few steps, one late survivor's body crunched beneath their heels. "So my phone's been off," Caroline said.

He looked down the hill at the lake, his face shining in the sunlight, his gray T-shirt beginning to darken between his shoulder blades, and wiped the sweat from his head. "But everything's okay with us?" he said, and then more embarrassed, "You're not like, I don't know, pregnant or anything, right?" His eyes were soft.

Caroline laughed. "No, I'm not pregnant." She was still on her period. Her tampon was itching her this very moment. He didn't return the laugh. Instead, he cocked his head to the left and turned toward her. She refused to look over, fixed her eyes on a branch by the dock that was stuck in the tall cattails, bobbing up and down in the shallow water.

"Okay, what is going on with you, then?" he said. Beneath their feet the dry grass gave way to rocky sand and then to the creaking wood of the dock. They walked closer together now—Taylor looking at Caroline, Caroline looking at the grayish water visible between the slats. She dropped down onto the edge and felt the warm boards through her denim shorts. He sat beside her, one leg hanging over, the other bent at the knee, close to his chest. She sat cross-legged, their legs less than an inch apart. "I know we haven't talked a lot in general, but I don't know. I thought sex might be kind of a big deal to you and, since you disappeared, I thought you might be mad at me or something." His hand hovered over her knee for a second as if to give her the chance to move her leg. When she didn't, he lowered it. His palm was smooth; his fingers were curled, barely touching her skin. It was only a hand on her knee, Caroline told herself, though she knew if her sister appeared, she'd swat it away like a wasp.

But Caroline couldn't focus on Taylor right now. She couldn't stop thinking about Abigail, about the set of her jaw when she'd glanced at her on her way out the door, about the darkness in her eyes, the concrete wall she'd already built in between them. They'd worked through these difficult moral dilemmas together this summer and then all it took was Connor's arrival for everything to fall apart. Their happiness seemed so fragile.

"I'm fine, Taylor—really." Caroline looked at him for the first time and saw the worry written across his brow. He seemed so much younger than her, naive and hopeful and a little dumb.

"I imagine it's a lot," he was saying. "With your sister and your dad and . . ." The water lapped gently at the shore, tiny waves carrying ripples of sunlight. The center of the lake was stained pink from the sunset, reflecting the orange sky above, the deep blue of a few scattered clouds. Taylor continued on but Caroline didn't hear much more of it.

Maybe, she thought, Taylor had always been a distraction. She hadn't known everything was crumbling back when Abigail first found out about their father's affair and started dating Matthew, but she could have felt it somewhere deep in her bones and reacted, craved another feeling to override it, choosing lust in her haste, in her desperation—and there he was. She watched as he pushed the hair off his forehead, his shoulders rippling with the motion, and she felt nothing. Her former desire for him was inaccessible now.

"I'm sorry about your dad," Taylor was saying. "Once my mom told me what happened, I thought you needed some space. But at the same time, I thought we were having fun, and didn't want you to be upset with me for peacing out like that."

Caroline nodded. She couldn't think of any other response. Taylor fidgeted, drumming his hands on the dock, tossing some small sticks he found into the lake, where they plunged into the water and disappeared.

"Do I need to apologize to you?" he asked.

"Taylor, no," Caroline said. "You don't need to apologize."

"Well, I might need to after I say this next thing, okay? So if you're mad, you can tell me."

"Okay," Caroline said, and she turned to really listen to him for the first time since they'd sat down, noticed his shoulders creeping toward his ears.

"I really liked you, Caro. I still do, kind of." *Kind of.* "But it doesn't seem like you want me around." He waited, looking out at the water.

"I'm sorry," Caroline said. "I really am." She didn't correct him, though. She didn't know what she wanted, but it seemed like he needed something from her that she didn't have to give.

"No, don't be." He patted her back like he was her Little League coach. She waited for the relief to flood her, but the lightness she'd expected never came. Instead her heartbeat rose up into her throat. She wanted to be the one to end things.

She looked back over her shoulder toward the house. It had seemed so far away before, and now his car seemed close enough to hit with a rock, the sky low enough to reach out and grab. If Taylor left her, she didn't have anyone left. She would be all alone. She wanted his crush and his lips and him wanting her even if she didn't want him back. She wanted to be the person someone, anyone, woke up thinking about in the morning and texted before they fell asleep at night. Caroline turned to him, grabbed a handful of his T-shirt, and kissed him square on the lips. His were soft and open, his body relaxed. He put the heels of his hands on her shoulders and gently pushed her away.

"Caro, I need to move on," he said. "I feel like I'm stuck in this." He gestured to indicate a cyclone, but she didn't provide the word for him. He hung his head. "I can't keep doing this thing," he said, still looking at the dock. "Another girl wants to date me and she, like, really likes me." He looked up at the sky, trying to avoid her eyes, "and I want to be liked back."

"Who?" Caroline asked. After she said it, she realized that he had been giving her the opportunity to say that no, she really did like him and would choose him. But she didn't. They both knew she didn't.

"Sarah Delvy," he said. She was a year younger than them at Hope High, a soccer player, with a ponytail thicker than Caroline's forearm.

Now Caroline was the one looking up and away, pressing her tongue hard against the roof of her mouth, trying not to cry. He turned his shoulders toward her, and with the sun behind him, his features disappeared. She felt the same power she'd harnessed when she'd climbed on top of him. He wanted her. She could ask him to stay. She could have someone of her own. But wasn't this exactly what she was trying to protect Abigail from? She let the moment pass. They sat listening to the lap of the water beneath them, not touching, legs swinging off the dock. "Oh, okay," Caroline heard herself say. "That's totally fine."

"Can I ask . . ." He waited for her to look at him, motioned toward the house.

"It's a long story, but it's my fault that he's here." Caroline told him everything as quickly as she could. Once it was out, she felt slightly relieved. "I'm miserable about it, though."

He laughed. How dare he laugh. "Why?" he asked. "It doesn't seem like that big of a deal." He was a good guy, Caroline thought, but a little dense about things. He did not understand her situation at all.

"It is," Caroline said. She looked right at him to convey her seriousness. She did not need his unconditional support here. Her actions were unforgiveable. She deserved whatever punishment Abigail chose for her.

"Don't be so hard on yourself," he said. "It was a mistake! She'll forgive you."

Caroline looked up at the house and remembered the dullness in Abigail's eyes, her grip on her arm, and knew that he was wrong.

"You don't have a sister," she said.

Taylor ran a hand through his hair and drummed his fingers on the edge of the dock. Caroline rested her elbows on her knees, her forehead in her hands. He tried to touch her shoulder to reassure her and she pushed his hand away. He pulled his leg up over the side of the dock and stood, reached down to help her to her feet. Caroline grabbed his hand and felt for the briefest of moments the spark that had faded between them.

"I should go," he said. "Seems like you want to be alone with your sister."

They walked up the hill to the house. Caroline's T-shirt was stuck to the middle of her back with sweat.

She saw Abigail and Connor saying their goodbyes on the front porch. Abigail stretched up to hug him, and not a side-hug either, a real one. Caroline averted her eyes. Taylor watched. She hit him on the arm with the back of her hand and he looked away.

They went straight to Taylor's car, changing their direction away from the porch. Caroline tried to focus her gaze on the canvas tear near the driver's-side window, the pine-tree air freshener that hung from the rearview mirror.

Taylor unlocked his Jeep, leaned over, and kissed her on the cheek. "Are we cool, Caro?"

"Yeah," Caroline said. "We're cool."

"Are you sure?" Taylor asked.

Connor was descending the stairs now.

"Yes," Caroline said, turning away from him before he'd even closed the door and running toward the house.

"Thank you," she heard Connor say as she hurried past him, but she didn't bother to stop. Abigail was turning the handle, stepping across the threshold, closing the door behind her with a thud even though she knew Caroline was coming right after her.

Caroline reopened the front door. She heard the sink running in the kitchen, the clanging of dishes being scrubbed. She ran to her sister.

"Abigail," she said. "Abigail, please talk to me. Please."

"I don't want to talk to you," she said, scrubbing the steel wool against the bottom of a pot.

"Abby, I need to explain. Please let me explain."

Abigail gripped the edge of the counter with both hands, bowed her head, and said a short prayer, speaking to the Lord instead of to Caroline. She had pulled her hair up into a ponytail that fell over her face. Caroline took another step toward her. Abigail reached over and turned off the water, raised her head, and threw her ponytail over her shoulder. She pivoted to look at her sister.

"What exactly do you think you're going to explain? You're going to somehow explain why you invited my ex-boyfriend to come here and talk to me like I'm some kind of child who doesn't know what she needs—and after all the conversations we've had about what I know is right and what I want for my life? Like I would want to be his sloppy seconds after his marriage fell apart?" Abigail paused to take a breath.

"Abby, that's not what I meant—" Caroline heard the whine in her voice.

"No," Abigail said, pointing a finger at her. "You don't

get to talk. I get to talk." Every line of her body was angular, pointed now.

Caroline bit her lip. She didn't deserve to argue. Abigail was right. Abigail could have slapped her across the face and she still would have been in the right.

"How dare you invite him here," her sister said, taking a step forward. It felt as if she were looking down her nose at Caroline. "I have been honest with you this summer in a way that I guess I probably shouldn't have." Her back was straight, one hand on her hip, the other emphasizing her words with a side-to-side motion like she was wiping away their time together. "I am happy," she said, enunciating each word. "And I do not need whatever it is that you think I need."

ABIGAIL MOVED AROUND Caroline for the rest of the night. Caroline was like a lamp, an unloved portrait, a glass whose water had evaporated. Her sister was silent making dinner. Afterward, she marched out the front door without asking Caroline to join her. Caroline followed along behind anyway, watching as her sister snapped twigs from trees. She felt her distance like a sunburn.

After they returned to the house, Abigail went to the kitchen to call Matthew. Caroline hovered in the doorframe until Abigail shot her a look mean enough to send her away. Caroline was washing her face in the bathroom when she saw Abigail walk by with her pillow pressed to her stomach. She rushed out into the hall right as her sister disappeared into the guest bedroom.

"You're leaving?" Caro said.

"Go to bed," Abigail said as she untucked the corner of the striped duvet, switched on the bedside lamp. "We have to be up early tomorrow and we don't need bags under our eyes onstage."

"Okay, but can't we talk about this, Abby?" Caroline began to cry. "Please, Abby. I need to talk to you. I need to talk about this."

She took a step forward, toes just inside the door. Abigail looked up then, her eyes like daggers. Caroline backed out of the room. Her sister walked across the hardwood floor. Caroline's heart rate increased.

"I do not want to talk to you," Abigail said, and closed the door in her face.

18

The next morning sleep followed Caroline around, burying itself in the pockets under her eyes and behind her nose. Outside, the sky was clear and relentless. She ran the water in the tub, dragged the razor over her calves up to her knee. She pulled on a new pair of underwear, latched a bra across her stomach and twisted it around. Her abdomen was nearly translucent. In the mirror, she could see her green blood traveling toward her heart around her breastbone, the veins circling. She traced her finger over them.

She'd always been taught that inside your heart, somewhere near your soul, was a very precise vacancy shaped like Christ. Pastors said He was the only one who could make a person feel complete—and Caroline had never known a life without Christ. She was a chosen child, redeemed. Now she knew that the space really existed because she felt it vacant and wanting there beneath her ribs. But it wasn't due to her loss of faith. It was the loss of her sister.

In the room they'd shared, she stepped into the blue dress

Abigail had hung on her door. Caroline found her in the kitchen, showered and dressed in a flowery button-up shirt over a long black skirt. She looked trendy, beautiful as always. Her hair was so blond it was almost white around her face. She'd straightened and sprayed it so it hung sharp and unmoving. Their mother, Caroline knew, would hate it.

"I like your hair," she said. Abigail sat at the kitchen table, hovering a finger over a verse in her Bible. She paused, took a sip from her mug, and continued reading.

"There's coffee in the pot," she said to the table, waving a hand toward the counter. "Matthew will be here soon." She did not look up. Caroline grabbed a mug from the cabinet, knocked it against the door, set it hard on the counter. Abigail was undisturbed.

"Wait, why is Matthew coming?" Her hands shook as she spoke, spilling her coffee onto the floor as she carried it to the table.

"I asked him to come for the reinstatement," Abigail said, still staring at the Bible.

"When?" *Please*, Caroline thought, *at least acknowledge that I'm here.*

Abigail didn't look up. "Last night," she said. "I want him here." She spoke as if Caroline were one of her students, annoying her for the hundredth time that day. Abigail grabbed a pen and underlined a verse.

Caroline sipped her coffee, tried to think of something to ask her sister that wouldn't annoy her further. She fiddled with the few remaining puzzle pieces on the table in front of her, hoped Abigail would finish reading and talk to her. She looked up every time her sister turned a page or sipped her coffee or breathed. She had fit three puzzle pieces into place when she heard the front door open.

Matthew let himself in, bounding into the kitchen. Abigail looked up, right past Caroline to where he stood in the doorway, a smile spreading across her face so bright and full that Caroline almost felt like she was being stabbed. Abigail rose from her chair and hugged him tightly. He kissed her on the cheek, his arm around her waist. She pressed her hips into his. Caroline wanted to get away, but now he was opening his arms to her. She stood and hugged him. Maybe this meant that Abigail hadn't told him everything.

"What's up, Caro?" he said, releasing her.

"Nothing, I guess," Caroline said.

"Yeah," he said, and his voice sounded a little sad. She could see in the way he shifted his weight that Abigail had filled him in on everything that was going on with their parents.

"Matthew and I are going to talk on the porch alone for a bit," Abigail said, grabbing his hand and brushing past her. "Fix your hair and makeup while we're out there. Be ready to go in thirty."

Abigail pulled Matthew around the corner. Caroline rose too, followed them down the hallway before they disappeared out the front door. Matthew pulled it closed behind him. Caroline peered through the blinds of her bedroom and saw that they were facing each other, their faces tight, voices a low murmur, a mirror of the fights she'd seen their parents have too many times. She couldn't read their lips, but their shoulders were tense. Matthew was frowning. Maybe he was taking her side, Caroline thought. He glanced toward her window right then, and she dropped the blinds, fleeing from view.

In the bathroom, she tried to apply her eyeliner, made a mess of it, and was forced to start over again. She smoothed some product in her hair. Now it looked even messier. It never looked neat. She gave up and twisted the top half into a clip as she'd seen her sister do a thousand times. Better, she thought. Acceptable.

Caroline had shoved the deodorant stick down the neck of her dress and under her armpit when Abby knocked twice. "Let's go. Car's running," she said.

Caroline swung open the bathroom door a moment later, but her sister was gone. The lights in the house were off too. She walked down the front hallway alone, saw the shadow of Matthew's car through the stained-glass window in the door. She grabbed her Bible out of the front room, untouched for weeks now, stepped out into the sweltering heat, and locked the door behind her.

In the car it felt as if any sudden movement might destroy the delicate truce. Matthew turned on the radio. Abigail seemed to be pulling away from them both. Caroline noticed Matthew shooting looks at her sister. Abigail stared straight out the window. Caroline closed her eyes and tried to focus on anything other than her sister and their father's reinstatement.

They arrived at the church at 9:45 on the dot. As Matthew pulled into the parking lot, Caroline began to feel sick to her stomach. She wasn't sure she could go in there and face everyone. She didn't want to make small talk and sing worship songs and pretend she was happy.

"You coming, Caro?" Matthew said, already standing outside the car. Caroline unbuckled herself from the back seat and opened the door.

THE CHURCH WAS solemn: the overhead lights dimmed to a dull orange, battery-operated candles flickering on the welcome booth and the table with sign-ups for the Men's Retreat. The curtains were drawn and an amber candle had been burned some time ago. It all felt surprisingly holy to Caroline.

In the entryway, Luke and Ruthie Nolan were surrounded by early arrivals, every one of them staring adoringly at Caroline's father, patting him on the shoulder. She counted every step they took toward their parents, thinking it was still possible to turn around and leave. But when Ruthie saw them it was over. Her eyes locked on Abigail and her smile dulled slightly. She looked both girls up and down as they joined the circle. Ruthie frowned at Caroline, licked her hand, and used it to smooth a few stray hairs. Caroline pulled away.

"There are my daughters," Luke said, his chest broadening. Their mother smiled up at him, patted him on the shoulder. He'd remembered this time. Caroline buried her scream so far beneath a pile of social graces that all that escaped was a *hello*.

Luke Nolan was back.

He hugged each of his daughters in turn. His body was stiff against Caroline's, arms wrapping around her but leaving room between them. Caroline felt small. It was clearly a hug for their audience. He held each of his girls by the shoulders for a moment. "It's good to see you," he said. "Thank you for coming." Caroline didn't respond. She took her cue from Abby and, once released, turned to talk to someone else.

He greeted them like they were guests, which in a way they were. This was the longest Caroline had ever gone without attending a service. While Abby laughed at anecdotes and bounced children on her hip, Caroline resisted the urge to turn and walk right out the front door. Maybe her happiness in this space had been completely dependent on her belief, or maybe her belief had blinded her to all of the things that should have been making her unhappy all along.

Everything was the same as it had always been—the kiosk with the photos, the stacks of Luke Nolan's books, the banners advertising the Youth Ministry's fall mission trip, the T-shirts with I GOT IT stenciled across the shoulders, the light snacks and the smell of burnt coffee, the knowledge that Caroline still had no idea what her father thought or knew or wanted. Luke disappeared as more congregants arrived. His daughters were not afforded that same luxury. They hugged. They said hello. They talked about the wedding as much as they could to avoid talking about anything else. Their mother flitted about like a bee from group to group.

"We've missed you two," women said to them both, while their tone said, *How dare you disappear instead of supporting your father.* Abigail smiled, her hand intertwined with Matthew's, at everyone except Caroline.

The worship pastor, a man in his midthirties with tattooed forearms showing beneath his rolled button-up, a brimmed hat perched high on his head, approached Abigail, placed two fingers on the top of her shoulder. "Ya got a second? I've got a proposal," he said.

Abigail excused herself from the circle of people, leaned close to whisper something into Matthew's ear. "I'll see y'all in there," she said to Ruthie, and turned to follow the worship pastor through the big double doors into the auditorium.

"I'll go grab our seats," Caroline offered, leaving the group before anyone could stop her and trying to catch up to her sister.

Caroline looked around the auditorium. Abigail wasn't by the stage or the sound booth or the nursing mothers' room.

The screens above the stage were black and candles had been lined up along the edge. A single spotlight illuminated the cross mounted on the back wall as congregants filed into their seats. Caroline went to their usual row and waited with her hands folded gently in her lap, her Bible on the chair to her left, two programs on those to her right. She did not stand and chat. She did not wave. A few women came through the row in front of her. "How are you?" they asked with questioning eyes. Caroline had no idea how she answered.

After a few minutes, her section began to fill.

"Can you scootch down one, Caro?" Matthew asked, and she did. Ruthie slid past her to her right and Matthew sat down on her left. Abigail would sit in the aisle seat, where she could best view the stage, the one farthest away from Caroline.

She waited a few moments before leaning over to ask Matthew, "Where's Abby?"

"She's backstage," he said.

"What? Why?" Caroline looked at the side door as if she could will her sister to walk through it.

He looked confused. "Oh, Pastor Aaron asked her to help with worship again today, since it's part of the process of, like, getting everything back to normal."

"And she said yes?" Caroline bit the inside of her lip. She had thought they were in agreement that this whole day was immoral. They hadn't wanted to come. Both of them. And now Abby was part of the service.

"I dunno, Caro. I heard him ask her and she hasn't come back, so I assume that's where she is," he said.

Next to her, Ruthie scrunched up her face and smiled at the toddler in front of her with the death grip on her pinky finger and chatted with the woman to her right. Caroline had wanted to believe that the revelations about her father would reshape the church, and here were the people she'd known all her life milling about, smiling, laughing, everyone so eager to forget. The chatter was quieter than usual in the darkened room, and when the light illuminating the cross switched off, each member said *excuse me*, and *so sorry*, and *thank you*, until they too were seated and facing the stage. Here it was: Caroline's old life, ready to slip back on like a broken-in boot. But did she want it? Did it want her?

Only the two of them emerged at first, a pair of dark figures on a dark stage. A guitar strummed three high single notes followed by a chord; a spotlight flickered on, pointing straight down, revealing Abigail Nolan front and center. Caroline heard the murmur of approval ripple through the crowd. The worship pastor stood to her right. His silver wedding ring gleamed as he carefully switched chords, his palm muting the strings.

Abigail's first note was flat. She took a step back from the microphone, cleared her throat, and he started again. She began lower this time. For the first chorus of "In Christ Alone," she sang unaccompanied. This was a hymn made for singers and she knew it, pacing it so that the echo of her voice had time to fully fade between each verse. She kept her eyes closed, three fingers on the microphone, her other hand patting out the beat against the hip of her skirt.

The lyrics came up on the screen, projected below her image, and the congregation joined in, voices breaking as they tried to keep up with her. In between verses, she opened her eyes and smiled at the audience. Caroline knew she couldn't see them through the light but they were smiling back at her just the same. Abigail jumped an octave above them for the line "Sin's curse has lost its grip on me."

Caroline sang along with her sister, her voice trembling. This felt like such an obvious endorsement of his reinstatement. She looked over at Matthew. He was staring up at Abigail, a proud look on his face. Caroline was confused. She wanted to march up on that stage and drag her down from there. Why would Abigail choose their father over her? She searched her sister's toothless smile, her gracious eyes for any hint of the girl she'd spent the past few weeks on the ranch with, and found nothing.

During a brief pause, as the worship pastor strummed, three more musicians joined them onstage—a bassist, a pianist, and a drummer.

Abigail looked straight at the camera in the back of the auditorium as she began her next song.

You caught me when I was in failure
When sin had won
And evil reigned.

Caroline's eyes darted to her mother, whose hand now covered her open mouth.

And there you found me at my weakest
And in my pain
You rescued me.

Matthew leaned over to Caroline, not taking his eyes off Abby. "Did you know she was going to sing this?"

"I did not," Caroline said.

Above them her sister's voice jumped another octave.

And without you I am worth nothing
And in your grace you loved me still
When fires burn, my soul will stay
Safe in your clutch
Your mercy reigns.

Abigail had finished writing the song two years ago, after spending hours in her bedroom pressing the notes on her keyboard until she was convinced each line was perfect. When it was done, she'd submitted it to the church's songwriting committee, who'd helped her add accompaniment and get it theologically approved by the senior pastors. They'd rehearsed it a few times, and then Abby had refused to let them perform it. The song was too difficult, she said, and she was right. She was the only one on the Hope worship team who could hit all its notes, and who had the confidence to sing the long belt at its emotional center. She said worship wasn't about showing off, and that the song was more for her glory than God's, and so she benched it.

Now here she was. The song was nine minutes long and she was nearing the end. She gripped the microphone with both hands, removed it from its stand, her eyes still closed. The worship pastor stood beside her strumming his guitar. He mattered so little to the performance that even the spotlight barely graced his shoulder. On the third repeat of the chorus, a drumbeat kicked in, and she began to bounce on her toes. Around them, hands rose. Caroline heard a woman behind her sobbing. Ruthie grabbed her hand and held it tightly. The drumbeat rose, the guitar stopped. Abigail's head tilted back and it began.

"Oh Jesus saves," she sang. "I do not deserve the presence of my Savior." And when she hit that last word, her voice rose for one octave, two, spiked at a note so crisp every hair on Caroline's body stood on end, and then her vocals fell down for one bar. Two. Three.

She was absolutely perfect.

And then the drums were gone and it was just Abigail again, repeating the same verse, quietly this time, her eyes open and full of power. The piano faded; the guitar next to her played its last chord.

"Dear Heavenly Father," she said, both hands gripping the microphone. Next to her, the worship pastor's jaw dropped. He forced it closed. Her mother's hand flew to Caroline's shoulder and squeezed. Caroline reopened her eyes and saw her sister at the center of the stage, her left hand raised high, her head bowed.

Everyone knows that a woman does not open a service in prayer. Pastors do. But here was Abigail Nancy Nolan with her eyes closed, the microphone pointing at her glossed lips, tucking a strand of hair behind her ear and saying, "We come before You today broken people, a broken church. Together we have been forced to recognize Your power and Your guidance in our lives. Perhaps before all of this we had forgotten that You are the one we should be lifting up, O Lord, that You are the first and true leader of this church. We come before You as Your bride, and beg that You allow those of us who are still in sin to see that and to repent. We ask that You remind us of who You are, O God, and use this sermon, this day, this space, for Your holiness alone. In Your Son's name I pray."

She waited one beat, two. "Amen," she said, and then looked up and out at the auditorium, her sun-bleached hair falling back over her shoulder, a tear running down her cheek, glistening on the screens behind her.

It wasn't beauty making her sister radiate on that stage, Caroline thought, it was fury. Abigail bent into a humble bow. Only Caroline recognized the rage in her eyes. She wasn't endorsing him. She was staking a claim to his pulpit.

The applause was deafening as she descended the stairs at the side of the stage. Abigail stared down at the floor and returned to the aisle seat her fiancé had saved for her, smoothed her skirt under her butt and sat beside him.

"Abby," he said, "that was so good. I'm so proud of you."

She shushed him. Luke Nolan was coming out from the wings, accompanied by Pastor Mark. They both wore blue button-ups. Their father's fit him better. The whole auditorium stood for him. Caroline did too. He smiled out at his congregation.

"I'd pray to open us," Pastor Mark said, stepping forward then, "but somebody better beat me to it." His tone was jovial, but there seemed to be resentment in his eyes. He exchanged a look with their father.

"We are thrilled to welcome back Pastor Luke Nolan," Pastor Mark said, hugging his friend and descending the stairs on the right, leaving their father alone on the stage.

Luke took a deep breath and let out a long sigh into the microphone, and then smiled using every one of his straight white teeth. He tilted his head, making eye contact with a dozen people around the room. "It's good to be back," he said. And the audience gave him the second round of applause he wanted.

"Four weeks ago, I brought my wife and my daughters up here on the stage and promised you—" He paused, waving to

Ruthie, who waved back with her left hand, her diamond ring flickering in and out of Caroline's vision, her eyes wrinkling at the corners with her smile. "Promised the Lord that we would seek Him through this storm, and continue to serve the people of the Hope to the best of our abilities."

He took a deep breath. "On Thursday, the elder board voted to formally reinstate me. We could spend a whole long time talking about what happens next. But the long and short of it is that I have repented. I have been forgiven more than I deserve, and I am blessed to have been helped through this struggle and this time of trial by the Lord and my community."

Caroline had to stifle a bitter laugh. She recognized some of the phrasing. It was lifted straight from the reinstatement announcement the Houston pastor had used. She had watched it many times on YouTube. She knew what came next and tried to get her sister's attention. Abigail remained facing forward, toward him, her jaw clenched. "The Bible tells us that Satan prowls like a roaring lion, seeking those he can devour. Our church has been attacked through me, but we will continue to seek the Lord."

His every word after that dropped like a stone. None of them floated like Abigail's. He said "fade" instead of "faith." He messed up in the middle of a verse and was forced to start again. To Caroline's left, her sister's knee bobbed up and down. Matthew rested his hand there until it stopped. Her sister must have contributed more to his sermons than she'd admitted, Caroline thought. Caroline leaned forward and tried to make eye contact with Abigail, but her mother's hand was firm on her shoulder, pushing her back.

"If it's all right with y'all"—the screens above the stage

were tight on his face—"I'd like to get back to talking about the Lord."

They applauded him again, and a few whoops rang out from the youth group section. Caroline looked around. Everyone was clapping. A woman behind her dabbed at a few tears with a handkerchief. "Turn to your Bibles with me, then," he said. "To Acts Nine."

Caroline saw her sister stiffen and recross her legs. Caroline flipped to Acts 9 and stifled a gasp. It was Paul. Their father's first sermon back and he was going with the redemption of Paul. He began to preach about the Lord meeting Paul and converting him, how He transformed this hateful man into one of His greatest disciples. Caroline forced her jaw to close. Their father was positioning himself as the only one who could lead Hope.

"'Day and night they kept close watch on the city gates in order to kill him,'" he read. "'But Paul's followers took him by night and lowered him in a basket through an opening in the wall.'" He paused. Beneath the spotlight, his forehead was beaded with sweat. "The Lord," he said, now reading from the teleprompter in the back, "protects His disciples, uses us for His Glory and His Holy Purpose even when we are at our worst."

He took hold of the podium with both hands. "I am so grateful that the Lord sent His only son to die on a cross for me. So that I can be redeemed and forgiven. So that I can continue to serve Him." Caroline rolled her eyes, but people all around her clapped. Onstage, he smiled. Once again, Luke Nolan, pastor of the third-largest evangelical church in the great state of Texas, had been redeemed.

Christians, she thought as he spoke, were called to forgive. *Bear with each other and forgive one another if any of you has a grievance against someone. Forgive as the Lord forgave you.* The Bible was clear on this point. Caroline rested her elbows on her knees and her head in her hands, and heard his voice drone on: "Now, I know this has been a time of struggle for all of us, and I am certain that we will come through this stronger in Christ together."

Caroline shook her head and knew she couldn't forgive him, and though she tried to bury the thought, it rose to the surface again and again. She had spent many years in Bible studies. Her brain provided her a verse that promised she could do all things through Christ who strengthened her. But could she? She hadn't prayed in months, and every time she tried to open her Bible she grew frustrated and gave up. She no longer had Christ to strengthen her, and she couldn't turn to the one person she'd always gone to with any crisis of faith because she no longer trusted his guidance. Tears began to fall down her face. She wiped them with the back of her hand.

Her mother patted the middle of her back as Luke asked everyone to bow their heads and pray. The acoustic guitar strummed along behind him, and when he said the word *amen*, the musicians began to play again. By the last song, Caroline too was standing, singing with the rest of the congregation until the final chord faded, and then she joined the crowd of people walking quietly to the atrium.

THE LIGHTS WERE turned back up and everyone around her seemed to be smiling, yelling over the person next to them.

Ruthie disappeared into the crowd, waving goodbye to the girls. Caroline stepped closer to Matthew and Abby. "Wasn't that a great sermon?" a woman asked, approaching the three of them. "Yes," they said. "Yes, it was wonderful. Yes, we are so happy to have him back." She kissed both Caroline and Abigail on the cheek and left before Caroline could remember her name. Another woman was coming toward them, tapping people on the shoulder as she pushed through the crowd.

"Do we have to stay for this part?" Matthew said.

"No," Abigail and Caroline said at the same time.

"But if we're going to leave, we need to do it before anyone notices," Abigail finished. So the three of them fled, pushing out through the double doors and practically running to the car, peeling out of the back entrance and onto the highway.

They rode in silence all the way back to the ranch, Abigail's knee bouncing, Matthew drumming his fingers on the steering wheel. Caroline tried to focus on the passing farmland outside her window instead of the discomfort growing inside her heart.

ABIGAIL WENT FOR their afternoon walk with Matthew, leaving Caroline on the front porch alone, tearing a piece of grass between her hands. She drank soda water from a glass bottle and tried to read a novel, but couldn't get her eyes to focus on the words for long enough.

She heard noise from inside the house—Abigail and Matthew clattering around the kitchen, pulling out pots and pans. They must have come through the back door. The sky was almost dark when Matthew popped his head out the front. "Dinner," he said.

The table was set with silverware and cloth napkins. Caroline sat in her usual seat, slicing into the chicken breast in front of her. There was asparagus with lemon and mashed potatoes on the side. Caroline had to stop herself from shoveling it all into her mouth at once.

"So, are you excited to go off to school?" Matthew said after they'd taken several bites in silence.

"Yes," Caroline said, a hand over her mouth, still chewing.

"What are you most excited about?" He looked her in the eyes. It felt too intimate. Caroline looked away.

"I don't know," she said, cutting another bite of chicken. "Leaving?"

She kept telling everyone, herself included, that she was excited to go off to school, and she was. Because at the very least she wouldn't be stuck in this hellhole her entire life.

Matthew laughed. "Yeah, I remember that feeling."

"Are you excited for Abby to come live with you in West Texas?" Caroline said. He looked back at her with a puzzled expression and then over at her sister. Abby was cutting her chicken into perfect cubes. He looked back at Caroline.

"I'm confused," he said, a line appearing between his brows. Caroline glanced at Abigail, but she didn't look up from her food.

"After the wedding? Are you excited that you and Abby will finally get to live together?" This was supposed to be small talk, she thought. It shouldn't be this hard to talk to someone who was about to become a part of your family.

"I'm excited to live together for sure," he said, and set down his fork. He pushed his plate forward and folded his arms on the table in front of him. "But Caro"—his voice was gentle, like he was talking to a child—"we've decided to stay in Hope."

Caroline sat up straight in her chair. "Abby," she said, turning to her sister.

Abigail tucked her hair behind her ears, put another bite of chicken into her mouth, and reached across the table to grab Matthew's hand.

"We really think it would be good for us to be here since all of this family stuff is going on." He waved his hand in the air as if "family stuff" were referring to a collection of parties he didn't want to attend and not to their father's affair. "We're thinking that after the honeymoon, we might move out here to the ranch so we can have some space and still be nearby."

Abigail pushed her mashed potatoes around her plate. Caroline waited for her to say something, noticed that Matthew was doing the same. She wanted to shove her sister's plate off the table and into her lap so she'd show some emotion, any emotion. She wanted to wad up her napkin and hit her in the face with it.

"When did you decide this?" Caroline asked her sister.

"Just today," Matthew said. And then quieter, "Abby, I thought you said you told her about this and that it was fine."

Now she looked up at him, her hand a fist around her fork. "I said she'd be fine with us staying here at the ranch. Because she will." Her head pivoted to face her sister. Abigail was looking at her as though she were a pane of glass. "Won't you, Caro?"

Caroline felt very far away from her then, as if the table in front of her were receding. "Yes, of course," she said. Of course she'd let them stay on the ranch. That didn't matter to her.

"Why, though? Why stay?" Caroline asked the space

between them. She thought Abigail had decided to leave. The girl who had convinced her to make the call to Pastor Mark hadn't wanted anything to do with their father. Sure, she'd always loved Hope, but they'd come out here to get away from all that. Caroline needed to talk to her sister alone and make sure this was what she really wanted, that she hadn't been persuaded by their father or some misguided family guilt. *Look at me*, Caroline implored her.

Matthew patted Abigail's leg beneath the table. "You should talk to her," he said. Caroline would have kissed him if she could have, she was that grateful.

But her sister seemed miles away, her voice small as she said, "Maybe later."

Matthew left after dinner to drive back to Midland, and it was only the two of them again. They washed the dishes by hand. All the while Abigail said nothing. She handed every plate and cup and spoon to her sister without a look or a word.

Caroline rinsed and placed the dishes on the drying rack. "I don't know what you want me to say. I've apologized a hundred times."

"I know," Abigail said, her knuckles turning white as she scrubbed the saucepan.

"Can we talk about it?" Caroline said, and her voice broke then. Her hands were shaking. She turned to face her sister. She needed to talk about the sermon and the church and Connor and that dinner. Abby was all she had. She had pushed everyone else away.

"Soon," Abigail said, still scrubbing. Caroline grabbed her by the shoulders and forced her to turn and face her. The saucepan slipped and clattered in the sink. Her hands dripped water on the floor.

"I just want to go back to a few days ago. I want it to be you and me again." Caroline's words were piling up, spilling out. "I hate this. I hate being separate from you. I hate that we aren't talking. I hate that I had to sit through that sermon and come home and you went and talked to Matthew about it and I had no one. I hate that you completely changed your plans for the future and I had to learn about it from *him*."

"You still have me," Abigail said, removing Caroline's hands from her shoulders. She turned off the water and wiped her hands on a dish towel. She picked up the pan she'd dropped and set it on the drying rack. Her face didn't move.

"No, I don't!" Caroline yelled. "I don't have you! You hate me!"

"I promise you," Abby said, her voice steady, "I don't hate you." She rested a hand on Caroline's shoulder for a moment and walked out of the kitchen toward the guest room.

"Then why won't you forgive me?" Caroline begged. Her sister stopped, her back to her, shoulders rising and falling. She seemed deflated. How could she refuse? Abby was a Christian, Caroline thought. She would have to forgive her.

"I will," Abby said. She turned around then, massaging her brow with her hand.

"But when? Can't we talk about it? Why won't you talk to me?" Caroline stepped forward.

"I'm stressed, okay? Give me some time." Caroline noticed the dull green of her sister's eyes, the haze of exhaustion that lay just beneath the surface of her perfectly made-up face. It was at least half-true. She turned to head to the guest room, leaving Caroline in the kitchen, a plate in one hand and tears streaming down her face. The wedding was only six days away.

19

The next morning, Abigail transformed into a tornado. Four days disappeared into a list of problems that she'd suddenly realized needed to be solved. Caroline helped her move the couches out of the living room to create more space for the rehearsal dinner. They spot-cleaned the kitchen and outfitted the second bedroom as a bridal suite with candles and her white rehearsal dress. They arranged flowers and made tulle bows and completed a dozen menial chores that felt more important than anything else they'd ever done. Abigail bossed Caroline around and Caroline listened, even though Abigail used these heavy, regret-laden sighs whenever she didn't do something exactly as instructed.

An enlarged photo of the happy couple now sat on an easel to the right of the kitchen table. In it, Abigail and Matthew were sitting on a giant rock. She was holding one perfectly manicured hand over her mouth as she laughed, eyes shining. He was looking at her, and she was looking straight into the camera.

The girls swept old photographs from the walls like cobwebs, stacking and carrying them away so quickly that later, when it was time to rehang them, no one could recall exactly where any of them went. Nearly fifty years of Nannie's magazines, letters, and coasters were hauled into her bedroom, where they created a dividing wall between the double doors that led outside and the bed. The television was placed on top of her dresser.

Tables that Caroline hadn't even known existed were pulled out of the garage and laid on their sides. Once their ribs were kicked into place, the tables were arranged in the living room, and covered with linen. Dozens of framed photographs of Abigail and Matthew as children sat on various surfaces. The floors were scrubbed, the fans dusted, the windows opened for one day to "freshen the air" and then closed the next to sufficiently cool the space.

"Isn't the groom's family supposed to host the rehearsal dinner?" Caroline asked. She was carrying a box of tiny flowerpots filled with M&M's that were the same blush tone as her bridesmaid's dress.

"Yes," Abigail said with a laugh, "but can you imagine Matthew's family doing all this?"

She couldn't. Matthew's family would have planned something simpler and cheaper—two words that were practically heresy to any good Texas bride. As a compromise, the Nolans had kept it as simple as they could manage, hosting the event at Nannie's ranch for a small group of thirty and delegating most of the decorating and cooking to family friends.

Abigail and Caroline spent their last day alone together dusting the edges of picture frames, straightening knick-knacks no one would ever notice. Abigail was looking at her again, even touching her as they worked side by side, though they didn't talk about anything other than the wedding and went off to their own bedrooms in the evening (Caroline miserably).

Ruthie showed up the day before the rehearsal dinner with her own list of tasks, carrying Abigail's wedding dress over her head like a state flag, its train folded up inside the zipped white bag. Her demeanor was the same as always, as if nothing had happened between them at all. Abigail's hair was in a low braid, her black T-shirt tucked into high-waisted oversized shorts. She looked ready for more deep cleaning. An hour before it was time to retrieve her fiancé's extended family from the airport, she locked herself inside the bathroom, applying makeup, curling the bottom of her hair with a straightener. When she finally emerged, her eyeliner had a sharp wing and her sundress had been steamed. Her movements were stiff again. Caroline had thought this version of her sister was gone forever, but it seemed she had only been hiding.

"You look cute!" Ruthie exclaimed on their way out the front door, keys in hand.

"Thanks," Abby said, leaving Caroline with the list of things that needed to be done before the rehearsal the following day.

THEY'D BEEN GONE twenty minutes when Caroline heard the creak of the cattle gate. She assumed they'd forgotten something. A car meandered up the gravel drive and parked outside the front porch; a door slammed.

There were boots on the porch before she noticed that it wasn't her mother and sister.

"Hellooooo," he came in yelling. "Ollie ollie oxen free!"

His boots clomped five times on the hardwood floor before he removed them with a thump. He was whistling.

"Anybody home?" he called, his voice projecting from his gut even without a microphone.

In the kitchen, Caroline ducked, a reflexive motion that left her sitting on the floor behind the island, the heels of her hands pressing into her eyes. But he didn't come around the corner from the living room as she'd expected him to, and so when he entered through the doors from the dining room, he saw her there in plain view, his own daughter hiding from him.

"Caroline!" He beamed. "What are you doing?"

"I just—" Only the lie was too far away for her to grab it easily, and so she stood, and accepted the hug her father was already offering, arms out, gangly and unwieldy, like hers. He smelled like the first cold day and hugged like he needed it.

Here was the man who had taught her to ride a bike and drive a car, who held her hand when she got scared at the movies and came to every one of her plays' opening nights, whose eyes filled with tears when she told him she wanted to become a Christian, and who'd clapped when she emerged from the pool of water in his arms blessed in the name of the Father, the Son, and the Holy Spirit. His vocal cadences pumped her blood and his pacing was the metronome of her breath, and yet she felt like she was greeting a stranger.

"It's good to see you," he said, and he sounded sincere, even if his voice clipped at the end like it couldn't quite clear the hurdle of his front teeth.

"You too," Caroline said. She hadn't been alone with him since before the affair had been announced, and she didn't want to be. She moved around him to the kitchen table, where she scanned desperately down the list of tasks, hoping to find one unchecked. Hanging banners would require his help. Place cards, that was it. If she was lucky, she thought, he'd leave her alone.

Caroline scooped up the place cards and carried them into the living room, where they'd set up the tables earlier that morning. She felt his eyes following her, watching her hands flit from the clipboard to the stack of cards, to the table and back again. Ostensibly, he was putting away the dishes, but she could feel him gearing up for one of his talks. Until finally, he set a giant glass punch bowl down on the counter a little too loudly and joined her in the living room.

"Can we talk?" he asked.

"Hm," Caroline said, though she really wanted to say no.

"I have some things that I'd like you to hear from me," he said, speaking to his youngest daughter as if she were a congregant. He was nervous. But she knew that wouldn't stop him from reprimanding her. This must be about the call, she thought. Who knew what Pastor Mark had told him.

"I'm not really in the mood to be lectured," she heard herself say in a tone she recognized as belonging to her mother.

"Hey, that's not fair," he said, raising both hands as if she'd aimed a gun at him.

Between them were dozens of objects: the chair in front of her and the place card for Matthew's mother, the spoon, the two forks, the two knives, a stack of three plates each smaller than the next, the lace tablecloth laid on top of the darker cream tablecloth, and the glasses (one for wine and one for water and one for anything else). And then there were the centerpieces: tall blue vases stacked with chrysanthemums and baby's breath and gentle green flowers that the girls had plucked from the hill where Abigail would be wed in only two days' time. There was a two-foot gap between the narrow tables. All of this between Caroline and her father and she still felt like it wasn't enough.

She finished arranging the cards around the table according to the chart Abigail had made before raising her eyes to finally meet his gaze.

"Okay, okay, fine," he said. "I guess I can do that sometimes."

She had plenty to say in response, but pressed the front of her lips together. The greatest mistake in any fight with Luke Nolan was to try to make the first move. If she began with a question, he would curve his answer. If she offered up any information, he would use it against her. She knew to smile and say nothing until he showed his cards.

Caroline fiddled with the place settings, scooted in chairs, lined up wineglasses as he stood on the other side of the table waiting. This was a game of chicken that she would always win now. Because she didn't care if she ever spoke to him again.

Eventually, he sighed and laid both hands on the back of one of the folding chairs they'd brought in from the garage and covered with fabric so they looked fancier, his torso bent, his hips back, like an Olympic skier waiting for the bell to push off down the hill. His head hung down as he rocked heel to toe until he gathered enough momentum to speak.

"These kinds of things don't end in an instant," he said.

"Mm," she said, pushing the sound out without opening her lips.

"You know what I mean."

"Do I?" She did, but she wanted to see him squirm.

"Caroline, I know you're mad, but your behavior lately—" He paused, shaking his head. "You're being cruel."

Cruel, she thought. *Cruel like lying to your family or cruel like betraying an entire congregation?* She could feel every vein in her body pulsing. Luke Nolan, she thought, deserved to have someone be cruel to him for once—and how apt that he'd interpret being held accountable for his actions as cruelty.

"What behavior are you mad about, exactly? Is it that I called Pastor Mark? Or that I didn't buy your lie the second time?" Caroline's hands shook. If no one else was going to ask him for answers, she would. She had nothing left to lose.

"Fine, Caroline, okay? I cheated on your mother. I had an affair, but I promise you on the Lord's name that it is over, and that I have repented." He raised one hand as if swearing an oath.

As a child, Caroline was always making promises to her father. Promise you aren't lying. Promise you'll come straight home from school. Promise. Promise. Promise. She'd promised with her body. Crossed her heart, hooked her pinky, and spit into the palms of her dirt-covered hands—and Luke Nolan had taught his daughters that promises, real promises, were holy. He'd taught them that God's promises never failed and neither did his. Then he'd broken all of the biggest promises he'd ever made.

The laugh came out of her before she could stop it. He knew so little about her that he didn't realize that swearing on the Lord's name meant almost nothing to her anymore.

"It's over," he repeated.

"When was the last time you saw her?" she said.

He took a deep breath. "In Pastor Mark's office, the day after you made the call."

She inhaled through her nose and reminded herself to stay calm. Every muscle in her body tightened, but she showed him none of it, merely nodded—giving him the space to lie if that's what he wanted. And though she knew better, she hoped he wouldn't.

"You were right that the affair went on for longer than I originally said. I lied to Abigail and I lied to you and I feel deeply ashamed of that. I hope you know that."

"I have the receipt and I have the book with her name in it," Caroline said, and he stiffened, his cheeks reddening.

"Yes, and like I said, I lied about how long the affair went on, and I've apologized for that."

"So you told the elder board that you lied and Mary told the truth?" She wanted to hurt him now.

"Yes," he said.

"Just to be clear: You confessed that you were at the grocery store with her in West Prairie last week playing house?" She watched his face fall. It was unclear whether he was shocked at his daughter's decision to grill him, or at how many details she had on hand to use against him.

"I went over to her house for dinner," he said slowly. "Just for dinner."

"Does Mom know you went to her house for dinner?"

"Yes, Caroline. She does." It sounded true, but she knew better than to trust him.

His emphasis that it had been only for dinner made her skin itch. There was something even more upsetting about him waiting in the car for her to run into the grocery store for supplies, the two of them cooking dinner in her kitchen while her son played piano in the background, the two of them pouring a glass of wine, their hands brushing, no obvious foul play in sight.

She placed the last card at the end of the last table and straightened the runner.

"Ah," she said. "So while in the process of repenting for falling into a sin that ruined all of our lives, you went over to her house for a friendly dinner? Or were those all promises you made so that you could preach again?"

It was too far. The red spread to his nose. "Sit down," he said through gritted teeth.

She thought about it, even pulled out a chair.

"No," she said. His face was red. She remained standing. Was this, she wondered, what it felt like to have power? No wonder he wanted it so much. Her head was light, her body tense, her mind quick.

"You may think you're better than me, Caroline, but we have all sinned and fallen short of the glory of God. I understand that you are angry." His words flew at her. "And I like to think I have been pretty permissive of you two living out here alone even though I disapprove of it, and I think I deserve some credit for that. I am still your father. You will not speak to me in that tone," he said, "ever again." His hands were gripped around a chair on the other side of the table. "Ya got that?"

"Yes, sir," she said. "I got it." But she'd used the forbidden tone, sarcastic and mocking.

"I don't understand why it's so difficult to talk to you about this," he said under his breath. And for the first time in their awkward conversation, Caroline stopped fidgeting and looked into his eyes. "We always"—he sighed—"I always thought we were good."

She didn't bother to tell him that they had never really been good. What was the point? He had always been *good* with her sister. But they would never have that, so she let him believe that they had been once, if that was what he needed.

"Now, what were you trying to ask me?"

How did he end up asking the questions? She took a deep breath. "I still don't understand how it happened," she said. "How you *accidentally* ended up in an affair."

"Caroline, I don't know. I was tempted."

It was the same idea Ruthie had used when she came to tell her daughters about the meeting with Pastor Mark: "being lured by the flesh," she'd said, as if his agency were only his inability to pay more attention.

"Why should I believe you?"

"I guess because you know me. You know who I've always been, my character."

"I thought I did," Caroline said.

"Caro, come on," he whined.

She scooted a place setting an inch to the right one piece at a time. Let him feel the discomfort that he had made her feel.

But he still didn't get it. "We all have areas of sin that are easiest for us to fall into—" he began.

"Sure," she said, cutting him off. "That's an excuse." She looked him square in the face. "But the rule in the house I grew up in was that excuses weren't good enough." She picked up his cadence with her rage. "Why. Did. You. Do it?"

Sin, he had told his daughters their entire life, was debilitating. Fall into a consistent sin, and the guilt created by the Holy Spirit would eat away at you until you were a shell of your former self. But here in Nannie's house, there was absolutely nothing different about him at all. He chewed a toothpick between his molars, laughed at his own jokes with as much ease and enthusiasm as he always had. He was, as her mother promised, still the same man.

"I guess that I was unsatisfied." He ran a hand through his hair. "I liked being with someone who didn't know everything about me."

Caroline's mouth soured.

Luke Nolan, the man who had brought the country Hope, who'd made his name off selling sexual purity, who stood beneath the spotlight onstage every week, was not the same man their mother had married, or who had parented her and Abigail. No. The man they knew had flaws, nightmares. He couldn't remember what he'd promised to pick up at the grocery store, wasn't always so charismatic. He was telling her that he liked the performance more than he liked the person. He wanted to be revered.

Three months ago, Caroline would have felt sympathy at this admission. Of course a person wants to be seen for their best self and not for their inability to close the kitchen cabinets correctly. But now she knew better. She knew that who he was onstage wasn't really him at all. It was Abigail. Abigail wrote his sermons. Abigail studied the Word with him. It was Abigail he wanted to be.

They had that in common too.

Caroline scoffed a little. If he wouldn't show her the same guilt he'd shown Abigail in his office, then she'd make him. She deserved to see it. "Okay. I mean, that doesn't work for me, really. What about the first affair you had? You weren't famous then, so that argument doesn't really make sense." It was a guess, but she said it confidently. From his quick intake of breath, she knew she'd been right. She moved each wineglass two centimeters from the other at the base, lined them up on a diagonal. She didn't have to look at him to feel his eyes widen.

"The . . . what?" he said. "What first affair?"

Their mother hadn't told him everything, then.

"The first affair you had. The woman before Mary."

"How—" he started.

"Does it matter how I know?" Caroline asked. "I think you probably owe me an explanation either way. It's kind of the least you can do."

"There's something broken in me, a thorn in my side," he said. "I have begged the Lord to take it away from me. Your mother, well, I mean, you know how your mother is." He smiled at his youngest daughter. She did not smile back. "Your mother doesn't really . . ."

"This," Caroline said, "is not Mom's fault."

"You're right, Caroline," he said. "It's not. It's not her fault at all. I made this decision, and I have to reckon with its consequences."

"What consequences!" She was yelling now. "Tell me a single consequence you've actually faced! I've faced consequences, and so have Mom and Abby, and so has the Hope." She pointed at him. Her voice was too high. She searched through her arsenal and chose the thing she knew would dent him. "Mary has faced more consequences than you *ever* have." His face crumpled, his eyes squeezed shut.

His discomfort fueled her. "You," she yelled, "are so selfish that you can't even *see* the pain you've caused all around you!" She breathed through her mouth. She had spent her life repressing all this anger that she hadn't known she was allowed to feel. Where had this girl who yelled at her father come from?

"Your buddies at the church may have forgiven you," she said, "but I haven't."

His mouth was open. She saw him take a deep breath, prepare to deliver a scolding sermon, right as the front door opened.

Abigail and Ruthie and Matthew entered the house, all smiles, ready for hugs and handshakes and attention. Caroline was out of breath, struggling to regain it. Abigail accepted their father's hug, let him kiss her on the cheek, glanced between him and her sister. Matthew shook their father's hand, looked him in the eye. "Good to see you," he said.

"Is everything okay in here?" Abigail said. The laughter that had filled the space a moment earlier had been replaced with air so tense it felt like if you snapped your fingers, you might burst into flames.

"Yep," Luke Nolan said, a tight smile on his face. "Everything's just dandy." He looked at each of the women in his family as if waiting for one of them to rush forward and come to his aid. When no one moved, he stomped out of the living room and into the kitchen. Ruthie followed along behind him.

Caroline tried to meet her sister's eyes. "I need to talk to you," she said.

"Okay, later," Abigail said, but there were so few times in the future that could be theirs.

LATER IN THE afternoon, after they'd finished all their preparations and Caroline stood in the kitchen drinking ice water from the fridge out of a tall glass, her father came in and stood beside her, one hand steadying him on the counter.

"I need you to forgive me," he said, and his voice wavered. "I need you to believe me when I say it's over."

Caroline could have said *I want to* or *I'll try*, but she said nothing.

She left him there, with his hands and heart on the counter, and headed out of the bright lights of the kitchen and through the darkened hallway. The women of the Nolan family were strong—and yet because they were quiet, their silence had often been mistaken for weakness. Blessed are the meek, well-meaning churchwomen who would beam up at him as she and Abby stood silently behind their mother as young girls, hair cascading down over their shoulders, for theirs is the Kingdom of Heaven. But heaven was not for her anymore and maybe it never had been.

20

After love, luck is the foundation of any good wedding. It is good luck to pray before the vows, bad luck to see the bride before the event; good luck to rehearse before the sun goes down, bad luck to have a perfect rehearsal. Losing the wedding license is good luck and so is pulling down your underwear to find them soaked with blood. And if someone had told Caroline right then that your mother ignoring your father's affair was also good luck, she wouldn't have been that surprised.

For these were the days of great promise, of joy and heart and love. This was the day before the most important day in a woman's life. To be single, the mythology promised, was an uncertain misery, and this was her sister's final day of it.

The sons of the Hope Church arrived at daybreak the morning of the rehearsal in a pickup truck, pulling a trailer filled with round wooden tables for the reception. They wheeled them to the prearranged spots Ruthie had marked with tape on the ground. Caroline stood at the top of the hill under the arch where her sister would pledge her life to a man Caro-

line still worried might be the wrong one, watching and waiting for the rehearsal to begin.

Abigail was too busy to talk to her, so Caroline dressed an
hour early and ran away from the endless list of incomplete
crafts and delegated tasks. She sat in a white folding chair in
the front row with her legs spread like she wasn't wearing a
skirt. The insides of her thighs were sweaty. This was the only
position that provided some relief. She tugged at the neck of
her rehearsal dress—a nice navy with eyelet windows on the
collar and a defined waist. Every now and then, she looked at
her to-do list and straightened the lines of chairs or adjusted
the ribbons. She was crouched on the ground checking a vase
at the end of an aisle to make sure it was secure when she heard
someone clearing his throat right behind her. She jolted at the
sound.

"Caroline, right?" the man said. She stood to face him.

"Coupla the boys found these out at the far edge of the area
we were mowing." He pointed. "Can you take care of them?"

Before she could say anything, the rings she and Abigail
had thrown into the darkness were back in the palm of her
hand, warm from the earth, their cutout crosses casting sun-
beams on her palm. She slipped them into the pocket of her
dress, where they pressed against her leg as two boys came up
the hill to secure the whitewashed arbor, now ready to be
adorned with flowers.

"What time is it?" she asked one of them. Half an hour
until the rehearsal, they told her. She turned toward the house,
shaded her eyes, and there she was, coming down the stairs
of the porch, hair long and loose, skin gleaming, dress white
and starched. Abigail turned to someone directing table place-
ment, and Caroline watched as that person turned and pointed

a finger up the hill to where she stood. Her sister was looking for her. Caroline tried to seem busy as she approached.

"There you are," Abby said.

"Yup," Caroline said.

"I just needed a break. Everyone is asking me questions and making me absolutely crazy," her sister rambled on. Her hands flitted around as she spoke, her hair shinier than it had been all summer, her eyeliner ending in crisp, aggressive points.

Was this it? Caroline wondered. Were they reconciling? Abigail trailed off. Caroline rocked back and forth on her heels.

"I'm sorry," Caroline said. And she was. For everything.

"Oh, it'll be fine," Abigail said, swatting Caroline's apology out of the air. But she was here, Caroline thought. "Everything will get done," Abigail said. "But if anyone needs me, we are doing very important wedding planning right now." She winked.

Caroline took the hint. "Yes, very important," she said. "We are soooo busy and cannot be disturbed." She would do whatever her sister asked of her, be whoever she needed, just to have her back.

"Exactly," Abigail said, and shifted her weight. The silence brewed between them, every moment a reminder of the thing they still hadn't resolved, Abigail's pointing finger, her lips saying "I do not want to talk to you." She crossed her arms.

Caroline looked out across the field past her sister and saw Taylor, his shoulders buckling as he held up a table and kicked out its legs. He noticed her and lifted his hand in a wave. Bingo, she thought. Why hadn't she thought of this earlier? Abigail followed her gaze and turned back toward her, an eyebrow raised. Caroline handed her sister the last secret she had left and prayed it would be enough.

"The night that Connor came," she said, and her sister's body stiffened, "Taylor was there, remember?" Abigail nodded. "He came by to make sure I was okay with the fact that he is going to date Sarah Delvy now." It was mostly true, at least.

Abigail grabbed her by the shoulders, acrylic nails digging into her flesh. Caroline felt herself filling with joy, and forced her face to remain serious, upset, even.

"Caroline, oh my gosh, I'm so sorry." Abigail pulled her into a tight hug. "That was so selfish of me. I didn't even think to ask, and here you were hurting and I was blowing you off. I'm so, so sorry." She was babbling. Over her shoulder, Caroline smiled. Abigail was the best person she'd ever known.

"It's okay. It's really okay, I promise," Caroline said as Abigail patted her on the back. In her sister's arms, she felt looser, her head lighter. "It's been hard. I didn't have anyone to talk to about it." She laid her head on her shoulder.

"Of course, I'm really sorry," Abigail said. It was as if all else had disappeared and it was only the two of them. Abigail held her at arm's length. "How do you feel? Are you okay?"

"Yeah, I think I'm okay," Caroline said. She paused.

"Mmm," Abigail said. "Maybe."

"I mean, we weren't actually dating," Caroline said. And suddenly, beneath Abigail's skeptical gaze, she did feel sad. Her sister took a step closer, looked at Caroline with a wisdom she would have resented under any other circumstances.

"It's still hard to be rejected, even if you weren't dating," Abigail said. "But you are a perfect angel." She placed her palm on Caroline's cheek. "A beautiful, perfect angel." Her eyes were soft with pity, but Caroline wanted them to shine with love.

"Nah, I had sex with him, so I'm a regular ol' slut now," she tried to joke.

"Caro, don't say that," Abigail scolded, but at least she was smiling now, shaking her head. "Are you really okay?" she asked, holding Caroline's gaze. She reached her hand forward and grabbed Caroline's.

"I'm okay," Caroline said, squeezing. A smile crept into the corner of Abigail's mouth, and Caroline returned it.

"Promise?" Abigail offered her other pinky.

"I promise," Caroline said, and gripped her sister's with her own as if she could hold her there forever.

"I'm so sorry," Abby said, swinging their linked hands between them.

For a moment, Caroline felt a little guilty at how easily she had manipulated her, but she also felt awake for the first time in days. "I'm sorry too," she said.

Caroline continued, "I do want to talk more later about the whole Connor thing." Her voice caught halfway through. "Also, uh, I kind of yelled at Dad."

She expected Abigail to chastise her. She only laughed, the echo of her happiness so long and loud that the boys setting up the tables turned to look. "So I heard," she said, her eyes fixed on the horizon. Her lips parted and Caroline leaned toward her, but right as she was about to say something more, a long, loud "Abby!" came from the ceremony space. Abigail's mouth closed, and she whipped around.

"Tonight," she said. "After the dinner, we'll make time. I promise." She squeezed her pinky one last time. Caroline felt the heaviness disappear from her stomach.

Both families were now swarming out of the house like fire ants. Caroline could see their mother and Matthew's, arms linked, their mouths moving rapidly, waving for Abby to come join them.

"Love you," Caroline said, but her sister had already turned away.

CAROLINE SPUN THE rings inside her pocket while Pastor Mark explained the basics of the ceremony. They had placed Post-it notes on the ground so everyone knew where to stand.

The wedding was a promise to be with each other forever in front of witnesses—legally, one, but in actuality, three hundred. Caroline wasn't worried that her sister's marriage would fail. She knew Abigail would never get a divorce. She was worried that her sister would be bound to Matthew forever, even if she was miserable. Pastor Mark explained the lighting of the unity candle, and how they'd pour two pitchers of colored salt into a vase at the same time, the knot they'd tie around their hands. It was as if her sister had been presented every option for the ceremony and, without hesitation, she'd chosen them all. Finally, he returned to the beginning and the procession, which they actually did need to practice.

The group stood in a huddle discussing the order, who the ushers should seat first, and when the songs would play. Matthew gripped Abigail's hand like he could save her. They were so young, standing exactly where they'd be wed the next day.

Matthew's family was a group of short, round-faced smilers. They hugged Caroline with both hands tightly gripping her back before she pulled away. There were tears in his parents' eyes as Matthew made his way down the aisle, a mock groom, his shirt untucked in the back. Only the families remained now. Matthew's brother, Chase, and Caroline were the sole members of the wedding party.

Caroline began her path from the house and down the aisle. She made it only halfway before both of the mothers started yelling at her. Luck, she'd forgotten, had rules. Abigail could not walk down the aisle at her rehearsal! It would curse the wedding! They had to switch places!

So, Abigail positioned herself where Caroline would stand, and Caroline was handed a paper plate decorated with the bows she'd sorted at the shower, ribbons threaded through a hole in the center like stems. She tucked her other arm through her father's where her sister would the next day, but she maintained as much space as possible from him. He could have pulled her in closer, but he didn't. They began to walk, each of them straining away from the other, their gait uneven and awkward.

This was what her sister would see tomorrow. The yellows of the prairie in the magic hour as the light grayed out, the sky desaturated. Caroline looked at Abigail, saw her smile fade as they approached.

At the front of the aisle, Luke Nolan said "Her mother and I," and turned to kiss Caroline on the cheek, handing her off to Matthew for the rest of the rehearsal. Caroline began to tremble. The whole rehearsal took no more than half an hour, but by the end of it, she was exhausted.

"Can you help me with something?" Abigail said, grabbing her by the arm and pulling her behind a row of chairs, saying "We'll be right in" and "See you soon" as everyone else trudged past them down the hill. The sky was rosy around the house. Abigail's skin was bathed in orange, her highlighter shimmering on the tip of her nose and along her high cheekbones. She waited until the last guest closed the front door behind them to face Caroline. "It looked like you might need a minute." Caroline would have died for her right then.

They stood in the blistering heat, sweat trickling down their backs. They did not say that they felt unsettled; they were silent, both girls shifting their weight, swaying from side to side until their mother finally yelled, "Girls!" from the porch and switched on the light.

Abigail squeezed her hand. "Are you ready?" She ran a hand through her hair, twisted it over her shoulder.

"I can be," Caroline said, and watched as her sister turned toward the house and set off down the hill without her, hair swaying with every step. The rings bounced inside Caroline's pocket as she followed her. At the bottom of the porch steps, Abigail turned and looked back. They both took a deep breath. Caroline could hear their father's voice from inside, even over the lightly playing classical music, the hum of conversation.

"Here we go," Abigail said.

Caroline looked at her sister in the soft light of the porch and knew that her smile was real this time.

DINNER WAS ALMOST ready, they were told. Everyone should head to the living room. "Make sure she eats," Ruthie told Caroline, as their guests searched the place cards for their seats. Abigail was so often up, chatting, smiling, that she had eaten maybe five bites by the time the toasts began. As maid of honor, Caroline would give her speech tomorrow. During the planning phase, when it had still been unclear whether their father would be reinstated, Abigail and Ruthie had decided that his should be relegated to the rehearsal dinner, to keep the focus of the big day on the bride and groom. Abigail told her that their father had pouted, tried to plead his case, but Ruthie had refused to budge until he raised his hands, saying "Okay, okay."

Napkins were dabbed at lipsticked mouths. Wine bottles glugged, first the whites and then the reds. Knives scraped across plates as steaks were cut. The overhead lights were turned off, replaced by tall candles that dripped onto the tables and rope lights that hung around the ceiling. Everyone's teeth shone as they laughed. When the tiny crème brûlées emerged, a few guests even clapped.

Champagne bottles popped and two men in white shirts and black pants filled everyone's glasses. "Not hers!" Ruthie yelled when one began to pour some into Caroline's. "She's eighteen!" The waiter returned with a flute of sparkling apple juice. Caroline frowned after tasting it. Abigail saw her, laughed, and switched Caroline's glass with Matthew's when he wasn't looking. They watched him take a sip, lick his lips, and glare at the two of them before calling over the waiter.

Matthew's father was the first to speak, a glass of champagne in his squat round hand. His knife dinged against the glass.

"Matthew was our little miracle," he said. He and his wife had tried for years. "When the hospital let us take him home, I was terrified. We prayed that we'd be able to do this, and that prayer brought us to the Lord. Matthew saved us." This too was a tale of faith, as are most stories about miracles. They'd prayed that their son would find someone who could hold his hand and lead him back toward his faith even on his darkest days.

"We've been praying for you, Abigail," he said, raising his glass, "every day of our Matthew's life, and we are so happy he finally found you."

Beside him, Matthew's mother was in tears. They ran in straight gleaming lines down her face. Abigail lifted her napkin from her lap and dabbed it at the corner of her eye. She smiled, a hand on Matthew's knee, their shoulders overlapping.

Everyone is on the home team at a wedding. Everyone wants the speeches to work, the jokes to land. The bride, they think, deserves it. And the witnesses, who want nothing more than to celebrate, feel that they deserve it too. But Caroline sensed some hesitancy around the room a few moments later when their father rose from his chair and buttoned his blazer, a champagne flute in his hand. He tapped it with the edge of his dessert spoon, and one clean, graceful, practiced chime rang through the air. Caroline couldn't decide whether she wanted him to succeed or not.

Abigail reached for her hand underneath the table, held it tight, her diamond solitaire engagement ring digging into the thin skin between Caroline's fingers. Two seats down from her, on the other side of their mother, Luke lowered his spoon to the table and took a deep breath. Caroline noticed his suit jacket was wrinkled from sitting so long.

Their father told family stories at every opportunity, but Caroline had never heard the one he told that night. After he and Ruthie were married, Luke began, he and his new wife slept in this house. They were young, younger than Abigail and Matthew, and had known each other only three months. As he spoke, he looked down at his wife, smiling, and Ruthie blushed like it was the eve of her own wedding, lifted her hand to the table to take his free one.

"They have a direction for their life," he joked, pointing toward Abigail and Matthew, bouncing on his toes. "Heck, they have jobs!" He looked around the room as the crowd of family and friends laughed. He pursed his lips in a tight smile and waited for the silence to resettle. He lowered his voice, released Ruthie's hand.

"No one," he warned, "is ever really in a perfect position to get married." On his first night as a married man, he'd woken in the middle of the night to an empty bed. He might have believed the whole thing was a dream—the love and courtship, the engagement and wedding. "It would have made sense," he said. "It had been so easy, blissful."

Luke paused then. Matthew's mother shifted uncomfortably and his father set his drink on the table, accidentally dinging it against his plate.

His marriage had been real, though, Luke continued. And when he'd turned to look out the window she was there, her pale skin shining blue in the light of the full moon, her oversized sleep shirt filling with the wind like a sail. On his walk out to her, he'd heard her crying. *How had things gone wrong so quickly?* he'd asked himself. And before he reached her, before she even turned around, she'd confessed.

Next to him, Ruthie's face was turned up to gaze at him, her thumb stroking his hand. She was proud of him, Caroline realized.

"Now, she was crying pretty hard, so it was a little difficult to understand her," he joked, "but I think she was saying that it didn't feel like she thought it would." He hadn't known what to do or say at the time, so he'd just hugged her until she was ready to go back inside.

"There is no happy ending here," he said, as Ruthie wiped two slow tears from her eyes. "It took us a while to figure that out. We are *still* trying to figure it out. Obviously. But loving someone isn't promising to never ever make a mistake. Loving someone is about seeking the Lord first in all that you do, and knowing that it will bring you closer together in the end."

Caroline finally understood what Ruthie had been trying to tell her all along. She remained at her husband's side even though he'd cheated on her, always holding tight to her gold cross necklace, because it wasn't Luke Nolan she was committed to—she'd made a promise to the Lord. "God never fails," Luke said, looking around the room. "And so love doesn't either. Love . . . is always worth saving."

Everyone smiled up at him. A man standing against the back wall shouted, "Amen." Abigail squeezed Caroline's hand beneath the table. Caroline wrapped her other hand around her sister's and squeezed back. Matthew sipped his replacement champagne, his other hand draped around the back of Abigail's chair. Her sister had chosen to share this moment with her, Caroline realized. And their father's pacing had been perfect. There was no catch, no stutter, no difficulty delivering a line. It was too good, actually.

"My daughter, my sweetheart, my firstborn," he said, pointing with his glass to Abigail, "you will fail, and so will he. I pray that as you learn to fail together, you also learn to lean on the Lord, and that your marriage will last as long as His love, and mine, for you both."

Glasses clinked. Caroline heard the guttural pop of another bottle being opened. "That was so good," a woman whispered, surprised. Fizzing golden liquid poured down throats, and when the conversation returned it was lighter, merry, celebratory, as if the room was relieved that Luke Nolan was back.

Caroline knew better. She turned to her sister.

"I cannot believe," she whispered, "that you wrote his speech for your own wedding rehearsal."

Abigail shrugged and smirked. "Well," she said, "I wanted it to be good." Then she threw back her head and downed the rest of her champagne.

After that, Abigail was pulled away for photos and hugs and congratulations. Luke Nolan's daughter at her own rehearsal dinner, smiling and thanking and laughing. She moved her father to one side as she made room for someone else. She did not even look at him as she did this. It was her spotlight, her weekend, and she didn't intend to share it with him. Caroline saw how well the spotlight suited her, how she inhabited it as easily as her own skin, and knew that Abigail would surpass their father someday.

Outside, the sun had long ago set in the distance and the few remaining crickets began to sing. Matthew stood at her sister's side, laughing, raising his glass to his mouth, egging on the other members of the party to tell more stories. Abigail shone under the soft light, her white dress immaculate, her hair smooth, her movements graceful. Caroline watched her closely, and noticed that her smile was a touch too rigid, her bottom lip drawn tight as a bow. It looked like she was performing for the crowd.

21

The girls spent the first hours of the best day of Abigail Nolan's life all alone. The rehearsal guests had departed; the cattle gate was locked behind them. The grass around the freshly cut meadow swayed in the breeze, sparkled in the moonlight. The air was too hot for comfort even at this hour. Still, the girls sat outside, drawn by memories of their summer together, already feeling nostalgic for it. They sat on the porch finishing off the remaining half bottle of champagne, along with a bag of Goldfish crackers. The outline of the moon, if you looked closely enough, was clear, even if only half of it was illuminated. You could just make out its dark edges against the even darker night. Crickets cried out in their mismatched harmonies all around them.

"I hate the sound of those things," Abigail said, crinkling up her nose as if she could smell them too.

Caroline listened to their chirping for a moment. It was so soft she had to strain to hear it. "Then why are you staying out here?"

Abigail shrugged. "I only wanted to leave because I was

mad at him." She gestured vaguely to indicate that she was talking about their father. "I'm still mad at him." She scooped up a handful of Goldfish and, before shoving them into her mouth, added, "But I think that means I need to stay."

Caroline had hoped her sister was staying because she wanted to—wanted, not needed.

She glanced over and fought the urge to question her further. She wanted to interrogate Abigail until she admitted that she didn't really want to stay and help Hope, but Caroline didn't want to ruin the mood the night before her wedding. Caroline shifted again, pulled her legs to her chest. "Are you still mad at me?" She directed the question at her knees. She picked at a loose piece of wood on the deck.

"Hmm?" Abigail said, dropping the strand of hair she'd been twisting with both hands, and faced her sister.

This was her chance. Abigail wasn't about to be called away by someone else or remember some other chore that needed to be done. Caroline felt like she might never have this opportunity again, so she said everything in one stream. "I thought you were saying something you weren't when we had that conversation about Matthew and I asked Connor to come out here and I'm really, really sorry. I should have talked to you about it first."

Abigail looked out at the land. Caroline watched for any sign that she might pull away from her again.

"No, I get it. Really, I do," she said. "And I'm sorry I freaked out. It makes sense why you thought that." She sighed. "But Connor hurt me so badly that it could never work between us. I didn't want to see him knowing he was separated, to be tempted."

Caroline's mouth fell open. "Were you?"

Abigail looked over at her. "No, Caro. Not like that. Nothing happened between me and Connor." She took a sip from the champagne bottle and passed it to her sister. "We had a long chat and he wished me well. But I am glad I had that moment. It made it easier for me to understand—well, to understand how someone could stumble into sin so easily."

Caroline wasn't sure if she was alluding to their father, or herself, or both of them.

"It's also part of why I decided that Matthew and I should stay here, to be honest," she added. "I want to keep an eye on him. Me being here gives him less opportunities to fail." *Him* being Luke Nolan. Her words slurred a little as she stood and moved to the porch swing, patted the seat beside her. Caroline had barely sat down before her sister's small head tucked itself into her shoulder.

"That's not your job, Abby," she said.

"I know," she said. "But Hope is."

The church. She had as much of a claim to it as their father did. Of course she was going to stay.

"I thought we were going to leave together." Caroline heard the whine in her voice, but her sister didn't comment on it.

"I wanted to marry Matthew and run away from all of this, but I was wrong. Just because moving would be the easier thing to do doesn't mean it's the right thing for me, ya know?"

"Yeah," Caroline said, but she didn't really. She couldn't imagine choosing the hard thing for the rest of her life. She was already so tired. "But won't you be bored? Won't Matthew be bored?" The bottom of the Goldfish bag was only crumbs now. Caroline poured them into her mouth.

"Eh, it'll be fine," Abigail said. "Matthew's going to work for his dad. He never really liked working on the oil field to begin with. He was just doing it so that he could save money for us to have a down payment for a house, and now we don't need that." She patted the arm of the swing and took the bottle from between Caroline's legs. She took a long swig and smiled, her whitened teeth gleaming in the porch light.

"There's something else too," Abigail said, tucking her knee up onto the swing and shifting to face Caroline. "Matthew and I are going to help you pay for school."

"No," Caroline said. Her sister's eyes were dancing now. "That's insane."

"We saved that money so that we could leave and now we're staying and you're going, and you'll need it more than we do." Her whole face smiled. She took another swig of the champagne. "I'm not actually asking. We're going to do it."

"Abby," Caroline said, and hugged her. Her heart felt heavy against her ribs. The swing rocked back and forth until Abigail stopped it with her foot. Caroline squeezed her. It wasn't a trade she wanted. She wanted them both to go. She wanted them to be together. "Abby, thank you," she said, releasing her sister, wiping the tears from her eyes. It was so much. Too much.

Abigail pointed the lip of the bottle at her. Caroline grabbed it and tilted it into her mouth. The wind built waves on the lake and rustled through the reeds. "But what will you *do* out here?" She knew what Abigail would do: the same thing they'd done all summer but without her sister. Matthew would hold her hand and take her for walks and hear about her day. He would do these things and Caroline wouldn't.

"Eh," Abigail said. "I'll be married. I'll have a couple of kids. I can write some more songs and maybe I'll even get to speak at women's conferences eventually." Her voice was small, though still optimistic.

"But there's no cell service out here," Caroline said, rolling her eyes. She knew Abigail hated her phone, though.

"After the honeymoon, maybe we can get Wi-Fi. With all these new subdivisions, there will be service soon. Plus, we gotta get cable so I can watch at least one of the dozens of shows you'll try to talk to me about."

They sat swaying on the porch, watching the reflection of the moon dance along the surface of the lake. The conversation trickled out as they passed the champagne bottle between them. Caroline looked over at Abigail and worried her sister might disappear, fade into the backdrop, the dark navy of the night. *She should be filled with light*, Caroline thought. *It's her wedding day.*

She pulled the rings from her pocket. Abigail glanced down at her hand, saw what she held, and choked on the champagne she was about to swallow, coughed twice, her face turning red.

"Someone found them in the field," Caroline said. "They're back."

"Oh my gosh," Abby said between coughs, smiling now. "That's too funny."

Caroline rolled the rings around in her hand, the two of them clinking together. "What should we do with them?" she asked. She wanted to throw them again, to bring out whatever had motivated Abby to do it in the first place. But her sister remained seated and just shook her head.

"I don't care," she said. "You do something with them." Caroline shoved them back into her front pocket. Abigail flipped her phone over on the railing. It was 1:00 A.M.

"Happy wedding day," Caroline said, but the joy she'd tried to inject didn't quite ring true to her own ears.

Abigail frowned. "I know you don't think I should marry him," she said, putting her feet back on the ground and facing the lake, away from Caroline. She'd turned too slowly, though. Caroline had caught the flash of tears in her eyes.

"No," Caroline started to say, before Abigail cut her off.

"Don't lie to me," she said. "Not today."

"Okay, fine. But it's not him. There's literally nothing wrong with him," Caroline said. Matthew was unimportant, and that was the problem—his personality was so small compared to her sister's. If Abigail really wanted to marry him, though, Caroline could accept that. "I just feel weird about it, I guess."

Abigail looked over at Caroline, her eyes bright like they had yellow suns around the pupils. "What does that even mean?" she said.

Caroline searched for the right words. She didn't know what it meant exactly. She only knew that when she saw them together, something inside of her twisted. She couldn't point out that her sister was different with him, how when they were alone, Abigail never checked her language, or her posture, or her tone the way she did with Matthew. There just wasn't a nice way to say that she liked her sister less when her future husband was around—and Caroline worried that she'd never have this time with her again. Matthew would always be in the next room, or waiting at home for her to return. The version of her sister that she'd seen evolve this summer, a woman who radiated confidence, who took what she wanted without asking, who had a tattoo and a sunburned nose, might never exist again. It was that loss that upset Caroline the most.

She imagined her sister pregnant, holding her new baby wrapped in its pristine white blanket. She saw her packing up her classroom, pushing a double stroller, pulling soccer balls out of an SUV and never standing on the stage again, one day telling her sons about how she used to sing during worship. "I just don't want you to end up like Mom," Caroline said, though she really wanted to say: *I don't want you to become one of those women who changes her name and forgets that she ever used to be someone else.*

Caroline had expected her sister to cry, but Abigail seemed calmed by her response. She wiped her eyeliner with her pointer finger and shrugged. "The scary thing is, I think Mom's happy. I think even with all of the mess this summer, her life with Dad has and will be better than it ever would have been alone."

Abigail believed that her best shot at ever leading worship and someday being more than Matthew's wife was to stay and tie herself to the church, and to their father, even if he never admitted she was the reason he excelled. But Caroline wanted more for her sister than her father's shadow.

"I don't understand," Caroline said. Her hands trembled in her lap. "I don't want you to have to stay here." She wanted her to have everything she ever wanted.

"But I don't have to, Caro," she said. "I'm choosing to. This is my decision. This is where I want to be."

Caroline felt the pressure building behind her eyes. When she raised her hands to rub her temples, she realized she was crying. She lifted her T-shirt and wiped away the tears, leaving a smear of mascara across her stomach.

Abigail tucked her hair behind her ears. "Matthew is the right choice," she said, emphasizing the word *right* just a bit too much. "It's the smart decision." Her voice trembled there at the end. Caroline wasn't sure if either of them believed her.

The girls went inside after that, the champagne bottle

empty, the same argument rehashed, the moon too high in the sky. After the wedding, Abigail and Matthew would leave for a hotel, and then to Hawaii for a week. Caroline would stay here alone for a few nights before driving herself to Austin and checking into her dorm. It was their last night together. Abigail followed her sister to the front room. They climbed into bed and lay there beneath the clicking ceiling fan.

Abigail was turned away from her. Caroline buried her face between her shoulder blades, locked her knees in behind her sister's, and said into her hair, "I want to stay here forever." *Here in this moment, this summer, with you forever.*

Abigail's breath left her body more slowly and softly until Caroline could no longer detect it. "Me too," she mumbled. "But we can't."

Caroline wrapped her arms around her sister as they drifted off to sleep.

22

It's unfair to say that Caroline Nolan was the first one awake on her sister's wedding day. Because she'd never fallen asleep. There was simply no space to slip into a state of help-lessness when so many fears and terrors appeared throughout the night. By the time she staggered out of bed with the rising sun, Caroline felt as if she'd spent the night wrestling with the sheets, her hair plastered to her face, her spirit bruised. The first things she saw were the two silver rings on the night-stand, shining in the morning light. She climbed out of bed, rifled through the pile of dirty clothes on the floor, and pulled on a pair of denim shorts. The house whirred with the sound of the air conditioner as she set the coffeepot to brew. It was too quiet, but she was afraid to make any noise. She carried her boots outside, careful not to slam the door behind her. At the bottom of the steps, she pulled on her shoes, their soles now bent to her feet, and walked in the opposite direction of the rising sun.

Caroline walked west until she reached the foot of Nan-nie's grave, the sweeping blue of the sky overhead now dotted with leaf clusters. The sun shone down on the marble cross coated with pollen and bird droppings. She was so tired and lay down next to her grandmother. Just for a moment, she told herself.

Out here the quiet was built of comfortable routine instead of anxious anticipation. She let the stillness rock her slowly; her limbs softened, her mind cleared. The air settled into the spaces between her legs and her arms. Her body was coated with an even layer of sweat; the grass dug into the backs of her bare limbs. When she looked up into the sky, so seamless and empty, snakes filled her vision, small thin cracks floating above. They only disappeared if she closed her eyes and waited for them to fade from gray to red to smooth black.

Two months ago, she had held everything she wanted in the palm of her hand: to leave Hope, to go off to college, to distance herself from the example of her sister. And all these dreams had materialized, but now she wasn't sure if she wanted them at all. She had assumed that by completely changing her life, she would end up in one she wanted. Everyone said that college was the time to find yourself, but no one ever talked about what would happen when you did. Who was she without all of this?

Caroline begged the sky above for something, a voice or spirit that would wrap around her like a lasso. She wanted to feel, for the first time since the affair, the guidance of a greater power—the Earth, an ancestor, God—and though she listened and pressed as much of her into the land as she could, she heard nothing. So she peeled herself off the ground, buried the rings in a shallow divot at the foot of the cross that marked Nannie's grave, and left them there.

She tripped over a stick on her way back to the house and

caught herself on a tree, her vision blurring, the house flickering like a mirage. Dehydration, she realized, and felt silly for the moment in which she'd hoped the day wasn't real. As she came closer, she saw her sister's silhouette in the kitchen window. She entered through the back door and Abigail met her with a mug of coffee, still hot, her hair wet.

They spoke of other things: their mother, when the ushers would arrive, whether they had remembered to clean out the buckets for the sparklers to sit in so they would look rustic and not just plain dirty. There was no buzz of excitement as there had been the past few days. Instead, the kitchen was as quiet as it had been on their first day together. The sun arranged itself into squares on the floor as they chatted. They ate cereal with their hands from a box they'd bought weeks ago, its crunch now dulled, and split apart when it was time for Caroline to shower.

Their hair was still dripping when the photographer pulled onto the property, unloaded, and began taking snapshots. In the first photo, it is just the two of them, laughing with hands over their mouths.

Through the window, the girls watched volunteers dress the tables with centerpieces and place settings and hand-lettered menus. Their mother was at the top of the hill, pointing with her clipboard at idle young men, assigning them jobs until morning turned into afternoon and Ruthie retired to her mother's room to shower and change into her dress. When she returned, Caroline thought she smelled the shampoo That Woman had forgotten in Nannie's shower on her mother's hair. But she said nothing.

Around four, the volunteers left and the silence settled in—the eye of the tornado. Abigail sat in front of a long oval mirror. Her makeup had been painstakingly painted on until every freckle from the summer's sun had been spackled over. Caroline had applied four layers of thick skin-colored paint to cover the rose tattoo on her sister's neck. Her hair had been straightened and then curled and now hung loose and wavy, half of it pulled back off her face in a clip. It was so long that when she turned to face the photographer, who hovered around her like a wasp, she flinched as the hairs tickled her back.

It was time. They watched Ruthie unzip the white garment bag. The crisp ivory fabric gushed out and onto the floor, where it lay in a puddle. Ruthie lifted the dress off its hanger and spread it into a glistening doughnut on the hardwood, where it no longer demanded reverence. There, it was only a dress.

Abigail stepped forward, holding her mother's and her sister's hands as they released her and lifted the heavy dress up around her. She clutched the dress to her chest while Caroline pulled the top together at the back and their mother wielded a hook like a sword, forcing each tiny button from the bottom of Abigail's butt to the top of her dress through its tiny satin loop, drawing the bodice and her guts tighter and tighter until the dress now held itself up. Caroline walked around the train as the bodice came together and watched her sister's face drop from laughter to severity to tension and finally into fear. When Abigail noticed her looking, she reached out her left hand, the diamond ring sparkling, her nails blush and oval, and pulled her closer. She cringed as their mother forced the final metal hook into its eye, holding on to Caroline's hand as the clip on her veil was shoved into her hair. Caroline dropped her hand to adjust it, and when Abigail spun to look in the mirror, her reflection showed her standing there all alone.

The shutter of the photographer's camera shushed and a holy silence reigned as Abigail was preserved in all her perfection. Caroline glanced at the clock that hung on the wall behind her and gasped.

"What?" Abigail asked, still smiling for the camera.

"It's just later than I thought," she said, and soon the calm of preparation was broken by the noise and scurrying of the final hour of Abigail's single life. Mrs. Marshall, the wedding coordinator, arrived with her horn-rimmed glasses and shooed Ruthie out the door. A few close friends entered and fawned over her sister, the photographer instructing them to shift an arm or turn a face toward the window, where the blinds had been opened facing toward the ceiling so no one could see inside.

Caroline went to the window and pulled one slat down to peek through. Car after car pulled through the balloon arch where the cattle gate stood open crushing the flowers and the high grass, directed by a young man in a suit and fluorescent vest. She watched the people of the Hope Church in their heels and dress shoes walk up the small hill, guided by the usher into their appropriate rows. The last half hour evaporated quicker than the signs of a July rain. Caroline heard the walkie-talkie announce that the gate was closing, that Matthew's grandparents were ready to be seated and the family lined up in the entryway.

"Okay, girlies," Mrs. Marshall said, looking at her watch. "It's time."

Caroline gathered the small train of her blush-colored dress in her fist and followed her sister out the door and into the hallway, where their parents were waiting. Abigail hugged each of them at a distance, turning her face so that her makeup wouldn't touch any of the dark suits, stretching up to kiss their father on the cheek, who beamed like it was the best day of his life, and not hers. From her spot at the back of the line, Caroline thought she saw a flicker of sadness in his eyes, though. Abigail motioned for her to scoot back so she could stand behind their mother, and even though that was not the order they were supposed to stand in, Caroline made room and followed her sister.

The walkie-talkie hissed again and two ushers swept the parents away. They went two by two from the dark hall into the stark golden twilight. Someone handed Caroline her bouquet. The ushers were ready for them. They stepped into the relentless heat, protected from their guests by a six-foot screen held by two hearty young men who both said "Congratulations," as if they'd been told it was the only thing they were allowed to say.

Mrs. Marshall stood in front of them on the porch, her clipboard tucked under her arm, her tone the same firm one she used in her day job as a flight attendant. She lifted her glasses from the beaded chain around her neck and set them back on her nose. "At the top of the hill," she said, pausing to make sure they were paying attention, "they will set down the screen. As soon as they leave, you go," she said, pointing at Caroline. "When she is all the way down the aisle, the song will switch, and Abby, your father will be at the beginning of the aisle waiting for you. Okay?" Mrs. Marshall looked them each in the eye. Caroline swallowed her nerves. "I'm so happy for you, Abby," she went on, and Abigail hugged her. "Moving in fifteen," Mrs. Marshall said into her walkie-talkie, and the five-piece band began to play louder and slower, the notes dying down as they reached the porch.

Mrs. Marshall lifted a finger and pointed at the boys with the screen. They bent their knees and lifted, pausing on each stair. Mrs. Marshall held Abigail's hand until she was safely on the ground. Caroline cradled the end of her sister's train, her own, and her bouquet. Their steps were so small that Caroline wondered if she would sweat off all her makeup before the ceremony had even begun. The strings grew louder as they approached. Caroline could feel the heat burning the side of her arm through the white screen. She did not look at her own shadow on the ground or at the men walking ahead of them. All she saw were the shimmering sharp edges of her sister's bones jutting out like angel wings above the upper ridge of her strapless gown.

The music grew louder and faster, and without warning, the boys set down the screen and the girls were left alone. The yellow roses in her bouquet were so fragrant Caroline's head throbbed with their scent. She wanted to take her sister by the hand and run back the way they had come. Her heart rate increased with each pluck of the cello. There were so many things she had wanted to say and had failed to, and now they were here, their shadows fully visible to the guests, facing each other.

Inches from her own face, Abigail's eyes were closed, her thick mascaraed lashes laid out like fans. Caroline blinked back the tears she felt starting to form; the beginning of a sob bubbled up in her throat, and her breath hopped as it escaped through her lips. Out of instinct or desperation, she prayed to a god she wasn't sure could hear her as their last seconds together slipped away.

"You know you don't have to do this, right?" Caroline said, her last word a tremble, her hand shaking where she held her sister's arm. Abigail turned toward the music and looked at the screen as though she could see right through it. She took a step back and Caroline saw that her mouth was open slightly, her jaw tight, and knew she was trying not to cry.

"Abigail," Caroline said.

Abby shook her head but didn't turn to face her.

"This is still your choice," Caroline said, her voice holding every doubt she'd ever had.

Abigail turned toward her then, forced her shoulders back to where they belonged. Caroline reached out with her mind, up and around, as far as she could stretch. *Please*, she thought, and tried to pull her sister tight against her.

"Caroline," Abigail whispered in her ear. "It's too late. I'll be okay."

Caroline swallowed down her tears. God had loved the world so much that he gave His only Son to save it. But they were only daughters.

Abigail squeezed her once more, and when she stepped back, she released her sister entirely. Caroline dabbed a tear from her eye.

"Don't you dare," Abigail said, smiling with the corner of her mouth.

Caroline couldn't look at her. She just kissed her on the cheek, lifted the short silk-hemmed veil over her head to cover her face, turned, and left her there, her breath catching in her throat.

As Caroline made her way down the aisle, Matthew smiled, and she smiled back. She worried someone might see the sparkle of tears in her eyes and figure out the real reason they were there, but no one was paying any attention to her. They had already turned to look over their shoulders as the music changed. Caroline took her position on the left side and turned just in time to see her sister step out from behind the screen, loop her arm through her father's, and float her way down the aisle.

Caroline stared over her sister's head at the sky, crisp and blue, scattered with bulbous cotton-ball clouds. This was the land that Abigail loved so much and that, in one summer, she'd taught Caroline to love too. Abigail was looking straight ahead at Matthew. She was the third generation of Nolan women to marry right here on this hill. Maybe the land really was cursed, Caroline thought. Her grandparents had both died here, and now her sister was standing before her, radiant behind the lace of her veil. Abigail had reached the end of the aisle and the guests settled into their seats.

In the front row, Ruthie caught Caroline's eye and smiled wide, tapped the corner of her mouth with her fingers. Caroline pasted on a smile.

"Who presents this woman?" Pastor Mark said.

"I do," their father said, with a hand on his chest as if he were pledging his life. He turned, lifted the veil over his eldest daughter's head, kissed her on the cheek, and traded places with the man about to become her husband. Caroline bent and adjusted her sister's train so that it lay flat on the ground behind her, plucked off the few pieces of dead grass it had picked up along the way. She stepped back into her spot, straightened her own dress, peeled her hand off the stem of her bouquet, and saw a dozen pinpricks of blood on the satin ribbon. She looked at her sister in profile, at the slight upturn at the end of her nose, the applied blush on her cheeks, the thin cross necklace that hovered right at the dip of her collarbone.

"You can face each other," Pastor Mark said, and Abigail

turned to Matthew, but then she paused and spun back around. Caroline's eyes widened, her heart thumped. Her sister had turned to face her instead. But it was only to hand off the giant, heavy bouquet. She thrust it toward her like a torch. Caroline wrapped her free hand around it—and there, in that one moment, their eyes met.

In her sister's eyes, Caroline saw the land to the west of the house, where yellowed grass swayed in the hot evening breeze and two crosses stood reluctant guard over all that happened before them. She saw the shell of a hot air balloon, the remains of a grasshopper. Abigail's hands released the bouquet to her sister, her lips parted slightly as if to say something, and then she thought better of it and turned back to the man who would be her husband.

Caroline closed her eyes. When she opened them again, all she saw before her was a tower of sparkling white silk and tulle shimmering in the twilight. She bent and pulled the train straight again, considered staying there in the painful grass at her sister's feet. But she stood and forced herself to smile. Her tears tasted like salt.

Acknowledgments

First and foremost, thank you to my talented, brilliant agent Dana Murphy. She read a messy early draft of this book in a single weekend and saw what it could be. She believed in this story and these girls, and she believed in me. Thank you for being tenacious and patient. Thank you for always being game to drink cheap beer and dream up a way to make a story better. Thank you for fixing my teeth.

Additionally, thank you to the entire team at the Book Group, who were always there to provide a second opinion or word of encouragement. Thank you to Jenny Meyer for her belief that people outside of Texas might care about these girls. And a big "Full eyes, clear hearts, Team Texas" thank you to Kristina Moore and everyone at Anonymous Content.

My editor, Jessica Williams, saw the better book within my draft and chiseled it out. She tore apart sentences and questioned my decisions and made this story tighter and stronger than I ever could have managed alone. I am in awe of the skill and attention she gave this book and me. Thank you, Jess.

Ploy Siripant, thank you for making me the cover of my dreams.

Eliza Rosenberry, thank you for publicizing my book so well and always messaging me back.

Thank you to every person at William Morrow and Harper-Collins who rallied around this book, sent me pictures of their dogs, and promised that one day (when all of this is over) we will raise martini glasses together. Thank you to Julia Elliott for your keen eye and Laura Cherkas for reading so closely. Thank you also to Liate Stehlik, Jennifer Hart, Elina Cohen, Andrea Molitor, Naureen Nashid, and Kaitlin Harri.

I wrote the first draft of this book on yellow notepads and hid them for months. Aleksander Chan, Hannah Smothers, Molly Fitzpatrick, Allison Pohle, Arielle Pardes, and Katy Waldman were safe havens where I knew I could share it. Thank you for reading this book when it was still young and giving me brutal (but encouraging) notes. Thank you for always being there for me.

Thank you to so many of my friends who read various drafts and pieces of this book and listened to me whine endlessly. Thank you Kelly Fine, Mike Case, Lauren Winchester, Claire Carusillo, Laura Wright, Alex Tanner, Lauren L'Amie, Elyssa Klann, Karl and Tressie Daum, Fran Hopfner, Lucy Junker, Jorge Corona, Liberty Riggs, Fred Tally-Foos, Shelby Hasten, Susannah Jacob, and Adrian White.

Thank you to Olivia Nuzzi, who talked me off several cliffs and walked me to the bank when I was too scared to deposit my advance check. And to Megan Greenwell and Kate Nocera, who put up with me being a baby all of the time.

Thank you to Chrissy Mullan, who read my juvenilia a million years ago and never doubted this day would come.

Thank you to Tahirah Hairston, who didn't laugh when I confessed I wanted to write a novel.

My friends in DC poured me wine and promised me it would all be okay. Thank you to Maya Rhodan, who always holds my hand. Thank you to Hannah Groch-Begley, Gaby Simundson, and Andrew Rutledge, who have cooked me more dinners than I can count. Thank you to Dylan Matthews, Evans Mullan, Molly Hensley-Clancy, Elite Truong, Quinn Dang, Andrew Prokop, Kim Vu, Allison Hollander, Sara McQuillen, and Dayana Sarkisova. Thank you to the Kalorama Dog Park crew—Ellen, Beth, Aaron, Leah and David, and Jen and Sam—for beers and long Friday afternoons. Thank you also to the staff of Tail Up Goat (especially Jill) in Washington, DC, who celebrated with me at every turn.

Thank you to all of my former work wives turned pals who keep me sane in an increasingly unstable industry: Danielle Henderson, Alisha Ramos, Chao Li, Elena Scotti, Alex Abad-Santos, Jenée Desmond-Harris, Sujay Kumar, and Katie McDonough. And thank you to all of my editors. There is no way to list all of you but thank you especially to Melissa Bell, Ezra Klein, and Matt Yglesias for taking a chance on me, to Lauren Williams for the blessing of great editing and guidance, to Emily VanDerWerff (and Libby Hill!) for loving me, to Dodai Stewart for teaching me to pitch, to Megan Greenwell for hiring me onto the best sinking ship, and to Joyce Tang, who hugged me on not one but two of the worst days of my life.

Thank you to my two amazing book clubs. Erica Brody, Danielle Corley, and Alyssa Davis: let's get a yurt. Gryte Verbusaityte, Betsy Law, and Aisha Wolo: I miss you all.

Thank you to the Terry Foundation, which paid for my college. That gift gave me a future in which I could afford to take the risk of trying to write for a living. Thank you to Dr. Janet Davis, Dr. Mia Carter, Dr. Lisa Moore, Dr. Robert Crosnoe, and Dr. Brian Doherty at the University of Texas at Austin for expanding my world and my mind. Thank you to Booker T. Washington High School for the Performing and Visual Arts in Dallas, Texas, and Cassie Benzenberg, Charlotte Chambliss, and Carolyn Reitz for teaching me that it isn't dumb to pursue something you love.

Thank you to my oldest friends: Bethany Hayes and Jessica Zetzman, who helped me remember the way we grew up with grace and honesty, and helped me move on.

To the idiots of Defector.com, present and future: I love you all; eat shit.

To Jess Goodman, who was my North Star through the publishing process, and Drew Magary, who reassured me everything would be fine.

To the members of Crossroads Bible Church in Double Oak, Texas: thank you for raising me.

Emilio Madrid, thank you for taking my head shot and making me look good despite my squirming.

I could not have written this book without Tricia, my longtime therapist, to whom I owe quite literally my life. Thank you for helping me. And in that vein, thank you to Kacey Musgraves for *Same Trailer Different Park*, which helped me reckon with leaving Texas. Thank you also to the drug Wellbutrin, Buc-ee's sour strawberry belts, and Trent Reznor's *Gone Girl* soundtrack, all of which I need to write anything at all.

Thank you to all of my family. Thank you to Jill and Shane Sentz, who are always, always there when I need them. I love y'all so much. Thank you to the Dondreas, for loving me too.

Thank you to my parents, Brent and Tracy McKinney,

who always believed I could be a writer. Thank you for taking me to the library and pretending not to see the reading lights in my room late at night. Thank you for always encouraging me, and for loving me so much.

Thank you to Sarah-Grace Sweeney. I couldn't survive without you.

Thank you to my sister, Shelby, who was this book's first fan and without whom I never could have written it.

And thank you to my first reader, Trey Dondrea: for everything, for ever. I love you.

About the author

About the book

Insights,
Interviews
& More . . .

Meet Kelsey McKinney

Emilio Madrid

KELSEY McKINNEY is a freelance features
writer and cofounder of Defector Media.
She previously worked as a staff writer at
Vox, Fusion, and Deadspin. Her writing
has appeared in the *New York Times*, *GQ*,
Cosmopolitan, and *New York* magazine,
among other publications. Raised
evangelical in North Texas, she now lives
in Philadelphia, Pennsylvania, with her
husband and dog. *God Spare the Girls* is
her first novel. ∾

A Conversation with Kelsey McKinney

A version of this interview was first published by Writeordietribe.com on July 26, 2021. The interviewer is Kailey Brennan.

Q: God Spare the Girls *explores the loss of faith and questioning of religion. I'd love to know why this was a topic you wanted to explore in fiction.*

A: There is no better artistic medium to explore the internal conflicts and concerns of a person than in writing, and faith is this personal, intimate thing. So much of belief in general is something we do internally in silence, so it's best on the page, and there's a long, beautiful history of writers working through questions of faith through stories. I knew I wanted to write about how it feels to believe something and how it feels not to, and the uncomfortable space when you aren't sure which side of that question you're going to land on.

Personally, I wanted to write about faith and questioning religion because both of those things have been fundamental to my development. With a project as long as a book, you need something that you really care about, and I knew really early on that this would be a book about a young girl trying to figure out what she believes because I don't think there's a ton of modern fiction grappling with faith. There are plenty of stories trying to answer questions about how to be moral or how to make ethical decisions, but not many for people who grew up with a set of codes and want to question whether those need to be followed at all.

Q: *The setting, North Texas, is a huge part of this novel. Do you have any advice for writing place? Did you face any challenges in this part of the novel process?*

A: I wanted every space in this novel to feel real and to be immersive enough that the setting itself could act almost as a character in the story. Part of that is because selfishly I like to read books with great senses of place, but it's also because ▸

A Conversation with Kelsey McKinney *(continued)*

I wanted this to firmly be a book in and of and about Texas. I think that there's a tendency in a lot of modern novels to be vague about where a story is taking place in the hopes that it will ring as universal, but the books that I've always loved do the opposite: they venture that, by being insanely specific, you will relate more easily and truly to these fake characters.

One thing my editor, Jessica Williams, told me that I've been repeating to anyone who will listen is that description, and florid language in general, only works for the reader (and not just for the writer) if it contributes to the tension of scenes. So that was something I thought a lot about as I tried to build out the physical landscape of the book, making sure that when I was describing a space or a horizon or a heat index, it was always for a reason and always meant to tell the reader something more than just the color of the sky. It forces you to be economical as a writer, but I think it also gives you a chance to be more creative, to use more metaphors, to describe the way sweat falls instead of just listing the temperature.

Q: *Since this is your debut novel, I'd love to know what the process looked like for you. Did you outline? How long did it take you to write this book?*

A: I started off writing scenes on yellow legal pads without editing. It was more of a vomiting than a planning. And I did that for a long time before I realized that these characters were evolving together and becoming something more than a bunch of scribbles in my terrible handwriting. Once I realized that, I edited it, and laid it out in piles on the floor and tried to make it better. But since it was my first novel, I didn't really know how. I tried, but honestly the early versions of this book were slow as hell! Nothing happened! Every single piece of action took place in the past and in the present there were just two girls sitting on their grandmother's property.

When I signed with my agent, Dana Murphy, she pointed this out and it was immediately obvious that she was right, that though I had a lot of beautiful passages, there was absolutely no engine to the book at all. So after that I learned to outline, and to set up questions and reveals to give the book momentum. I knew I wanted to write a book that people could and would read in a couple of sittings, so it was important to me to build that motor. I think from the first words I scribbled to the book in hardback in my hands was something like four years. Hopefully, I've learned enough that it won't take that much time in the future, but a novel is a place you live for a long time before anyone else gets to visit you there.

Q: Were there any misconceptions about novel writing that you discovered along your writing journey? Or anything new you discovered about yourself as a writer?

A: Oh, absolutely. I thought that people wrote novels in one pass. I thought that everyone who had written a novel was this genius who just kind of typed for 90,000 words and then had a book, and that's not at all the way writing a novel works. Or at least that's not how it worked for me. For me, writing a novel is a process in infinite revision. You have to write at first for yourself, but over time the book becomes its own object separate from you and you have to start making decisions for the book to be the best it can be.

As a writer, I learned that I use way too many filler words. I cut maybe five hundred instances of words like "just" and "really" and "very." I have a tendency to use adverbs instead of ever fucking describing anything, but I'm getting better. I'm growing.

Q: Can you share your writing routine with us? Take us through a day in your life.

A: So, I have a full-time job writing nonfiction. I work for a site called Defector.com where I write sometimes reported pieces and sometimes blogs about houses I find on Zillow.com. What that means is that I work too much, but almost all of my work is about words and typing them with my silly little carpal-tunnel-ridden hands into the computer. That doesn't answer your question, let me start at the beginning. ▸

I wake up at 7:30. I need a lot of sleep because I'm neither a genius nor a superhero. I have one cup of coffee and scroll on my phone and then I try to read during my second cup of coffee. I walk the dog. I sit down at my computer at 9:00 for my blogging job and I work until about noon. Then I have lunch at my desk. At 2:00, I take the dog for a walk again. Then I work more. At 6:00, I log off, but then I have to exercise because otherwise my clinical depression will get out of control. Terrible. I hate doing exercises, but I do it. Then (you guessed it) I walk the dog again. Usually I will make dinner after this, and then I will read on the couch or I will watch some trash television.

If you are wondering when the hell I ever write fiction, same? But really I think most of writing is about thinking and only some of it is about actually writing. I'm always writing. I sometimes have to sit down on my dog walks and frantically type something I think is good into the Notes of my iPhone. Usually it is bad, but it's the work that counts. When I'm in the middle of a fiction draft, like I am now, I'm usually avoiding it. I work in like accidental marathon sprints, where I will sit down on a weekend or an evening and just pound words out for, like, five hours. I motivate myself to do this by laying out sour candies on my desk. If I'm revising, I'm more methodical and less insane. I'll set days to revise or work on structure or write out plot points on the windows of my study and figure out what order they go in, but mainly I feel like most of my work happens in random bursts. I go to bed at 11:00 unless I fall asleep on the couch before then.

Q: *What was a piece of craft advice that helped you while writing this novel?*

A: My editor gave me a hack that I love for writing really anything, and it's that every section needs to have a main source of tension, a question, and a reveal. As long as you are doing that, the plot will move forward. How well it works is a product of how good you are but it's an easy check when a section isn't working. Usually, if I ask myself what each of those three are in a chapter or a scene, I'll realize one is missing, and then I can figure out how to solve it.

Q: *If you could make a playlist for* God Spare the Girls, *what are a few songs you might put on it?*

A: The playlist for *God Spare the Girls* is just two albums back to back and that's Semler's *Preacher's Kid*, which absolutely destroyed me the first time I listened to it, and Lucy Dacus's *Home Video.* ～

Losing My Religion— and My Virginity
by Kelsey McKinney

A version of this essay was first published by Elle.com on June 22, 2021.

Everyone took their teenage daughter to the same store to buy her abstinence ring. The store was in a newly built outdoor shopping mall, and the air-conditioning was on so high that I remember my hair blowing back when stepping inside from the triple-digit heat. Inside their glass terrariums, the rings were cradled in little pillows, each propped upright, begging to be purchased. It was the first time I had been into a jewelry store, and I tugged at my shorts, worried they were too short. In the cases shone silver rings with crosses cut out, crosses forged roughly, crosses horizontal on the tiny bands. Too obvious, my parents and I decided. We laughed together at the one with the words TRUE LOVE WAITS engraved on it. Tacky. We chose something subtle: a stacked silver ring. But there's nothing really that subtle about a fifteen-year-old wearing any jewelry on her left-hand ring finger. It was Texas, after all. Everyone knew exactly what it meant.

The ring was a finale to a multi-week program in which I had to listen to my parents speak vaguely and uncomfortably about sex more than I had ever wanted to. The idea was that by putting everyone at our evangelical church through the same True Love Waits abstinence pledge program, we would break down the barriers in communication around sex. This, of course, was a complete and utter failure because the whole premise of the program was that I was agreeing to not have sex until I was married. More than agreeing, I was *promising*.

In all honesty, it wasn't that hard of a promise for me to make. I was fifteen years old. I didn't think I'd ever want to have sex very badly, so I promised not to do it. This made me good, moral, admirable. Worthy of praise by the adults in my community. But it also tied up my faith with sexual purity, so that without one, I could no longer have the other. In retrospect, I can barely even remember which I lost first: my faith or my virginity.

The preservation of girls' virginities is nothing new. Human history and the church in particular have long been obsessed with women's purity. The Bible is clear that one should flee from "sexual immorality," and American culture latched on to that suggestion as a beacon of truth. The Reagan administration had the Chastity Act in the 1980s. The Southern Baptist Convention introduced True Love Waits in 1993. A spin-off, Silver Ring Thing, was founded in 1995. An estimated 2.5 million teenagers pledged to stay abstinent. When I was a teenager, half the hot young celebrities had purity rings: the Jonas Brothers, Selena Gomez, Jordin Sparks, Demi Lovato, and Miley Cyrus.

The pledges, generally, ask you to sign a card, vowing that you will abstain from sexual encounters until marriage. It's not just a pledge to stay a virgin, but a pledge to stay "pure." Most people take these pledges in late middle school or early high school, when they are more children than adults—young enough to not really know what they are agreeing to. As a child, I learned in church that lust was a sin boys struggled with, not girls. Sex, I was taught, was something men wanted and women reluctantly agreed to. In the journal I kept around that time I wrote, married women "are always talking about how great sex is and how precious it is inside marriage, but it sounds like they're trying to convince themselves, not me."

Maybe I didn't think I would ever want sex because I was too young when I took the pledge, or maybe it's because I was ▶

Losing My Religion—and My Virginity *(continued)*

so closeted I didn't recognize the feelings I had for girls as more than friendly. I was surprised when I learned a bit later in life that the pulsing tension and lingering looks I had experienced were in fact about sex. I had matured enough to realize I wanted more than someone to date; I wanted someone to touch me. It was a feeling I had been told was wrong, but in that moment, it certainly didn't feel like it. More than feeling guilty, though, I felt confused.

I knew men wanted sex. I knew married women had sex. But wanting sex myself surprised me. "Making women the sexual gatekeepers and telling men they just can't help themselves not only drives home the point that women's sexuality is unnatural, but also sets up a disturbing dynamic in which women are expected to be responsible for men's sexual behavior," Jessica Valenti wrote in her book *The Purity Myth: How America's Obsession with Virginity Is Harming Young Women*. It did feel unnatural; I felt strange for wanting more than just my hand held. And I also felt broken somehow, as if a screw had popped loose inside the machine of my body and pieces of myself were rapidly collapsing.

When I first started working on my debut novel, *God Spare the Girls*, I knew that I wanted to write about purity culture and how it's adapting to fit the modern era. How churches now are more willing to admit that young girls want sex, but they still condemn it—insisting that to even want sex, much less to pursue or acquire it, is something to be ashamed of. It's a form of policing young women's bodies and desires that seeks to control them, but more importantly, it puts young people in an easy space to be manipulated. Maybe you're sixteen years old, as I was, and always had a hard time relating to the gospel preached that you are broken and sinful and in desperate need of a savior. I had straight As. I was a model child. I did everything in my power to be perceived as good. Until I started desiring sex, there wasn't much in my life that a pastor could allude to that was meant to make me feel guilty.

There has been a lot written about how purity culture and abstinence pledges can ruin people's relationships with sex for life, how they can build up a heavy guilt in a person's gut that threatens to drown them in their own shame, and how they make most young women feel unempowered and trapped. I had dozens of calls with friends of mine who grew up with the same program, grew out of it, and called me in the middle of the night crying when they failed. I have seen firsthand the difficulty they had balancing the thing they believed with the decisions they wanted to make.

For me, though, it was more complicated than that. Sex, and sex-adjacent activities, never felt wrong to me. I never felt the guilt I was promised, or the shame I was supposed to feel, or the dread that was supposed to consume me. In fact, it was the discussions about God that more often began to feel that way to me.

In her book *The Years*, Annie Ernaux writes that "the church no longer terrorized the teenage imagination or ruled over sexual exchange. Women's bodies were freed from its clutches. By losing sex, its main field of endeavor, the church had lost everything." When I read this a few months ago, my book was already finished, but it was a perfect encapsulation of why I began writing it in the first place. Because I had been taught so firmly and so adamantly that sex outside of marriage was a sin and an affront against God, when my body failed to feel those things, it wasn't myself I questioned, but the God I had been promised.

The power dynamic of my relationship to myself shifted when I started having sexual experiences. Because I was the one in control and because I was the one making the decision, I felt stronger. Like the protagonist of my novel, it was in the eyes of people who were attracted to me that I saw reflected back how strong I could be, and how much power I actually had. It wasn't the sex itself that made me feel empowered as much as the realization that I was an individual who could choose which rules to follow and which to ignore.

Teenagers today are better at that. Many of them realize that sex is a choice for them to make, and because they also realize that having sex can be a painful and hurtful thing, they're more cautious. According to a 2020 report from the Centers for Disease Control and Prevention, American teenagers are having less sex than ever. Only 42 percent of teen girls and 38 percent of teen boys reported having sex. That number is down significantly from 2002 when it was 46 percent for both. In 2019, teens ▶

interviewed didn't say this was because of religion or a desire for abstinence, though, they said it was because of awareness of disease and access to more information on the internet. So that decline isn't because of purity rings and abstinence pledges; it's not fearmongering making young people today choose to wait longer to have sex—it's their own empowerment.

Purity culture fails at everything it tries to accomplish. Studies have found teens who take purity pledges are almost twice as likely to become pregnant while not married. Teens who take purity pledges also often have guilt and shame that affect their sex lives and the future. And the whole intent of the pledges in the first place—to convert people to Christianity—is a massive failure on every front. While teens attend church regularly, young adults do not. The Pew Research Center found in 2019 that the share of Americans who consider themselves white evangelical Protestant has declined from 19 percent to 16 percent of the U.S. adult population in the last decade.

The bet purity culture didn't realize it was making is that young adults would choose God over sex. They didn't and they won't. But in setting up that dichotomy, the church has failed young evangelical women on every front. The hardest part for me about losing my virginity wasn't guilt or shame; it was the recognition that what I was really losing was the faith I had held close to my heart my entire life.

I wore my abstinence ring every day, long after I stopped believing or abiding by the message it projected, because I didn't want to answer questions and because I didn't want to allow myself to ask the biggest question hiding in the back of my mind. If I didn't believe it mattered at all what I did with my body, why did I believe any of it? I don't know where my abstinence ring is now. Like my virginity, I lost the ring slowly, over time, in incremental steps, and in the end, both it and my virginity were so much less important than I'd at one time thought they might be. ∾

Questions for Discussion

1. Have you ever experienced a fundamental shift in your worldview or had your preconceptions shatter with age and understanding? How did you react then, and how has it changed you?

2. How does Caroline and Abigail's relationship evolve over the course of the novel? Did you relate to one of the sisters more? And why?

3. How does each member of the Nolan family respond to the scandal? Who do they reach out to for support and why? How does crisis reveal which bonds are worth protecting?

4. What were your first impressions of these characters, and how did your understanding of them change as the cracks in their facades were revealed?

5. How do Abigail and Caroline decide which values to uphold? Have you ever made the decision to walk a different path than the one set out for you? Why can this decision be so difficult to make?

6. How does Abigail's impending wedding force the girls to reconsider what love and commitment really mean for each of them? By the end of the novel, do you feel they've found the answer?

7. How did *God Spare the Girls* illuminate your definition of faith?

8. Caroline considers a passage from the Bible: "True love is not only forgiving but forgetting." How do you interpret this statement, and do you think it is true?

9. Several characters are accused of committing sins. Did this book challenge your understanding of sin and what it means to be forgiven? ▶

Questions for Discussion *(continued)*

10. How does *God Spare the Girls* highlight the disparity in the treatment of men and women in the Hope congregation? How does the ideal of purity differ among genders?

11. Did you feel every character received the ending they deserved? Why or why not?

12. What do you think the title *God Spare the Girls* means? Is anyone in this novel truly "spared" or "saved"? ❧